# CADENCE CREEK COWBOYS

*They're the rough Diamonds of the West...*

Sam and Ty Diamond—*trouble is these two cowboys' middle name. With chips on their shoulders the size of hay bales, these rough and rugged men think they need a woman like they need a lame horse. Little do they know...*

Don't miss any of the action in Cadence Creek!

Sam's story, **The Last Real Cowboy** is out in May 2012

With a tip of his Stetson and a lazy smile, Sam Diamond can charm anyone. Except prickly Angela Beck...

Ty's story, **The Rebel Rancher**—*available in June 2012*

Ty Diamond isn't exactly known for his mild reputation. But if he wants to be with Clara Ferguson, he's going to have to show her his gentle side....

Dear Reader,

Welcome to Cadence Creek—home of the sprawling Diamondback Ranch and two very sexy men: Sam Diamond, rancher, and his cousin Ty, a real down-to-his-boots cowboy. These two bachelors need two good women to make them settle down, and I've got just the pair. These girls may come with baggage, but they're made of strong, resilient stuff. Angela Beck is a social worker on a mission, and Clara Ferguson's a sweet, nurturing soul looking for a place to call home.

It all starts with the launch of Butterfly House, a special women's shelter for victims of abuse. Angela won't let anyone stand in the way of her plans—not even Sam Diamond, who saunters into a board meeting with a devilish smile. She and Sam don't exactly see eye to eye. But, as we all know, things are rarely as simple as they seem. Turns out Sam is exactly the kind of man Angela needs—and Angela is the woman he's been waiting for his whole life.

I loved writing this story from start to finish, and I hope you enjoy it too. And don't forget to look for Ty and Clara's story, coming in July!

I love hearing from readers—you can find me at my website, www.donnaalward.com.

Until then—happy reading!

Donna

# DONNA ALWARD

## *The Last Real Cowboy*

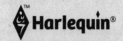

TORONTO NEW YORK LONDON
AMSTERDAM PARIS SYDNEY HAMBURG
STOCKHOLM ATHENS TOKYO MILAN MADRID
PRAGUE WARSAW BUDAPEST AUCKLAND

ISBN-13: 978-0-373-17807-0

THE LAST REAL COWBOY

First North American Publication 2012

Copyright © 2012 by Harlequin Books S.A.

The publisher acknowledges the copyright holder of the individual works as follows:

THE LAST REAL COWBOY
Copyright © 2012 by Donna Alward

THE RANCHER'S RUNAWAY PRINCESS
Copyright © 2009 by Donna Alward

Recycling programs for this product may not exist in your area.

A busy wife and mother of three (two daughters and the family dog), **Donna Alward** believes hers is the best job in the world: a combination of stay-at-home mom and romance novelist. An avid reader since childhood, Donna always made up her own stories. She completed her arts degree in English literature in 1994, but it wasn't until 2001 that she penned her first full-length novel and found herself hooked on writing romance. In 2006 she sold her first manuscript, and now writes warm, emotional stories for Harlequin Romance.

In her new home office in Nova Scotia, Donna loves being back on the east coast of Canada after nearly twelve years in Alberta, where her career began, writing about cowboys and the West. Donna's debut romance, *Hired by the Cowboy,* was awarded the Booksellers Best Award in 2008 for Best Traditional Romance.

With the Atlantic Ocean only minutes from her doorstep, Donna has found a fresh take on life and promises even more great romances in the near future!

Donna loves to hear from readers. You can contact her through her website at www.donnaalward.com, her page at www.myspace.com/dalward, or through her publisher.

**Books by Donna Alward**

HOW A COWBOY STOLE HER HEART
A FAMILY FOR THE RUGGED RANCHER
HONEYMOON WITH THE RANCHER
PROUD RANCHER, PRECIOUS BUNDLE

**Other titles by this author available in ebook format.**

To Jayne, who rescued a very special kitty. And to Chippie—truly one of a kind.

# THE LAST REAL COWBOY

Donna Alward

# CHAPTER ONE

ANGELA Beck tapped her fingers against the boardroom table and frowned. The seat across from her was noticeably empty and she grew more irritated by the moment. They'd held things up long enough, though why Molly Diamond was running so very late was a mystery. Molly was usually right on time.

"Angela, we really can't hold off any longer." Charles Spring, the President of the Butterfly Foundation board, folded his hands and looked down the table at her, his gray eyes stern over the rims of his glasses. "We need to get started."

Charles had graciously agreed to let the foundation meet in the boardroom of his oil and gas company's headquarters. It meant a drive into Edmonton, but Angela knew it was easier for her to commute than for the entire volunteer board to drive to Cadence Creek for a meeting. As a result she'd put together a list of things she needed for the renovations, determined to make the most of the trip. She didn't have any time to waste if she wanted to make her projected opening date.

"I know." Angela forced a smile and made herself remember that every person in the room was volunteering their time. She was the only one drawing a salary from the foundation. The reminder was enough to ensure her patience. The shelter was her dream, but success relied on a lot of people—people who didn't have this project as their top priority the way she did. She couldn't afford to alienate any of them—she'd come too far and invested too much.

"I'll call the meeting to order, then, at 2:18."

For an hour the board members discussed the latest fund-raising campaign; Angela outlined the latest PR push and upcoming open house, adding her input to the proposed operating budget and counseling services she'd organized for residents of Butterfly House. She'd thought she'd worked long hours before as a social worker for the province, but that was nothing compared to her days lately, especially as she was a staff of exactly one.

"And now," she said, "I wanted to bring up the suggestion that we hire some short-term help for the minor renovations still needed to the house."

Charles tapped his lip and looked over at the board treasurer, a graying woman with glasses and a stern demeanor. "Iris?"

"Leave it with me," she suggested. "But don't get your hopes up. The budget is already stretched. What's allocated is barely going to cover the cost of materials. Start adding in labor costs and I start seeing red ink."

"Perhaps if we can get more donations…" Soliciting sponsors was definitely not Angela's favorite part of the job; she hated feeling like the center of attention and preferred to be behind the scenes. But it had to be done and so she did it—with a smile and an eye on the big picture.

The talk then turned to drafting up letters requesting sponsorship. Angela pinched the bridge of her nose. The place needed paint and window coverings and the floor in the living room was in dire need of replacement. Who would come good for all of that?

She straightened her back. She would do it, somehow. She was thrilled that her vision was becoming a reality and it was worth the long hours, the elbow grease and the worry. It would be better when the house was actually ready for residents. In its present state it looked the way she felt—tired and droopy. She'd make it right if she had to do it all herself.

They were down to the last item on the meeting agenda when the door opened and *he* sauntered in. Sam Diamond needed no introduction, Angela thought with disdain. *Everyone* knew who he was. She resolved to keep her expression bland as she looked up, wondering why on earth Sam had shown up instead of his mother, Molly, the Diamond family representative to the board.

Sam turned a slow smile on the group and Angela clenched her teeth. He was going to be trouble—with a capital *T*. She'd known it from the first moment he'd sidled up to her at the Butterfly House fundraiser and had asked in his smooth, deep voice, "Have we met?" Her tongue had tangled in her throat and she'd hesitated, feeling stupid and predictable as a purely feminine reaction warred with her usual timidity when it came to dealing with members of the opposite sex—especially in social situations. Well, maybe he'd had her at a disadvantage during their first meeting, but she'd kept the upper hand in the end and she would today, too. She was far more comfortable in a meeting room than at a cocktail party.

But she'd have to do it delicately. His family had made Butterfly House possible, and it wouldn't do to bite the hand that was feeding her project.

"Mr. Diamond." Charles lifted his head and offered a wide smile. "I'm afraid we started without you."

Started without him? Angela silently fumed. He was over an hour late and had just walked in as though he had all the time in the world! And Charles Spring…she felt her muscles tense. Old boys' club, indeed. Spring might frown at her over his glasses, but to Diamond he was as sweet as her mother's chocolate silk pie!

"I got held up." Sam gave the board a wide, charming smile and removed his hat. "I hope I didn't inconvenience anyone."

"Not at all! There's always time for the foundation's biggest supporter." Heads around the table nodded. Sam shook Charles's hand and then put his thumbs in his pockets.

"I didn't realize I'd be in the company of such lovely ladies," he drawled, popping just the hint of a dimple. Angela swore that she could hear the sighs from three of the board members old enough to be Sam's mother. "I would have made a better effort to be here earlier."

Angela thought she might be sick from all the flattery stuffing up the room. Where was Molly? Why had Sam come in her stead?

"I do hope your mother's okay," Angela said clearly. She took off her reading glasses and put them down on the table. Sam pulled out his chair and met her gaze as he took a seat. Recognition flared in his eyes for a moment, then cleared as if they were perfectly polite strangers.

"She's fine, why do you ask?"

There was an edge to his voice and Angela didn't like it. Maybe he was still nursing a bit of hurt pride where she was concerned. She blinked. Men like Sam Diamond weren't used to being refused. Especially when they bought a lady a drink and told her she was a pretty little thing.

She'd simply said, "No, thank you." It was only afterward that she'd realized that she'd given a Diamond—a pillar of the community—his walking papers. It put her in an awkward position. She needed his family's support.

She ignored the uneasy glances from the board members and pasted on a cool smile. "Molly hasn't missed a meeting yet. She's been so supportive of the foundation. So I'm a bit surprised to see you here today, Mr. Diamond."

Dark eyes met hers, challenging. "And you are?"

Oh, the nerve! He knew exactly who she was. She could see

by the gleam in his eye that it was a deliberate cut, intended to throw her off her stride. She lifted her chin and rose to the challenge. "Executive Director of Butterfly House, Angela Beck."

"You obviously didn't receive my message. I called this morning."

And this morning she'd been outside chasing Morris around, trying to get the infernal creature indoors before she had to race into Edmonton. She hadn't stopped to check messages. She resisted the urge to bite down on her lip. She wasn't feeling quite as in charge as she'd like. She was well aware that the Diamond family had a place on the board; after all, they'd donated the building and land for Butterfly House and promised an annual donation toward maintaining the facility. Which was all down to Molly's generosity, she knew. The younger Diamond had a reputation that preceded him and it wasn't all favorable. The fact that he'd tried his charms on her only made it more awkward. Maybe the deed was already signed, but without the continuing support the program would die a quick death unless she could find another sponsor with deep pockets.

"I'm so sorry, I didn't receive it. I've been in the city for several hours already."

Angela was aware that every pair of eyes were on the two of them and that everyone seemed to be holding their breath. Everyone knew Sam. He was a big man, with big money and a big ego. Most of the residents spoke of him as if he were a god. Men respected him and women wanted him—until he trampled on their affections. She'd had her ears filled about that already.

But Angela could see the appeal. He was over six feet in his boots, sexy as sin and looking scrumptious in jeans and a shirt with a sport jacket thrown over top as a concession to business attire. Paired with his unassailable confidence, he made quite the package.

Just because she could understand the attraction did not mean she was interested, though. He was too… Well, he was too everything. She'd known it from the moment he'd tipped his hat and looked down at her with his bedroom eyes. And after she'd refused his overtures, he'd gotten this little half smile. "Do you know who I am?" he'd asked. Clearly she hadn't. But she did now. They both knew exactly who had the upper hand—and he was enjoying it.

How kind, gentle Molly Diamond had spawned such an egomaniac was beyond her. Did he really think his transparent charm would work on her now when it hadn't the first time?

"My mother won't be attending any board meetings for the foreseeable future. My father suffered a stroke last week and she'll be looking after him for the time being. She requested I sit on the board in her place."

Oh, brother. Sympathy for the lovely Molly and her husband Virgil warred with annoyance at the turn of events. Angela and Molly had hit it off from the start, and she'd so looked forward to talking things over with the older, friendly woman. Molly had insisted that she'd love to be involved with turning the house into a real home and had even helped plan the upcoming open house. Angela couldn't imagine Sam helping with those sorts of things. Undoubtedly his impression of "service to the community" was throwing money at it, then smiling and shaking a few hands and feeling proud of himself.

"I hadn't heard." Angela forced herself to meet his gaze. "I'm very sorry about your dad, Mr. Diamond. Please tell Molly that if she needs anything to give me a shout."

"Thank you."

But the words came out coolly, without the warm flirtatious charm he'd used on the other board members. Great. It seemed his pride was still smarting from her response that night. His question—*Do you know who I am?*—had struck a nerve and made her so defensive that goose bumps had popped up over her arms. "Should I?" she'd answered, looking over her shoulder as she walked away. Her insides had been trembling, but she'd covered it well. She was done letting domineering men run roughshod over her.

She'd utterly alienated Sam and she'd done it in front of the board. He turned his head away now, effectively ending the conversation. And why wouldn't he? She'd been prickly as a cactus. Both times they'd met.

Charles wrapped up the meeting, but before he adjourned he smiled at Sam.

"I'm sure Angela would be happy to fill in the gaps, Sam. She knows more about the project than anyone."

Angela felt the blood rush to her face as Sam's gaze settled on her again. "Of course," she murmured. She would just have to suck it up. What was important was getting Butterfly House off the ground no matter how often she had to smile. Maybe Sam wouldn't even be interested in the details and this would be short and relatively painless.

She could afford a few minutes as long as she could make it to the hardware store in time to pick up her supplies. By the time she finished running her errands, it would be evening before she returned to Cadence Creek. Her whole day would be gone with little accomplished.

The meeting adjourned and the board members filtered out of the room. Sam pushed back his chair just far enough that he could cross an ankle over his knee. Angela organized her papers, avoiding Sam's penetrating gaze as long as possible. Finally she put her pen atop the stack and folded her hands. She looked up and into his stupidly handsome face. "Shall I bring you up to speed, then? Or will you be on your way?"

\* \* \*

Sam forced himself to stay relaxed. Lordy, this Ms. Beck was a piece of work. She looked as though she had a perennial stick up her posterior and she clearly didn't approve of him any more now than she had two weeks ago when he'd offered to buy her a drink and she'd flatly refused, looking at him like he was dirt beneath her heel. Which was of no great importance. He didn't need her to like him. In fact, he didn't need anything from her. She needed him, especially now that his mother was otherwise occupied.

He ignored the shaft of fear and concern that weighed him down when he thought of his father and focused instead on the budget in front of him. He was only here because his mother had asked and he couldn't say no to her. Especially not now. In his mind, today's meeting was supposed to be a token appearance and then he could be on his way attending to more important matters.

Instead he found himself sticking around. Aggravating Miss Prim and Proper was a side benefit he hadn't anticipated, and it took his mind off the troubles at home.

"By all means," he said slowly, letting a grin crawl up his cheek purely to irritate her. "Educate me."

Damned if she didn't blush, he thought with some satisfaction. He tilted his head, studying her. Pretty, he decided, or she could be if she let her hair down a little. Now, as it had been at the fundraiser, it was pulled back into a somewhat severe twist, with only a few nearly black strands rebelling by her ears. Her eyes were a stunning color, too, a sort of greeny-aqua that he'd never seen before and he wondered if she wore tinted contacts. As he watched, she put her glasses back on—armor. He recognized the gesture. He was the same way with his hat.

"Is your father going to be all right?" she asked quietly, surprising him. He'd expected facts and figures from Miss Neat and Tidy.

"I think so," he replied honestly. "He's home from the hospital and Mom insists on nursing him herself. Since he requires round-the-clock care, something had to give in her schedule. Your foundation was it."

"Of course. Please give her my best and tell her not to worry about a thing."

Sam uncrossed his legs and leaned forward, resting his elbows on the table. "Let me be honest, Ms. Beck. I don't want to be here. With my dad sick, the running of Diamondback Ranch falls solely to me. I don't have time to sit on charity boards and shake hands, okay? All I'm concerned about is the responsible management of the foundation so my mother's donation is held to a…certain standard."

She looked like she'd just sucked on a lemon. "The Diamonds won't be associated with anything substandard," she replied sharply. "I get it, Mr. Diamond."

She made it sound as though it was a bad thing. Four generations had gone into making Diamondback what it was—the biggest and best ranch in the county. The standards set by his ancestors were a lot to live up to. And it wasn't just the responsibility of taking the ranch into the future that he carried on his back. Lord knew he loved his mother, but at age thirty-seven he was getting tired of the question of when he was going to provide a fifth generation. When the hell did he have time? His father was seventy-two, his mother in her late sixties. The ranch was bigger than ever and facing new challenges every day. His latest idea—making Diamondback more environmentally friendly—was taking up the rest of his waking hours. And now, with his father being so ill, it made him think about what would happen to Diamondback. To the family. He rubbed a hand over his mouth. Good Lord. Now he was starting to think like his mother. Men weren't supposed to have biological clocks, were they? So why did he suddenly hear ticking?

Now his mother had lassoed him into sitting on this silly board because the Diamonds had donated some land and a house for Miss Goody Two-Shoes to turn into a women's shelter. And he had said yes because Molly had looked very tired and worried and family was important. He didn't plan on being actively involved. He'd write a damned check and keep his hands off.

"Look, we provided the location. What more do you want?"

He hadn't thought it was possible that she would sit up any straighter but she did—her spine ramrod-stiff as her nostrils flared. "The spot on the board was your mother's condition, not mine."

"I know that," he answered, his annoyance growing. What had he done that had made her so hostile? Surely offering a smile and a glass of wine wasn't a crime? And he hadn't meant to be late today. "What I mean is, what in particular do you want from *me*?"

He heard the sharp intake of breath and could nearly hear the words spinning in her head: *not a thing.* Instead she put down her pen, looked him dead in the eye and said, "Your assurance that you won't withdraw funding and that you'll stay out of the way."

"That's blunt."

"Would you rather I was less direct?"

There was a glimmer of respect taking hold in the midst of his irritation. "Not at all. Please. Be honest."

But his invitation was met with silence. He wondered what she wanted to say, what she was holding back.

"Perhaps I should mention the elephant in the room," he suggested. "The fundraiser."

"What about it?"

But now he heard it—a tiny wobble, the smallest bit of uncertainty. "You really didn't know who I was?"

"And that surprises you, doesn't it? Because *everyone* knows Sam Diamond."

He raised an eyebrow at her sarcastic tone. "Frankly, in this area? Yes."

"You really do have an inflated ego."

Sam chuckled. "Are you trying to hurt my feelings, Ms. Beck? Look, you passed up the opportunity for a free drink. I'm not going to cry in my beer over it." But the truth was he had felt snubbed. Not because he thought he was God's gift but because she'd been standing alone and he'd taken pity on her. She was too beautiful to be hidden in a corner all night. And all he'd got for his trouble was a cold *no, thank you* and a chilly breeze as she left his presence in record time.

"Well, that's settled then." She ran a hand over the side of her hair, even though he couldn't see a strand out of place. It probably wouldn't dare be so impertinent. "Now if you'll excuse me, I have more important things to do."

"More important than impressing your main benefactor? Tsk, tsk."

He didn't know what made him say that. Sam didn't usually resort to throwing his weight around. Something about Angela Beck rubbed him the wrong way. It was as though she'd sized him up at first glance and found him wanting. And that grated, especially since he was already in a foul mood. He'd been late when he prided himself on punctuality. His last meeting with the engineers for the biogas facility had gone well over the time expected and had had less than satisfactory results. Sam was used to being ahead of the curve, not behind it.

He was set to apologize when she stood, placing her palms flat on the table. "This is about helping abused women, not stroking your ego. Your mother understands that. Perhaps you can suggest an alternative proxy for the board position as clearly you do not care about the cause."

Well, well. She had fire, he'd give her that. And it was all wrapped in a package that momentarily took his breath now that he could see her from head to…well, mid thigh, anyway. She had curves under the neat and tidy librarian clothes—straight black skirt and plain buttoned-down blouse. But she had him to rights and he knew it. And they both knew that Molly had stipulated a Diamond family member sit on the board and not the other way around. He was the only other Diamond in Cadence Creek. There *was* no one else.

He stood slowly, reached for his hat and put it back on his head. "Ma'am."

He was nearly to the door when he heard her sigh. "Mr. Diamond?"

He paused, his hand on the door handle. He turned his head to look at her and realized she'd taken off her glasses again. Her eyes really were stunning. And he shouldn't be noticing.

"Your mother didn't believe in simply throwing money at a problem," Angela said quietly. "She believed in being part of the solution. I find it strange she'd ask you to take her place if she didn't think you'd hold up that end of the bargain."

It wasn't that he didn't care, or that Butterfly House wasn't a good cause. He just had too much on his plate. Angela Beck was being far too smart. She'd worded her last statement in just the right way to flatter and to issue a finely veiled challenge at the same time.

A challenge he wasn't up to accepting. The foundation had its land, had its house free and clear. That would have to be enough.

"Good day, Ms. Beck," he replied, and walked out, shutting the door behind him.

# CHAPTER TWO

SAM pulled into the yard and killed the engine, resting his hands on the steering wheel. He hadn't been going to come. He had planned simply to leave well enough alone, go home to Diamondback, grab something to eat and collapse in bed so he'd be on his game for his daybreak wake-up call. Instead he'd found himself turning off the main road and driving through Cadence Creek, putting on his signal light and turning into the Butterfly House driveway. Angela Beck's last words bothered him more than he cared to admit, and he couldn't escape the need to make things right. He didn't necessarily want to apologize. He just wanted to explain why he'd acted the way he had today.

Angela was right. His mother *was* counting on him to step in now that she couldn't. He was a Diamond, and family was everything. He'd learned that at a young age, and it had been reinforced daily as he grew up alongside his cousin, Ty. Blood stuck together—no matter what Ty insisted these days. The ranch wasn't the same with him gone, and Sam wished both Ty and Virgil would mend fences.

Sam was only doing this for Molly—Lord knew she'd sacrificed enough over the years for the Diamond men. It didn't sit well that he was probably going to let her down, too. So when Angela had accused him of just that, it had smarted more than he wanted to admit. He hadn't exactly acted like a gentleman by walking away. So now he'd just smooth things over and ease his conscience.

Resolved, he hopped out of the truck and shut the door. The rambling yellow Victorian house was full of add-on rooms, giving it a boxy, unsymmetrical appearance. It had once been in its glory but now the gingerbread trim beneath the eaves was dull and the paint was chipping. The front porch sagged as he took the first step. This was what the Diamond money had paid for? This falling-down monstrosity was going to be a progressive women's shelter? He frowned, then jumped as a train whistle sounded to the west, followed by the faint rumble of the cars on tracks. What a dump! And on the fringes of town. What had his mother been thinking, endorsing such a place?

He knocked on the door. It would be better if he just explained and left. He'd find the right time to deal with his mother. If he bided his time, she might even be back on the board within a month or two.

The door opened a crack. "Mr. Diamond?"

Ms. Beck's voice came through the crack, clearly surprised at seeing him standing on the ramshackle verandah. "Sam," he corrected, angling his neck to peer through the thin gap between door and frame.

"Sorry. If I open it further, Morris will get out. Again."

Morris? Sam sighed. Who on earth was Morris? *Give me strength*, he thought. He was starting to think that growing a conscience had been a big mistake. But he was here now. Might as well press on and then put it behind him. He had far bigger things to worry about when he got home. Like how to save the family that was falling apart.

"May I come in, then? I'll shut the door behind me."

Indecision twisted her face. She didn't want him inside Butterfly House. He knew it as sure as he knew he was breathing. What he didn't know was why. Maybe he'd been a little heavy-handed this afternoon, but nothing that should keep the door barred against him.

"I only want five minutes of your time," he said. "I don't like how we left things this afternoon."

She opened the door and he stepped inside, only to find it quickly shut again.

There was barely room to move around in the foyer. Plastic bags were scattered everywhere, along with cans of paint in various shades, the colors announced by dots on the silver lids. He sidestepped around them and pressed against the wall to allow Angela to move past and ahead of him. When she did, the panels of his sport coat brushed against her blouse. Something slid through him, something dark and familiar that came as a surprise. Angela sucked in a breath, clearly wanting to keep from touching him in any way, her eyes wide with alarm.

Just as well. She was pretty tightly wound and he preferred his women to be a little more easygoing. Angela Beck was the kind of woman who was work, and he had enough of that to last him a lifetime.

"I just got home a while ago," she said, leading the way into the kitchen. "Excuse the mess."

"I dropped in uninvited. No need to apologize." He walked around boxes stacked with linens and came to stand in the middle of the room.

"I was just having something to eat. Can I get you anything?"

He looked down at the concoction in cardboard she held in her hand. It appeared to be some sort of chicken and rice in a brownish sauce. "Not if it looks like that," he replied.

She performed a perfect shoulder shrug and said, "Suit yourself." She took another bite, but then got a strange look on her face and put the meal down on the counter. He wondered if she was going to ask him to sit down as the silence wound out awkwardly.

"So this is the house," he said casually, trying to put things on an even keel. He looked around the kitchen and then ignored his customary good manners and took a seat at the table, hoping she'd follow his lead and they could stop standing in the middle of the room. Small talk. He could manage a few minutes of that, couldn't he?

"It is."

"And how many residents will you have?"

"We split up the master bedroom and added a bathroom. At full capacity, we'll have five women and myself." She remained stubbornly standing, which made him feel even more like an unwanted guest she'd rather be rid of.

He nodded, wondering where to go next. Five tenants weren't many, but the shelter was only meant to be temporary—for as little as two months with a maximum of a year's occupancy. It would mean that a lot of abused women could find help in the run of a year. She was doing a good thing. He just didn't fit into the picture.

"Begging your pardon," she asked, "but why are you here… Sam?"

"Are you always this abrasive?"

Her mouth dropped open and she stared at him. "Are you always this blunt?"

"Yes," he replied without missing a beat. "What's the point in dancing around anything? I tell it like it is. Makes it much easier to deal with issues."

Her mouth twisted. "In answer to your question, no," she admitted. "I'm usually not."

"Should I be flattered?" He couldn't resist asking. Flapping the seemingly unflappable Ms. Beck was an intriguing pastime.

"Hardly. You seem to bring out my worst."

Sam couldn't help it, he laughed. A low, dry chuckle built in his chest and the sound changed the air in the room, made it warmer. He looked up at her, watched as her gaze softened and her lips turned up the slightest bit in a reluctant smile. Desire, the same feeling he'd had as they'd brushed by each other in the foyer, gave a sharp kick. Angela Beck was an attractive woman. But when she became approachable, she was dangerous. The last thing he needed was to be tangled up in something messy and complicated. He'd been there and done that and it wasn't fun.

"Careful," he warned her. "You might smile."

"It's been known to happen. Once or twice. I'll try to restrain myself."

He was starting to appreciate her acid tongue, too. It spoke of a quick mind.

"Look," he said a little more easily, "I didn't feel right about how I spoke to you this afternoon. I have nothing against you personally, or your project. It's simply a case of hours in a day and only so much of me to go around, and I was in a bad mood when I arrived at the meeting. I meant what I said," he continued, "but I didn't put it in a very nice way."

"You're stepping back from the board then?"

She didn't have to sound so hopeful about it. He frowned. "I didn't say that. I just mean that the Diamond family assistance will be more of a behind-the-scenes kind of thing."

He didn't like the way her lips pursed. She should be glad he was still amenable to signing the checks.

"Your mother…"

"I know," he replied, cutting her off and growing impatient with the constant reminder of his mother's wishes. He stood up and faced Angela, wondering how it was possible that she could be getting under his skin so easily—again. "But I'm not my mother. My mother is in her sixties, her family is grown and she was looking for a cause to champion, something to fill her day with purpose. I don't need such a thing. Surely you can see how our time demands are completely different? My being here is entirely because it means something to her. But don't ask for more than that. I don't have it to give."

"That's what most people say," she responded. "I thank you for wanting to mend fences, but you're really just repeating yourself, Mr. Diamond. Butterfly House is low on your list of priorities."

Why did she have to make it sound like a character flaw? Sam bit his tongue, but she was making it hard with her holier-than-thou stance.

"What if I asked you to come out to the ranch tomorrow? Spend the day, take a tour?"

"I can't afford to take a day away from here!" Her lips dropped open in dismay. "There's too much to be done!"

He sat back, pleased that she'd taken the bait. "Exactly my point."

"It's hardly the same," she argued, wrapping her arms around her middle, the movement closing herself off from him even further. "You can hardly compare the Diamondback Ranch with this place. The differences are laughable."

She thought the Diamondback ranch was a joke? His blood heated. "Why do you disapprove of me so much?"

"Please," she said, contempt clear in her tone. "I've worked with people a long time. I know your type."

He bristled. His *type*? What exactly was his type? He didn't profess to be perfect but all he tried to do was put in an honest day's work. He knew he had a bit of a reputation for being single-minded, but what was so wrong with that? He knew what he wanted, and he went after it. There was something else in her tone, the same negative inflection she'd used the night of the benefit. It grated that she made that sort of snap judgment without even getting to know him at all. She had no idea of the pressure he was under these days.

"Really. And you came to this judgment somewhere between me offering you a drink at the fundraiser and walking through the door at the meeting today?"

She looked slightly uncomfortable and he noticed her fingers picked at the fabric in her skirt. "Among other sources."

"Ah, I see. And these other sources would be?"

She lifted her gaze and something sparked in her eyes. "You are not going to turn this on me, Mr. Diamond."

"Oh, don't worry, Ms. Beck." He put particular emphasis on the *Ms.*, hoping to get a rise out of her. Snap judgments that she wouldn't even qualify annoyed him. He was gratified to see her nostrils flare the slightest bit. "Because I know your type, too, but I'm too much of a gentleman to elaborate."

"A gentleman!" she exclaimed. Sparks flashed in her eyes. "From what I hear, you're far from a gentleman."

Sam wasn't in the mood to defend his character as well as today's actions. He had never, not once, been dishonest with a woman. He wondered where she'd gotten her information from and if it had anything to do with Amy Wilson? Dating her had been a mistake and he'd done her a favor by setting her free. But Amy hadn't seen it that way and had felt compelled to complain all over town. Most people knew to take it for what it was—sour grapes and hurt feelings. But Angela was new here and Amy could be very persuasive.

He had come here to apologize only to have his good intentions thrown back in his face and his character maligned. His temper flared. "Before you say anything more, think very carefully," he cautioned. "I'm sure you don't want to lose Diamond funding. If I recall, even with the house bought and paid for, there are operating expenses to consider. Not to mention your salary."

He saw her face go pale and felt his insides shrivel. Dam-

mit. They were right back where they'd started despite all
his resolve to smooth out the wrinkles. It was beneath him
to threaten funding and yet he couldn't bring himself to back
down. He'd look even more foolish. He should have put a stop
to Amy's gossip ages ago, but he'd felt bad after the breakup,
knowing he'd hurt her without intending to.

Now he'd gone and acted like a bully. He sighed and wiped
a hand over his face, uttering a low curse. "What is it about
you that brings out the worst in me?"

"The truth?" she replied acidly.

Angela's stomach seemed to drop to her feet as the words slid
from her lips. She couldn't take them back and they echoed
through the kitchen. He had just confirmed her opinion.
Everything Amy had said about him really was true. He was
caught up in himself and no one else, wasn't he? She really
should learn to shut her mouth. More than anything else, the
need to smooth the waters rather than make waves was the
one thing she'd never quite eradicated from her own life.

Her head said to placate him because his funds were crucial to the project. But her pride—and her heart—wanted
to tell him exactly what she thought. What sort of example
would she set if she allowed him to threaten her job, the very
existence of the project? The whole purpose of the shelter was
to help women stand on their own two feet, to be strong. How
could she allow herself to be weak? She certainly couldn't
give in to the urge to back down every time she faced a challenge.

While she was contemplating her response, Morris chose
that moment to strut through the kitchen. Lord of the house,
master and protector, the orange-and-cream-colored cat
stopped and regarded Sam with a judgmental eye.

"The infamous Morris?" Sam asked.

"I should have called him Houdini," Angela responded.

"He's quite the escape artist." It was unusual for Morris to come out when strangers were around, and she watched as he made his way over to Sam. Maybe she'd judged Sam too harshly before. You could tell a lot about a man by watching him with animals.

Morris went directly to Sam, surprising her, and he sniffed at Sam's jeans suspiciously. Sam looked at Angela helplessly, shrugging his shoulders. Angela saw the fur on Morris's back stand up and his tail stiffen. She took a step forward, opening her mouth to warn Sam. But she was too late. Sam shouted and looked down at his leg, rubbing the denim just above the top of his boot.

Morris scooted away, but Angela knew exactly what had happened and wanted to sink through the floor. She hadn't thought this meeting could get any worse, but Morris had taken matters into his own...teeth.

"Your cat bit me!"

Heat rushed to her face as his words moved her to action. She scrambled after Morris and picked him up. Cursed animal, he snuggled into her arms sweet as honey. "He has a thing about strangers. Particularly men." She rushed to the half bath and locked Morris inside. "I think he was abused as a kitten," she continued, wondering if there was anything more she could do to make Sam Diamond more aggravated. "The vet said his tail was broken in three places, that's why it's crooked. But he really isn't a bad cat, he just has a protective streak. He..."

Her voice trailed off. Sam was staring at her as though she was crazy. "I'll shut up now," she murmured.

"Really," Sam said drily, as if she'd stated the impossible.

Morris meowed in protest, the howl only barely muffled through the door.

"You're a real bleeding heart, aren't you, Ms. Beck?" He

glowered at her. "Maybe I need to come up with a better sob story, eh? Maybe that'll get you off my back."

That did it. "Since when did helping others become a flaw, Diamond?" She took a step forward, feeling her temper get the better of her. "Maybe if you took your head out of your charmed, privileged life for two seconds you'd see someone other than yourself. And as far as Morris goes, maybe I am a bleeding heart because I can't stand to see another creature abused. And if he's a little leery of men, he has good reason. I consider him a fine judge of character!"

Sam's dark eyes flared. "A fine judge of…" He made a sound like air whistling out of a tube. Morris howled again. "You know nothing about me. Nothing."

"I know you're a big bully who thinks I'll dance to his tune because I need his money. But I won't pander to you like Charles Spring and the others on the board. You can threaten, you can take funding away. Go for it. Because I would rather that than me betray all Butterfly House stands for by letting myself be pushed around by the likes of you." She finished the speech out of breath.

"Without the funding, this place never opens."

"Don't be so sure." Several times today she'd allowed Sam Diamond to mess with her confidence. But she was done with that. She'd faced worse than Sam Diamond over the years and come through with flying colors. Besides, she had an ace in the hole. She knew Molly Diamond was dedicated to this project. Molly believed in it and in her.

"You think I haven't faced adversity before?" She pressed her hand to her collarbone, felt her heart pounding against her fingertips. "I'm stronger and more resourceful than you think. So go for it. Pull the funding."

She wasn't sure what made her dare him to do such a thing when they clearly pushed each other's buttons so completely and quickly. That had only happened to her once before when she'd been seventeen and so very vulnerable. She'd fallen for Steven in record time and found herself smack in the middle of a volatile relationship. Her mother had taken one look at Angela's face and said quietly, "Passion burns as hot as anger, dear." But that wasn't the kind of passion Angela ever wanted, and her parents certainly hadn't set a shining example for her to follow.

It took everything she had to stand toe-to-toe with Sam Diamond now without cowering. And yet, as she looked into his handsome face, she somehow knew that she wasn't being entirely fair. She was making connections, assumptions without basis. All through her career she'd worked very hard to be objective. She'd had to be.

So Sam Diamond shouldn't be any different. But he was. And she admitted to herself that he had been from the moment he'd sauntered over and spoken to her in his slow, sexy voice at the benefit. Nerve endings had shimmered just at his nearness. He posed a different threat than physical fear. And that threat came from inside herself and her own weaknesses.

He hooked his thumbs into his pockets. "I'm not going to pull the funding. The Diamond family made a commitment, and we honor our commitments despite what some may think."

The tension in the room seemed to settle slightly, no longer at a fever pitch amplified by sharp words.

"I appreciate that."

He took a step closer and her heart started a different sort of thrumming. Earlier she'd taken great care to make sure she didn't touch him as they passed in the crowded hallway. She stood her ground. She didn't want him to know she was afraid. Goodness, she was a strong, capable, resourceful woman. It was ridiculous that one person could make her forget all of that just by breathing. She tried to remember what it was that Amy had said. That Sam Diamond took what he wanted until he was done and then he tossed it away like yesterday's garbage. Amy's words were completely opposite from Sam's pledge, so which should she believe?

"You're tired," he noted, and to her shock he lifted his hand and ran his thumb along the top of her cheekbone. She knew there were dark circles beneath her eyes. Makeup had concealed it for most of the day, but it was growing late and as the makeup faded, her fatigue came to the surface.

But more than that—he was touching her. She flinched slightly at the presumptuous yet gentle touch, but he didn't seem to notice. His thumb was large, strong and just a little rough. She was tempted to lean in to the strength of his hand for just a minute, but she held her face perfectly still instead as her insides quivered with a blend of attraction and fear. "I've been putting in long days," she breathed. "There's a lot to do."

"I won't keep you, then," he replied, dropping his hand. She missed the warmth of his thumb and took a step backward, shocked at her response. No one ever touched her. Ever. And certainly not in such an intimate way.

"I'm sorry about Morris. He's a very naughty cat. Did he get you very badly?"

And then it happened. Angela saw the barest hint of a smile touch his lips. Not the smooth, charming grin from this afternoon. A conspiratorial upturning of his lips that Angela couldn't resist. It sneaked past all her misgivings and lit something inside her. She found herself smiling in return and chuckling. He joined in, the warm sound filling the kitchen.

Angela sighed as the laughter faded, looked over at Sam's face, now holding a spot of devilishness that made her understand why the women of this town all swooned in his presence.

"I'll live," he said, the earlier hostility gone. "It was more of a surprise, really." He lifted an eyebrow. "Just as well I have a tough skin. Maybe he smelled our dog or something. Buster has a way of putting cats on edge."

Was he teasing her now? The idea made an unfamiliar warmth curl through her. She had to admit, knowing he was a pet owner added to his appeal. She had a momentary image of Sam on a huge horse with a dog following at their heels....

Dangerous. And trouble. At the very least, Amy had that part right.

"Don't take it personally," she offered weakly. "It's not you..."

"If you say so."

"I couldn't just leave him," she continued, not knowing why it was important that Sam understand about her cat but feeling compelled just the same. Another meow sounded behind the door. "He was hurt, and just a baby."

Sam's face was inscrutable. "Do I strike you as the kind of man who kicks puppies, Ms. Beck?"

Did he? Lord, no. He might use charm as a weapon, and he might have a ruthless streak—that single-mindedness he'd mentioned—but she found it hard to believe he'd be deliberately cruel. There was something about the way he'd touched her face...

She shook her head, not quite trusting her judgment.

"Well, that's something, then."

He turned to walk down the hall, back toward the front door, around the bags of home-renovation supplies and paint and everything else that would take up all her waking moments for the next several days. Perhaps weeks.

Maybe she could sweet-talk someone local into donating their time. School would be out for summer soon. Maybe a couple of students at loose ends... There was so much to do before the open house. The logistics of organizing that alone were taking up so much time and energy, and she'd already drafted the press release and sent it out....

The press release. The media was going to expect to see Molly at that, too. New nerves tangled as she thought of dealing with the press alone. She looked up at Sam. Getting more from him would be like getting blood from a stone. She'd figure something out. She had a little bit of time.

"I'd better let you get back to your dinner," he said, putting his hand on the doorknob.

Her dinner. The tasteless glazed chicken that she'd popped in the microwave in lieu of a real meal.

"I trust that I'll see you next month at the board meeting, then?"

His hat shadowed his eyes in the dim light of the foyer, so when he nodded briefly Angela couldn't read his expression. Something between them hesitated, seemed to keep him from opening the door, made it feel that there was more to her question than she'd voiced—and more to his answer.

When she finally thought he must be able to hear her heart beating through her chest, he opened the door. Angela let out a deep sigh of relief, until he turned and tipped his finger to his hat in farewell.

A gentleman.

She shut the door behind him. Perhaps. But not like any gentleman she'd ever known. And maybe that was the problem.

# CHAPTER THREE

SHE'D been kidding herself.

Exhausted, Angela sank down on the lopsided front step and put her head in her hands. For ten days she'd worked her tail off, and there was still so much to do her head was spinning. Having to do the renovations herself meant no time for working on the embellishments, the little special touches she'd had in mind. The basement was littered with used paint cans and rollers, and she'd missed a stud trying to install a curtain rod and ended up having to do a substantial drywall repair in the yellow room. Yards of material gathered dust waiting to be sewn into curtains and duvet covers. Boxes of supplies were still taped up, needing to be unpacked. The carpet was torn up in the living room but the local flooring business had postponed installation of the new hardwood until tomorrow. The place was a mess.

The open house was only four days away. She needed Molly's help. Molly had been on board to look after feeding the crew from the youth center on Saturday. She was also supposed to be a spokesperson to the media so Angela could stay in the background, where she liked it. Angela had been so annoyed by Sam's attitude that she'd squared her shoulders and determined she'd show him and do it all herself.

But she'd been wrong. She needed help. And she needed *his* help if Molly wasn't able. It wasn't just about a pair of spare hands. The press release had gone out before that horrible board meeting and the local angle had been playing up Diamond involvement. To go ahead with the day and have the Diamonds conspicuously absent…to stand in front of a camera and have her picture taken, her words put into print…

Her stomach tied up in knots just thinking about it. This wasn't about her, it was about *them*—the women the foundation would help. The last thing she needed was anyone digging around in her past. She closed her eyes. It was truly a bad state if she was relying on the likes of Sam Diamond to be her ally!

She wiped her hands on her overalls, resigned. It came back to the same thing every time, no matter how much she didn't want to admit it.

She needed Sam Diamond's help.

She found him coming down a beaten track on horseback, sitting a trot effortlessly while a golden retriever loped along behind. Growing up in the city she hadn't really believed that cowboys and ranchers, like those in storybooks and movies, really existed. But they did. The Diamondback Ranch sprawled over the foothills, dotted with red-and-white cattle. The house was a huge log-type mansion that reeked of money and Western tradition at once. Just beyond a gigantic barn was a paddock where half a dozen gleaming horses snoozed in the warmth of the summer sun. And Sam Diamond was getting closer by the second, all six foot plus of him in his own über-masculine element.

She'd never felt so out of place in her life, and she'd been in some pretty uncomfortable spots over the years.

"Well, well. Must be important to tear yourself away from Butterfly House on such a gorgeous day."

She had to squint against the sun to look up at him. "You manage to compliment the weather and antagonize me all in the same sentence," she said. She forced a small smile. "And I might get mad, except for the fact that you're right. It is important."

He'd slowed to a walk but she still had to hustle to keep up with him.

"And it has to do with me…why?"

With a slight shift of the reins, horse and rider came to a stop. The dog, sensing home, bounded off in the direction of the house. Angela held her breath as Sam turned in the saddle and looked directly at her. On horseback he was an imposing figure, and he had a direct way of looking at a person that was intimidating. She wasn't comfortable being one hundred percent of his focus, but she made herself meet his gaze. He looked far too good for comfort in his jeans, boots and dark Stetson, and she took her sunglasses out of her hair and put them on, shading her eyes.

The horse Sam rode was big and black, and the way he tossed his head made his bridle hardware jingle. He was exactly the kind of mount she'd expect Sam Diamond to ride— big and bossy and used to having his way. But Angela refused to be intimidated.

When she didn't answer, he grinned. "Let's try that again, shall we? Good mornin', Ms. Beck. To what do I owe the pleasure?"

There was a mocking note to his words and Angela felt his gaze drop over her clothing and back up again. She'd considered changing out of her paint-streaked overalls and sneakers but decided not to. She felt safer in the shapeless garment rather than her work clothes that skimmed her figure more closely. Besides, the scale of work that had to be done was enormous. Fixing herself up would have taken valuable time she couldn't afford to lose.

"I need your help."

There, she'd said it, and it only hurt a little. Mostly in her pride.

"My help? My, my. That must have been hard to say."

"Yes. I mean no. You see…I had counted on your mother's help and without it I've fallen behind. I know it couldn't be helped," she rushed to add. "I don't blame Molly. She belongs with your father, of course. I've tried for the last week and a half to keep pace on my own, but we've got a press opportunity happening this Saturday and I'm not ready."

"As you can see, I've got my hands full here."

"Surely you can spare some time? I've been doing the renovations myself but there are some things I'm just not equipped to do. The front step is a hazard and the furniture needs to be moved into the living room before Saturday and somehow I have to have refreshments on hand for a dozen teenagers who will be at the house. Not to mention the press."

She was quite breathless at the end and felt a blush infuse her cheeks as Sam merely raised one eyebrow until it disappeared from view beneath his hat.

"Come to the house. I'll write you a check and you can hire some help for a few days."

Her blood began to simmer. For most people she would have said *put your money where your mouth is.* But for Sam, writing a check was an easy way to rid himself of the inconvenience of her and of Butterfly House. Her annoyance temporarily overrode her personal discomfort.

"You don't understand. This isn't just about slapping on some paint. It's about perception."

"Perception?"

"Yes, perception." She sighed. "It's not even so much the renovations. When you replaced Molly on the board, the press releases had already been sent and the arrangements made. You're the foundation's biggest sponsor, Sam. And everyone expects to see a Diamond presence this weekend. If there's no one there…"

"If it's perception you're worried about, I'm not sure I'm the image you want to present to the public. You'll do fine without me."

He laughed, but Angela wasn't amused. This project was about more than helping women reclaim their lives. It was about changing attitudes. And Sam Diamond, with his money and swagger, was the perfect test case. If she could bring him around, she figured she could accomplish just about anything.

"I won't say no to the check because the foundation needs it. But we need more than that, too. We need a showing of support. We need the backing of the community. I don't like it any more than you do. I wish I didn't need your help. But I sat on the step this morning trying to figure out how I was going to manage it all and I kept coming up blank."

"Maybe I can spare a man for a day or two, but that's all. Now, if you'll excuse me."

But that wasn't all. How easy was it for Sam to solve a problem by scrawling a dollar amount and washing his hands of it? "All I'm asking for is one day. One day for you to show up, be charming, give a visible show of support. As much as it pains me to admit it, the people of Cadence Creek follow your lead."

He rolled his eyes. "Here we go again. You don't give up, do you? Do you ever take no for an answer?"

She gritted her teeth. If he only knew how much she hated confrontation! She lifted her chin. "Do *you*?"

A magpie chattered, breaking the angry silence. "From the look of the house, it needs more than a slap of paint. It needs a demolition order. You'll never get it fixed by Saturday." Sam adjusted the reins as his horse danced, impatient at being forced to stand.

Angela got close enough that she had to tilt her head to look up at Sam. She wanted him to see what was at stake. It wasn't enough for him to sit atop his ivory tower of privilege—or his trusty steed—and bestow his beneficence. It was too easy. And the women she wanted to help hadn't had it easy. Their lives couldn't be fixed by a blank check.

"I have to. The house has been neglected, that's all. It just needs some TLC."

"Ms. Beck." He sighed, looking down at her from beneath his hat. "Do you want me to do everything for you?"

She felt her cheeks heat. "Of course not. But, for example, I was going to look after the painting and minor renovations while your mother lent a hand with some of the aesthetic needs—like window fashions, linens. On Saturday she was not only going to represent your family to the community and press, but she was in charge of all the refreshments. That's all fallen to me now. I do need to sleep sometime, Sam. And then there's the issue of what to say to people on Saturday when they ask about our biggest sponsor and their conspicuous absence."

"You tell them we're busy running a ranch. You tell them we're occupied with adding a new green facility to our operation. Or that we're busy employing a number of the town residents. All true, by the way."

"Have you heard of volunteering, Mr. Diamond?"

His dark eyes widened as his brows went up. "I beg your pardon?"

"Volunteering—offering one's time with no expectation of reimbursement."

"I know what volunteering is," he replied, impatience saturating each word.

"Millions of people volunteer every day and still manage to work their day jobs. Most of them also have families of their own—and you don't have a wife or children that I can see.

You can spare Butterfly House the cash, but can you spare it the time?"

Angela swallowed, took a breath, and stepped forward, grabbing the reins of his horse with far more confidence than she felt. She stood in front of the stallion's withers, her body only inches away from Sam's denim-clad leg as it lengthened into the stirrup. "What are you so afraid of, Sam?"

He slid out of the saddle and snatched the reins from her hands, his movements impatient. "You can save the holier-than-thou routine. I've made up my mind."

She could sense success slipping away from her and frustration bubbled. "You go to great lengths to avoid personal involvement. Why is that? Maybe it's true what they say about you."

"And what's that?" He stood before her, all long legs and broad chest. She felt incredibly small and awkward next to his physicality, dumpy in her overalls next to his worn jeans and cotton shirt that seemed to hug his shoulders and chest. She felt a little bit awed, too, and it irritated her that she should be so susceptible to that because, despite the fact he was a pain in the behind, Sam Diamond was also drop-dead sexy. The sad thing was she was nearly thirty years old and had no idea what to do with these feelings. She'd gotten very good at presenting a certain image, but inside she knew the truth. She had no idea how to be close to anyone.

"Never mind." She turned away, hating that he was able to provoke her without even trying.

He reached out and grabbed her wrist. "Not so fast. I think you'd better tell me."

Her heart seemed to freeze as her breath caught for one horrible, chilling moment. Then, very carefully and deliberately, she reached down and removed his fingers from her wrist and stepped back. She wasn't sure which emotion was taking over at the moment—anger or fear. But either one was enough to make the words that had been sitting on her tongue come out in a rush.

"That you're a cold-hearted…" She couldn't bring herself to say the word. She kept her gaze glued to his face for several seconds.

Finally the hard angle of his jaw bone softened a touch and he said quietly, "Where'd you hear that? Let me guess, Amy Wilson?"

She had, and her lack of response confirmed it.

"You shouldn't judge someone by what you hear."

"I don't." At his skeptical expression, she sniffed. "I don't," she insisted. "I form my own opinions. I deal with people all the time, you know. And I judge people by what I see them do." And right now he wasn't scoring many points. Her wrist still smarted from the strength of his fingers circling the soft flesh. She touched the spot with her fingers.

His gaze caught the movement and then lifted to meet hers. There was contrition there, she realized. He hadn't really hurt her; he'd merely reached out to keep her from running away. It was her reaction that was out of proportion and she suspected they both knew it. Awkward silence stretched out as heat rose once again in her cheeks.

"And so you've judged me." The horse got tired of standing and jerked his head, pulling on the reins. Sam tightened his grip, uttered a few soothing words as he gave the glistening neck a pat. "I suppose you won't believe me if I say I'm sorry about that." He nodded at her clasped hands.

It was a backward apology, and did nothing to change the situation. That was what she had to remember. "Sam, you give from your pocketbook if it means you don't have to get involved. I just haven't figured out why. Is the ugliness of real life too much for you?" She kissed her last hope of success goodbye, knowing she was crossing a line but needing to say it anyway. How many times over the years had people turned a blind eye to someone in trouble? How many people had avoided the nasty side of life because it made them uncomfortable? How many people had known what was happening in front of their faces and hadn't had the courage to make the call? Angela's life might have been very different. It was the only thing that kept her moving forward in spite of her own fears.

"That's ridiculous." He turned his back and started leading his horse across the barnyard.

"Then prove it. Try giving of yourself." She went after him, desperately wanting to get through. "These women have been through it all, Sam. They've been beaten, degraded, raped…" She swallowed. "By the men who professed to love them. Despite it all, they got out. They sought help, often leaving everything they owned behind. This house will help bridge the gap between overcoming an old life and building a new, shiny one. What in your life is more important than that?"

He didn't answer. But she sensed he was weakening, and she softened her voice. "All I'm asking for is a few hours here and there. You have a gorgeous house, food on the table, a purpose. I just want to give these women the same chance. If you show the people of Cadence Creek that you support these women, doors will open. They'll have a chance to be a part of something. People look to you to lead. Lead now, Sam. For something really important."

She took a step back, uncomfortable with how impassioned her voice had become. For a few seconds there was nothing but the sounds of the wind in the grass and the songbirds in the bushes.

"You realize how busy this ranch is, right? And that I'm going it alone now that Dad's sick?"

"But you have a foreman, and hands. Surely they can spare you for a few hours?"

"You're forgetting one important detail."

"I am?"

"If I help you, we're going to be seeing more of each other." He made it sound like a prison sentence. "And I don't mean to be rude, but we're kind of like oil and water."

She felt her vanity take a hit before locking it away. Her personal feelings weren't important here. It shouldn't matter if Sam liked her or not. She only needed his support.

"Don't worry. There's lots of house to go around. We hardly have to see each other. I can stand it if you can." Besides, there were lines she didn't cross, ever, and it was a big leap from noticing the fit of a man's jeans to personal involvement. They rubbed each other the wrong way. Then she remembered how he'd brushed by her the other night and how her body had suddenly become attuned to his. The real trouble was in the few moments where they had rubbed each other exactly the right way. At least on Saturday there would be tons of other people around and she'd be too busy keeping the kids busy and the food on the go to worry about Sam.

They were at the fence gate now and there wasn't much left to say. He threw the reins up over the saddle horn and mounted, settling into the saddle with a creak of leather. "I'm not afraid," he said. "Two hours. I'll give you two hours Saturday afternoon to talk to whatever press you've lined up. Just keep your social-worker analysis to yourself, okay? I'm not interested. Save it for your clients."

"Scouts' honor," she replied, lifting two fingers to her brow. She couldn't help the smile that curved her lips. It wasn't all she'd asked for, but more than she'd dare hoped and she counted it as a significant victory. Perhaps she'd be spared the public face after all.

He shook his head and gave the horse a nudge. As they were walking away he twisted in the saddle, looking back at her. "I'll send over a check. I'd advise you to cash it before

I change my mind and stop payment on it. Maybe you can cater your food for Saturday with it."

He showed her his back again and they took off at a trot, stirring up dust.

Sam looked up from his desk and realized it was nearly dark outside. That meant… He checked his watch. It was going on ten o'clock. He'd been at it longer than he realized. But he wanted to start the construction on the new project before the end of summer, marking a new era for Diamondback. As he got older the more he realized he was caretaker not only of the Diamondback name but the land. The environmentally friendly initiatives were exciting, and he loved the idea of reducing Diamondback's footprint. But his father's stubborn refusal to sign off on the contracts was stressing him out.

He sighed, rubbed a hand over his face. It grated on his nerves, having the responsibility of the ranch without also having the authority to make the changes he wanted. And with Virgil's health so precarious, he was doing some fancy footwork these days trying to get his way without upsetting the proverbial apple cart. Between his father and the everyday running of the ranch, he hadn't been lying when he'd told Angela that he didn't have a moment to spare.

But then she'd had to go and challenge him and he'd been suckered in. It rankled that she knew how to push his buttons without really knowing him at all. He didn't think he was usually so transparent.

She'd looked exhausted. There was the annoying realization that she'd been right in just about everything. A Diamond family member *had* promised to appear and her assertion that Butterfly House would need community support was valid.

But for Sam it had been more than that. It had been the look in her eyes, the way all the color had leached from her cheeks in the split second he'd grasped her wrist within his fingers. The expression had been enough to give even his jaded heart a wrench. There was more to Angela than the prim and proper businesswoman he'd met at the board meeting. This was personal for her and he wanted to know why.

He scowled. It was none of his business. The last thing he needed was to get sucked into someone else's problems. If only his mother would agree to a hired nurse, she could go back to being Angela's right hand and cheerleader. He worried about Molly, taking on all of his father's care herself and refusing any help. With a sigh he closed his eyes. He was trying to hold everything together and not doing a great job of it.

A light knock sounded at the door and he turned in his chair. "Mom. You're still up?"

Molly Diamond came in, and Sam thought she looked older than she had a few short weeks ago. There were new lines around her eyes and mouth, and she'd lost weight. The light sweater she wore seemed to hang from her shoulders.

"I just got your father settled. You're up late."

"Just going over the latest information on the biogas facility. I'm close to finally having the details nailed down. The sooner the better, we've had enough delays. I'm excited about it."

"Sam…" Molly's brow furrowed. "Right now those plans are more like building castles in the sand."

"Then help me convince him," he replied easily. "He won't listen to me. This will take Diamondback into the future."

"What sort of future? Who for, Sam?"

There it was again. The constant tone that said *when are you going to start a family?* Surely she realized it wasn't a simple snap of the fingers to find the right woman. There had to be love. Whoever he married was taking on not only him but Diamondback as well. He gritted his teeth. "Two different subjects, Mom. And right now this facility is the right thing."

Molly sighed. "It's a big undertaking. And your father sacrificed a lot to make Diamondback what it is. He's just… cautious. Please don't trouble him about it. Not now."

"It's the way of the future. And I've spent a lot of hours putting this together." Disappointment was clear in his voice.

"And it's taking its toll," she said, coming to the desk and pulling up a chair. The desk lamp cast a circle of cozy light and despite the recent troubles, Sam thought how lucky he was to have grown up here. It hadn't always been easy, and there'd been a good many arguments and slammed doors, especially in younger years.

But he'd never once questioned their love, never once felt insecure. He thought of Angela, standing in the farmyard in paint-smeared, shapeless overalls and dark glasses. He wondered what her upbringing had been like, thought about the women who would benefit from Butterfly House. Not everyone had had the advantages that he'd had.

"What's really on your mind, Sam?"

"Nothing, really. Just trying to keep up."

"You met Angela Beck," Molly said, leaning back against the cushion of the chair and crossing her legs. "She's a worker."

"A dog with a bone, more like it," he muttered. Molly laughed and it was good to hear the sound. Ever since she'd found his father on the floor of their bedroom after his stroke, there hadn't been much to laugh about.

"She's doing a good thing, Sam."

"I know. But you're much better at this kind of thing than I am. I belong out there." He lifted his chin, looking out the window. In the darkness, only the reflection from the lamp looked back at him. "We totally rub each other the wrong way. We can't occupy the same space without arguing. I have intentions of being nice, and I end up being an idiot."

To his surprise Molly laughed. "At least you acknowledge when you're an idiot," she answered, "which puts you a step ahead of most of the population."

"Mom, why don't you let me hire some help for you?" He leaned forward, resting his elbows on the desk. "Then you can still work on this project. It'll be good for you." Plus it would mean he wouldn't be pulled away from the farm, and he wouldn't have to come face-to-face with Angela's acute observations—never mind her smoky eyes and delicious curves. She'd tried to hide them in the overalls, but they were still there. He didn't like that he kept noticing. Didn't like that she seemed to be on his mind more often than not.

"Because I want to be with your father." Molly looked tired, but Sam noticed how her eyes warmed. "You'll understand someday, when you're married and you've been in love with that person for most of your life."

Sam sighed. "Mom, I'm thirty-seven. Don't count on it, okay? At this rate, Ty's your best chance for a grandkid."

Ty. Sam's cousin by blood but also his adoptive brother. Any child of his would be considered a grandchild. But Ty was barely on speaking terms with the family. Neither said it but they knew it was true. He hadn't even come home for Virgil's seventieth birthday.

"I'm not saying that, don't panic. I'm just saying that I need to do this for Virgil. And that leaves Butterfly House up to you. It's not a long commitment. Once it's fixed up, the management of it will be in Angela's fine hands. A board meeting here and there is not too much to ask."

"You failed to mention the open house this weekend. She was here today, demanding I show up."

Molly put a hand to her head. "Oh, my word, I'd forgotten

about that. I promised to help. We wrote the press releases together, before your dad…"

Her voice broke and Sam's heart gave a lurch. "It's okay. I told her I'd show up and do all the official handshaking. But, Mom, I can't go on doing this forever. I'm too busy. Maybe Dad will improve enough that you can step back in after a month or so," Sam suggested, shutting his folder.

"Maybe. But, Sam…"

He looked into Molly's dark eyes, eyes that reminded him of who he saw in the mirror. She was the strongest woman he knew, and he liked to think he'd inherited some of that strength.

"You've been brought up to believe that Diamondback is everything, but it's not, not really. Sometimes I think your Dad and I sheltered you too much, made it too easy on you. We wanted things to be better for you than they were for us starting out, but you've never really seen what it's like to be hurting, and struggling, and wondering if life will ever be good again."

"So this is for my own good?"

She chuckled. "You'll thank me one day, you'll see."

"Don't count on it." But he couldn't help the smile that curved his lips.

"I know you didn't sign up for this, Sam. But it would mean a lot to me if you could help out." Molly put her hands on the arms of the chair and boosted herself up. She gave a small stretch. "Well, I'm off to make a cup of tea before bed. Tomorrow's another day."

"I think I'll look in on Dad before I turn in."

"He was awake when I left. He lives for your updates, Sam. I know you're butting heads right now, but keep talking. He needs you. He needs to feel a part of this place."

Sam nodded, clicked off the light and followed his mother to the office door. They parted ways in the hall—Molly to the kitchen, Sam to the main level spare room, where his parents had slept ever since Virgil's stroke.

When he looked in, his father was asleep. Sam's heart gave a hitch. His larger-than-life father was reduced to a bed and a wheelchair. His words were muffled and unclear and he seemed so different from the giant who had slain boyhood dragons, from the man who had built this ranch, living for—and off—the land.

Now it was all up to Sam.

He could understand his father going crazy. He could even understand why Virgil was fighting so hard to remain in control. Because Sam couldn't imagine a day where he didn't wake up under a Diamondback sky and smell the Diamondback air. Why couldn't Virgil see they were fighting for the same thing?

## CHAPTER FOUR

THE smell of paint hung in the air as Angela took another pin out of the curtain hem and carefully kept her foot on the pedal of the sewing machine. She'd planned simple curtains, tab-style that would thread through the pretty café rods she'd bought. Maybe it was the fabric that was causing the trouble, or maybe it was the fact that she'd been up and working for nearly twelve hours. Either way, she'd ripped out two seams already, and then indulged in an uncharacteristic spate of cursing when the bobbin thread tangled on the bottom.

She reversed, finished the seam, cut the threads and closed her eyes. There was still so much to do before Saturday. She was never going to make it this way.

"Is it safe to come in?"

She started in her chair as the deep voice echoed down the hall. "Sam?"

"None other." The screen door thumped into the frame and she pressed a hand to her pounding chest. She shouldn't be so jumpy, but it was an automatic reaction she'd been conditioned to years ago.

She hastily folded the fabric and put it on the kitchen table with the rest of the sewing bits. What on earth was he doing here? She hadn't expected to see him until Saturday afternoon.

His boots thumped on the wood floor and suddenly there

he was, larger than life, in his customary jeans and boots but he'd traded his button-down shirt for a black T-shirt. The way the cotton stretched across his chest made her want to rest her hands against the surface to see if it was indeed as hard as it looked.

"What in the world?" His eyes widened as he took in the sight of the table.

She followed the path of his gaze. Not a glimpse of wood table was visible beneath the strewn-out cloth, pins and thread. More fabric hung over the back of one of the chairs and Morris batted a scrap along the floor, too entranced with the way it slithered over the tile to worry about Sam's presence.

"I'm not a neat seamstress," she remarked.

"I hope you have something else for me to do," he said, folding his arms. "Though I've been known to pick up a needle and thread before."

Angela swallowed. She tried to picture him in a chair, a tiny needle in his strong, wide hands, and it wouldn't gel. Sam was more untamed than that. She looked up at his glittering eyes and decided *untamed* was a good word indeed. There was a restless energy about him that made her uneasy. Especially when what she needed from him was reliability.

He shrugged. "Of course, I'm usually stitching together hide and not dainties."

She would hardly call the blue damask *dainties*, but she didn't bother correcting him as now her mind was full of the image of him doctoring horses and cows. He was stubborn as a mule—she could see that plain as day. But she couldn't shake the idea that he'd treat his animals with capable and gentle hands.

Oh, dear. It wasn't a good idea to think of Sam Diamond in those terms. He was already looking a little too attractive.

"Do?"

"Yes, do. You didn't finish everything on your list, did you?"

Gracious, no. There was still lots to be done, but his sudden presence threw her utterly off balance. "I wasn't expecting you," she stammered.

"I thought you could use some help before the big day."

She kept her mouth shut for once, biting down on her lip and feeling a bit bad for all the nasty thoughts she'd had about him. She scrambled to come up with something he could do on the spur of the moment.

"Of course I can use the help. Um…I'm not exactly sure where to start."

"I brought some tools and supplies in the truck," he suggested, resting his weight on one hip. "You mentioned the other day that the porch steps and floor needed some work. Maybe I could tighten them up, replace a few boards. I don't think anything's rotted, but I won't know until I have a good look. In any case, you can't paint until it's repaired."

"That'd be fine," she replied, relieved he'd thought ahead and she wouldn't have to show him anything. It also meant he'd paid attention and given it some thought. It was what she'd wanted, right? For him to notice that Butterfly House needed help? So why was getting what she wanted making her so flustered?

"It'll give me a chance to clean up in here. I finished painting the blue room today. Your mother helped me pick out the fabric. That's what I'm sewing…"

"My mother and I have different skill sets."

She smiled, trying to imagine Sam debating the benefits of certain colors and fabrics or chatting about recipes. The image didn't fit. But visualizing him using his hands was something entirely different. For all his untamed energy and irritating ways, Angela was beginning to see that Sam was the kind of man who formed foundations. He shored up the weak spots and made them strong—at Diamondback and now here. She didn't want to be relieved at passing off even just a little of the responsibility, but she was, just the same.

"I'm happy to have your skills, since I'm not adept at construction. Some light carpentry work would be wonderful, Sam, thank you."

The words were friendly and for a moment neither of them said anything. Friendliness was a new vibe between them and Angela didn't quite know what to do with it. But wasn't it better than being at each other's throats all the time? If they could make peace, maybe this tight feeling in her chest that happened every time he was around would disappear.

"If I need anything I'll give a shout."

"I'll be here."

He treated her to one long, last look before turning on his heel. He was out of sight when he called out.

"Oh, and Angela? Be careful. You smiled just now. You might want to get that checked."

She balled her fingers into fists as the door shut behind him. Oh, he was impossible! Just when she thought they were coming to some common ground, he had to provoke her again. And yet there'd been a teasing note in his voice that made warmth seep into her. It was foreign, but it wasn't an unwelcome feeling.

She folded the finished panel and yanked out the second, all pinned and ready for stitching. At least he was out there and she was in here and she didn't have to look into his sexy, teasing face!

But the sound of the hammer could be heard over the hum of the machine, and Angela's brows knit together. Sam Diamond was not going to be an easy man to ignore.

He was still working on the porch when she finished pressing the last completed panel. Carefully she laid the curtains over the ironing board so they wouldn't wrinkle and tidied up her sewing mess. Twilight was starting to fall and he'd soon have to quit as he lost the light. Angela took a breath, considered, and then went to the fridge for the jug of lemonade she'd mixed up earlier. She poured two glasses and started for the front door. Whatever her misgivings where Sam was concerned, it would be nice if at Saturday's event they appeared as a team rather than on opposing sides. In hindsight, the incident earlier in the week had been pure overreaction on her part. Sam had made the first step coming here today. Now it was her turn.

She opened the screen door with a flick of her finger and a nudge of her hip. Sam looked up and for a moment Angela's heart seemed to hesitate as their gazes locked. There was a gleam of sweat on his forehead and as he stood, he hooked his hammer into his tool belt, a thoroughly masculine move that sent her heart rate fluttering.

*Oh, my.*

She'd never been particularly susceptible to the rugged workingman type before, but Sam was in a class of his own. And when he smiled and asked, "Is that for me?" the only thing she could do was extend her hand and give him the glass, careful not to let their fingers touch.

She held her own lemonade in her hand, forgotten, as he took two big swallows, tipping his head back so that she could see the movement in his throat. Her tongue snuck out to wet her lips. She'd bet any money the skin on his neck was salty and warm from his hard work.

He lowered the glass and Angela snapped out of her stupor, hiding her face behind her own drink as she took a sip. She was no better than the other women in town, was she? There was no denying that Sam had a certain appeal, but she'd always prided herself on being immune to such things. She'd always been a "keep your eye on the prize" kind of girl—that philosophy had held her in good stead through many, many difficult years.

And so it would now, too. Besides, Sam wasn't interested in her. He'd made enough disparaging comments during their first few meetings for her to know that she was not his type.

"Thanks, that hits the spot," he said, leaning against the porch post.

"I finished my sewing and thought you might be thirsty," she replied. She'd just go inside now before she embarrassed herself. She consoled her pride with the fact that she was human, after all, and her eyes were in perfect working order. It was nothing more than that. She turned on her heel but his voice stopped her.

"Stay. The boards are sound now and I dusted the cobwebs off the chairs."

The invitation was tempting. Sitting in the warm purple twilight with Sam Diamond and sipping tart lemonade sounded like a good way to end the day. Too good. "That's okay. I still have things to finish up inside."

She dared look up at him, and she was surprised to see concern softening his hard features.

"You've been burning the candle at both ends." He moved his hand, gesturing at the chair. "Let it wait until tomorrow."

She raised an eyebrow. Did he want to spend time with her? Had he cleaned off the chairs for this specific reason? Her heart sped up thinking about it. Besides, Sam was a bit of pot calling kettle. "Would you leave it 'til tomorrow if you had things left to do?"

Delicious crinkles formed at the corners of his eyes as he gave a small smile of acquiescence. "Touché."

But he was right, she admitted to herself. She had been working hard and she knew part of her sewing trouble had come from being tired and inattentive. "Well, maybe just for a minute."

She took her glass and sat in one of the Adirondack chairs, letting out a sigh as she sank into the curved wooden back. They needed scraping and repainting like everything else, but for right now it was perfect. Sam likewise sat, took off his hat, and stretched out his impossibly long legs. He took a sip of what was left of his lemonade and turned his head to look at her.

"Can I ask you a question?"

A mourning dove set up a lonely call and Angela rested her head against the chair. "It depends."

"Is this project personal for you?"

She turned her head and studied his face. When his gaze met hers, she knew. He'd guessed. The invitation to sit had been deliberate, she knew that now. And she was scrambling to come up with an appropriate answer that would appease him and yet tell him nothing. Her hesitation spun out, weaving a web around them consisting of what she didn't say rather than what she did.

Finally she sighed. "Of course it is. I've put a lot of energy into it. I couldn't have done that if I weren't committed to its success."

Sam put his glass on the arm of the chair. "That's not what I meant."

"I know," she admitted, meeting his gaze.

"The other day, when I grabbed your arm…"

She saw his Adam's apple bob as he swallowed. A sinking feeling weighed down her chest. Was that why he was here tonight? Guilt?

"Don't worry about it," she murmured, lowering her eyes.

"I can't stop thinking about it." His voice was husky now in the semi-darkness and it sneaked past her defenses, making her vulnerable. She didn't want him to care. Didn't need him to. And yet it felt nice to have someone see beyond the image she showed the world every day.

"All the color drained from your face, and your eyes…" He cleared his throat. "You recovered quickly, but not before I saw. And it suddenly made sense. I'm sorry, Angela. I never meant to frighten you."

He met her gaze fully now, and she was surprised at the honesty in his eyes. He looked different without his hat— more approachable, more casual. Probably too casual to be sitting here alone with her. And now they were sharing something. It created an intimacy that felt a little too good. It would be so much easier if she could simply treat Sam like a client! She never lost her objectivity with clients.

"Is that why you came back? Because you feel guilty? Because it was nothing, Sam, really."

He hesitated. "It made me think about what you said about the foundation, that's all. Put it… Well, put it into context, I suppose."

It was a good answer and Angela leaned her head back against the chair. It felt odd to be talking and not butting heads, but good. It was progress. His voice was quiet and hopeful and it touched Angela's heart. She'd accused him of not wanting to face the ugliness of life, but here he was anyway. On some level he cared.

But could he handle her personal "context"? She doubted it. Nor did she care to tell it, so she tailored her response to satisfy his curiosity while only truly skimming the surface. She didn't want to go all the way back. Not ever.

"Before I became a social worker, I found myself in a bad situation, yes. But I left. So you see I'm not so bad off after all. You just took me by surprise the other day."

"Did he…you know. Hit you?" He struggled over the words.

How to answer? Her story was not simple or easy. She could see where his assumptions were leading him and it was probably the easiest, cleanest way out. "Once," she admitted, hearing the crack in her voice. She cleared her throat. "It had been bad for a while, but after he hit me I left."

It barely scratched the surface of her tangled history but it did the trick. "So when I grabbed your wrist…it was thoughtless, Angela. I'm sorry."

"It was the reaction of a moment. And already forgotten. Don't worry about it." She tried a smile that didn't quite feel genuine.

"I'm glad," he replied. "The last thing I'd want to do is…"

He let the thought trail off, but it didn't matter. She understood. This was a different Sam and Angela wasn't sure what to do with the change. Being aware of his physical attributes was one thing. But starting to *like* him? Bad news. All the same, she needed him as an ally. She wanted to trust him—especially this Sam, who was currently without the self-important edge she'd sensed from him at the beginning. A man who was thoughtful and caring.

But she didn't want to be the foundation's poster child. Rather she wanted him to make the connection to the women who would call this place home. She felt a moment of sadness, wishing her mother could be one of those women. She knew it would never happen, but she couldn't extinguish the tiny spark of hope that still flared from time to time.

"The women coming here have gone through the hardest part—leaving their particular situation. Now they're ready to rebuild their lives and need a nudge and helping hand to get started. Our first resident is already lined up. Once she's settled our first task will be to help her find a job. When our residents are on their way to a new life, then they'll go out on their own."

"Like a butterfly out of a cocoon."

"Yes, exactly like that." She smiled, glad he'd connected the dots. "We hope they'll leave with a little cash in their pockets, as well as some confidence and hope for the future."

Silence fell for a few minutes as the shadows deepened. Angela sipped her drink while they watched a pair of squirrels race through the yard and up a poplar tree. She was ever aware of Sam sitting next to her, the length of his long, strong legs, the way his T-shirt sleeves revealed tanned, strong forearms. He'd reached out tonight. Nothing could have surprised—or pleased—her more. Even if it had cost her a corner of her privacy.

"It's a good program," he admitted.

Sam was saying all the right things, but there was a little voice in the back of her head saying that she shouldn't be too quick to believe. All her training, all her life experience had taught her that she had to be clear-headed and objective. To feel compassion and a need to help, but not to insert her personal feelings into a situation.

"This situation," Sam said carefully, "was he your husband?"

"No," she replied, making the word deliberately definite so as to close the subject. She kept her private life private. She'd learned to be skeptical years ago, somewhere between the fear and the anger. Home life had been frightening and fraught with anxiety. Sam's question made her feel that he could somehow see right past her barriers and it made her uneasy. No one needed to know how personal this cause truly was to her heart. How close she'd come to history repeating itself before she got out.

She couldn't meet his eyes now. She'd always made a point of judging what she saw, but she hadn't with Sam. She'd formed an opinion because of things she'd heard and then read that into her impression of him rather than giving him the benefit of the doubt. She didn't very much like what that said about her.

* * *

Sam watched Angela lower her eyes. He knew very well he hadn't made a good impression the first few times they'd met, but he was trying to make up for it. His reasons for being abrasive in the beginning had been his own stress talking. But his sincere questions tonight had taken the snap and sparkle out of her eyes. He found he missed it.

"You're doing a good thing here, Angela."

"I'm pleased you think so." She looked up briefly.

"I'm not a liar, and I wasn't trying to be mean before. I do have my hands full—we're trying to finalize details on a biogas facility at the ranch. Let's just say it hasn't gone as smoothly as I'd like. I haven't had many moments to spare. I probably could have been more tactful." He offered a smile, hoping to change the subject. He didn't like seeing her look so sad.

"Biogas?"

Gratified she'd taken the bait, he continued. "We can turn our organic waste into energy. Specifically, enough energy to run our entire operation and then some without touching the power grid. But it's newer technology and it doesn't come cheap." Even talking about it made him excited. The initial capital was what his father kept harping on, but Sam knew their coffers could take it. The reason for his dad's worry he suspected was not as black and white and had to be handled more delicately. And Sam wasn't used to dealing that way. There'd been a lot of adjustments since his father's sudden illness.

"You? A 'green' farmer? I never would have guessed it."

"I get the feeling that you formed a lot of opinions about me that may turn out to be wrong."

She blushed a little and he watched the way the breeze ruffled her hair in the increasing darkness. The last of the June bugs were starting to hit the porch door as the light from within glowed through the rectangular window.

"Our ranch has been in the family for generations. Each new generation bears a responsibility—to the family, to the land. I'm nothing but a steward, until…"

"Until the next generation? But aren't you an only child?"

He rested his elbows on his knees. "Yep."

It was the one way he knew he'd disappointed the family, but he refused to enter into a marriage that wasn't real, that wasn't based on love and respect. He was probably foolish and an idealist, but that was where he drew the line. He imagined admitting such a thing to Angela. He suspected she'd laugh in his face. It was rather sentimental, he supposed. He wanted the kind of marriage his parents had.

The only reason he hadn't pushed harder about the development was that Virgil's stroke had made Sam suddenly aware of the fact that his dad—who'd always seemed invincible—wouldn't always be there with him. Coming to terms with that was a hard pill to swallow.

"You've gone quiet all of a sudden."

He smacked his hands on his knees and pushed himself to standing. "Just tired. I should get a move on." *Before I say too much*, he thought. He was finding her far too easy to talk to.

"I appreciate the help tonight, Sam. I know you're busy."

He chuckled. "That must have been hard for you to say."

"Maybe a little." Her lips twitched. "I probably haven't been entirely fair. If we hadn't sent out press releases and set up media…"

"It's okay. I handed off a few things to my foreman. It's a few days, nothing more. I'll manage."

Angela drained what was left of the lemonade from her glass and stood up. "Well, thanks for coming. At least I won't have to worry about anyone falling through the porch on Saturday."

"No problem." He picked up his glass and followed her

into the house. He put it in the sink as Angela draped the blue curtains over her arm. "You don't have more to do?" he said, hooking his thumbs in his pockets.

"Just hang these curtains. I have to put them up tonight because I don't want to fold them and crease the fabric, and I can't leave them out or Morris will be sure to have fun playing in the material hanging over the ironing board."

Ah, the devilish Morris. Sam figured he should consider it an achievement that he'd gone from being bitten to simply being ignored. The cat was nowhere to be seen. "I'll give you a hand."

"No, really…"

"Which room?"

She met his gaze and he knew she was exhausted when she gave in without too much of a fight.

"Upstairs, first door on the left."

# CHAPTER FIVE

ANGELA followed Sam up the stairs, staying a few steps behind and trying to avoid looking at the worn patches on his jeans. She failed utterly. They'd learned more about each other tonight and it had created some common ground—ground that Angela wasn't sure she was comfortable treading. He was far harder to dismiss when he was like this.

"Do you have the rods installed?" Sam's deep voice shimmered in the darkness of the stairway. How he could sound so good saying something so banal was impressive. She pushed the reaction to the side and told herself to remain focused on practicalities.

"They're not up yet. They're ready though, and my tool box is in the closet." They reached the landing and Angela let out a sigh of relief as they emerged from the confined space of the stairway. "Here we are. Hang on and I'll flip on a light. The last bracket I installed I made a mess of and had to fix the drywall."

They stepped inside the room and she hit the switch. Light from the overhead fixture lit up the room and she looked at Sam, standing there with soft blue fabric draped over his arms. It looked out of place against his tanned masculinity, and the effect of the contrast was appealing. She paused to enjoy the picture. She might be immune to his charms but she could still appreciate his finer points. And they were *very* fine.

"Let me take those from you," she murmured. "This will only take a minute or two."

She moved to take the panels from his arms and as he slipped them into her hands their fingers touched. His were warm and rough and it tripped her personal distance alarm big-time. The tips of his fingers grazed the inside of her wrist and butterflies winged their way through her stomach as she snatched her fingers away.

Okay. The last thing she expected to feel around Sam Diamond was this flicker of physical awareness. She slid the fabric the rest of the way out of his hands and stepped back. She wasn't sure if he had touched her deliberately or not. But she was positive of one thing. He couldn't ever know that he affected her in any way. She simply didn't *do* touching. It hit too many triggers.

Instead she inhaled, and counted to ten as she exhaled.

Sam didn't seem to notice her reaction; instead he looked around the room. Angela felt an expanding sense of pride. "It's pretty, isn't it?" she asked, seeking level emotional ground again.

"The color—it looks like something my mother would pick out. Like the old chinaware she's got."

Angela smiled. "She did pick out the color, and the material, too. I think it's kind of classic, don't you?"

"She's classic," he replied, smiling, and Angela tried to ignore the way his eyes warmed when he spoke about Molly. Sam was clearly devoted to his mama, and he always spoke of her with love and respect. But Angela had to wonder if there was a reason why someone as handsome and well-established as Sam hadn't been snapped up off the market? He was a good-looking, successful guy. Amy had said that he'd given her a line about not wanting to lead her on and give her false expectations and made it sound as if it was merely an excuse to be rid of her. Angela now wondered if he'd been sincere while ending the relationship, and if the wonderful example Molly set had created a standard that other women simply couldn't live up to.

Not that she was inclined to try to reach the mark herself. She'd never really bought into that idea of married bliss, two halves of one whole and the whole nine yards. So far she'd done just fine on her own.

"Well, the curtains are the finishing touch. Shall we?" She nodded toward the two large windows on the north wall, suddenly impatient to see the final effect. Looking around the room, she was struck once more with a sense of satisfaction. She'd done a good job here if she did say so herself. The hardwood only needed a good cleaning and polishing and then Angela was leaving the room be. The women would want to put their things there, make the space their own. She knew very well how important it felt to have a say. For years she'd been forced to keep her room just so. She'd longed to change the paper, the color, put things on the walls. None of it was allowed. She'd never been able to have anything that smacked of individuality. But the residents here deserved a room of their own for the duration of their stay, and she was determined that they would get it.

"The rods are in the closet. Just a sec." She laid the curtains over the bed and went to get the café rods and her toolbox. In a few short minutes Sam had measured, marked and screwed the brackets to the wall. Angela slid the tabs over the rod and stood on tiptoe, arms above her head, holding it steady while Sam threaded the rod through the hole and screwed the decorative finial on the end. As he reached to do the other side, his hands slid over hers. The electricity from the touch rocketed through Angela's body and she lowered her hands quickly, stepping away from the window. That wasn't supposed to happen again!

This reaction—this attraction—was just wrong on so many levels. She didn't even want to like him, let alone feel…what was it she was feeling, anyway? Desire? It couldn't be. Desire meant wanting, and she didn't want this. She didn't know what to do with it.

It was just some weird chemistry thing. It must be, because nothing like this had ever happened to her before. Touches, even simple ones, always made her want to shy away. But Sam's left her wanting more and that scared her to death.

And there was still another curtain to contend with.

There was no sound in the room now and it put Angela more on edge. Did he know what he was doing to her? Was he playing a game? The moments ticked by and she wished he'd say something. If he provoked her she could at least respond. As it was she was beginning to think that he'd felt it too. Heavens, one of them being jumpy was enough. It was easier to deal with him when he was teasing or baiting her. In the silence her body still hummed from the innocent contact.

It was akin to torture to lift her arms again, holding the rod while he threaded it through the first side. She inhaled a shaky breath, Sam looked down at her, and the finial dropped to the floor and rolled a few feet away.

"Hang on," he said, his voice soft and husky. She stood, frozen to the spot while he retrieved the curled knob, and when he came back to put the second end through the bracket he stood behind her, his hands raised above hers as he reached for the rod.

His chest pressed gently against her back and she shivered, aware that with her arms up her breasts were very accessible. All he'd have to do was slide his hands down over her shoulders and he could be touching her. There was a pause—just a breath—but she was as aware of a man's body as she'd ever been. She was trapped in the circle of his arms, blocked by his body, telling herself she had no reason to be afraid and yet trembling just the same. There was an intimacy here that she wasn't prepared for. And yet neither of them had spoken a word or made an overt move.

She couldn't breathe. She had to get out of here, get away from the hard warmth of his body and his scent…oh, for goodness' sake, when did the smell of fresh-cut lumber and lemon become so appealing? "Have you got it?" she asked, hoping her voice didn't sound as shaky as she felt.

"I've got it," he replied.

She let go of the curtain rod as though it was burning her hands and slid out from beneath his arm. The air around her cooled and she exhaled with relief. What surprised her most was the empty sense of disappointment that rushed in where moments ago desire and fear had battled.

He cleared his throat and resumed screwing the finials on the rod as if nothing had happened. When he was done, he smoothed out the panel so that it lay flat. "There you go," he said, turning around.

When she looked at him something seemed to snap in the air between them. All it would take was one step and she could feel the heat of his body again. One step and she could explore the sensations that rocketed through her body when he was near. She saw his eyes widen as the moment spun out and the air seemed to ripple between them. He was so powerful, so forceful without any effort, and Angela knew he could swallow up a little wallflower like her in the blink of an eye.

"That's unexpected," he acknowledged quietly, and Angela wished he'd never spoken at all.

"I don't know what you mean," she countered, picking up the screwdriver and dropping it in the toolbox, hoping it would put him off. Being close to him set off tons of personal boundary alarms, but the truly terrifying thing for Angela was her own betraying reaction to him. She was back to not trusting herself or her judgment, and it made her stomach twist sickeningly. She'd made too many mistakes to risk making another.

"I mean whatever it was that just happened." He pursued the subject, and she wished he'd just shut up and let the matter drop. "And it obviously scares you to death. I suppose, considering your past…"

She forced herself to face him, schooling her features into what she hoped was an unreadable mask. This was why she didn't talk about her own history. Suddenly it defined her and everything she did. "All that happened here is that you helped me install some curtain rods. And that's all that can happen, Mr. Diamond," she added significantly.

The corner of his mouth turned up. "So we're back to Mr. Diamond again. You're plenty rattled."

"Are there no bounds to your ego?" She snapped out the question, but it stung because he was one-hundred-percent right. Had he provoked her deliberately in those long moments when he'd let his chest ride so close to her back? She didn't want to think so. Whether it had been intentional or not, she'd fallen for it. She straightened her spine. Now she felt vulnerable *and* ridiculous, not to mention transparent. "I appreciate all of your help with the project, but if you're looking for more than that…"

"Ms. Beck." He took a step closer and her heart started beating strangely again. "I have just about all I can handle with Diamondback and my other commitments. I'm not 'looking for' anything."

"Then…"

The rest of the question was silently asked. What was going on between them? The pause deepened and so did his dimple. "What do *you* propose we do about it?"

"Do about it?" There was a definite squeak in her voice now and she wasn't sure if it was fear or anticipation. She cleared her throat. "We don't do anything. You're the one playing games, Sam."

"I don't play games," he replied, standing taller. "You don't strike me as someone into casual relationships, Angela." His smile faded. "And I'm not looking for anything serious. So that pretty much takes care of that, right? We'll just forget it ever happened."

"Right," she parroted, so completely off balance now she wasn't entirely sure what he was saying and what he wasn't. She didn't do casual relationships because she didn't do *any* relationships. She could never let anyone close enough. Not that he needed to know that.

"Now if you'll excuse me, it's getting late and I'm sure we both need our rest."

"Of course."

He brushed by her. Moments later she heard his truck door slam and the engine start. She sagged, resting her flaming cheek against the cool blue wall, watching through the window as he drove away.

He'd been utterly sincere in his last words. So why didn't Angela quite believe him? He'd certainly been in an all-fired hurry to leave.

He was right about one thing—she was dog-tired. But she suspected sleep would be a long time coming tonight. Sam Diamond had a way of challenging everything. And what freaked her out the most was realizing that even knowing her past, he hadn't run. She had.

Sam pushed his mount harder over the trail, enjoying the feel of the wide-open gallop and the wind on his face. Nothing had prepared him for the jolt he'd suffered the moment his body had touched Angela's. And then she'd had the nerve to accuse him of playing games.

It had bothered him ever since he'd left her standing in the bedroom, her face pale and her greeny-blue eyes huge as they stared at him. He couldn't get her off his mind. He could still see the spark in her eyes. He'd seen something else, too—fear. She was afraid of him and he'd had the strangest desire to pull her into his arms and tell her it was all right.

Knowing her past, though, made him question every action, wondering how it would appear to her. So instead of following his instincts, he'd got himself out of there. Angela wasn't a woman he could trifle with. And anything more than trifling scared him witless.

To top it off, his father had truly dug in his heels about the biogas facility, flat-out refusing to sign any papers so they could release the money and begin construction. Sam had been so angry he'd nearly yelled at Virgil—a man still recovering from a stroke. He'd managed to hold on to his temper, but it had only taken one small mention of Power of Attorney and Virgil's eyes had blazed at him. Despite his verbal difficulties he had very clearly made his point as he shouted, "Not crazy!"

Sam had slammed out the door instead, deciding that a good, old-fashioned hell-bent-for-leather ride was in order to work off the tension. Nothing was going right. Everything felt unsettled and off balance. Every attempt he made at holding the family together was a flop. He'd come terribly close to telling his father to start walking and get back where he belonged, but he'd reined in his emotions. It wasn't Virgil's fault. It wasn't anyone's fault. They were all just trying to cope the best they knew how.

His horse started to lather and Sam knew he couldn't push him any harder.

As he started over the crest of the hill, Sam stared at the

flat parcel of land marked with surveyor's stakes. Seeing it waiting, so empty and perfect, made his shoulders tense. He was a grown man, for God's sake. A man who could make his own decisions, not a boy beneath his father's thumb. The whole issue made him feel impotent and ineffectual. Was this how Ty had felt before he'd taken off for parts unknown? Once more Sam wished his cousin were here to talk things over with. It wasn't the same with him gone.

The more nagging problem was that he was still thinking about Angela. That wasn't a good sign.

He slowed and let the gelding walk, the restlessness unabated in himself. He remembered the guarded look on her face as she'd admitted she'd gotten out of a bad relationship. Something had happened in that moment. More than knowledge—he'd guessed as much when she'd blanched after he'd grabbed her wrist. It was something else.

It was trust. And the moment in the bedroom had taken that delicate trust and shattered it. Maybe she was right. Maybe he had played games because he'd indulged in the attraction even knowing their connection was fragile at best.

He dug his heels into the gelding's side. He needed to get away from here for a while, clear his head. The least he could do was make it up to her, right?

Angela counted down the hours. Less than twenty-four now and everyone would be here. A reporter and photographer from the local paper, someone from the town council, even the Member of the Legislature was slated to attend. The very idea of being front and center made her lightheaded with dread, but she reminded herself that it was part of her job. And with Sam here, she could stay under the radar.

The more important problem was that she didn't even have a chair for them to sit on beyond the somewhat scarred table and chairs in the kitchen. Somehow she had to get the sofa and chairs from the garage into the living room without scuffing the new floor.

She was struggling with the first armchair when she heard the steady growl of a truck engine. She peered over the top of the chair and saw Sam's face behind the wheel, cowboy hat and sunglasses shading his face. Her heart began pounding and she nearly dropped the chair. What was he doing here? After the curtain incident she'd been sure he wouldn't be back. And she'd considered that just as well.

He got out of the truck, shut the door, and took off the glasses, letting them dangle from one hand for a moment before folding them up and tucking them into the neck of his shirt. Oh, boy. He was Trouble with a capital *T*. Maybe he'd shown a softer side the other night, but it hadn't exactly ended well. So what was he doing back here?

He knocked on the screen door as Angela's arms started to scream in protest. She waddled the half-dozen steps it took to get into the living room and put the chair down as Sam called, "Angela?"

She brushed her hands off and walked to the door, trying to steady her pace and her pulse. "Sam. What on earth?"

"It occurred to me you might be a bit shorthanded trying to get ready for tomorrow."

Shorthanded. So he was only here to help? She paused, torn between needing his help and needing to be honest. "You left in an awful hurry the other night. I didn't expect to see you until tomorrow."

He looked at her through the screen door, watching her steadily and making her feel about two inches tall. How could she turn away a pair of willing, strong hands?

He held out the appendages in question. "And yet here I am."

"Aren't you too busy at Diamondback?"

"I needed to get away for a bit. Got in the truck and ended up here, thinking you might be able to put me to work."

"I…uh…see."

*Oh, brilliant response, Angela*, she thought, shifting her weight on her feet nervously. Having him show up while she was thinking about him didn't help matters at all.

One eyebrow raised. "Are you going to talk to me through this screen door all day?"

She sighed. Of course not. She was ashamed to admit that she was far more concerned with her own behavior than his. As the social worker, she was supposed to be the well-adjusted one, so Sam could never know about all the unresolved feelings he stirred up. "No funny business," she said, opening the door and inviting him in.

He burst out laughing. "Funny business?"

Her face heated. Despite her intentions to the contrary, she was making a fool of herself. "Oh, never mind. I do need help so don't say you weren't warned." He couldn't be that much trouble with six feet and a hundred pounds of sofa between them, could he? That little atmospheric moment was a one-off. "I was wondering how I was going to get the furniture moved in from the garage." A perfectly good, safe activity.

"The boys could have done it tomorrow."

"That's what I originally decided. But then I thought, what if it rains? And people are coming. I need somewhere for them to sit if we can't be outdoors, right?"

He looked into the empty living room and back to her again, his eyes disapproving. She knew it was silly to think of doing it all herself. And she hated that she somehow felt she needed his approval when she didn't.

"You should have called."

"So you could have said you were too busy? No thanks." His eyes widened with surprise at her quick response, and then seemed to warm with a new respect. "You know, sometimes it beats me why I keep coming back here."

"Maybe you're a sucker for punishment." She tilted her chin. Enough was enough. She kept letting him get the upper hand and it was time that changed. At the same time, there was a new edge to the words now. Not the angry, spiteful edge that had been prevalent in their first meetings. But something else. It almost felt like teasing. Banter. Right now he was looking at her like he was up to something. The boyish expression made him look younger than she expected he was and very, very sexy.

"Maybe I am," he replied slowly, and punctuated it with a wink.

Angela burst out laughing. "Okay, you had me until the wink. Seriously?"

Sam shoved his hands in his pockets. "Over the top?"

"Yeah. A bit."

"Then I'd better stop making a fool of myself and get to work, huh?"

She led him to the garage while a new, unfamiliar warmth expanded inside her. It was a surprise to find that she was slowly growing to trust Sam. How could her first impression have been so wrong? She'd thought him all swagger and arrogance, but there was more to Sam Diamond than what she'd first thought was a huge sense of self-entitlement. He had a generous spirit and a sense of humor, the humble kind that meant he didn't mind poking fun at himself a little. She'd been wrong to accuse him of ego. What had happened was as much her fault as his.

As he lifted the other wing chair effortlessly, Angela swallowed, staring at the way the fabric of his shirt stretched across the muscles of his chest and arms. It was just as well that the project was getting closer to launch. Once things were underway their paths would rarely need to cross. Perhaps a chance encounter in town, or at a board meeting of the foundation.

Besides, after Butterfly House was well-established, she had plans. If she had her way, there'd be several houses like this one scattered around the country. It was going to take all her energy to make that a reality. There wasn't room for sexy distractions in those plans.

While Sam took the chair inside, she grabbed an end table and followed him. Together they positioned the chairs and put the table between, and Angela brought out a lamp to place upon it. It made the corner of the room cozy. Next they manhandled the sofa.

"We're not going to trip over your cat, are we?" he asked, puffing a little as they hefted it up.

"He's been hiding in the basement most of the day. I think you're safe."

"Okay, now tilt it a little," Sam suggested, "to fit the arms through the doorway."

It was heavy and Angela braced the weight against her knee as she fought for a better grip and turned it slightly for a better angle. "Easy for you to say."

"Shout if you have to put it down."

As if. Her competitive spirit rose up and made her determined to carry her weight. She gave the sofa a boost and said, "I'm fine. Go."

It wasn't done gracefully, but they managed to get the sofa into the living room and put into place without scratching the new finish on the floor. "It's starting to look like a room," she said, brushing off her hands.

"What's left?"

There were two footstools and a coffee table still in the garage, and within moments they had the room organized. A quick polish and vacuum and it would be fine.

Angela looked at Sam. He'd left his customary hat on

the coatrack by the door and his hair was slightly mussed and damp from lifting in the July heat. She looked down at herself—a smear of dust streaked across her left breast, light beige against the navy T-shirt. She dusted it off and rubbed her hands on her jeans. The room was done but she didn't want him to leave yet. She'd have too much time on her hands to fuss and flutter and worry about all the things that could go wrong tomorrow. Sam made her focus on other things.

"There's a mattress and box spring that just arrived yesterday," she piped up. "I don't suppose you'd care to help me get them up the stairs?"

"Sure. Might as well use me while I'm here."

"Use him" indeed. Angela ignored the rush of heat at his innocently spoken words. They took the mattress up first and leaned it against the wall of the sunny yellow room. The box spring was harder to manage. The rigid frame made it unwieldy to get around the corner of the stairs, and it took three tries to get the angle lined up correctly to get it through the door of the bedroom. Angela's face was flushed and her breath was labored as they finally got inside and shifted the box spring so that they could lay it on the bed frame she'd put together. She nearly had it when the corner slipped and it started to slide. A splinter from the wood dug into her finger and she let go as a reflex.

"Ow!"

Sam's face flattened in alarm as he tried to take as much weight of the box spring as possible, but it was too unbalanced. It tipped and dropped, landing squarely on her toes.

"Oh!" There was a sharp pain in her big toe that began radiating out in waves. Despite the splinter, she bent to lift the box spring off her foot as her eyes watered. She took a step toward the bed and gasped out a curse.

"Put it down," Sam instructed. "Just lay it down, Angela. I'll put it on the frame later."

They laid it across the frame and she exhaled fully as Sam rushed around the corner of the bed. "Did you break it? I thought you had it…"

"I did have it, until this." She held up her hand with the splinter still sticking out.

"Let me have a look."

She wasn't about to argue, and held up her hand for his examination.

"You should sit down," he suggested, looking into her face. She tried not to wince but wasn't entirely sure she was succeeding.

The pain in her toe was horrible and she wanted nothing more than to get off her feet. But there was nowhere to sit in the bedroom. "We'll have to go downstairs."

"Come on, then. Put your arm around my neck."

She looked at him, so shocked at his suggestion that she temporarily forgot about her toe and splinter. What would it be like to be picked up off her feet and held against his wide chest with his strong arms? It made something inside her lift up and go all fizzy. She couldn't quite make the leap between the idea and actual physical contact, though. Oh, how she wished she were one of those confident women who could slide their arms around a handsome man and be comfortable doing so. Instead Angela felt a cloying sense of claustrophobia, as if she were pinned—a butterfly under glass, vulnerable and unable to escape.

She shook her head. "That's okay. I can walk."

She hobbled to the stairs and used the banister for support as she made her way down the steps one by one. She refused to look at Sam, who stayed beside her on each step. She appreciated the solicitude but he was too close and she was too aware of his body blocking her against the stairway. At the bottom she grimaced but refused his arm when he offered it.

"Stubborn as a mule," he muttered, following her into the living room.

She sank into the chair. "You got that right. Did you forget?"

"I guess I must have." He was looking at her with concern and it made the parts of her that weren't throbbing with pain go all squishy. It was inconceivable that he might actually care about her, wasn't it? It was only a few weeks ago that he'd pointed a finger at her in the boardroom in Edmonton and told her not to expect a thing from him.

And now here he was. Doing a very good impression of being there for her and she was afraid she might be getting used to it.

The pain wasn't so bad now that she was off her feet and she sighed. This was just what she needed. How was she going to supervise a dozen energetic teens tomorrow if she could hardly hobble from one room to the next? Tears of frustration stung her eyes as she contemplated the to-do list. She hadn't even begun on the refreshments yet...

"Do you think it's broken?"

"I don't know. I hope not."

Sam's troubled gaze met hers, and then he reached in his pocket. He took out a Swiss army knife and plucked out a set of tweezers. "Let's see your hand first," he said, pulling over a foot stool and sitting on it. She held out her hand and winced as he gently squeezed the skin around the splinter. With a few quick plucks she felt the wood slide out of her skin. "It's a good one, but it's out."

"Thanks," she replied. And was going to say more but realized that Sam's hands were on her ankle, lifting her leg to rest across his knee.

"Let's have a look at that toe," he said quietly.

She held her breath as his warm hands circled her ankle and carefully removed her shoe and rolled her sock down over her heel. Every nerve ending in her body was aware of his gentle touch and she bit down on her lip. She could do this. She could handle being touched, even if it did feel far too intimate. The sock slid off into his fingers and he dropped it on the floor. His careful examination was intensely uncomfortable—a mix of shooting pain, uneasiness at the personal nature of his probing and delicious pleasure as he touched gently with his fingers. His thumb was along her instep and rubbed the arch as he turned her foot. It felt wonderful and she relaxed against the back of the chair.

"You've bruised it good," he said quietly. "I don't think it's broken. Even if it is, there's not much you can do for it but stay off it. We should try to get the swelling down, though. Got any ice?"

"There's an ice pack in the kitchen freezer," she said, and watched with her senses clamoring as he put her foot carefully on the footstool and disappeared, only to return a moment later with the pack wrapped in a dish towel.

"You need to keep it elevated and the ice on it. Take some ibuprofen. It's an anti-inflammatory."

"I don't have any. I have a policy about not keeping any drugs in the house, even over-the-counter ones." She had a first aid kit but no medication.

"Then I'll go get you some."

She leaned back against the chair, finally admitting defeat. Up until now she'd been sure she could have everything put together. She couldn't now.

She was going to look like an amateur.

Her bottom lip wobbled. Just a little, and she sucked it up, but not in time. Sam's brows pulled together.

"What is it?"

"There's no way I'll be ready now. I have reporters and politicians coming—" that very thought caused her heart to stutter "—and a dusty living room and no food. I have a dozen teens coming from the youth center to do yard work, and how am I going to supervise if I can't even walk around the property?"

She felt so very vulnerable, and it was truly a bad state of affairs if she was confiding in Sam Diamond. The last time she'd given him a personal glimpse it hadn't turned him away as she'd expected.

"It'll be ready, I promise."

"Please don't make promises you can't keep, Sam. I can't bear it."

She'd heard too many promises, had too many broken over the years, especially by people she was supposed to trust. She'd heard a lot of apologies, all of them sincerely meant. And then she'd felt the blistering rage when something didn't go her father's way. She'd heard it all from Steve, too, until one day he'd backhanded her across the face.

He'd done her a favor because that was the day she broke free of the pattern forever.

But she didn't believe in promises and assurances. Not even from someone like Sam.

"I do not make idle promises. I'll be honest and walk away before breaking my word."

Her heart surged at the sincerity in his voice. She *wanted* to believe him. So badly.

"Sam, I…" Her throat thickened. She didn't want to depend on him to make this right. She didn't want to depend on anyone.

"Hush," he said, bending over and putting his hands on the arm of the chair. "You'll have everything you need. It'll go off without a hitch. Can you trust me?"

His eyes searched hers and she noticed tiny gold flecks in the irises. He was asking her to trust him with Butterfly House, the one thing she cared about most. Could she? She wanted to. She wanted to so badly it hurt inside. But she was afraid—of everything he was making her feel. Her hesitation was slowly melting away—the armor that she'd used to protect herself for years. In its absence came a whole host of other problems. She had no idea how to handle a situation like this.

But in the end she had no choice. She lifted her eyes to his and took a breath. "Yes," she breathed. "I trust you."

There was a long moment where their eyes met, accepted. And then Sam leaned in and did the one thing she feared and longed for most: he kissed her.

# CHAPTER SIX

ANGELA'S heart skidded as his lips touched hers. She wasn't prepared for how they'd feel—gentle, warm and seductive. She remembered reading a book once where a character described kissing the hero as feeling like sliding down a rainbow. Angela had thought it a silly comparison at the time. Now she understood what it meant. It was *heavenly*.

She sighed a little as his mouth nibbled at hers, teasing and making her forget all about her throbbing toe. Hesitantly she responded, not quite comfortable with the intimacy of it all but wooed just the same. There were no demands made. There was only the whisper of his lips on hers. How long had it been since she'd been kissed this way? Had she ever been? It was as if he somehow knew she needed patience and tenderness.

But when his hand slipped from the arm of the chair to her shoulder, she pulled away, breaking the contact. This couldn't happen. She couldn't let him this close. For a tense second their mouths seemed to hover, only scant inches apart. Then, to her surprise, he leaned his forehead against hers. There was an openness in the gesture that surprised and touched her. Where was the irascible rancher she'd butted heads with at the beginning? The man who'd claimed he didn't have time for her or her cause? She knew he was still in there somewhere.

The most worrying thing was that she liked this new side of Sam. When was the last time she'd felt pretty, desirable, cared for? He made her feel all those things and more, without the crippling anxiety that usually accompanied any sort of romantic overture.

"I'm sorry, Angela. I wasn't going to do that today."

*Today.* Nerves bubbled up as she realized his words confirmed that he'd thought about it before. When? When they were hanging the curtains? Drinking lemonade on the porch? Arguing at Diamondback? She swallowed. It might have been easier to pass off if it had just been a spur-of-the-moment impulse. But knowing he'd considered doing it—that he'd ostensibly told himself he wasn't going to kiss her and now had—that changed things.

Something was going on between them, something bigger than she was comfortable with. Was he interested in a relationship? That was impossible. He'd made it very plain he didn't have time for romance.

"Then why did you?"

He squatted down beside the chair, leaving his hands on the arms. "Maybe because today you were human. Today you admitted defeat. I know how hard that was for you to do. I know what it cost you." He sighed. "Boy, do I know."

She swiped her tongue over her lips; now they held the tang of bitterness. Why did she have to fail in order to be attractive to him? She never wanted anyone to pity her ever again. She'd come too far for that. "You felt sorry for me."

"No!" He shook his head. "For the first time, the cold veneer you wear all the time slipped."

Was that how he saw her? Cold? She curled her arms around her middle. Is that how *everyone* saw her? She knew she was focused and she was guarded. She had been wary of letting anyone in, giving them any power over her at all. She refused to be beneath anyone's thumb the way she'd been

under her father's. Every insult and slap had eroded her child-
ish confidence bit by bit until she'd nearly believed she was
nothing. She'd had to fight her way back. But this was the
first time she'd really sat back and thought about how she
must appear to others. Each time she saw a neglected child or
a woman who'd lost her hope for the future, her heart broke
a little more. If she appeared that way it was because she refused to let her compassion be a weakness for someone to
exploit.

"I don't trust easily, that's all," she said quietly, wanting
to explain in some small way. "When you trust someone and
they betray that trust… I don't mean to be cold. Just careful."

She couldn't explain it any better than that. She didn't trust
anyone with her secrets. She supposed being considered aloof
was a small price to pay for her privacy.

"And you don't trust me, either, do you?" He frowned.

"I don't want to, no."

He got up and lifted her foot so he could sit on the footstool again, putting her feet on his thighs. "That implies that
you do, on some level."

Angela closed her eyes briefly. She didn't want to have
this conversation. She wished Molly had never stepped away
from the board. As exciting as Sam could be, he complicated
things. He managed to see her the way no one had seen her
before and that was terrifying. The truth was ugly.

"You don't even want to be here. You said so," she defended. "And you keep coming back. You said you don't want
anything romantic." She forced herself to say the word; they'd
just kissed so it wasn't as if it was taboo now. "And now you're
here and you're kissing me. What do you want, Sam? Because
I can't keep up with your mixed signals."

"I want to help." His hand rested warmly on her ankle and
she fought not to pull away from what he probably considered
a casual touch but what meant so much more to her. "I know

I came on strong at first. I was overwhelmed at the ranch and feeling stretched to the max. Lately…" He seemed to consider for a moment, then forged ahead. "All the responsibility for Diamondback is on my shoulders, but Dad still pulls the strings and we're not seeing eye to eye. Today I had to go for a ride to blow off some steam."

"What happened between you?"

"He doesn't agree with putting in the biogas plant. I've showed him all the research. I've crunched the numbers. But he's dug in his heels and crossed his arms and said no."

Angela longed to reach out and touch his hand, but knew she didn't dare. "He's going through a difficult time. From what I gather, he was a vital workingman and now he's stuck inside and doing rehab."

"I know that. Seeing him this way is killing me, so arguing is making it all worse. My family's falling apart. Hell, I even called my cousin Ty to get his take on the whole thing."

"Ty?"

"Dad's nephew. Mom and Dad adopted him when he was a baby. He's a Diamond through and through. He reminded me that Dad is like a brick wall. There's just no easy way to break through."

"You'll figure it out," she assured him. "Diamondback means everything to both of you. It's natural that you're both very passionate about its direction."

"You're right. Diamondback—it's my life. I want to take it into the future, and Dad, he's just scared." He tilted his head and looked at her suspiciously. "Did you just go all social worker on me?"

She couldn't resist smiling just a little. "Of course not. You just needed to get it off your chest."

His hand rubbed absently over her foot, and he seemed completely unaware of the effect it was having on her. "Thanks for letting me vent. When I'm here, it's…"

"It's what?"

"Simpler. I can look at it with different eyes, and it makes sense. When I'm here I feel like even the smallest thing I do might make a difference to someone."

It did make a difference—to her. His words touched something inside her. She knew what it was like to need to act. She supposed that her feelings about her mother were similar to how Sam felt about his father. Beverly Beck would never leave her own personal hell and there was nothing Angela could say or do to change her mom's mind.

Sam had shared a part of himself with her today. She didn't want to care; she didn't want to rely on someone only to be disappointed. And she was in grave danger of relying on— and caring for—Sam.

"What you do matters," she finally replied. "To your family. Your mother worships you, Sam."

"I know that. And I love Diamondback. I love the open space and I take pride in what we do. It's in my blood."

Of course it was. It only took seeing him in the saddle to know he was a rancher through and through. "But?"

"I don't know. I'm not satisfied. Maybe I need a constant challenge to keep me from being bored."

Was that all she was, then? Angela took her recently budded feelings and buried them again. She wasn't anyone's challenge. She knew she wasn't exciting and adventurous. Certainly not dynamic enough for him. He was all strength and energy and restless ambition.

"I guess Butterfly House is the lucky beneficiary of your boredom, then," she said carefully.

"Perhaps it is," he admitted. "Now, what are we going to do about tomorrow? What's left?"

Angela swallowed thickly. Maybe Sam was right. Maybe she did shut people out. Maybe there was a way to be friendly without divulging deeper secrets. Her confession that she'd been in a bad relationship had seemed to appease him. Angela felt her own sting of shame. How could she profess to be brilliant at her job when her own mother refused to leave her abuser every day?

Instead of talking about it, Angela chose to do the only thing she could—help the hundreds of other women looking to start again. Now, just as things were coming to fruition, she was forced to rely on Sam to get the job done. She didn't like the pattern that was forming, but she had no choice at this point.

"I need to run the vacuum over the floors."

"Consider it done."

"And organize all the food. There are a dozen teenagers who will need lunch, not to mention others dropping by."

And she had to start on that now. She knew how much food hungry teens could eat. There would be sandwiches but she'd planned on making sweets as well as a pot of homemade soup. She took her leg off Sam's lap—instantly missing the warmth of his body touching hers—and put her arms on the chair, pushing herself up. She took two steps and caught her breath. Maybe she could hobble around, but she couldn't stand on her feet for long and carrying anything was out of the question. Frustration simmered. Why now? Why couldn't this have happened next week?

Because she'd let Sam distract her and had suggested moving that silly box spring and mattress. It was her own fault, plain and simple.

"You need to keep that foot up."

"I need to get things ready."

"Do you ever accept help without fighting it every step of the way?"

She turned around, bracing her hand against the wall. "I'm not used to having help, to be honest. And when I do have it, it usually comes with conditions. Heck, you're only here because your support came with a seat on the board."

His eyes darkened. "Ouch."

It wasn't fair, not after all he'd just told her. "Sorry. I guess I'm not a very good patient."

He shrugged. "Maybe it was true, at first anyway. But I'm here now and I'm offering, string-free."

They were not in this together and she didn't want to feel as if they were. Her insides quivered. How many times had she wanted to stand side by side with her mother? To fight together? And each time she'd thought they were close to escaping, Beverly had backed down. Angela had ended up disappointed and alone. Not just alone—but with wounds that cut a little bit deeper. Feeling more and more alone and losing all faith and hope.

Sam was standing beside her now, but once this project was over he'd be gone. And she'd be standing alone again. So it came down to which was more important: Saving face or saving her feelings?

She already knew the answer. She was strong and resilient. She could withstand the loss of Sam Diamond. She couldn't lose Butterfly House, though. It had to succeed no matter what.

"I'll make you a list."

She hobbled to the kitchen and grabbed a notepad. Sitting at the table she began to write out what she needed. "I have the makings for sandwiches here and I can make those sitting down," she said, "but I need sweets. Cookies, brownies, and I was planning on making butter tarts. A few dozen muffins. And I was going to make a pot of soup in the slow cooker."

"That's it?" His brows lifted, studying the list over her shoulder. "That shouldn't be too much trouble. I don't know what you were making such a big fuss over."

The fuss was less over the items and more about needing

his help once more. He was making himself indispensable and she didn't like it. Add into that the fact that she could still taste him on her lips and she needed to get him out of here as soon as possible.

She fought the urge to close her eyes. The warning bells pealed with a suffocating warning. Sam was taking over. Things with Steve had started the same way. He'd ingrained himself into her life until one day she woke up and realized he'd begun controlling it in a way she swore would never happen.

"I bought drinks but forgot cups." She wrote on the pad once more, trying to keep her hand from shaking. "And get paper ones, please, so we can recycle them."

"Leave it all to me. What about set up in the morning?"

"Clara, our first resident, is arriving first thing. She'll help me set up. But, Sam, really…"

"Sweets and soup. Consider it done." He ripped the list off the notepad and tucked it in his pocket.

She felt as though she was giving away control of the situation and it was killing her. This was her baby. If anything went wrong it was all on her. The trouble with it all was that she *wanted* to trust him. And that made her weak.

He put his hand on her shoulder and squeezed. "You don't believe me, do you?"

There was no accusation in the words. She turned her head and looked up at him. "It's not you, Sam. I don't really trust anyone."

"Maybe someday you'd care to share why that is." He said it quietly, a soft invitation. But she was already liking him too much. There could be no more kisses. No more shared intimacies. Definitely no sharing of dirty secrets.

"I doubt it," she answered truthfully. "But thank you. You're going above and beyond, and I do appreciate it." And after tomorrow she'd be able to breathe again.

"It's been known to happen once or twice. Once I commit to a thing, I give it one hundred percent. Don't worry about tomorrow. I promise."

He gave it one hundred percent, but, by his own admission, he got bored and moved on. That was what she had to remember.

"I'll be back in half an hour with the cups and some pain meds for that foot." He came back and took the pen from her hands, scribbling a number on the top. "If you need anything, that's my cell number."

"Got it."

"See you soon."

He left once more and Angela sat in the quiet. She touched her fingers to her lips.

She was usually so good at figuring people out from first impressions. She'd learned to read people. But the more she got to know Sam, the harder it was to reconcile him with the slick charmer who'd barged into their board meeting.

She closed her eyes. The worst of it all was that she had enjoyed being taken care of today. And that wasn't a good thing at all.

The rain Angela feared would ruin the day stayed well to the west, cushioned in the valleys of the Rockies. Instead, the summer day dawned clear and sunny with only a few cotton-ball clouds marring the perfect sky. She showered and hobbled to the kitchen to fix some tea and toast, waiting for Clara to arrive. She was due at nine, the teens at ten. For now there was little to do. True to his word, Sam had returned yesterday with a bottle of ibuprofen, paper cups and a willing hand as he gave the vacuum a turn around the downstairs. It was a leap of faith, but she was trusting him to deliver on the rest of his promises. So far he'd come good and it was either trust or blind panic. And she really didn't want to panic. She'd leave the hyperventilating for later when she had time for it.

At five to nine Clara arrived. Angela met her at the door. "Oh, you look wonderful," she exclaimed, standing back and examining Butterfly House's first official resident. It was really happening. After all this time, it was hard to believe. But seeing Clara on her doorstep with a suitcase made it real.

"I feel good," Clara admitted. Her brown hair fell in curls to her shoulders, and Angela noticed she'd put on some of the weight she'd lost during the first months she'd been in a shelter in Edmonton. She had lovely curves now, and dressed in denim capri pants and a loose blue shirt she looked casual and attractive. Angela wondered if the plain, slightly baggy style and understated color was intended to deflect attention. Trying to avoid being noticed—unconsciously or consciously—was common.

"Bring in your things, Clara. Three of the rooms are ready and you can have your pick. Then we can set to work."

Clara brought in a suitcase and carryall. Angela held open the door but Clara immediately noticed her limp. "What did you do to yourself?"

"Dropped a box spring on my toe yesterday."

"You should have called. I would have come early to help."

Heat rose in Angela's cheeks. "I had some help, but thanks. And I'm certainly going to put you to work today. I don't think I'll be very effective herding teens."

Morris popped into the kitchen through the basement cat door and Clara put down her bags. "Well, hello there," she cooed, and a delighted Morris rubbed his head against her hand. "Aren't you handsome?"

"Be careful. He can be a biter."

"Don't be silly. What's your name, kitty?"

"Morris," Angela replied, watching with fascination. After

the first incident with Sam, Morris had either hid out in the basement or simply stayed out of the way. He certainly didn't warm up to people as a rule. But here he was, snuggling up to Clara as if they were old friends. Perhaps her instinct about it being a man thing was dead-on.

"I'm glad you have a cat. Pets are so nonjudgmental. All they want is love."

Angela laughed. "Oh, I'm afraid Morris is typical cat. He judges on sight and has many demands. But it looks like you've passed the test. I'm glad. I rescued him and hoped he'd go over well here. I don't think I could bear to give him up now."

"He'll be great company. Now let's drop my things so we can get to work." Clara lifted her bags again and threw Angela a smile. Suddenly the day seemed full of possibilities.

They went upstairs and it was no surprise to Angela that Clara picked the sunny yellow room that matched her personality. Angela was glad that they'd finished it yesterday, and Clara could make the bed up with the new bedding later.

They'd just managed to set up the banquet table on the porch and put a tablecloth on it when Sam arrived. He lifted a hand from the steering wheel in greeting and Angela waved back, the now-familiar swirl of anticipation curling through her tummy. There was no doubt about it—she'd gone from dreading his appearance to looking forward to it. Something had changed yesterday and not just because of the kiss, but because they'd shared glimpses into their lives.

She resisted the urge to touch her hair, determined that any reaction she felt was kept inside and not broadcast for Sam or Clara to see.

He opened the back door of the truck cab and took out a plastic bin. "Someone call for food?"

"Morning," she said when he came closer. He smiled. It

was ridiculous that a smile should make her feel giddy, but it did. He'd come, just like he'd promised. She looked over to see if Clara was watching them, but she was busy putting drinks in a cooler on the porch. All in all, a sense of celebration and the feeling that everything was going to turn out all right was in the air.

"Good morning. How's the foot?"

"Sore," she admitted.

He lifted his hands a little. "Where do you want it?"

"Inside on the counter." She turned around and waved at Clara to come over. With the way she was feeling, a little interference would be a good thing. "Sam, this is Clara Ferguson. She's moving in today. Clara, Sam Diamond."

"Miss Ferguson." Sam put down the bin and held out his hand.

"Mr. Diamond."

Angela noticed the happy light dim in Clara's eyes for just a moment, and she didn't come forward to shake Sam's hand. Sam kept the smile on his face as he casually dropped the hand and looked at Angela.

"Sam's family is our biggest sponsor, Clara. His mother, Molly, sits on the board of directors. But his father's been ill, so in the meantime Sam has stepped in. He's been invaluable in getting the house ready for today."

As she said the words she knew they were true. Today couldn't have happened without him. She couldn't ever remember depending on someone so heavily. But she'd never taken on a project of this magnitude, either.

"It's an important project," Sam replied, and looked back at Clara again. "I hope you'll be happy here, Clara."

Clara lifted her chin. "I haven't been happy in a long time, Mr. Diamond. I'm looking forward to it."

Angela smiled at the fledgling confidence in Clara's voice. Yes, she'd do very nicely. Sam nodded at them both, picked up the bin and started up the porch steps. Angela followed at a slow hobble, wishing that Sam didn't look quite so good from the back view.

Sam was taking packages out of the bin when Angela arrived in the kitchen. He'd been unsure of what to say to Clara, especially when she seemed to withdraw into herself at his introduction. What should he have said? Was it better to address the issues plainly, or avoid the topic altogether? He was a rancher, no good at diplomacy, and today he was going to be put on the spot about Butterfly House. A few days ago he had considered today an annoying interruption in his schedule. But he felt differently now. He wanted to do and say the right thing. He wanted to be helpful. How could he when he couldn't even figure out the right way to speak to the women most affected by the project?

"Thank you, Sam, for bringing the food."

He put a tray of bakery muffins on the counter. "It was no trouble." He paused and turned to face her. "Delivering food is easy. But with Clara just now I didn't know what to say. I didn't want to say the wrong thing and offend her."

"You did fine," she replied, and the small half smile he was growing to look for tilted her lips. "You read the signs, which is good, and you didn't press her into shaking hands. It's a long process, Sam. When you've been abused, it stays with you forever. It's not surprising that she's not comfortable with close contact. Clara's come a long way and now she's ready to start over."

She sounded so logical, so professional. And perhaps a little bit distant. This was her element, he realized. She was more like her boardroom self today and he wasn't sure what to make of it. It was impressive, but he missed the flustered and slightly messed woman who huffed and puffed carrying furniture. Who sighed just a little when their lips touched.

Whose lashes fluttered onto her cheeks when she opened up just a little about her past. Sam felt his heart constrict. How any man could treat a woman badly angered the hell out of him. "My mother would be better at this sort of thing."

Angela looked up at him. She looked so fresh and lovely in linen trousers and a cute white top—all airy and summery. Her glossy hair was pinned up today, and he missed the way the waves fell over her shoulders as they had yesterday when he'd leaned in and kissed her. His body tightened just thinking about it.

"Maybe she would, but maybe not. It might actually be better if it's you. Molly would have set an example for the women of Cadence Creek and that support system is crucial, it's true. But you could make a real difference, too. Over half the businesses in town are owned by men. Men who look up to you, and to your father. Men who might just have employment opportunities."

His hand paused on a bag of chocolate chip cookies. He thought back to the conversation he'd had with Angela in the Diamondback yard—that his presence was important here today for PR reasons. Was that all he was to her, then? It surprised him that the idea bothered him, when weeks ago he hadn't wanted anything to do with her—at all.

"Angela? The first of the kids are here." Clara's voice came through the screen door.

"I should get them organized," Angela said, and his annoyance grew. He wanted to gather her into his arms and kiss her again to see if her cool and collected demeanor was genuine or if he still had the ability to frazzle her. Right now, despite the limp, she seemed implacable.

"I'll bring in the rest of the things. Mom wanted to help so she sent a batch of her taco soup and insisted that store-bought brownies couldn't compare to her recipe." Indeed,

Molly had seemed more than happy to take the time to cook for the event.

"Oh, how nice of her! I'll be right back to plate everything."

He watched her limp down the hall and frowned. Yesterday's kiss had done nothing less than fire something in him that he hadn't felt in a long time. And he discovered he was far from being done with it.

# CHAPTER SEVEN

ANGELA ladled out soup to the line of kids, every now and then glancing up to watch Sam speak to the local Member of the Legislature. He looked so comfortable in the situation, his weight resting on one hip and his shoulders down and relaxed. She envied how easy he made it all look. The idea of being in the spotlight just about made her blood run cold. She was so much better behind the scenes. It had been Molly who had pushed for an open-house day. She'd been right—the foundation needed the exposure. But it definitely put Angela out of her comfort zone.

Sam had been so great today. First with providing the food she'd needed, and then hanging around to speak with people while she spent her time supervising and organizing, all at a snail's pace as she hobbled about on her sore foot. She handed over another soup bowl and Sam looked over and smiled, gave a little wave. She fluttered her fingers in response and then tucked a stray piece of hair behind her ear.

She knew very well she shouldn't be so happy he was here. It was the reaction of the moment, it wasn't real. Her future was with the foundation and her plans, not with Sam. It was just hard to remember that when he was around.

Sometimes she wondered what it would be like to truly be a part of someone's world, rather than a series of people simply passing through. What would it be like to be part of *his* world?

The very idea sent a curl of warmth through her, tempered by a touch of fear. It would be easy to lose herself in Sam. He was so charismatic, so dynamic. His outgoing personality would swallow her whole.

"Ms. Beck?" One of the kids said her name and drew her out of her thoughts. "Can I have more soup? It's good."

She shook the troubling thoughts away and smiled. "Sure you can." The teens had worked up an appetite and Clara had kept them in line throughout the morning, trimming dead branches off shrubs and clearing out the old flower gardens at the base of the porch. A local garden center had donated some bedding plants—the season was ending and it hadn't been difficult to convince them to part with their leftover stock. Now flats of brightly colored geraniums, marigolds and petunias waited to be planted. One more thing to make Butterfly House home, to add some color and zip that was missing in so many of their lives.

She handed over the soup. "You've been a huge help. Thank you all for coming."

"It's been fun," one girl said, breaking off a piece of cookie. "I'd just be hanging around at home watching TV anyway."

The group of them belonged to an after-school club organized to keep local kids out of trouble. Now, in the summer months, they were left to their own devices more often than not. Giving them a project had been a good idea. Angela planned on speaking to the director again about partnering up. There was no reason why the two projects couldn't help each other.

"Yeah, me, too," said one of the boys. "Maybe we could take turns mowing the grass here or something. Whaddaya think, Ms. Beck?"

"I think it's a great idea. Tell you what. Come see me on Monday and we can set up a schedule."

"Cool."

She'd been so involved with talking to the group that she hadn't noticed Sam coming up the porch steps. "What plans are you concocting now?" he asked.

She wished she didn't get that jumped-up feeling every time she heard his voice. It didn't help that he was behind her and essentially blocking any escape off the veranda.

She began to lift her hands to her warm cheeks but stopped, dropping them to her sides. "The club is going to help out on a more regular basis. Isn't it great?"

"Sure it is." Sam smiled, but Angela sensed an awkwardness to his expression. He nodded briefly to the kids and then grabbed a paper plate.

His cool response seemed to have dimmed the enthusiasm, so Angela smiled broadly. "Hey, if someone is prepared to do my yardwork, I'll happily provide snacks." She grinned as sounds of approval came from the group. She looked at the lot of them. She knew their lives could be touched by a variety of problems—poverty, neglect, alcoholism—providing some home cooking was the least she could do. For some of them it might be the best meal they got all day.

"And have you taken time to eat anything?" Sam gave her elbow a nudge. "You haven't stopped all morning. A bird can't fly on one wing, you know."

His intimate smile was disarming and rattled her further. He'd noticed her movements even though they'd been doing different things. And his words weren't critical. Instead they felt caring. "Not yet," she replied, realizing her tummy was feeling a little hollow. "You?"

"Nope. And Mom's taco soup is one of my favorites. Let's get some before this crowd drains the pot."

While Angela got their soup, Sam loaded his plate with a

ham sandwich, a handful of potato chips and a selection of raw veggies. He led her away from the teens to a quieter spot on the porch steps. "What?" he asked, as they sat balancing the food on their knees. "I'm a growing boy."

She snorted. "Sam, if you grow any bigger you'll be..."

"Be what?"

She stared into her bowl. Even what was intended as easy banter flustered her beyond belief. She struggled to find a word and grabbed on to one she'd heard the kids use this morning. "Ginormous."

He chuckled. "You haven't met my father, have you?"

"No."

"My mom always said he was as big as a barn door." The warmth dropped out of his voice a little, replaced with sadness. "He's not as big as he used to be."

She wished she could say something to make it better, but she knew that there were times that words simply couldn't fix what was wrong. There was no other comfort she could give other than a paltry "I'm sorry, Sam. It must be so hard for all of you."

"Yes, it is. After yesterday...I talked to my mom. I think she's finally starting to realize she needs help."

Angela felt guilt slide down her spine. "I never meant that she should have to cook for today," she said quietly. "I know she has enough on her plate looking after your father." Sam had pushed and made it impossible for her to say no. If she'd known he was going to go home and foist it on Molly, she would have insisted on doing it herself. "Please thank her for me, will you? If I'd known that was your plan, I would have made a different suggestion."

"She wanted to," Sam replied easily. "She's been so wrapped up in Dad's recovery that it was good for her to focus on something else—something positive. I was going to go out and buy everything and she insisted she help. So don't feel the least bit bad, Angela. You were right. It's more meaningful when people put themselves into a project rather than just 'throwing money at it,' as you said."

She stared at her toes. Oh, how she wished she'd never said those words! "I'm sorry I said that to you," she replied quietly, putting down her empty bowl. He held out his plate, and she took a chip from it. "Thanks."

"No, you were right to. I've been like Mom. So absorbed in the issues at Diamondback that I couldn't see anything else. There are other things—important things—going on. I've enjoyed helping the last few weeks. I care about..."

Hope seemed to hover in the middle of her chest. After their first disastrous meeting she'd wanted him to appreciate what Butterfly House meant. That was *all* she wanted, she reminded herself. "You care about what?"

He popped a chip in his mouth, chewed and swallowed. "I care what happens to this place and feel invested in its success. That's new for me."

"I'm glad." And she was. The sinking feeling in the pit of her stomach was inconsequential. There was not a single reason why she should be feeling disappointed.

"That's what I told our MLA, and the reporter from the paper, too. That we as a community need to get involved."

Angela looked over at him. He was still wearing his Stetson and the way it shaded his face made him look mysterious and delicious. He was so different from anyone she'd ever known. No matter how confusing her feelings were regarding him, she was, for the moment, glad that Molly had stepped away from the board and Sam had taken her place. If he meant what he said, she'd managed to bring Sam around after that horrible first meeting when he'd been so dismissive. She remembered thinking if she could accomplish that, she could accomplish anything. Today was a victory in every sense of the word. But it felt hollow somehow.

"Thank you," she whispered. "For getting it. For helping."

"You're welcome."

There was a finality to the word that was a letdown. It occurred to her that after today she'd hardly need him around. Clara was here now and could help with the final touches to the house. The yard work was done. By the first of August, a few more beds would be occupied. Angela would be filling her days with the day-to-day management of the house and liaising with support programs. Sam would be back at Diamondback, overseeing the ranch and the new facility he was planning. It was as it should be. The sooner things got back to normal the sooner she could stop having all these confusing feelings. Sam Diamond was a distraction she didn't need.

But even as she knew deep down it was for the best, she was going to miss the anticipation of seeing him walk through the front door and hearing his voice challenge her.

"I'd better get back. I should make another pot of coffee and get those kids going again."

"They working out all right?"

She met his gaze. "Sure, why wouldn't they?" She realized he'd worn the same awkward expression when talking about Clara this morning. "Is there something wrong with having them here?"

He shook his head. "Of course not. I'm just not used to any of this. I don't know how to talk to people who…"

"Who weren't brought up by Molly and Virgil Diamond?"

He looked so earnest that her heart gave a little thump. "Maybe," he replied honestly. "I had a sheltered life, I guess, with advantages. I don't know what to say to people. You have a way that I don't, Angela. I admire that."

She was shocked. "But you handled the people part so well today—you looked totally at ease!"

He chuckled. "That's different. It's… Aw, heck. It's easier

to put on an act when it's something official. But you—you're genuine. That's special."

Her? Special? He had no idea how much easier it had been to deal with troubled teens than face the press. "You played to your strengths today, Sam, and I appreciate it. As far as the kids go—they're just kids. There's no secret code. They just want to feel visible, important to someone."

She looked up and saw Clara waving her over. The photographer from the paper was standing close by and Clara's face looked absolutely panicked.

"There's something wrong with Clara, will you excuse me?"

Clara's eyes filled with relief when she arrived.

"Oh, good. I was trying to explain that I don't want my picture taken," Clara said to Angela in a low voice.

"Of course," Angela assured her. The last thing residents needed was their faces plastered over the media. "Why don't you get some lunch? I'll take it from here."

She spoke briefly to the photographer, who was undeterred. He wanted a picture for the paper to go with the story. Angela's insides froze when she thought about standing before a camera lens. After a few moments of strained diplomacy, she heard Sam's voice at her back.

"Anything I can help with?"

Sam was close by her shoulder and she looked up at him. "The photographer wants a picture for the paper."

"So what's the problem?"

"I don't do pictures, Sam."

Sam's brow puckered. "Will you excuse us a moment?" he asked the photographer pleasantly. Then, with a light hand at her back, he led her aside.

"You don't enjoy having your picture taken?"

If he only knew. She was so much better in the background. It was why she had wanted to be a director but not the face of the foundation. "It can be a fine line between starting over and trying to keep under the radar, you know? Worse for Clara. But I don't do photos. I just don't."

"Is that reasonable? You're the director here."

But the reasons went bone deep. There was the privacy thing, and perhaps she should be past it by now. But there was that horrible slap she hadn't expected, the one that had snapped her head around so quickly she'd dropped to her knees.

Steve had taken a picture of her and waved it in her face. She recognized the young woman in the photo all too well and she hated that person. "A reminder so you don't step out of line again," he'd said, taking a magnet and sticking it on the fridge. She hadn't posed for a photograph since.

She shuddered at the memory. "You do it," she suggested.

"But you're the director," Sam argued. "This is your baby. You should be in the picture."

Her throat constricted. "I can't," she whispered, her voice raw. That would make her public. It would make her feel… exposed. And she had no idea how to explain it without breaking down.

Silence spun out for several long seconds. Sam's gaze never left her face and she blinked rapidly. Then he put his hand on her shoulder, warm and strong. "Then let's do it together. We can both be in it."

As compromises went it was a good one. "I don't know."

"At some point you need to step out of the shadows, sweetheart. Otherwise he's still winning."

Sam was right. Nothing would sidetrack her from making this a success—not even her own fears. She was depending on Butterfly House to set the bar. A brilliant track record would follow her when she went to set up similar houses in other towns, maybe even other provinces. Maybe one day the one person she hoped would need help most would take that step. If her mother ever wanted to break free, a place like Butterfly House should be waiting for her.

"We just need to show a unified front for a few minutes. A couple of snaps and we're done."

A couple of snaps that would put her face in print. Angela wondered what Sam would think if he knew the real truth. She'd made it sound so *over* when they'd spoken earlier in the week. But beneath the businesslike social worker there was a victim still struggling to overcome her own issues. She was a complete fraud and terrified of being found out.

So today she would stop acting like a victim. "Okay," she agreed, feeling slightly nauseous but glad Sam was there beside her. "Let's do it and get it over with."

The photographer stepped in. "Are you ready?"

"Oh, yes. Sure." Angela pasted on a brittle meet-the-press smile. "This is Sam Diamond, one of our board members. He'll be in the photo with me."

"Mr. Diamond, of course. Thanks for sparing the time. Let's make it a nice casual shot, shall we? Maybe you can sit on the picnic table here, with Miss Beck beside you? That way the height discrepancy is minimized."

Sam shrugged and perched on the edge of the wood table.

"Right. Put your foot there, perhaps?"

Sam put his left foot on the bench seat of the table, while his right leg balanced on the ground. All it did was emphasize the long length of his legs.

"Now, Miss Beck, if you'll move in closer and stand beside him…"

Butterflies dipped and swirled and she fought to keep the professional smile glued to her lips. She moved closer to Sam until she was standing beside him. But not touching. Sitting beside him on the step during lunch had been close enough.

The photographer looked through his lens and then lowered his camera again. "Not quite right. If you could slide in a little, please. Maybe put your hand on Mr. Diamond's shoulder, Miss Beck."

Touch him? In a personal way? For a photo? Angela was suddenly at a loss as to how to express the inappropriateness of it without sounding offensive. This whole thing was growing more uncomfortable by the second. She scrambled to come up with an alternative. "What if I stand a little behind him, like this?" She moved in behind his shoulder and instead of placing her hand on his shoulder, placed it on the top of the table instead. The bulk of Sam's body hid her from the camera lens which suited her just fine. There was no doubt in her mind that he'd be the focal point of the picture.

"That's good," he replied, lifting the camera again.

She wasn't touching Sam but their bodies were close enough that it felt warm and intimate. His morning exertions had magnified the scent of his aftershave. It filled her nostrils, the clean, masculine scent making her mouth water.

She wanted to touch him. That was the heck of it.

"One more," the photographer said. "The Butterfly House team," he chattered on. Sam turned his head and looked up at her briefly.

"A team," he said, a grin lighting his face. "Imagine that."

His smile warmed her all over and she began to relax. "Pretty impossible if you ask me. You did drop a bed on my foot."

"You dropped that yourself, but nice try."

It really wasn't so bad after all, she realized. Sam's easy posture relaxed her as well. "Turn around and pay attention," she scolded.

He dutifully turned around. Angela couldn't hold in the little snort that bubbled up at his sudden obedience.

"All done. Thank you both." The photographer lowered his camera and smiled.

"That's it?" She looked up in surprise. It had been painless after all! She'd nearly forgotten that there was anyone behind the camera.

"That's it," he confirmed.

Sam's teasing had made Angela forget the awkwardness of being so close to him, but it came back tenfold when Sam leaned back against her for just a moment, his shoulder pressed lightly up against her breastbone. It was an odd moment where she suddenly felt very much like a part of a team, and something more. Intimacy. There was awareness, but there was also an increasing level of comfort with the way his body fitted against hers or the way his skin felt when they came in contact with each other. She'd never really experienced that kind of intimacy before and she wasn't sure what to do with it. She surely didn't want it—even if it did feel nice.

"Thanks for this," she murmured.

"My pleasure," Sam said, seemingly unaware of the turmoil he created within her. "Don't work too hard, now."

Hard work was just what she needed to forget about Sam—and her confusing feelings.

The flowers nodded their bright heads, perhaps a little unevenly but cheerfully nonetheless. The mess from the buffet lunch was tidied and Clara and Angela were packaging up the leftovers in the kitchen. The house was strangely silent after the commotion, and when Angela heard a distinct meowing, she went to the cat door and unlocked the flap. "It's safe now," she said soothingly as Morris stuck his orange head through the hole.

She'd locked him downstairs with full bowls of food and water shortly before Sam's arrival, knowing he'd hide in his basket anyway during the ruckus of people running in and out all day. She'd also worried about doors being left open in the chaos and him getting out. When Morris was out, he was a terror to try to get back. And the longer he was with her, the more Angela couldn't bear the thought of parting with him. He'd been her company on long nights. He never judged. He just did his thing and came for a cuddle when it suited him. Angela understood it perfectly.

Clara looked out the kitchen window and gave a little sigh. "Well, there's a sight."

Angela went to the window and looked out. Sam was working on the old woodpile that had been created when the previous owners had cut down a birch in the backyard. He'd taken off his cotton shirt and now wore a plain white T-shirt and jeans. Beside him were two of the boys from today's group, stacking the cut wood in even piles. One of them said something and Sam laughed, tipping back his head. For a guy who was so awkward around the teens, he was fitting in incredibly well.

"He likes you," Clara said quietly. "I can tell. It's in the way he looks at you."

"I'm not interested," Angela replied, turning away from the sight. But it was too late. She already had the picture of him in her mind, blended with the leftover reactions from their picture-taking episode. Sam was persistent, she'd give him that. And he'd seen the day through, which was great. But it was time he went on his way. It was time to take the next step—the day-to-day running of the house. The last thing she needed was Sam underfoot and distracting her with his slow swagger and sexy smile.

"Yes, you are," Clara contradicted. "What you are is scared."

Angela looked at Clara. The other woman's pleasant smile was gone. Instead she looked worried—and sympathetic. Clara seemed to understand things a little too well. And while she wanted to be friends with the women here, that couldn't extend to examining her own problems.

Angela forced herself to smile. "Which one of us is the social worker?"

Clara's shoulders relaxed and she resumed packing vegetables into a plastic container. "You know the saying about walking in someone else's shoes?"

"Sure."

"You've walked in mine. There's a big difference between appreciating how a man looks and acting on it. There's an even bigger gap between wanting it all and being brave enough to go after it."

*Amen,* Angela thought. Clara put it all so succinctly, summarizing the quandary in a way that Angela hadn't been able to because her emotions had gotten in the way. For the first time Angela admitted to herself that she had been flirting with other dreams. Dreams in which she had a perfectly normal happily ever after. But Clara was right. It was not the same as taking the bull by the horns and going after it. She wasn't even sure it existed in real life. She picked up a platter and opened a bottom cupboard, hiding her face from Clara. "I guess neither of us are there yet."

Clara shook her head. "I know I'm not. It's too soon. But what's stopping you, Angela? How long…" She paused. "Forget I asked that. It's not my business."

"I'm happy as I am. I made my choices and I don't regret a one." She grinned, determined to change the subject. "And now you're here. This is what I've been working toward all along. So don't worry about me. I'm exactly where I want to be."

Angela looked out the window as she passed by to the fridge. Sam was shrugging his shirt back on and she watched the play of the muscles in his shoulders. He shook the boys' hands before sending them on their way. Clara was right. She was scared. Of Sam. Of her feelings which seemed to grow stronger every day. Of everything. This job was the only place where she felt she had absolute control and confidence and that was how it was going to stay. She couldn't be rational about Sam, and she had to be. Her life depended on seeing things clearly.

Sam knocked on the back door and Clara let him in. "Do you ladies need anything else?" he asked.

Angela put Molly's slow cooker back in the bin. "No, I think we're good. We've washed up Molly's dishes and they're all here for her. Please thank her, Sam. Everything was delicious."

"Thank her yourself. She told me to ask you to dinner when things were through."

He had left his shirt unbuttoned and the tails hung around the hips of his jeans. Angela didn't know how to answer. An invitation to Diamondback! That hadn't happened before, even when Molly had worked with her on the project.

But it was different somehow. This felt personal, and it was crossing a line. Especially on the heels of Clara's observation. As much as Angela was tempted to accept, she knew she couldn't. "I'm sorry, but I can't. We need to get Clara settled and everything."

"Clara, you're welcome to come, too. It's just a barbecue on the deck. You both deserve a break after today. Surely you have all day tomorrow to get settled?"

Silence fell on the kitchen as Clara looked at Angela and Angela looked at Sam. He was making it awfully hard to say no. The idea of a dinner full of conversation and laughter— Molly and Sam both had such an easy way about them—was hard to resist. When was the last time she'd sat around a table with friends enjoying a meal? Relaxing? And she'd just determined that it was a good thing that they'd barely see each other after today. He was really hitting her in a vulnerable spot.

"It would mean a lot. Mom feels badly for leaving you in

the lurch and not helping more. And it would cheer her up to have people around. You know my mother, Angela." His dark eyes pleaded with her. "She is usually so outgoing, but she hardly leaves the house nowadays. It's so rare that she looks forward to anything. Surely you can spare an hour or two?"

Angela was still debating when Morris stalked in from the living room and halted a few feet from Sam as if to say *hey, what's he doing here?*

Then, to Angela's great surprise, he came forward and rubbed on Sam's pant leg. Sam knelt down and stroked between Morris's ears. Angela could hear the purrs clear across the kitchen.

"Looks like your cat's had a change of heart," he said. He stopped rubbing and instantly Morris leaned against his hand, looking for more. For a moment Angela was transported back to yesterday, and the way Sam's hand had felt on her ankle, warm and reassuring. The way his lips had rubbed against hers. She couldn't blame Morris for wanting more—even if it did make him a bit of a traitor.

"So what do you say about dinner? If we had company, I think Mom would bring Dad outside to eat with us. He could use the change of scenery."

It was the mention of his father that tipped the balance. She knew Sam was struggling with the changes happening in his family and especially with his relationship with his father. She'd be small and insecure if she let a few misgivings keep a sick man from an enjoyable evening. "Oh, all right," she relented. It's not like it was just the two of them. There'd be other people around. Goodness, she'd hardly have to speak to Sam if she didn't want to. She could catch up with Molly, after all. She'd missed Molly, who'd been such a blessing during the early stages of the project. "We'll finish here and meet you at the ranch."

"Great."

He gave Morris one last pat and stood. "I'll take that with me." He held out his hands for the bin. Angela picked it up and placed it in his hands, careful not to touch him in any way. The earlier resolve stood. Dinner changed nothing.

"Tell Molly not to go to any fuss," she said, looking up at him.

"It'll just be casual, don't worry. See you in an hour or so."

She saw him to the door and watched him drive away until the sound of his truck engine faded. She sighed, wondering how on earth this had happened, and the bigger question: What on earth was she going to wear?

# CHAPTER EIGHT

For an hour Sam wondered if Angela was truly going to show up. It was nearly six o'clock and he'd had a fresh shower and changed clothes, helped move Virgil out onto the deck overlooking the valley, and now he turned the chicken over in the marinade even though it was already evenly coated.

He wrinkled his brow. Little things about Angela didn't add up in the usual way, and he wondered if there was more to the story than she was telling him. If? He was sure there must be. Nothing could be as cut-and-dried as she'd made in sound in a few short sentences.

Her lips were soft and sweet when he'd kissed her, but she'd pulled away first. She was fiercely dedicated to the project but panicked when it came to being the center of attention. She bantered easily with the teenagers but froze when it came to the press. And most miraculous of all—she'd managed to get him talking about himself. And yet she'd always kept the topic of conversation away from herself, only revealing what he suspected was the bare minimum.

All in all it made him wonder how best to proceed. The last thing he wanted to do was frighten her or come across as intimidating. He wasn't sure if a casual touch to him was equally casual to her. All in all, being involved with Angela in any way was a bit like walking through a minefield, not wanting to make a single misstep lest everything blow up in his face.

He was beginning to think he was in big trouble.

"Muss be sommme girrrl."

Sam looked over at his father. Virgil's speech was getting better but he still had trouble enunciating clearly, and often his words were drawn out. There was no mistaking the sparkle in his eyes, though, or the grin on his face—even if it was lopsided because of the lingering paralysis. It felt good to have the old, easy teasing between them again.

"I'm hungry, that's all."

The rusty laugh that came from Virgil warmed Sam's heart. It had been too long since he had heard his father laugh. Too long since they'd had a conversation without arguing, or lately, because of the speech difficulty, without disapproving grunts. "Uh-huh," Virgil replied.

"I know. Can't kid a kidder, right?"

A gleam of approval lit Virgil's eyes. Sam hadn't brought a girl home for a family dinner for years. If Angela knew what his parents had to be thinking, she'd be halfway to Edmonton by now. Sam had to tread carefully. "This isn't a date, so go easy on her, Dad. She's skittish."

"Like yrrr motherrr."

"Mom?"

Virgil nodded. "Shy when we met. Hard work."

Sam chuckled, then sobered. Without knowing the full details of Angela's past, Sam knew something terrible had shaped who she'd become. It was more than shyness.

In the end he wanted what his parents had. Virgil's illness had not only affected Sam's parents but Sam himself. Suddenly he was very aware of mortality. Molly and Virgil wouldn't be around forever. It wasn't just the responsibility of Diamondback that Sam worried about. It was the legacy. Things couldn't go on, fractured the way they were, with all the arguing and with Ty wandering all over the continent. Family needed to stick together. And it was Angela who'd shown him that.

"You warm enough, Dad?" He changed the subject, not wanting to delve into things any deeper. He hated that his father had to sit in a wheelchair. Physio was working with him with a walker, but he could only use it under supervision and for short periods of time. He looked so frail, unable to get up and take charge in his usual good-natured, blustery way. The stroke had altered Virgil in so many ways. He was short-tempered and while Virgil had always been stubborn, he'd also been open-minded. Not now. Sam was pretty sure that fear was making the old man hold on too tight.

"Isss thirrrty degrees. Fine."

The annoyance was back in Virgil's voice and Sam backed off, not wanting to cause any trouble when guests were expected. "Okay, okay."

A car door slammed, followed by another. His heart gave a leap.

He tested the grill and found the temperature just right and when Molly brought the ladies back through the French doors, he was busy putting chicken breasts on the grates.

"Virgil, this is Angela Beck and Clara Ferguson." Molly made the introductions as Sam turned around.

Angela had changed her clothes. Sam's mouth went dry looking at her. She was pretty as a picture in a floral linen skirt and a cotton sweater the color of the prairie sky as the sun came up. She kept her hair off her face with a simple cream headband, the dark waves of it falling gracefully to her shoulders. She looked so young and fresh it made him feel all of his thirty-seven years. And yet the nerves that centered in his belly made him feel like a teenager again. He'd never met anyone who could make him feel that way before.

Perhaps having her over for a family dinner was a mistake. He was afraid he was going to be horribly transparent, gawking at her the way he was right now.

Molly's speculative gaze lit on him and he went back to the barbecue, shutting the lid. Yes, a family dinner probably wasn't the smartest move. Molly had been pushing him for grandkids for years and would read more into it than it was. Sam knew Angela well enough by now to know that she could easily be chased away by well-meaning innuendoes. She reminded him of a skittish colt who needed a gentle and strong hand. He should have asked her out somewhere private. But where would that be in Cadence Creek? There was only the Wagon Wheel Diner and tongues would set to wagging the moment they walked in the door. She'd hate gossip. As would he.

"Mr. Diamond, it's so good to meet you. Thanks for inviting us to your home."

Sam schooled his features and stepped away from the grill in time to see Angela take Virgil's hand in hers and squeeze. Sam saw his father's eyes light up and she smiled. "Oh, goodness," she teased, "now I see where Sam got that wicked grin."

"Chip offf old block." His sideways smile was back. Angela laughed in response and Sam saw a touch of color bloom in her cheeks.

"Hmmm," she replied, raising a knowing eyebrow. "I see I'm going to have to watch out for you."

Sam's heart turned over at the happy expression on Virgil's face. She couldn't possibly know how much this one moment meant to his father—or to him. He'd watched over the weeks as his father's dignity—his manhood and vitality—had been stripped away. He'd been helpless to change it, and had made it worse at times with their arguments over ways to make the ranch more environmentally friendly. With one smile and a few words Angela had given something back to

Virgil. Did she have any idea how well she fitted here without even trying?

Sam put his hand on the deck railing. He was a fool. He kept telling himself that he was doing it for his mother, or that he was after friendship, but there came a time when a man couldn't lie to himself any longer. He was in the precarious position of falling for Angela Beck completely. All it would take was the slightest push and he'd be over the edge. The most shocking thing of all was that he almost welcomed the leap.

"Mr. Diamond, this is my friend Clara. She's the first resident at Butterfly House."

"Thank you for making me feel so welcome here," Clara said. She didn't move to take Virgil's hand, and Sam remembered what Angela had said about close contact. Sympathy for her mixed with respect for what Angela was doing. Whatever had happened in the past, Clara was getting a fresh start in Cadence Creek. Angela met his gaze and gave him a sweet smile. He knew it was a thank-you for including Clara in the evening. But for Sam, the smile meant more. It tethered them together as architects of something good. Angela was the driving force, but Sam had long stopped begrudging the time spent away from Diamondback. Somewhere along the way he'd started believing. In the foundation. In *her*.

"What do you do, Clara? What sort of job will you be looking for?" Molly spoke up.

Clara looked over at Molly, who was laying out napkins on a glass-topped table. "I'm a licensed practical nurse," she replied. "I'm hoping to find a job close by, maybe at a nursing home or clinic. I'm not sure how long my car can withstand a long commute, but right now anything would be wonderful."

"I see," Molly replied. Sam stared at Clara. She could be

the answer to his prayers. He'd been after Molly to hire some help with Virgil and Clara would be perfect.

But Molly would take convincing, and he needed to speak to her as well as Angela before any offer was made. Surely Angela would be pleased?

"And what do you have cooking there?" Angela left Molly and Clara chatting and came closer to the barbecue as he opened the lid and grabbed a pair of tongs to flip the chicken. She was still limping but not as badly as she had earlier in the day. She even smelled good, like outdoors and the soft lily of the valley that grew in the shade of Molly's weeping birch grove. He tamped down the wave of desire that flared and focused on brushing the meat with leftover marinade. "Mom's Greek chicken."

"It looks delicious," she replied lightly.

He looked down at her, staring at the top of her head. "You're late. You weren't going to come, were you?"

She shrugged, but still didn't meet his eye. "I thought twice about it."

"But here you are. And looking mighty pretty." He couldn't resist the compliment. Besides, he knew it would make her look at him, and she did. Her blue-green eyes met his and he felt the alarms go off all over again. Falling for her would be so easy. He should put an end to it right now. It hadn't been difficult in the past. The attraction he was feeling now was simply physical and would go away in time, wouldn't it?

The difference was that he wasn't willing to explore that attraction with her as he had been with other woman. She wasn't the sort of girl a man could be casual with. And so he looked away and absently flipped the chicken even though it didn't need flipping.

"I came because I thought it would be good for Clara to meet a few more people. Especially people who are support-ive and not prone to judge."

"That's the only reason?"

She lifted her chin. "Should there be another one?"

It was his turn to shrug as he closed the lid on the grill again. "Not necessarily."

"Molly invited me. Isn't that enough?"

He didn't answer. Molly hadn't invited her at all. It had been Sam's suggestion. At his continued silence she grabbed his arm. "Sam, tell me you didn't foist us on your mother after all she did to help today?"

"She said it was a great idea." Those hadn't been her precise words, but the meaning was the same.

"What do you want from me, Sam?" She lowered her voice so that it was barely a murmur at his side.

He couldn't help it; his gaze dropped to her lips. They were full and a slight sheen of gloss made them look soft and supple.

"I don't want anything," he replied quietly. "I'm playing it by ear here, same as you. Maybe I just wanted to see you away from Butterfly House and get to know you better. Isn't that what friends do?"

There, well done. He'd played the friends card. That would help dial things back a notch. It was bad enough he was looking at her lips as if they were coated in sugar and he had a sweet tooth. She didn't need to be getting any notions of her own.

Her eyes cooled and her lips formed a thin line. "Butterfly House makes me tick. And that's probably all you need to know."

She turned away and went to join Molly and Clara who were setting the table. Sam caught his father's gaze and felt a flash of kinship as Virgil gave him a familiar look that said *you've got your work cut out for you with that one.*

As the meat sizzled on the grill, he watched Angela work her magic. The three women talked as they worked and the tired tension around Molly's mouth seemed to evaporate as her smile became more relaxed. Angela had a way about her that put everyone at ease, he realized, and she did it all effortlessly. She'd worked that skill on him, too, getting him talking when normally he held his problems close to his chest. There was a burst of laughter and Sam watched as Molly put her hand along Angela's back, a kind of pseudo-hug that spoke of comfort and affection. Angela's dark head was next to his mother's gray-streaked one, and a sense of certainty struck Sam right in his core.

Through the years he'd spent time on unsatisfying relationships without knowing why. Now it made sense. None of those other women could measure up to Molly. None of them had her grace, wisdom or strength. She'd led by example and set the bar high—a standard no one had been able to meet.

But Angela did. And the hell of it was she wanted nothing to do with what he had to offer.

The sun started its slow descent as they lingered over dinner. Angela couldn't remember a time when she'd felt this relaxed and hyped up all at once. There was something different here tonight. She was so used to being an outsider but tonight she had been welcomed and more importantly—she'd actively *accepted* the welcome. She'd opened her heart, just a crack, to the Diamond family. How could she help it? Her heart had gone out to Virgil the moment he'd teased her and his smile had shown her what Sam's would look like in thirty years. Still charming. Still powerful. It had grabbed her and had yet to let go. A lump formed in her throat as she watched Molly cut Virgil's chicken into tiny pieces because managing two utensils proved beyond his abilities. When she finished he patted her hand and the look they shared spoke of so much love it made Angela want to weep.

It was hard to believe such trust and devotion existed but

she had living proof tonight. It was rare. She knew that well enough. It would be easy to believe herself a part of it, but she wasn't. She was on the fringes, always the outsider looking in and wishing. For a moment she was angry with Sam. Didn't he realize how much he had here? How lucky he was? And he was determined to argue with his father over it. Molly and Virgil had given him everything a son could want while she'd been hiding in her clumsily mended secondhand clothes, scrimping and saving so that she could one day simply get out and choose her own life.

All the fluttery feelings she got when Sam was around couldn't disguise the truth. They were from different worlds and wanted different things. She should never have come tonight. It only made her wish for things that she would never have.

"Penny for your thoughts." Sam was seated across from her and his low voice sent shivers of pleasure along her skin.

"They're lovely, aren't they?" she replied, nodding at his parents and then meeting his gaze. Sam's dark eyes were watching her steadily and it made her pulse start knocking around like crazy.

"They've been there for each other as long as I can remember," Sam murmured. He glanced over at his parents holding hands while they chatted with Clara. "Even when my cousin came to live with us, there was no question or debate. Mom wanted to adopt him and Dad said yes without blinking an eye—even though Ty was a handful."

"Where's Ty now?"

"Here and there." Sam frowned. "He and Dad didn't see eye to eye and Ty rebelled by becoming a rodeo star." Sam gave a half smile. "He loves it but considers it a perk that it drives Dad crazy." The smile faltered. "He hasn't been back since Dad's stroke, either. I think it's bothered Dad more than he wants to admit. Especially since we've been at odds more and more often over the biogas thing."

"Why can't you let it go, Sam?" Surely it wasn't worth destroying their relationship.

His gaze never flinched. "Because I'm right. Because sustainability is important. And because he knows it and doesn't want to admit it. It isn't really about the development. It's about him, and how he's dealing with things changing. I'm trying to be patient, but I'm not doing a very good job."

She chuckled. "I confess I'm a bit relieved."

"Relieved?" He paused with his fork in midair.

"Your family was looking rather perfect, Sam, with a complete lack of dysfunction. It's quite intimidating for a social worker."

"Nothing to fix?"

She couldn't help but laugh at his wry expression. "Something like that."

He smiled. "You've already helped, did you know that?"

She felt her cheeks heat and she dropped her eyes to her plate, but his encouraging words warmed her during the rest of the meal.

Virgil tired as they sipped tea; Molly enlisted Sam's help to get him to bed while Clara and Angela insisted on clearing the table. Angela couldn't help but marvel at the state-of-the-art appliances, the solid pine cupboards and soaring ceilings. It was a stark contrast to the dingy kitchen Angela and her mother had kept in Edmonton, where the winter drafts froze up the kitchen window and nothing ever quite gleamed. She'd dreamed of having a place like this someday, dreamed of sharing it with her mother; the two of them living in peace. The shelters she had planned would never be this grand, relying as they did on donations and general goodwill. And her mother would never come, would she?

And yet Angela stared at the wealth around her and knew

she couldn't stop trying; it was just like Sam felt about Diamondback. To give up Butterfly House would mean giving up on her mom. And giving up would break her heart.

She was aware of Sam returning but he went out on to the deck as Molly joined them at the sink.

"Oh, thank you, girls. My goodness, you've got it all cleaned up."

"The least we could do after such a great meal, Mrs. Diamond." Clara folded her dishcloth.

"You call me Molly. Everyone else does."

"Molly." Clara hung the dishcloth over the faucet. "I noticed the quilt on the back of your sofa. It's beautiful."

"Do you sew, Clara?"

"I used to. I like doing things with my hands."

"I've got another one on the frames in one of the spare rooms if you'd like to see it. A wedding-ring pattern in wine and cream."

"That would be wonderful."

Molly looked over at Angela, but for once Angela was unable to read the older woman's eyes. "I think Sam wants to speak to you about something, Angela."

"Oh, are you sure?" There was something about being alone in the twilight with Sam that made her hesitate.

"You go ahead," Molly replied. "I'll look after Clara."

How could she refuse without looking desperate or like a coward?

She paused at the French doors, gathering her courage. She could do this. His commitment to Butterfly House was over and so she just needed to reset the boundaries. They could redefine their relationship. If it even was a relationship—it was really more of an acquaintance, wasn't it?

She stepped outside and held her breath.

Sam stood at the top of the steps leading down to the garden. His arms were spread, his hands on the rail posts and she watched, transfixed, as he stretched, the pose highlighting the lean muscle that made up his body.

For the first time in years, Angela felt the ground shift beneath her feet. After focusing on her career, on the lives of others for so long, she wanted something for herself. And what she wanted—*who* she wanted—was Sam. It didn't matter about the justifications or reasons or differences in their lives. Nothing stopped the wanting. The only thing holding her back was that it scared her out of her wits. She wanted to believe in him so badly it terrified her.

"Sam?"

He turned. "You came. I wasn't sure you would."

Her pulse hammered in her wrists, her throat. "Why?"

"You avoided me all night."

Her voice came out at a whisper. "I wish you didn't always have to be so honest."

"I don't make it easy for you, do I?"

She shook her head. An owl hooted in the distance, a soulful cry that echoed through the garden. The sweet summer scent of Molly's rosebushes filled the air. Somewhere in a pasture to the right, a couple of cows lowed mournfully. This was Sam's world. And for tonight she'd gotten a taste of it. A bittersweet taste.

"Let me make it easier." He held out his hand. "Come for a walk with me."

She hesitated, but he waited, holding out his hand. Finally she took it, loving the feel of his warm fingers encircling hers. She followed him down the steps one at a time, only feeling a twinge of pain in her toe when she put all her weight on it. She expected him to let her hand go once they reached the bottom. But he didn't. He kept it firmly in his grasp as they wandered through the garden with slow steps.

"You didn't mention Clara was a licensed practical nurse," he finally said, halting and turning to face her.

Clara? He'd brought her out here to talk about Clara? Angela was glad that dusk prevented him from seeing the rise of color in her cheeks. Thank goodness he couldn't read her mind and the romantic notions she carried there. It all became clear now. It should have made things easier but it didn't.

"No, I didn't. She only arrived this morning, Sam."

"Still, you've known her for a while. She would have gone through screening, right?"

"Of course."

"She's perfect, Angela. Mom was incredibly easy to convince."

Angela pulled her fingers from his grasp. She came back to earth with a crash. Of course. A man like Sam—a woman like her. She was building castles in the air that didn't exist. She had never had to worry. Her feelings were her own and not returned, and therefore easily managed. She schooled her features and struggled to move back into professional mode. "Perfect for?"

"You know Mom needs help with Dad. Clara needs a job. And Dad likes her. He said so when we took him back to his room. For once he didn't argue with us. It took me a long time to convince Mom that she needed to hire help, but after meeting Clara... Her qualifications are perfect for what we need. What do you think?"

It was a wonderful opportunity and she was happy for Clara, of course. It was exactly what the program was designed for, and Molly would be a wonderful boss. Angela had no reservations about that whatsoever, except the sinking sensation that Clara would be spending her days in the glorious house surrounded by the warmth of the Diamonds. She didn't begrudge it one bit—Clara deserved it after what she'd been through. But Angela couldn't help feeling the tiniest bit envious.

"I think it's a terrific gesture and very generous of you," she replied, staring out over the dark fields. "I'll talk to Clara about it tomorrow."

"Thanks. It's been a productive day, hasn't it? First the open house, now this. Your project is off to a roaring start."

It was true, so why on earth was she feeling so empty? She should be happy, energized, raring to go. And instead she was weary. The fulfillment she expected wasn't as bright and shiny as she'd hoped.

"Thanks to you and your family."

He took her hand again and his dark eyes were earnest in the shadows. She froze the image on her mind so she could recall it later. This was feeling very much like a cutting of the strings, and it was necessary. But now and again she'd like to remember how he looked at this moment.

"It's all down to you. Being able to help was an honor," he finished quietly.

"Sam..." Tears pricked her eyelids and she looked down at her feet.

"I want to stay on the board."

Her gaze snapped to his. He what? But today was supposed to be the end. Especially if his parents hired Clara, there was no reason why Molly couldn't resume her position. Why on earth would he want to stay? And how difficult was it going to be seeing him on a regular basis? She didn't have any experience with this type of longing. Surely it would fade over time, wouldn't it?

"What about Diamondback, and your own concerns?"

"I've managed so far. A lot of the worry has been about Mom. If she has help now, that will take a load off my mind."

"But what about the biogas facility? I know how much that means to you."

"I doubt it will happen now. Mom has Power of Attorney, but there's nothing wrong with Dad's mind. And even if she could, she wouldn't go against his wishes. I don't know how to convince him. I've tried everything. I don't want to give up, but I've stopped having a timeline about it. It's too frustrating."

"I'm sorry."

"You control the things you can and let go of the rest, right? You made me see that it's not worth losing my dad over. We need to look after him first and then perhaps revisit the idea. So, you see, I will have some spare time to give the foundation. I thought you'd be glad."

Glad? The idea that she'd see him regularly was sweet torture. She was smart enough to know he wasn't doing it for her. They had no future. They were committed to different things in different places. They needed things that they couldn't provide for each other.

"Of course. My first priority is the foundation, and the connection to your family has been so beneficial." She wondered if she sounded as cold as the words made her seem.

"Beneficial." The word was flat. "That's all you have to say?"

She fidgeted with her fingers, unsure of what he wanted her to say. "Today couldn't have happened without you. I just hope you're doing it for the right reasons."

*And not because you kissed me*, she was tempted to add, but didn't. The less they referenced that kiss, the better. Men like Sam didn't set as much store in a simple kiss as she did. He'd probably already forgotten it.

He reached out and took her fingers loosely in his. "I'm doing it because helping you this last month has changed me. I enjoyed it. I realized today that I am proud of what we've done. What you're doing is so amazing, Angela. I just want to be a part of it a little longer."

His fingers were warm and strong. "You thought I was a hoity-toity do-gooder," she whispered.

"I was wrong."

"Sam, I…"

"We make a good team, Angela. Admit it."

She took a step backward, needing to put a few inches between herself and his seductive voice. She bit down on her lip. Sam Diamond could convince her of nearly anything, she realized, and that scared her. It made her feel weak and malleable. But she could not admit to him just how much he meant to her. The idea of having him on the board, involved with the house, made her feel weak. There was no way to explain it to him, either, not without revealing her true insecurities and she'd rather die than do that. "But your mom. The board position was hers."

"The deal was that a family member must sit on the board. It doesn't have to be Mom."

The owl hooted again, the sound lonely and mysterious.

"What are you so afraid of?" he asked quietly, squeezing her fingers.

She inhaled, decided on the truth. "You."

The air around them seemed to pause until Angela realized she was holding her breath, and she let it out slowly. Sam hadn't released her hand. She was so very aware of his body only inches from hers and the urge to step closer fought with her long-time instinct to flee. She'd let him get too close already.

"Me? Don't you know by now I'd never hurt you?"

She didn't mean that way, though perhaps it was easier. After all, that sort of fear was a tangible thing. Admitting she was afraid of her own feelings would be like touching a match to paper.

"You d-don't understand," she stammered, pulling her fingers away again and taking a step backward.

"Then make me understand. Make me understand what

happened that night with the curtain rod. What happened yesterday when I kissed you? What's happening right now?"

He was asking questions that she didn't know how to answer, questions she'd spent years avoiding by not getting close to anyone. She shook her head. "I thought we were talking about board positions."

"Only if you're trying to avoid what's really happening here," he said, taking a step toward her and closing the distance once again.

"You said you wanted to be a part of Butterfly House."

"And I do. But not just that. Don't you understand? It's you, Angela."

"No." The word came out stronger than she expected. "You can't use the position to get closer to me. I don't come with the package."

"What has got you so terrified?" He reached out and laid his palm against her cheek. She wanted to trust him. She wanted to so much it hurt in places she hadn't let herself feel for years.

"I care about you," he murmured, taking one more step so that their bodies hovered a mere breath apart. "I didn't want to. You know that. But I do. I don't know what to do about it, but I know I don't want to stop. When I'm with you everything makes sense."

He was going to kiss her. She knew it even before he began to dip his head. Her lips started to tingle in anticipation and they parted as her eyelids drifted closed.

She would let him kiss her one last time. And then he'd walk away. She'd make sure of it.

# CHAPTER NINE

THE heat of his body warmed the air between them as he drew her closer, while the cool summer breeze ruffled the hem of her skirt. Hot and cold, light and dark. They were as different as two people could be, and maybe that was part of the attraction. Sam was all the things that Angela had never been—strong, confident, sure of his place in the world. It was no wonder she was drawn to him like a moth to a flame. As his lips grazed hers, she caught her breath and decided to enjoy the moment. She could always pull away before she got singed by the fire.

He cupped her face in his hands. So softly she could hardly bear it, he kissed the corner of her mouth, her cheek, her temple. His long fingers slid down over her jawbone and he paused. Angela put her hand on his shoulder and felt the tension vibrating there. He was holding back. The idea of all that leashed energy was vastly exciting and a very feminine part of her was wooed by the consideration that was costing him so much.

She wound her arms around his neck and placed her mouth on his.

Taking the initiative changed the dynamic of the contact instantly. After a heartbeat of surprise, Sam opened his lips and kissed her fully, wrapping his arms around her middle and lifting her off the ground until only the tips of her toes touched the grass. There was no hope of surviving unsinged now. Her whole body felt as though it was on fire, with the soft sounds of their kisses in the dark fanning the flames.

She let her fingers run through his short hair, adoring the silky warmth of it and feeling a jolt of desire as he made a sound of arousal deep in his throat. He held her against the planes of his workingman's body, long and lean and muscular, until she felt they must be imprinted on her own. It was the most glorious thing she had ever experienced. Even as she knew they had to stop, she didn't want to. Just a few seconds more before she had to give it all up. She was hungry and hadn't yet had her fill.

Slowly he lowered her to the ground so she was standing on both feet again. He linked his hands at the hollow of her back, holding her in the circle of his arms while he continued to sip from her lips.

Finally she broke away, knowing she couldn't let it go on any longer and still retain her dignity. She'd practically thrown herself into his arms, conveniently forgetting all the reasons why it was a mistake. Heat rushed into her face and she pressed her hands to her cheeks. Her heart drummed insistently against her ribs. His wary eyes watched her but the rest of his body remained completely still as she took a step backward.

He was too much, too powerful, too attractive. He made her want things, different things than she'd wanted for as long as she could remember. She'd known from the beginning he was going to be trouble. She just hadn't thought he'd be *this* kind of trouble.

"Sam," she chastised quietly. "We can't."

"Why?" He crossed his arms over his chest. The pose highlighted his muscled arms and she licked her lips. She wouldn't respond to his physicality. She had to keep her head. One of them had to.

"This is too complicated. There are so many reasons why we shouldn't."

"Is that right?" His voice was soft and seductive. "You know, I've been trying to figure out what it is about you that sets me off."

He put his hands in his back pockets, highlighting the breadth of his chest and shoulders. That restless energy that couldn't be tamed was sparking through the air again, making it come alive. Making *her* come alive, and she wasn't prepared for it.

"I don't mean to set you off," she replied in a small voice.

"But you do," he said softly. "You challenge me. You're *work*. You have firm opinions, and I respect you for them."

He took a step forward, relaxing his arms, treating her to a small, sideways smile. He reached out and ran a finger over her arm, raising the delicate hairs and goosebumps beneath his touch. "Something's happening between us, Angela. It started that night with the curtains. Don't deny it."

She stepped back. "Don't, please," she said, embarrassingly aroused and horribly tempted to give in. She imagined what would come next, out here in the soft darkness. She hadn't been intimate with a man in… She blinked as she stared into Sam's determined face. In a very long time. It had nearly cost her everything—and she'd nearly lost herself in the process. She couldn't do that again.

"It's not just wanting you, you know that, right?" His eyes gleamed at her. "It's the way you see the world. It's how you make me stop and think. Like with the kids today. I looked at them and saw trouble but you made me see something else—potential. With Clara, too." He smiled gently. "I never considered myself narrow-minded, but you make me look beyond the surface. That's why I'm fall…"

"Stop," she commanded, cutting him off before he could say any more. Her pulse hammered at her throat. She didn't know how to do this. She didn't know how to care about someone this much or—worse—accept that they might care about her. She was as emotionally stunted as any of her clients only she was able to give it a proper name and she'd had years of practice at covering it. He couldn't fall for her, and she couldn't fall for him either.

"You're afraid."

Sam knew nothing about what really drove her, and it took her breath away to realize how close she was to telling him the whole truth. To trusting him. Her heart told her she could but her head kept her mouth shut. She'd learned long ago that her heart had flawed judgment.

"I'm not afraid," she replied, forcing herself to stand tall as she lied. "What I am is leaving."

She turned to walk away and he reached out, his strong fingers circling her wrist. "Don't go. Talk to me."

This time there was no fear, only temptation to fall back into his embrace. A part of her thrilled to hear the words. But a stronger, more rational part had a bigger voice. She wrenched her wrist out of his grasp, panic rising at the dull pain that shot through her arm as she twisted it away. Panic that he would somehow see through her, leaving her vulnerable and exposed. He wanted more from her than she could ever give.

"I have to. I got carried away in the moonlight for a minute but it's over." She began to back away, feeling the cool grass against her toes as she stepped off the path. "Please, just let me go. Don't come after me and don't call, Sam."

"But, Angela…"

"Just don't." Her voice choked. "I can't, don't you see?"

"No, goddammit, I don't!" He ran his hand over his hair and heaved out a breath. "Tell me what you're so afraid of. Let me help you."

"I can't." She gave him one last desperate glance before

turning and fleeing. Not even the twinges in her toe slowed her down until she reached the steps of the back deck.

The glow from the kitchen lights filtered weakly over the grass and there was a muffled bark that sounded from inside—the Diamonds' dog was in for the night now that dark had fallen fully. Angela saw Molly's figure pass in front of the French doors and she hesitated, knowing she had to go in and collect Clara and her purse, needing to catch her breath first.

The motion light over the door came on as she climbed the stairs. She hurried to school her features into what she hoped was a pleasant smile before turning the handle on the door and entering the warm kitchen that still smelled of fresh bread and chocolate cake.

No one would ever know just how close she'd come to losing her head tonight. And even though she knew leaving was the right thing, she'd hold the sweet memory of this eve-ning—all of it—inside during the months ahead. She was so used to being on the outside, staring longingly through the window at the perfect life she'd never have.

For one magical night, Sam had shown her what it could be like on the inside.

To Angela's surprise, Sam heeded her plea to leave her alone as July turned to August and Butterfly House became a buzz of activity. He was nowhere to be seen as three more ten-ants arrived and Angela's days were full with the day-to-day running of the project. Clara began working days at the Diamonds', looking after Virgil. She came home at night with stories about the family, tidbits that made Angela feel con-nected to Sam in some small way.

They also made her miss him horribly. She kept telling herself it was for the best, but there was no denying that she got an empty feeling every time a car turned into the yard and it wasn't him.

Then there were the handymen.

The first day the crew arrived Angela was in her office, conducting a session with her latest resident, Jane. She excused herself to see what was going on and found three men unloading scaffolding and paint.

"What do you think you're doing?"

"Mornin', ma'am. Just about to start working on your trim. We'll have it spruced up in no time."

She didn't want to sound rude but there was clearly some mistake. "But I didn't hire you."

"No, ma'am. Mr. Diamond did. We're to paint the gingerbread trim and stain the porch and railings." He put down the gallons of paint in his hand and straightened, wiping his hands on his coveralls. "Might want to use the back door until it's done."

She hesitated. Sam should have asked her first before going ahead with anything. The trouble was the trim did need a coat of paint and the porch, while sturdier since his repairs, made the house look shabby. A tiny voice inside her head asked her what she'd expected. Why would Sam ask her approval if she'd told him flat out to leave her alone?

Sending the men away would cause more trouble than it was worth. "All right then, go ahead. I'll be inside if you need anything."

"Yes, ma'am," he replied, and motioned to the others to begin setting up the scaffolding.

Angela had firmly believed that the whole out-of-sight, out-of-mind thing would work, but she felt Sam's presence constantly. After the workmen finished, one of the local teens came by to mow the grass and asked if he could put the new pushmower Mr. Diamond had provided in the shed when he was finished. The house and yard looked better than ever but, inside, her emotions were churning. Mr. Diamond this and Mr. Diamond that. Exorcising him from her thoughts proved harder than she'd expected. He'd helped with the fixing-up, and now it seemed that his handiwork was all around her, whether she asked for it or not.

The final straw was the feature in the local monthly paper. It had carried a wonderful spot on the project, but it was the picture they'd used of her with Sam that made her heart catch. It hadn't been one of the posed shots. Instead the black-and-white photo that stared up at her from the newsprint was one where Sam was looking back at her and she was grinning down at him—when they'd been teasing each other. He'd been a royal pain in the behind and a bright light in her life all at once, and now everything was gray and dull in his absence.

She folded the paper and put it in a desk drawer. The feature was good, though she wished it had focused more about the foundation and less about her. Sam had done a bang-up job singing her praises and her name was everywhere. She told herself she shouldn't worry. No one in Edmonton even cared where she was now. And the two people who might—well, Angela had stopped deluding herself long ago. The chances of Jack Beck actually reading a small-town rag were slim to none. The anxiety was natural, she supposed, but not necessarily rational.

But the picture of her with Sam was branded on her mind. She lay awake one hot summer night, her window open as she listened to the sounds of the peepers in the nearby slough and the rustle of the leaves. Coyotes howled, the sound so plaintive and lonely that she felt like howling along with them. She flipped over, punching her pillow, but her eyes remained stubbornly open. She couldn't erase the image of Sam in the moonlight, his lips still slightly swollen from her kisses. She had to do something, so she got out of bed and went downstairs in her pajamas. When she couldn't sleep, she baked. And when she was this twitchy, only one recipe would do.

She was careful to be quiet as she whisked together the cream, sugar and cocoa over the burner for the chocolate silk filling. A baked crust cooled on the counter as she stirred, wishing she could stir away her thoughts as easily as the whisk smoothed away the lumps in the mixture.

She poured the thickened filling into the crust and scraped the sides of the pan with her spatula. She gave the plastic surface an indulgent lick—the secret was in the melted dark chocolate—and then put both pot and spatula in the sink before turning back to the fridge and sliding the pie in to set. She stretched and gave a huge yawn. Baking always did the trick. Tomorrow morning would be time enough to whip up the cream for the top and they could all have a treat.

She was just wiping the pan dry when there was a horrible pounding on the door.

For one terrified second she couldn't move, flooded by a hundred memories crowding her consciousness all at once. This was the reality she knew—that no amount of therapy or time ever completely erased the fear, especially the reflexive reaction in that moment before rational thought took over. The pounding persisted and she forced her feet to move, grabbing the handset to the phone on the way by. Just in case.

Steps echoed behind her as Clara, Jane, Alyssa and Sue rattled down the stairs. When Angela reached the door, she turned and looked at the women standing behind her, their eyes wide, cheeks pale. Whatever Angela was feeling, it had to be a hundred times worse for them. It was fresher for them and they were looking to her to set an example. She squared her shoulders and peeped through the Judas hole.

What she saw turned her knees to jelly.

She flipped the locks and opened the door, her stomach

turning and heart pounding as she looked down at the woman on her knees on the front step.

"Mom?"

Beverly Beck lifted her head and Angela's soul wept at the sight of her. One eye was so swollen it was closed, while the opposite cheek sported an angry red bruise. Her bottom lip was cracked and when Angela knelt and touched her arm, she started to cry.

Angela felt an anger so profound she thought she might explode out of her own skin with it. This woman—this kind, caring woman who had done nothing but give blind devotion to her husband—had been repaid with *this*.

"Come inside," she whispered, going out carefully. "Let me help you."

Gently she helped her mother get to her feet and led her inside. She shut the door and locked it and nodded at the group of women still standing in the kitchen. "It's all right," she said, trying to sound reassuring while the conflicting mass of emotions tied knots in her belly. "We'll be in my office," she said, leading Beverly into the small room off the entry.

Beverly was still crying quietly and Angela led her to a small couch. They sat side by side and she simply waited for her mother to speak. When Beverly was ready, she patted Angela's hand and sighed.

"Help me, Angie," she said.

Angela had waited her whole life to hear that simple request, and her heart seemed to burst hearing the words.

No matter the hurt or blame that she had held inside over the years, this was her mother. The woman who had cut flower shapes out of sandwiches with cookie cutters when she was a child, the one who had taken her on weekly trips to the library until Angela was old enough to go on her own. She was the one who, no matter what, tucked Angela into bed at night and promised that tomorrow would be better even if she never kept those promises. Somewhere inside this broken body that beautiful woman still existed, and Angela opened her arms. "Of course I'll help you," she murmured, kissing her mother's graying hair. "It's all I've ever wanted."

There was a discreet knock on the door and Clara poked her head inside. "I made a pot of tea," she said quietly. "I thought you might like some."

"That'd be lovely—thank you." Angela sat back, wiping her fingers under her eyes and then took Beverly's hands in her own. She noticed that her mother's nails were short and chipped, her hands chapped. How many horrors had she suffered in the years since Angela left? Not for the first time, she felt unbearable guilt for leaving her mother to face things on her own.

Clara returned with a tray containing a teapot, mugs, milk and a plate of toast with a jar of jam. "In case someone would like a bite," she offered.

"Thank you, Clara." She offered a small smile, wanting to inject as much normalcy into the evening as she could. "Is everyone okay?" Clara was turning out to be a truly nurturing soul. The Diamonds were lucky to have her.

"A little shaken, but okay. They're going back to bed now."

"I'll see you in the morning, then."

Clara shut the door with a quiet click.

The new silence was deafening.

Angela poured two cups of tea and added milk to each. "Here," she offered, holding out the cup. "Drink this. You'll feel better and you can tell me what happened."

Beverly offered no resistance as she wrapped her hands around the warm mug and Angela wondered if she'd simply been used to obeying for so long that she didn't know how to do anything else. For the first time since becoming a social worker, Angela felt as though she was in over her head, flying by the seat of her pants.

The tea was hot and reviving, and she caught her mother's gaze focused on the toast. Angela wondered when she'd eaten last. She knew very well that there wasn't always money for groceries. "Jam?"

She spread a triangle with saskatoonberry jam and handed it over.

When the piece was gone, Angela sat up straighter. "You're not here for tea and toast. Can you tell me what happened?"

Beverly nodded. "I left your father."

"After he did this to you." The words came out tightly, like the string of a bow held taut, ready for release.

Another nod.

"Have you left him for good?"

Angela held her breath. The answer had to be yes. Beverly couldn't come this far and then go back, could she? But Angela knew she could. How many times had they talked about packing a bag and disappearing? It was always too good to be true. She had to attempt to keep her own feelings out of the mix right now. She had to if she were truly going to help.

Fear widened Beverly's eyes but she nodded once more. "I packed a bag tonight when he was at the bar. I took the car and came here."

Oh, Lord. Beverly hadn't had a driver's license for over fifteen years. If she'd been stopped she would have ended up right back home again. And Angela wouldn't put it past her father to report the vehicle stolen. Wouldn't it be ironic if the police were the ones to deliver her back to her doorstep? Angela looked at Beverly's downturned head and said slowly, "Does he know *where* you've gone?"

Agonized eyes met hers. "I don't know."

Something in the tone, and the way her mother's eyes dropped once more to her lap, made a line of dread sneak down Angela's spine. There was something more. "What set him off this time? What changed?"

Beverly's gaze skittered away again. "It doesn't matter."

"Mom."

Beverly's fingers picked at the frayed hem of her blouse. "I cut out that picture of you in the paper. I couldn't believe it was you, honey. You're so grown-up and pretty. I read all about this place and I was real proud, you know?"

Everything came crashing down. This was her fault, wasn't it? She hadn't realized the story had been picked up by the city paper. The words were like little knives cutting through Angela's skin, sharp and stinging. Why couldn't this have happened years ago when she'd begged and pleaded? Maybe they could have done this together. Maybe…

But Angela knew that the world didn't run on maybes. She forced the useless wish aside. "And?"

"Your dad, he found the picture and got right ugly."

"And he took it out on you."

There was no answer to give. They both knew she was right. Ever since the day Angela had left, there'd been no one but Beverly for him to use as a punching bag.

And ever since that day Angela had worked so hard, trying to atone for it.

"He told me to remember my place, and…" Her throat worked but no words came out for a moment. "When he was done with me he took off to the usual watering hole. I wasn't going to come, but he said he should have made you pay years ago. I was so scared, Angela. Afraid of what he might do. Afraid that he'd…he'd use me to get to you again."

Another thick silence fell. Neither of them needed to say the words. They both knew he'd already used Beverly to get to Angela.

"So he knows where I am. What I do?"

"It made him some mad."

A cold finger of fear shivered down Angela's spine, followed by anger. She couldn't let him have this power over her anymore. Not just her, either. There were four other women—five counting Beverly—looking to her for strength and leadership. She couldn't let them down. She didn't know what to do—everything seemed to be crumbling inside. Beverly put her hand over her face and started weeping again, the sound full of despair and hopelessness.

Angela's insides were quaking and she knew she couldn't do this alone.

Her first call should be to the police, but she couldn't make herself dial the number. The very thought of it was exhausting and left her emotionally drained. There was only one thing—one person—she wanted. It probably wasn't wise, and it definitely didn't make sense after their last conversation, but right now she would give anything to see Sam's strong face.

She got up from the couch, went to the desk drawer and pulled out a scrap of paper that she'd kept since the day she'd dropped the box spring on her toe. *If you need anything,* he'd said, *call me.*

With a tangle of nerves in her stomach, she dialed Sam's cell number.

# CHAPTER TEN

THE shrill ringtone of his cell dragged him out of a dead sleep and set his heart pounding. He reached for the phone beside the bed and fumbled with the buttons. A sane person never called at this hour unless something was wrong.

"Yuh, hello," he said into the phone, rubbing his hand over his face.

"It's Angela."

His eyes snapped open. There was something wrong. It was in the tight, odd sound to her voice. Like she was trying to sound normal but there was an edge to it that hinted of hysteria. He sat up in bed, fully alert, and reached over to turn on the bedside lamp. "What's going on?"

"Can you come over?"

There was a quiver in the last word as her voice caught. No preamble, no explanation, no wasted words, just a plea that put a cold shiver into his heart. The Angela he knew would have been rational and explained. She never would have been so raw and vulnerable. Or afraid. He was sure she was afraid for some reason. "Are you all right?"

"I just…I need you."

Goddamn. The last time they'd spoken she'd told him to leave her alone and he'd granted that request. For her to turn to him now had to mean something was desperately wrong. "Give me ten minutes," he replied, hanging up at the same time as he launched himself out of bed and reached for his jeans.

He drove far too fast in the dark, trying to think of plausible scenarios for why she'd call him in the middle of the night. Running the sort of place she did, his first reaction was that an ex-husband or boyfriend had caused trouble. He swallowed, putting his foot on the gas. Was someone hurt? Angela? Or Clara? She'd been such a bright spot around the house. Clara's help had made such a difference with Virgil. The very thought of her being in trouble was horrible. But when he thought of Angela, it was different. There was fear for her, but something more. A desire to protect her. Even though weeks had passed since they'd kissed in the garden, it was far from over. Not for Sam. It was time he admitted the truth to himself. He'd fallen in love with her, he'd blown it and he had no idea what to do next.

He was there in seven minutes flat. He knocked on the door and then tried the knob. It was locked, so he knocked a little louder. A strange car sat in the driveway and he set his jaw. If someone didn't answer soon, he'd break in the door if he had to.

Clara answered, wrapped up in a housecoat and slippers. Her face was pale but she offered Sam a weak smile. "She called you. I'm glad. Come in, Sam."

He followed her inside, glad she was clearly unhurt. "What's going on?"

Angela's office door opened and she stepped into the hall. For a moment all he could see were the tearstains on her cheeks. In the next heartbeat she was in his arms.

He took a step backward as the force of her embrace took him by surprise. He closed his eyes and put his arms around her. Lordy, she felt like she'd lost weight, she was so small and fragile. Her shoulders rose and fell and he heard her sniffle against his shirt. She was not a woman who surrendered easily; now she was crying in his arms. He held her tighter, wanting to protect her from whatever was pulling her apart at the seams.

There was no sense denying it now, no sense fighting what he'd been trying to ignore for weeks. He'd do anything for her. And right now he sensed that what she needed was a gentle touch. "Shhh," he offered, rubbing her back through her thin T-shirt. "What's wrong, Ang? You have to tell me what's wrong."

She lifted her head. "I…" She drew in a shuddering breath. "I shouldn't be so glad to see you, but I am."

A woman stepped out of the office, peering timidly around the corner. Sam saw the cracked lip and bruises and felt as though he'd been punched in the gut for the second time in as many minutes. She looked startled as she met his gaze and went back inside, but she turned a little, showing her profile. A profile that was remarkably similar to the woman in his arms, if she were a few decades older.

He ran his hand over her hair, suddenly understanding why she was so upset. "Is that your mom?"

Angela turned her head quickly but the woman had already gone back inside, shutting the door with a quiet click.

"Yes," she answered. "Yes, that's my mother. She showed up tonight after my father lit into her. For the last time, if I have anything to say about it."

Shock rippled through him as she admitted the truth. He knew how passionate she was about Butterfly House, how committed she was to ending abuse and helping these women start over. But her own mother… She had to be devastated. He was gutted just looking at the bruises. How must she feel as her daughter? How would he feel if it were Molly? Questions zinged through his mind, piling one on top of the other. Had she known? Had it been going on all through Angela's child-hood? Had she been a victim of her father's abuse, too? His stomach turned. How much had she suffered? And then there was the relationship she mentioned. How did that fit into everything? How much had she truly hidden from him?

But the answers would have to wait. They had to deal with the right now first.

Angela wouldn't push him away this time. No matter what it took. No matter how much she might fight him on it. The days of her standing alone against the world were done.

"Tell me what you need," he said, tipping up her chin with a finger and meeting her gaze. "Tell me what I can do to help and I'll do it."

Angela lost herself in his dark gaze for just a moment. Never before had she let herself need someone this much. Not just need—but she'd willingly placed herself in the hands of another and it was terrifying and a relief all at once.

It was scary to surrender when she'd spent her whole life avoiding that very thing. But also terrifying in how *right* it felt. It filled her with a sense of certainty that she'd never experienced before. She knew that Sam would be there. She'd known it the day he'd given her his cell number and told her to call if she needed anything. It had gone beyond items on a grocery list. It had even gone beyond a kiss in the moonlight.

She reached up and circled his wrist with her fingers, drawing his hand away from her face. Right now she was just happy to have him there. "I need your advice."

She wanted someone objective to look at the situation, someone whose life hadn't been colored by abusive situations. It stung her pride to know that she'd lost her objectivity. But some things were more important than pride. Like safety for all of them.

He looked startled, uncomfortable as he drew back a little and furrowed his brow. "Are you sure I'm the right person to ask? I have no experience with this."

She didn't share his doubts. "I can manage my mom. I think. But it's my father." She filled him in on the events of the evening. "And so you see, she took the car. She has no license, no insurance. He could report the car stolen. He'll be angry, Sam, and I'm not sure what to do next." She fought against the finger of fear that trickled down her spine and the backs of her legs. "He'll be really angry. And…" She swallowed. "He knows where I am. Because of the article and my picture."

"This is my fault," he murmured, his face flattening with shock. "I pushed you into being in that photo. You didn't even want to do it. Oh, Angela."

"It's not your fault, I promise."

"But…"

Things became very clear for Angela in that moment. Sam was blaming himself just as she'd blamed herself for years. "Look at me," she said, her voice stronger than she thought possible. "It's easy to blame yourself. You play the 'if only' game. 'If only I had done something differently.' 'If only I hadn't said that.' But the truth is abusers like my dad don't really need reasons. It is not your fault, Sam. It's his, and his alone. I promise."

There was freedom with the words, but she also felt her energy being sapped from the high emotion of the events. "But that doesn't change what we're dealing with." She pressed her fingers to the bridge of her nose, feeling the beginnings of a headache. "It won't take him long to figure out where she went."

"Did you call the police?"

"I've only called you. He won't realize she's gone until he gets home from the bar, maybe not until he wakes up with a hangover."

She couldn't help the bitterness that flavored the words. She knew the routine well. Jack would come home smelling like tequila and cigarettes and pass out. It was the next morning that was the worst. When the shakes set in along with the anger.

"But he needs to be arrested."

Nausea turned in Angela's stomach. "I…"

Her voice abandoned her and she looked at her feet.

Sam didn't speak for several long seconds. Finally he said the words down low. "Are you still afraid of him?"

"I left, didn't I?"

"Oh, honey. It's not the same thing, and we both know it. Look at me, please."

She lifted her head and met his gaze, hot shame filling her as she bit down on her lip.

"It's one thing to accept you're not to blame, but quite another to look down the barrel of the gun, isn't it?"

She didn't want to agree, so she kept silent. There were too many years and too many scars. She wanted to say she didn't care, that she wasn't afraid. But she was.

"If this were any other woman, would you hesitate to call the police?"

They both knew the answer. She'd made the phone call many, many times over the years.

"I can't," she whispered. "Oh, Sam, I'm such a hypocrite. I run this place and pretend I'm all whole and everything. But when it comes down to it, I'm still…" Tears clogged her throat. "A victim."

"Those women have you as their champion. But you had no one." He cupped her chin in his fingers. "Until now. You have me. And you are not going to do this alone."

She wouldn't cry. Not anymore. She needed to be strong and deal with what needed to be dealt with. And right now her first priority was her mother.

"I've got to be with her," she murmured. "She's so fragile right now. So scared."

"You look after your mom and I'll look after the rest," Sam said, drawing himself up to his full height. He was an imposing sight, her protector. She had never wanted to admit she needed a guardian, but she was glad to have him tonight. There wasn't a spare ounce that wasn't solid muscle and the glint in his eye and angle of his jaw spoke of determination. She'd pegged him as being stubborn before, blindly so. But now she knew he was not. He simply fought for those things he believed in. And tonight she was fortunate he believed in her and Butterfly House.

"I need to get her settled. This isn't the place for her. In the morning I'll need to get her to a different kind of shelter. It's a different sort of help here. And she's going to need me beside her."

"You do that and I'll make some phone calls. Don't worry, Ang. I won't let him hurt either of you. I promise."

She swallowed past the lump in her throat. Sam always made good on his promises. She knew that by now.

"You'll wait for me, then?"

He nodded. "Of course I will."

"There's tea in the kitchen."

His lopsided smile nearly popped a dimple. "I think I could use a whiskey, but I know the rules. Tea will do."

She stepped away from him and took three shaky steps back to her office before turning back.

"Thank you for coming," she murmured, her hand resting on the door frame. "I don't know how I would have gotten through this without you."

Then she turned away before she could hear his response. Because the look in his eyes was so tender and caring she suddenly felt at risk of exposing everything.

And that was something she just couldn't do.

When Beverly was settled in the last unoccupied bedroom, Angela shut the door gently and finally let her shoulders slump. If they could get through this first night it would be better. For a few panicked minutes her mother had insisted on going home, saying that it would be better than Jack's fury when he found out what she'd done. That he'd forgive her—as if she somehow needed forgiveness. Jack—Angela had long ago stopped thinking of him as Dad—was the one who should be on his knees. It had taken all of Angela's energy to stay calm and logical when she still felt her own fear and anger.

But she bit her tongue and was soothing and rational and all the other important things she needed to be, knowing that Sam waited. She might be weak but she would do this. They hadn't come this far to mess it up now.

She had tended to Beverly's wounds and helped her to bed, assuring her mother it would all be fine, while inside she held no such guarantee. This wasn't the end. It was only the beginning. And she still listened with one ear, wondering if Jack would come along and pound on her door and start making demands. That couldn't happen. Not just for Beverly but for the other women. This was supposed to be their safe place. She leaned back against the bedroom door and closed her eyes. That open house was supposed to be such a positive thing. Something to build awareness and support. And now because of her, it could all come tumbling down.

When she entered the kitchen, she was shocked to see Sam casually washing up the dishes from the tea and toast. A dish towel was slung over his shoulder as he washed out the teapot and rinsed it beneath the hot spray. There was something both masculine and nurturing about it and she knew she was in horrible danger of falling in love with him despite all her precautions. The phone call and embrace had been simple reactions to an extremely stressful situation, but even Angela, in her emotional state, realized that she never would have done either if something deeper weren't at work.

Love. A lump formed in her throat. It was impossible.

"I can do those in the morning," she said, wrapping her arms around her middle. She was still in the pink boxers and T-shirt she'd worn to answer the door and while perfectly modest, felt quite exposed beneath his dark gaze.

He slid the dish towel off his shoulder, gave the pot a wipe and put it down on the counter. "It was no trouble. I needed to do something while I waited."

"I kept you a long time."

His gaze was far too understanding for her to be comfortable. "You had a good reason. Do you want tea? I can make a new pot."

She shook her head. At the moment, his earlier suggestion of whiskey sounded just about right, but she had a policy about alcohol on the premises. "No, I'm fine. I had some earlier."

"Is your mom asleep?"

Angela shrugged. "I don't know. I figure she'll either lie awake a long time, or she'll be so exhausted she'll conk out completely." She moved farther into the room, forcing deep breaths to keep from feeling overwhelmed. "She's here, and that's the main thing."

"Well, no one's going to bother you tonight."

There was an edge to his voice, a defiance that sent a little fizz through her veins. "You don't have to stay, Sam. You've done so much already." She felt obligated to say it even as the thought of him leaving made an empty hole form inside her.

"You can't get rid of me that easily," he replied. He hung the dish towel over the oven-door handle. "I called a friend of mine. The car's been towed and it'll be delivered back to Edmonton like it had never gone missing. Then I called Mike Kowalchuk. He was here at the open house, remember? The constable. He's aware of the situation and he's contacted the police in the city. Someone's going to be watching the street until your dad is picked up. No one will get within a hundred yards without Mike knowing."

Relief swamped her. "I had no idea…"

"We take care of our own around here."

And he included her as one of them. The fact that he'd gotten people out of bed and into action with a few simple phone calls wasn't lost on her. When Sam wanted something done, he didn't stop until he made it happen. It was intimidating—and embarrassing that he'd had to do what she normally would have done in this situation. She was thankful for the support even as she felt like he was taking over.

She didn't like being the one not in control.

"I don't know what to say."

"Don't say anything." He stepped forward and cupped her face in his palm. "Keeping you safe comes first," he said simply.

She stared at his lips, wondering if he was going to kiss her, wondering if she even truly wanted him to.

Instead he pressed his lips to her forehead. They were firm and warm and reassuring. "You must have been so scared," he murmured.

"Not the first time. Or the worst," she said quietly.

He uttered a curse and ran a hand over his jaw. "I didn't know."

She took pity on him then, not liking the awkward silence that had fallen over the kitchen. "How could you? I've never told anyone. Don't worry about it." She sighed, feeling so much older than her years. "My mother has been in the same situation for as long as I can remember."

"I'm worried about you. You're pale and exhausted. You should rest."

"I'm fine. Everything's fine now." She pushed away and

wished she had a housecoat, a hoodie, anything to make her feel less naked.

"If you're fine, why do you look like you're about to collapse?"

He had her there. She wasn't fine. She was nowhere near fine. And she wouldn't be for a long time. Most days her energy went into current projects and she could forget—or ignore—those very real incidents that had shaped her past. But tonight she'd come face-to-face with her demons again. And relived every moment when she'd opened the front door and wondered what she'd find inside.

She blinked rapidly as his shape blurred. All the adrenaline abandoned her and exactly what had happened truly, finally, sank in. The life she had left behind had caught up with her. But her mother was out and had made that important first step. It shouldn't hurt this much to get what she'd always wanted.

"It's okay," she heard him say gently. "Aw, baby, come here."

He opened his arms.

She went to him because now that it was over she was fragile. He hugged her close and she drank in his smell—a bit woodsy, a bit like citrus and the blankety-soft scent of sleep because she'd dragged him out of bed.

"Come sit down before you fall down." His breath was warm on her ear and made her body shiver in an instinctive reaction. She had no energy left to fight him with, and, her hand tucked inside his, they went into the living room and sat side by side on the sofa.

"It's so hard," she confessed, and it felt so good to finally confide in someone. "It's not the same when it's your own mother, you know?" She closed her eyes and leaned against his shoulder. "At one point I thought she was going to get up and walk back out the door. I wanted to beg her not to go. I wanted to get down on my knees and plead with her not to let it happen again. But I learned a long time ago that begging doesn't work. So I sucked it up and put on my best social-worker hat. I was very professional on the outside," she continued, chancing a look up at him.

She realized for the first time that his shirt was buttoned incorrectly. She stared at the uneven buttons and her heart melted just a little. She'd frightened him that much, then, that he'd rushed into his clothes and raced over here without a second thought. She hadn't deserved that, not after the way she'd treated him. Not after the way she'd treat him before this was all over.

"And on the inside?"

She sighed. "On the inside I'm a mess. I'm supposed to be objective and smart and helpful. And you know what I am?"

He shook his head.

She looked down at her hands, not wanting to see disappointment in his eyes. "I'm a coward."

"You're the bravest woman I know," he replied, putting his arm around her shoulder, cuddling her in more as he leaned against the arm of the sofa. "Look at all you've accomplished here. Look at Clara, and the other women you're helping. Ang, at one time they arrived somewhere looking very much like your mother does tonight. Now look where they are."

Tonight was the first time he'd ever shortened her name. No one had ever called her Ang. Not ever. Not friends, not her mom, not even Steve when he'd been at his charming best and had sucked her into a controlling relationship. She liked the way it sounded when Sam said it, maybe too much.

"You don't understand."

"Then help me to."

Why did he have to be so wonderful? The last time they'd spoken she'd left him standing in the moonlight and told him to leave her alone. He'd followed her wishes to the letter, but he'd been taking care of her all along, she realized, helping her project when she refused any other sort of contact. He couldn't do that forever. At some point the emergency would be over and they'd have to get back to their regularly scheduled lives.

"Sam, what you saw tonight—that was my life, too. It was my daily existence from my first memories until I finished high school. I got a scholarship, packed my bags one night when my father was passed out, and never looked back."

"I wondered," he said quietly. "Tonight I was shocked, but not really surprised. There is something about you. A distance, a protective layer you never let down. You are always so determined to stand on your own two feet, never to back down. Like you have something to prove."

"Maybe I do." He was being rather insightful and she wasn't sure if she was glad at not having to explain or unsettled that she was so transparent.

"The only other time you let your guard down was the day before the open house."

Yes, the day she'd seen all her plans crumble before her eyes when that cursed box spring dropped on her foot. The day he'd turned her into a puddle of feminine goo and scared the hell out of her when he'd kissed her. "I felt safe, I suppose. Doesn't mean it was easy."

His hand rubbed along her arm, warm and reassuring, anchoring her to the present. After a few minutes, he spoke again. "He beat you, too, didn't he? That's why you were too afraid to make the call tonight."

"I don't want your pity," she warned. "There are a lot of ways to hurt a person, and not always with fists, though I had my share of those, too. I went to school and was around other people so Jack was careful not to leave any marks where they'd show. Those bruises healed faster than the hateful words and names he called me."

Sam didn't answer. She knew it was a lot for him to take in, but maybe now he'd finally understand why things could never work between them. "A father is supposed to be a provider and protector, you know? He broke trust with my mother and with me."

"Yes, he did."

"And I left rather than confronting him about it. He was my father. I thought I should love him. That he should love me. But love isn't supposed to be like that. It was easier to leave than to deal with it. With him."

He seemed to consider for a moment. "But when you studied, when you became a social worker…"

"You mean that I should have figured this all out then, right? Fixed myself?" She gave a short laugh. "I thought I had, but that was before I really understood what…"

She stopped. She'd been about to say *what real love feels like.* It would have been a slip that was tantamount to a three-word declaration. And a big mistake. Maybe she was in love with him. And maybe it did change everything. But it didn't mean it would ever work and it was better to leave the words unsaid.

"Before I really understood," she repeated, hoping he wouldn't pursue the *what.*

"You must be happy that your mom has taken this step, then."

She sighed. "Of course. But that's not easy, either. I don't want to be angry with her but I am. She broke trust with me, too, Sam. I needed her to stand up. To leave. To put me first. She stayed, insisting that he loved her. I've been so angry, so helpless." Her lip wobbled. "So guilty."

"Guilty? What on earth do you have to feel guilty about?" He twisted a little so that he was looking down at her face. "That's crazy talk."

She shook her head. "I left her there, Sam. I left her alone to deal with Jack all by herself. How many beatings did she endure when he realized I was gone? How many since?" She put her head in her hands, feeling the awful truth wrapping its cords around her neck. "I was angry and I gave up on her."

"You listen to me," Sam said, taking her hands in his and removing them from her face. "Look at me."

She couldn't. She was this close to falling apart and looking at him would ensure it. Nothing he could say would convince her that this wasn't her fault. It was all true. She had given up on her mother. She'd written her off. She'd dedicated her life to helping abused women and she was an absolute farce.

"I said look at me."

She looked up.

He looked angry, she realized, but not in a frightening, threatening way. In a way that made her heart take a ridiculous leap. "You did not give up on her. What you did was survive."

"I sacrificed her for myself, Sam. It was utterly selfish."

"That's garbage and you know it. You just got finished telling me that it was not my fault. Well, it's not yours, either, and deep down you know it. You relied on her to protect you and when she didn't, you protected yourself. That's courageous and smart, and don't let anyone tell you differently. You were a *kid*. You dedicated your life to helping women like your mom. And I'm guessing there are a lot of people out there thankful for whatever selfishness, as you call it, that you demonstrated. You've saved lives, Angela Beck. So do not sell yourself short because you are human."

"My penance," she whispered.

"You started Butterfly House because of her, didn't you?"

"I had to do something or go crazy. She wouldn't let me help her. Oh, Sam, she wouldn't help herself. I couldn't go back there. I thought about sneaking back and trying to convince her, but I couldn't get within two blocks of home without feeling sick to my stomach."

"Then this relationship you spoke of…"

"Classic pattern. Steve seemed wonderful at first, and I was young and alone. And then I started losing myself bit by bit, molded into what he wanted. I became a carbon copy of my mother until the day he hit me and then took my picture and stuck it on the fridge so I would remember what would happen if I put a toe out of line. That was my moment. I packed my things and walked away."

She'd conquered the demon by getting her degree in social work and proving time and again that she was stronger than the fear. But all the while she knew in her heart she was a coward. An imposter.

"I'm going to tell you something and I want you to think about it, Angela." He squeezed her fingers. "What you did back then made today possible. Every decision you've made brought you to this day, in this place, and put you in the position to give help when she finally decided to seek it."

"I want to believe you." It sounded so good, so logical, so exonerating. But was it true?

"You can't force someone to do what they don't have the strength to do. You can't force them to feel what you want them to feel. What you can do is be ready, so that when the day comes, you're there with open arms."

That sounded to Angela like the voice of experience. Sam was thirty-seven. Had he been waiting for someone to come to their senses all this time?

"And who are you waiting for, Sam? Who broke your trust?"

For a long moment he looked into her eyes, as if deliberating whether to speak. Finally he relaxed a little, his lips curving just the tiniest bit. "I'm not waiting for anyone."

And that was where he stopped. All kisses and tender moments aside, he finished his sentence there and said no more. Angela had turned to him tonight because she'd needed him. And he was there because they were…what exactly? More than friends? But he'd had chances to kiss her tonight and the closest he'd gotten was a peck on the forehead, like a brother might give a sister. She'd screwed it up big-time at Diamondback when she ran away.

Because she'd lied. She did want him. She did care and the truly astonishing thing was that she trusted him. With anything. With her life. And she could tell him so or she could let him walk out the door.

# CHAPTER ELEVEN

WHEN Angela woke, sun was streaming through the kitchen windows. The throw from the back of the sofa was soft against her skin and a cushion had been placed beneath her head. She felt as though a weight had been lifted even though she knew there was so much heartache to come. But it was going to get better. She just knew it.

She rolled slightly and looked toward the kitchen. Sam. He was standing at the counter in front of the coffeemaker, staring out the window at the backyard as the coffee brewed. Had he slept at all? His jaw was darkened with a layer of stubble and his hair was usually a bit messy so it was hard to tell if he'd slept or not. But she noticed his shirt was now buttoned correctly, and she gave a small smile.

He'd stayed all night. Looked after her in a way no one ever had before. Listened to her, and she'd opened up and let him see all the dark, hidden corners. And yet here he was, making coffee, humming tunelessly, completely oblivious to the changes he'd wrought in her.

She would be okay. She'd be more than okay and so would her mom. Because they would face what needed facing and she wouldn't be afraid.

She shifted on the sofa and he turned and smiled. The sight of him grinning at her made her warm all over, and if the wattage of his smile missed any spot, his easy greeting found the shadows. "Hey, sleepyhead."

Oh, my. Sam's morning voice was husky with the rasp of sleep. "Hey yourself," she replied, trying to keep her pulse under control. "How long have I slept?"

"A few hours. We were talking and then I looked down and you were out like a light."

The idea of falling asleep curled up against his side made her feel all hot and tingly. "Sorry about that."

"Don't be." The coffeemaker beeped and he held up an empty mug. "Want some?"

She pushed herself up to sit, leaving the blanket over her bare legs. He was trying to keep things easy and she needed to follow his lead, even if she was feeling a bit shaky. She didn't quite trust it, but had to admit it felt amazing to let someone look after her for a change. She smiled up at him. "Love some. Black's fine."

He brought her a cup along with one of his own and sat down. "I thought you'd want to know right away that I heard from Mike. They picked up your dad just south of Leduc. He was hitchhiking, on his way here."

She sipped her coffee, trying to sort out her feelings. Relief, certainly, that Jack would not show up. Hope that Beverly was truly on the road to a new life. And simple sadness. This was what her family was reduced to. And it was a mess. It would be for a long time, until things with both her parents got sorted. It certainly wasn't fair to drag Sam into it. He'd done enough last night.

"Mike wants to see you and your mom this morning. They need to interview you both if they're going to press charges. He can only stay in the drunk tank for so long before they have to release him."

"I know." She would face this—face him—after all this time. She had to.

"I can go with you if you want."

The offer was unexpected and generous but unsettling. She knew he was trying to help but couldn't escape the fear of being smothered by his involvement. She ran her finger around the rim of her cup. Didn't he trust her to see it through? She had needed him last night, but she was made of stern stuff. She stopped circling her finger and looked up at him. "To make sure I go through with it?"

He frowned. "Of course not. For support. I know this is going to be very difficult and painful."

Her hands felt cold and she curled them around the heat of the cup. "You're a strong person, Sam. You see a problem and you fix it. You aren't afraid of anything. And it would be easy for me to let you fix this for me, but if last night showed me anything, it's that I need to fix it for myself."

"I wasn't planning on fixing it for you." He sounded put out about it. "It was for moral support, but if you don't want me to go, I won't."

The gap that had narrowed last night started to widen again.

He put his cup down on the table and then took hers and put it down as well. He clasped her fingers in his hands and met her eyes. "But for the record, I do get afraid now and again. I'm not always as strong as I should be."

She doubted it. He was so very perfect, so masculine and approachable with his chocolate eyes and hint of stubble and wrinkled shirt. It wasn't fair that she should find him so attractive when she needed to gather the wherewithal to keep her distance. It would be too easy to let him take the lead.

At that moment Morris jumped up on the couch, stepped carefully across the cushion and curled up on Sam's lap. He started purring instantly while Sam's surprised gaze met hers.

"Well, I'll be," he murmured, letting go of one of her hands and dropping his to stroke the soft orange fur.

He'd won over Morris. Her timid, cranky boy hadn't just accepted a touch but had sought it out. He hardly ever sat in her lap, let alone curled up in a contented ball. And here he was cuddling with Sam. Traitor.

It shouldn't have irritated her but it did, adding to her sense of feeling alone. She was used to being the one who made things happen, but when it counted she'd frozen. It all came so easily to Sam. Even Morris seemed to have forsaken her this morning, choosing Sam instead.

Sam rubbed his wide hand down Morris's back. "Will you at least promise to call me if you need anything? Or just let me know how it goes later? I'll be worried."

"I appreciate it, Sam, but there's no need for us to take any more of your time. I know you have your own concerns." She would be strong. She would prove it—first to herself, and then to everyone else who had ever doubted.

"There's every need," he contradicted.

Something in the warm timbre of his voice set off alarm bells. "Why?" she asked, trying to pull her fingers away but he held them fast.

He seemed to consider for a moment, then relaxed as if he'd come to some silent decision. "When this is over, we need to talk."

The bells were ringing madly now. "I don't know if that's a good idea. I need to get my mother settled and there'll be legal matters to sort out…not to mention the running of Butterfly House." Nerves flickered in her voice but she was determined. If she relied on Sam now she would never know if she had it in her to defeat her own demons.

"Angela."

The soft but firm way he said her voice cut off her babbling.

"I understand you need to do this by yourself. I really do.

But I will worry about you whether you want me to or not. That's what happens when you love someone."

Oh, no, he hadn't just said it. Hope slammed into her chest quickly, followed by despair. His gaze never left her face and time stood still for just a second as she absorbed the words. No one had ever said them to her before. And she knew Sam well enough that she knew he wouldn't say it if he didn't think he meant it. Hearing the words filled her with a momentary, glorious happiness. It was a revelation to know she was love-able.

But they were both going to be so hurt at the end of all this. He wanted to care for her and shoulder her burdens. And what she needed was someone who could step back and let her fight her own battles. When she'd thought it was only her feelings involved it had been better. But now he'd gone and said it out loud without even hesitating or choking on the words. He couldn't take it back even as a small part of her acknowledged that she didn't really want him to.

"You…" She couldn't bring herself to say it, but she couldn't look away from the honesty and emotion in his eyes. She knew he meant it even before he spoke the confirmation.

"I love you, Angela. You drove me insane the first time we met and you haven't stopped. I didn't know what to do with you and your sharp tongue and tidy little suit. I wanted to throttle you and kiss you senseless at the same time. But then something changed. I kept telling myself my feelings were all wrong and you told me to stay away and I thought that would solve it. But when I heard your voice on the phone last night I was so afraid and I knew. Your past doesn't matter. I love you. I just do."

She was without words. Never in her life had she been the recipient of such a speech. And he meant every word. She didn't doubt that for a second.

He leaned in and touched her lips with his and she felt him

tremble beneath her hands. She curled her fingers around the cotton of his shirt and held on, absorbing the taste of him so that she could remember. He was always so unspeakably gentle. So gallant and courteous. And she deserved none of it, because she was letting him kiss her even though she knew in the end she'd turn him away.

Morris got cramped and with a meow of complaint jumped off Sam's lap. Sam slid a few inches closer until their bodies brushed. Angela gave herself this moment to cherish because even though she refused to say the words in return, she knew in her heart that she did love him back. She loved his loyalty and strength and the compassion that he sometimes kept hidden behind his hardworking exterior. The hands that worked the land and branded cows and broke horses were as gentle as a butterfly's touch on her skin. And yet she could not give in to it all the way. Because she would ask things of him that were not fair to ask. Things he could not give. She would ask him to stop being himself, and there was no way she could ask that of anyone.

And perhaps—just perhaps—she was afraid that if she forced him to make a choice between Diamondback and her, it wouldn't be her.

She pulled away from the tender embrace and sighed. "Oh, Sam."

The words were wistful and sad and needed no explanation or elaboration. The betrayed look in his eyes said it all for him. She hadn't said it back. They both knew that his declaration was not the beginning of something but the end.

The moment dragged out until he got to his feet, took a few steps, squared his shoulders and turned back to face her.

"This is why I didn't want to talk right now. You've got too much on your mind, too much you have to focus on. Once the dust has settled…"

"It won't change anything." She folded her hands on her

knees and looked up at him. He had done so much for her. She'd needled and accused him of some unjust things and in the end he'd come through, every single time. He deserved better than what she had to offer. He was looking for a wife who would move into the position of chatelaine of the ranch. That was his history and legacy. He needed someone who would put his needs—and Diamondback's—first, and that wasn't her. Because Butterfly House was *her* legacy and it was just getting started. She couldn't do both. And if the last twelve hours had taught her anything, it was that she had a lot of work left to do—both personally and professionally. She wasn't ready for what a committed relationship would mean.

"So you don't love me," he said, challenging her.

Could she lie? Could she look him in the eye and say *No, I don't love you, Sam*? She couldn't do it. He would see right through her.

"Where do you see this going?" she asked instead. It was an important question. A flicker of hope still burned. There was a chance she was wrong, after all, a chance that he might say the sorts of words that would give them a chance.

He came closer and squatted down in front of her, the denim of his jeans stretching taut across his long legs. She longed to reach out and lay her hands on his knees, just to feel connected to him again. She clenched her fingers tighter together to keep from doing it. She had to be strong.

"I saw you at the ranch the night of the open house, remember? You and Clara and mom all together in the kitchen, laughing. It felt so right, Ang. It's never been that way before. For a long time now it's been like living in black and white. And then you walked in and everything was in color again. I want you there, with me. I want you to make a life with me. I want us to face those challenges together."

Angela could think of a half dozen women who would give

their right arms to hear such a speech from Sam. What he had to offer any woman was a fine life. A beautiful, stable home, a prosperous living, and an incredible man capable of a lot of love. It was a dream come true. Except it was his dream and not hers.

She shrank back against the cushions. She was horribly afraid that if she said yes she'd end up losing the very best part of herself in the process, making them both miserable. They wouldn't make it. While she knew that Sam would never mistreat her the way Jack and Steve had, she was terribly afraid of losing the part of her she was just beginning to find.

In the end losing Sam would be so much worse than leaving Steve. That hadn't been about love at all. But Sam—he was unfailingly honest and deserved someone who could be as open with him. This time her heart was well and truly involved.

"I'm sorry, Sam. Your life is Diamondback. And mine is not. And that leaves us at a bit of an impasse."

He stood up, looked down at her and made her feel very small. "You'd have me walk away from the ranch?"

"Of course not. Diamondback is who you are. That's what I'm saying, you see?" She couldn't stand being on the sofa anymore and got up, letting the blanket drop to the floor. "You have built your life there. You are a part of the ranch and it is part of you. You need someone to be there by your side, to have a big family. I know you want that; I can see it every time you speak of your parents or your cousin. Family will always be at the center of your life—it's what drives you. And this foundation drives me, don't you see? You can't imagine walking away from the ranch so you must understand how it would be for me to walk away from this."

"You could still help," he offered. "You wouldn't have to give it up." But he looked away, knowing it was a paltry solution next to the absolute truth she spoke.

"I've dreamed of this foundation for most of my life," she said quietly. "If I walk away from this now, I leave the best part of me behind. I leave behind the part that makes me *me*. If you love me at all…"

"You know I do."

Her heart thudded. This was so hard. "If you love me at all," she continued, "you love me because of this place. Because of who it makes me. Because of who it will allow me to become. What is left if you take that away?"

"I would never want you to change who you are!" His eyes blazed at her. "You know that."

"I know you wouldn't mean to. But I have plans. It hasn't ended because of my mother, you know. Yes, I'm hoping this provides us with some healing and closure, but I believe in this project more than ever. I still want to expand and open up other shelters. And you need a wife who won't be traveling around all the time putting something else ahead of you. That's no way to run a relationship. I'd hurt you in the end, Sam, and that's not fair to either of us."

A door opened and shut and shuffling footsteps echoed in the hall. Beverly appeared in the doorway of the kitchen and Angela's heart hurt just looking at her. Dressed in an old nightie and a borrowed housecoat, she looked old and stooped and the fresh wounds on her face had deepened, giving her a tired, battered appearance.

"Mom. I hope we didn't wake you."

"I smelled coffee." The woman tried to smile but her cracked lip started to split and halted the smile in mid curve. Instead she moved to the coffeemaker and took a mug from a hook on a cup tree.

"I can't deal with this right now," Angela whispered to Sam, not sure if she was relieved by the interruption or not. Once he was gone it would truly be over. But sending him away was as close to breaking her heart as she'd ever come and she wasn't sure she was prepared for it. A part of her wanted to put it off as long as she could.

"Of course," he answered, but she detected a chill in his voice that hadn't been there before. Perhaps he was accepting the truth in what she said. It was an impossible choice for either of them to make. She was glad now that she hadn't said the words back to him. It would have made this even more unbearable.

"Mike will be expecting you at his office later this morning. And perhaps you can tell Clara that we can manage today without her. You need her more."

He grabbed his keys from the table and nodded at Beverly while Angela looked on helplessly.

"Mrs. Beck," he said, "I'm Sam Diamond. If you need anything, my family's here to help. Angela's going to take really good care of you. You can trust her to do the right thing."

Oh, the sting in those words, especially now that doing the right thing was costing them both so much. She blinked back tears and walked him to the door.

He paused for a moment on the steps, putting his hands in his pockets. Angela held on to the edge of the door, putting off shutting it, knowing it meant goodbye. Finally he looked up.

"You won't reconsider?"

She swallowed. "I can't," she whispered, looking down at her feet so he wouldn't see the glistening in her eyes.

"I want you to know that I meant what I just said to your mother. Same goes for you. If you ever need anything, I'm a phone call away. Got it?"

She nodded dumbly, still unable to look up at him. Her willpower was hanging by a thin thread. "I've got it."

He spun and jogged down the steps to his truck. Angela shut the door and locked it, then leaned her back against it. She couldn't bear to watch him drive away this time.

\* \* \*

Virgil was sitting in the late-August sun, a magazine in his lap. He hadn't even turned the cover. Instead Sam found him staring out over the pasture. Sam followed the path of his gaze and took a deep breath. Angela was right. This was more than home. Diamondback was something he felt through the soles of his feet straight to his heart. He and Virgil both did. And because of their love for the ranch, Sam was determined to give it one last try. There had to be a way to bring his vision for the future and the family all together.

"Dad."

Virgil started at the sound of his voice and Sam smiled wistfully. His father was improving slowly but there was no denying how much he'd aged since his stroke.

He pulled up a chair and sat beside his father. "Where's Clara?"

"Told her I wanted to sit outside for a while. No more fluttering."

Sam chuckled. Virgil's speech was improving, still slow but with fewer slurs. "She's good for you."

"Gives your mother a break. And she's a good woman." Virgil threw Sam a meaningful glance.

"Sorry, Dad. Barking up the wrong tree."

"I know." Virgil nodded. "You and Angela."

Surprise made Sam's mouth drop open. "How did you…"

"I see things. Slow. Not blind."

Sam sat back in his chair. Had he been treating his father as if he was blind? Had he underestimated how sharp his father's mind remained while his body betrayed him? He blew out a breath. "Of course. I'm sorry, Dad."

"I know that, too."

The dry August breeze blew across their faces, bringing with it the smell of fresh-cut grass and manure and the hundred other aromas of a ranch at its seasonal peak. For a few minutes Sam was quiet, gathering the words he needed.

Hoping that this last time he could break through and make his father understand.

"Dad, I need to say something and I want you to hear me out. Without jumping all over me." Virgil gave him a skeptical look and Sam's lip curved a little. "Okay, at least wait until I'm done."

"Say your piece."

He took a breath. "I think you're afraid, Dad. I think you hate what's happened and you're frustrated and you feel like you're losing control." Virgil's eyes blazed but Sam pressed on. "I think it has got to be hell on earth having to let go of your life's work and I think the fights we've had this summer have been a way for you to make sure you are not forgotten. That you are still a vital piece of Diamondback."

Virgil remained silent. Sam took that as a good sign, an affirmation without Virgil having to say the words.

Encouraged, he leaned forward. "Dad, you *are* Diamondback. I know it's been in the family for generations but you are the one who built it into what it is today. You are the one who took chances and became a leader in this industry. You are the fearless one. And it kills me to see that fearlessness taken away. I don't want to be the one to do it."

A magpie chattered beneath the caragana bushes and Sam watched it bob awkwardly along the grass, weighted down by its cumbersome tail. "I could never cut you out of Diamondback. I want us to do this together. And I know in my heart that this is the right thing. The right thing for right now and the right thing for the generations to come."

"What generations? Don't see any wives or babies runnin' around here."

Sam crossed an ankle over his knee. "Not for lack of trying, okay?" Irritation clouded his voice. The truth was, he hadn't been able to stop thinking about Angela. The bits and pieces he'd got from Clara over the past weeks were paltry crumbs. It had taken all his willpower to let Angela handle the changes in her life on her own, but he'd done it. Because he knew she needed to, for herself.

Besides, she hadn't even said she loved him. And that drove him crazy, because he could see her here, by his side. See their children running around in the hayfields. See himself teaching his son or daughter how to drive a tractor, ride a horse. For years he'd viewed children as a practical necessity, but not now. For the first time ever he could see it all and it wasn't his for the taking.

"You ask her?" Virgil reached out and touched Sam's arm. "Can't say yes if you don't ask."

"I told her I loved her. But it didn't make any difference."

Virgil started laughing. It was wheezy at first, rusty-sounding, and after a few moments he coughed, gasping for air. Sam started to feel alarmed once he got over the shock of seeing Virgil laugh. But Virgil grinned, sat back in his chair and sighed, catching his wind.

"Son, you can be so smart. And so stupid." He took a deep breath, unused to speaking so much. "What's really important here? You pestered me all summer like a dog with a bone. Now at the first sign of trouble with a woman, you run away with your tail between your legs."

"My tail!" Sam burned with indignation. "You don't know, Dad."

"I know enough. I know you gave up. Sad excuse for a Diamond."

Dammit. Sam hated to admit it but Virgil was right. He had given up. Angela had sent him away and he'd let her. He never wanted to seem pushy or overbearing because of her past. But the truth was, he'd been ornery before he knew anything of her history and she'd risen to the challenge, not cowered.

If anything, he'd let her down by not showing her how a man should stand by a woman.

"This project appears to be more important to you anyway," Virgil remarked. "So maybe it's best."

Sam sat back in his chair. He knew exactly what his father was doing and wanted to call him on it. But the truth was smack between his eyes. He'd fought for this but he hadn't fought for her. He thought back over all the reasons he'd just given his father for fighting the ranch development, and realized he could have been speaking to Angela about Butterfly House. She *was* afraid. She had been the one to realize her dream and now she was terrified of losing control. Of losing the most vital part of herself. She'd said it and he hadn't been listening.

"Sam, I'll sign the papers if you want me to. I know you'll do right by Diamondback. But I want you to remember something. This place—this life—means nothing without your mother. Make sure you make the right decisions and for the right reasons."

Virgil was giving Sam all he'd wanted and the victory felt hollow. What stretched before him was a cutting-edge, prosperous future and an empty one. It had taken him thirty-seven years to fall in love and he knew it was going to stick. So what was he going to do about it? Let her go without a fight? Spend the rest of his days at Diamondback, a man of property but with a hole in his soul?

He got up and put his hand on Virgil's shoulder. "Appears I have some thinking to do."

Virgil nodded. "Yessir."

"I'll send Clara out if you like."

"I don't mind sitting a little longer."

Sam gave the shoulder a squeeze before heading inside. An idea was beginning to form, the seedlings of a plan to bring the family together *and* have the woman he loved. Virgil wouldn't like it, but it might just get him the daughter-in-law and grandkids he'd been harping about for years.

# CHAPTER TWELVE

THE house seemed horribly quiet. The Cadence Creek Rodeo was on and Clara and the other girls had gone to enjoy the festivities, including entering their own pot of chili in the chili cook-off. It had been a bright spot, seeing the women come out of their shells as they got further acquainted. Angela had heard them giggling over the chili-making, speculating on how many employers they could entice with their secret ingredients.

Angela felt lonely listening to them. She was on the outside yet again and by her own choice. They'd invited Angela along, but she wanted the time alone. Moments of quiet were fewer and farther between these days and she was seldom in the mood for company.

A week had passed since Beverly had moved to a different shelter in another town. While Butterfly House helped women ready to start over, the assistance Beverly needed was different. And as much as Angela wished she could help her mother all on her own, she was wise enough to know she couldn't be objective. Leaving Beverly in someone else's care had been very, very hard. But wounds were healing. They'd hugged and cried a little as Angela had promised to be back to visit soon.

She wished she could say the same about Sam, but she hadn't spoken to him. The only time she'd seen him was when Jane had invited her to go along to church one Sunday. Sam and Molly were in the fourth pew from the front and she'd caught her breath at the sight of him in dress pants and a freshly pressed white shirt, open at the collar, his face smooth from a recent shave but with his hair still the same sexy, unruly mess.

She hadn't gone back to church the next Sunday.

So this afternoon she was spending the afternoon cleaning her room and listening to Patsy Cline. The wistful music suited her mood perfectly. She'd gotten what she wanted, hadn't she? So why did she feel so empty? Maybe it was time to start looking into the next project, scout new locations.

And then Sam's words came back to haunt her. That once he met a challenge he got bored and moved on to another. Was that what she was doing? Except instead of boredom she was running away from her problems.

She didn't have a magic solution, so she put her energies into the job at hand. Her sheets were on the clothesline and she was dusting off her dresser when his voice behind her scared her out of her skin.

"Busy?"

She nearly threw the duster at him as he laughed. Her heart raced from the shock. She'd been thinking about finally decorating this room and listening to Patsy singing about "Walkin' after Midnight" and then there he was. "You should know better than to sneak up on a person like that."

"May I come in?"

She lifted an eyebrow. Mercy, he looked good in new jeans and a crisp Western shirt, his customary Stetson atop his head. "You're going to anyway." She flourished the duster. "Go ahead."

Sam stepped inside, as calm as you please, removed his hat and held it in his hands. Her bedroom was the smallest of the six and he seemed to fill it with all his larger-than-life glory. Why did it seem as if nothing had changed? Maybe he'd realized he was wrong about his feelings. Surely if he still thought he was in love with her it would be more awkward, wouldn't it? Instead it felt as if he'd done this hundreds of times before.

He looked around the room. "You didn't decorate this one like the others."

She shrugged. "The money is allocated for the residents. Those rooms had to come first. I've been thinking about it, though…" She let the thought trail off. The truth of it was Butterfly House didn't feel like home. She wasn't sure where that was—or what it would feel like when she got there. But she'd put off decorating a room for herself just the same.

The CD shifted and "Crazy" started playing.

"Nice music choice." Sam waved his hat in the direction of the turntable. "My mother would approve. She loves Patsy Cline. Bit melancholy for a summer afternoon though, isn't it?"

"There's never a bad time for Patsy," Angela replied, putting down the duster and ignoring his observation about her state of mind. "Are you going to make me ask why you're here, Sam? Is this official Butterfly House board business? Because I figured you'd be at the fairgrounds with everyone else in town."

"I was, for a while." That explained his "dress" Western clothes, then. "My cousin's retiring after this season. But bull-riding's the last event of the day and he's not up for a few hours yet. I ran into Clara and the ladies in the church tent surrounded by Cadence Creek's finest chili. They told me you were stuck at home."

She'd stayed home because the thought of running into him at the rodeo put knots in her belly. Avoiding him wasn't the answer, but she figured one day it would get easier.

"That still doesn't tell me why you're here."

For a long moment he seemed to consider. Finally he said, "How's your mom?"

It touched her that he asked that first thing. "She's doing okay. We filed a report with Mike, and she's in a different place now getting the help she needs. The court date isn't going to be much fun, but we're going to be there together." She smiled a little. "She's going to be okay, and that's the main thing."

"And you? Are you okay?"

"I'm getting there." The truth was she couldn't have done this without his help that first day. It wasn't a magic solution, but she was working on making peace with things. With people.

The music changed, and the opening notes to "I Fall to Pieces" filled the room. Slowly Sam took a step forward, then another. He put his hat back on his head and held out his hand. "Care to? Since you're missing the festivities?"

"Sam…"

"Please, Angela. I've worked myself up to coming here all day and you're not making this easy. Dance with me."

She only complied because she knew how difficult it had been doing without him the last while and didn't want to make it any worse for Sam. She stepped tentatively into his arms, placing one hand in his and the other on his broad muscled shoulder.

His hand rested firmly on her waist as he pulled her close. In the tiny floor space his feet shuffled in small steps, but it was enough that she felt the movement of his thighs against hers, the rise and fall of his chest as he breathed, the warmth of his lips next to her hair that was shoved carelessly in a ratty ponytail.

"I'm sorry." He whispered it next to her ear, sending shivers down her spine as they swayed to the music.

It was not what she'd been expecting. "What do you have to be sorry about?"

"That I gave up."

"I told you to, remember?" Her heart started beating abnormally. She'd been the one to send him away. And she'd been the one to cry into her pillow at night because of it. Her reasons had been right, so why had it felt so wrong?

"You were scared and you should have had a friend by your side. Not to go through it for you, but with you. Instead I let you push me away, and I'm sorry I wasn't stronger."

Her lip quivered. "You scare me, Sam. You make me doubt everything."

"Why?"

His feet stopped moving for a moment and he drew back, looking down into her eyes. She gathered courage, knowing she'd faced her demons alone and she'd been strong enough to do it, but that she'd also missed him every moment. She'd been very wrong to push him away when she should have trusted him. "Because of the intensity I feel when I'm with you. I'm so afraid of getting lost in it."

"I know you are."

"You do?" She looked up at him with surprise. He hadn't understood before. He'd had his eye on a perfect Diamondback life where she could "help" with the Butterfly Foundation. The fact that she'd been at all tempted still frightened her to death. Was she so weak that she'd trade in her dream so easily?

"Of course I do. When you open yourself up to someone, then you allow them the opportunity to hurt you. To disappoint you. And you've already been hurt enough, sweetheart."

His feet started moving again, but slower, and she had the weirdest sensation that they were snuggling. He'd called her sweetheart again, she realized with a sigh. And despite trying to hold her feelings inside, she knew that she'd shared things with Sam already that she'd never shared before with another person. She trusted him, believed in his goodness. That was a brand-new feeling.

"By the way—Dad signed off on the biogas project."

She furrowed her brow, confused at the abrupt change of subject but willing to follow along if it meant she could stay within the circle of his arms. "How did you convince him to do that?"

"I was honest with him. I finally realized that he was afraid of being invisible, afraid of losing all he'd worked so hard to build. Holding out was the one thing he could still control when everything else was flying to pieces. But I told him that he would never be unimportant or ignored. Because we're in it together. That's what people who love each other do, you know?"

"No, Sam. I never had a family like yours so I don't know."

But he persisted. "I think you do. Look at what you've done for your mother. You are standing beside her even though she hurt you. You do the right thing, Angela, always. You give people a voice who otherwise don't have one. And yet your voice goes unheard."

Their feet stopped and her throat swelled. How could he see all of that? How could he know? She stumbled back, out of his arms, but he caught her fingers and held on.

"I didn't hear you." He captured her gaze and held it. "I didn't listen to what you were saying. It wasn't until I understood my dad that I got it."

He reached over and cupped her cheek. "You're a butterfly that needs to fly, not be shut up in a jar somewhere. I hear you now," he said softly, "and it's high time someone fought for you. I love you so much, Angela. And I was a fool to let you push me away. I told you the morning after your mother arrived, do you remember? That you can't force someone to feel what you want them to feel. What you can do is be ready, so that when the day comes, you're there with open arms." His forehead touched hers. "My arms are open now, Ang. Hoping you're ready."

The floodwaters broke and she went into his embrace. Oh, he felt so good, so strong, so right. His shirt smelled like detergent and the outdoors and the spicy scent that was distinctly Sam. "I love you, too," she said, her voice muffled against the cotton.

This man—this gorgeous, humbling, incredible man before her—was offering her the moon. How could she not take it? As her eyesight blurred through her tears she realized that surrendering to her feelings only made her more, not less. That over the last few difficult weeks she'd wanted him by her side not to bear the burden for her but to share it with her. Somehow, by some miracle, he'd restored her faith.

She leaned back and laid her hand on his tanned cheek. "I do love you, and it's hurt me so much to hold it inside."

"I never wanted to hurt you." He put his hand over hers, holding it there against the warmth of his skin, turning his head a little so he could kiss the base of her palm. His eyes closed for a second and his thick lashes lay against his cheek. Angela was swamped by a love so whole, so complete, she knew she'd remember this moment forever.

"I know that," she whispered, and he opened his eyes.

"I have a plan," he said. "Would you hear it? Please?"

Staying away from him hadn't solved a thing; she'd been utterly miserable. Besides, Sam wasn't the kind of man who said please often. He was used to having his own way. He was the kind of man who took charge rather than be at anyone's mercy. And that strong, forceful man was holding her in his arms saying please. Hope glimmered as she nodded just the tiniest bit, encouraging him to go on.

"I spent my whole life focusing on Diamondback. It meant everything to my mom and dad and then to me, too. It defined the Diamond family. I remember when times were tight. How we were looked down upon rather than up to. When things started to change, when the years of careful management paid off, I got cynical."

He squeezed her fingers. "I'm getting to the romantic part, I promise. I saw the love between my parents and knew I could never settle for anything less than the example they set. No one ever measured up—until I met you. Angela…"

Oh, lord. His dark eyes were wide and earnest and her heart was pattering a mile a minute.

"You really don't know, do you?" A soft smile touched his lips. "You walked into that benefit and it was like someone hit me right here and stole my breath." He pressed a hand to the middle of his chest. "And when you get talking numbers and figures and demographics it's a sight to behold. But it's not just that, either. You're compassionate, and strong."

She swallowed past the tears thickening her throat. But he wasn't done yet.

"And then I thought maybe you did care for me. I could see our life together. But it was still about me. It wasn't until I talked to Dad that I truly understood. He said something to me that day that brought it all back to one. He said that Diamondback and his life would have been nothing without Mom. And I realized he was right. I've been miserable. I holler at people and spend too much time brooding in the barn. I'm no quitter but I'd given up on us. I had to be willing to fight for us. And that meant putting us first. The only way to do that is to share your dreams with you. Because Diamondback be damned, Ang." His dark eyes shone down at her. "My dream is you. The rest of it doesn't matter if I don't have you."

He lifted her hand to his lips and kissed it, the gesture so chivalrous and tender that if she hadn't before, Angela would have lost her heart completely.

"I was looking for a way to put my family back together, and I couldn't see that you are doing it just by being you."

"I am?"

He nodded. "You made me see things from my dad's side. You helped my mom ask for help, became her friend. The only thing missing now is Ty—he belongs home rather than roaming the country. And now even he has a reason to come back."

"He does?" She was trying hard to keep up, but she couldn't see how she'd had anything to do with Sam's cousin whom she'd never met.

"I'm asking you to compromise," he said. "Make Diamondback the home base for something extraordinary. You don't belong running one single house, Angela, you deserve to be heading up the whole foundation. Hire a director for here, and oversee the start-up of each and every house built to help those who need it. I don't want you to give up your dreams. I want to share them with you, be with you every step of the way. And I hope that in the end, you'll share mine. Make a home with me at Diamondback. Maybe raise a family. A ranch is a good place to have kids. Hard work and open spaces and two parents who love and respect each other."

"You want to marry me. And have babies." Her mind was spinning, with the words he was saying tumbling about like little miracles and bubbles of possibilities she hadn't even considered before.

He tucked a piece of hair behind her ear, smiling softly. "Yes, I want to marry you." He grinned. "And have babies. Maybe I'm not great with teenagers but I'm guessing I'll learn, especially with you there beside me. What will it take to convince you?"

The CD had long since run out and the room echoed with expectant silence.

"I know you want to make this happen, but, Sam, you

can't be gone from the ranch all the time and your father is in no shape to go back to work." She wanted to believe him. Wanted it desperately.

"This is the best part. My cousin is retiring and coming home to run Diamondback with me. A full partnership. That means that I don't have to be at the ranch 24/7. I know that I can go away from time to time and the ranch is in good hands. It's where he's belonged all along anyway. The family all together."

"Your cousin?" she asked. "But I thought he was estranged from the family."

Sam grinned. "Convincing him to come back wasn't easy. He and Dad haven't seen eye to eye in a long time. Peas in a pod, that's why if you ask me. But Ty's sharp and he's a hard worker. If it hadn't been for one big blow-up I don't think he'd have gone in the first place. Even so, it took my trump card to make him say yes."

She risked a smile. "Of course you have an ace up your sleeve. You always do."

His lips curled in a sexy, private smile. "A long time ago we made a pact that we'd never lose our heads over a woman. I told him I had fallen in love and wouldn't have as much time to dedicate to the ranch. He said he didn't believe it and that it was something he needed to see in person. But it's just an excuse. I think he knows it's time he came home."

Sam had turned his life upside-down to make this happen. All for her. It was everything she wanted and it made her want to weep.

She put her hand on his chest and tipped her face up to his. "I had to face some things on my own, had to prove to myself that I was strong enough to be me and come out of the shadow that's been hanging over me for so long. But I missed you the whole time, Sam. I wish I could have done that without sending you away. I don't feel like I deserve you. I asked too much, I…"

"Hush." He placed a finger over her lips. "You taught me that it's about what you give, rather than what you get. You deserve far more than you think, and I'm going to spend my life showing you—if you'll say yes."

There was no other possible answer to give. He was offering her everything—the Butterfly Foundation, a home, brown-eyed and dark-haired babies to call her Mama. She just had to be brave enough to trust, and believe and reach out and grab it.

She cupped his face in her hands and kissed his lips. "Yes," she whispered. "Yes."

# EPILOGUE

THE fall day was gilded in hues of gold—the ripe harvests in the field, the drying grasses in the meadows, the gold coin-shaped leaves rustling on the poplar trees. The guests sat in rented chairs on the lawn while Sam stood at the top of the newly painted porch, where he'd shared lemonade and those first confidences with Angela in the twilight.

Sam watched as she made her way up the path, walking slowly in a simple white dress with her hand on Virgil's arm as he took small steps behind a rolling walker. When they'd announced their engagement, Virgil had insisted on walking her down the "aisle," and he and Clara had kept it a secret as they'd worked over the past weeks. Sam's throat thickened at the sight and he ran a finger between his neck and the tight collar of his new shirt. Angela smiled up at him and the world stopped. It was just the two of them now as she took the steps with her small train gliding behind, the long veil floating in the fall breeze.

"I, Samuel, take you, Angela..."

"I, Angela, take you, Samuel..."

She smiled at the use of his full name and he smiled back, full of a happiness he hadn't known existed. Within minutes it was done—the ring was on his finger where he planned to keep it forever.

The reception was held at Diamondback in a huge tent set

up in the garden. The asters, chrysanthemums and dahlias were still blooming, their spicy scents mixed with the delectable smell of Diamondback's finest prime rib.

Clara, Angela's only bridesmaid, came to offer her last congratulations before taking Virgil inside after the excitement of the day.

"I'm going in now, but I wanted to say happy wedding day to you both." She gave Angela a quick hug. "I'm going to miss you around the house, but you're going to have a wonderful time."

Sam had booked them in a chalet in Quebec's Eastern Townships for a week's honeymoon, to be followed by a week in Ottawa where they'd be in meetings about federal funding for the Butterfly Foundation. A new director of the Cadence Creek house had been hired, and a temporary office had already been set up at Diamondback for Angela to use until construction finished on their new house. He intended to keep his promises.

Sam hugged Clara as well—she'd gotten over her physical shyness with him shortly after their engagement. "Have you met Ty yet?" he asked. "Your paths will be crossing a lot from now on as he'll be staying in the house. Hang on."

He waved his cousin over. "Ty, come on over here."

Ty looked out of place in his suit. His jaw sported a faint bit of stubble and the suit coat hung awkwardly on his rangy frame. Sam hid a smile. Ty was back but he was still determined to do things his way. Thankfully that didn't mean butting heads with each other. But Sam had his doubts where Virgil was concerned. Ty and Virgil seemed to set each other off without trying. The next few months would be interesting. Still, he was convinced they'd work through it.

"Ty, this is Dad's assistant, Clara."

"Mr. Diamond," she said, and Sam saw the defiant set of her jaw as she held out her hand. It was more than she'd done with him at their first meeting, and Sam shared a look with his new wife. It was good progress.

"It's just Ty," he replied, taking her hand and shaking it. Sam saw Clara's eyes widen at the contact before she pulled her hand away. "Or Tyson if I'm on your bad side."

"Right. Well, I'd better get your dad inside. Goodnight everyone."

When she was gone, Sam saw Ty's gaze following her to the house.

"Go easy," Sam warned.

"Did I do anything?" There was a hint of belligerence in Ty's voice. Boy, he did still have a chip on his shoulder.

"Of course not," Angela stepped in with a smile. "Clara was our first Butterfly House resident, that's all. Sam just wants you to respect that."

Ty's gaze narrowed as he watched Clara's sage-green skirt disappear through the deck door. "Her husband abused her?"

"They weren't married, but yes," Angela confirmed. "But we know you'll be considerate, Ty. Don't worry."

Ty hesitated a moment, then to Sam's surprise excused himself and started toward the house.

Sam started forward but Angela stopped him with a hand on his arm. "Let him go. She'll put him in his place if need be. I'm not worried, Sam. Ty's a good man underneath all his cockiness." She grinned. "Like his cousin."

"Like your husband," he corrected, pulling her into his arms.

"Don't worry," she said, standing up on tiptoe and touching her lips to his. "I know how lucky I am. There's no other Diamond like you, Sam."

"Damn right," he confirmed, and picked her up, spinning her in a circle of happiness.

\* \* \* \* \*

# THE RANCHER'S RUNAWAY PRINCESS
Donna Alward

# CHAPTER ONE

"IN TWO hundred meters, turn left."

Lucy grinned lopsidedly in the direction of her GPS sitting on the dash. "Thank you, Bob," she replied with mock seriousness, looking up the long stretch of road for the intersection her "companion" kept insisting was approaching. The freedom—this wide-open space—was a revelation compared to how claustrophobic she'd felt lately.

"In one hundred meters, turn left."

She obeyed the monotone instruction and put on her turn signal. A small sign announced a numbered road. Thank goodness she'd been able to program in a waypoint for the Prairie Rose Ranch. Otherwise she would have kept driving the rented SUV through this fairly empty landscape for God knew how long. Not that she'd have minded; there was something comforting in the rolling green hills, their undulating curves broken only by random fences and trees.

She turned onto the road, only to discover after the first few seconds it had gravel instead of pavement. She rolled up the window against the dust curling up from her tires.

Prairie Rose Ranch was out in the middle of nowhere, just as Mr. Hamilton had said in his e-mail. All that isolation and space had sounded wonderful to her ears after the scrutiny she'd experienced the past few months. She couldn't wait to get there, away from all the prying eyes and whispers from behind hands. In Canada there would be no expectations, even for a short time. At Prairie Rose she would just be Lucy Farnsworth.

Whoever that was.

She frowned as Bob announced he'd lost the satellite signal, grateful he'd got her this far. She was here to buy horses, to look into Hamilton's breeding program and negotiate stud fees. It was her first real responsibility and one she was more than equipped for. Granted, she couldn't shake the feeling that King Alexander was placating her, but it didn't matter. For the first time in a long time she felt in control of something. No one to tell her who she was or how to act.

And no one at the ranch need know who she really was. The last thing she needed—or wanted for that matter—was for everyone to look at her as if she had some invisible tiara perched on her head.

No, this was her chance to get away from all of the curiosity and assessments and do what she knew how to do. Nothing made sense to her anymore, but at least this trip, short as it was, might offer her a bit of a reprieve. Might offer her a chance to shake off the pervading sadness. She'd been thrown from one unimaginable situation into another without time to catch her breath. When Alexander had suggested this trip, she'd left a vapor trail that rivaled the one from the 777 she'd flown in.

On the left up ahead she caught sight of a group of buildings…big buildings. With a rumble of tires, the SUV ran over a Texas gate, leading her up to a graveled drive. A wood and iron arch embraced the entrance, and she knew she was in the right place when she looked up and saw a uniquely shaped iron rose in the centre. Bob came back to life and announced she was arriving at her destination, but she reached over blindly and shut the unit off.

Her eyes assessed the ranch as she drove slowly up the

long, straight lane. It was neat, well kept, with a rambling two-story farmhouse hidden behind a long barn and corral. The immediate fences were in good repair and freshly painted; nothing seemed out of place. So far so good.

The land here was different from where she'd grown up, yet somewhat the same, and very different from the sun-baked countryside in Marazur. The sky here was broad and robin's-egg blue, in contrast to the piercing blue of the Mediterranean sky. Horses dotted the landscape, up a hill and beyond, grazing on rich grass, reminding her of her childhood home in Virginia. It was comforting and unsettling at the same time. It was what she knew. Yet everything she thought she knew about herself had been a lie, and she wanted to run away even as the ranch beckoned to her. Maybe this wasn't such a good idea after all.

Nothing made sense, and that was the *only* consistent thing these days.

She pulled in next to a white truck with the same Prairie Rose brand painted on the side, got out and shut the door. The polite thing to do would be to introduce herself at the house, she supposed. But then what? The west wind buffeted her curls about her face and she pushed them aside. The wind carried with it the sound of voices, coming from the open sliding door of the barn. Thankful she'd changed clothing before the drive, she straightened her T-shirt. At least someone in the barn could point her in the right direction.

Lucy heard the man before she saw him, his voice a low, warm rumble as he spoke. Her sneakers made soft padding noises on the concrete floor; for a moment she stopped and closed her eyes, drinking in the mellow smell of hay and straw and the warm pungency of horse, the one true thing that she associated with home. Perhaps that was what kept her going during all the dark days and uncertainty. The one constant she'd always had. The one place where she'd always belonged, no matter where she was. In a barn with the horses.

She knew it, and resented it. Resented that it was the only thing she seemed to have left. The male voice said something else, punctuated like a question. He was answered by a distinctly female voice, who laughed a little, though Lucy couldn't make out what they were saying. She paused, wondering again if she should have made herself known at the house first. She didn't want to intrude. But she turned a corner and suddenly two pairs of legs were before her and she couldn't pretend now that she hadn't come in.

He…the owner of the voice…stood upright, his weight planted squarely over his booted feet. One hand was resting on the withers of a splendid-looking chestnut mare. Lucy was first aware of his considerable height. Which made her realize how long his legs were in his faded jeans. Which led to his T-shirt. And how the worn cotton emphasized an impressively broad chest.

Color flooded her cheeks. Her assessment had taken all of two seconds, but it was complete, right down to the hot rush of appreciation.

"Can I help you?"

Lucy swallowed against the spit pooling in her mouth. She shot out her hand. "Lucy Farnsworth." *Please, please let him not be Brody Hamilton,* she prayed silently, with her hand suspended in midair. It wasn't possible that the man she'd just been caught blatantly staring at was the man she'd been sent here to broker deals with.

At her revelation he removed his hat, revealing a dark head and even darker eyes that crinkled at the corners with good humor. Her heart thumped at the courtesy…it was natural, not a put-on gesture, she was sure. He smiled as he stepped forward and took her small hand in his large one. "I beg your pardon, Miss Farnsworth. I'm Brody Hamilton. You made good time."

So this *was* Hamilton. So much for answered prayer. His fingers wrapped around hers and her tummy turned over.

Prairie Rose was a reputable operation. She'd expected the owner to be older. Certainly more plain looking, like most of the ranchers she'd grown up knowing. She hadn't expected him to be tall and sexy and all of what, thirty? Thirty-five? She kept the polite smile glued to her face, but inside she was growling to herself. Acting like a blushing schoolgirl. She was beyond that, wasn't she? And she was here to do a job, for Pete's sake!

"My flight was a little early."

She withdrew her hand, giving it a small tug. His fingers were warm and callused and had covered hers completely. She'd enjoyed the sensation, too much. Knowing it made her uncomfortable. There was no reason on earth why a single handshake should cause all this commotion within her.

*It's just a physical reaction,* she told herself. He *was* a fine-looking man, there was no sense denying it. She'd always admired that rugged, large, capable type, and he certainly fit that category. Any woman would have reacted the same way.

"This is my farrier, Martha," he introduced the woman holding the halter of the mare. Martha was taller than Lucy, sturdy, with slightly graying hair and was at least forty-five.

"You're from Marazur," Martha announced, releasing the halter and shaking Lucy's hand. "The Navarro family is renowned for their royal stables. It's a pleasure."

Why Lucy felt a tiny shaft of pride at that statement she had no idea. She'd been in Marazur all of two months and certainly couldn't take any credit for the stock owned by His Highness. It wasn't as if she belonged there or anything. Alexander had merely indulged her by letting her potter around; she'd heard him telling his eldest son that very thing.

He'd let her come on this trip just for appearances. He hadn't known what to do with her and this was easy. But that didn't matter. She was here now, and she would surprise them all by making the visit a success. Hamilton didn't know who she was. He wouldn't suspect her credibility, and she'd make sure it stayed that way.

"Brody's been telling me about you coming," Martha continued.

"It's not every day we get to do business with a royal family," Brody admitted, smiling down at her. It was slightly crooked, and her heart gave another traitorous thump.

Brody Hamilton was a charmer. With the realization of it, Lucy immediately felt better. Charm she could deal with. Charm only went so far, like good looks. It was blood that would tell. And unlike her mother, she wasn't going to fall for a wink and a smile. His would be wiped off his face soon enough, when he realized she actually knew what she was doing.

"Yes, well, I'm far more interested in the stock." She moved ahead and rubbed her hand on the hide just above the mare's nose. She closed her eyes briefly, smiling at the way the mare rubbed into her hand, enjoying the attention. "What's up with you, lovely? Hmm?"

"A bruise, nothing more. She stumbled during a trail ride yesterday."

"Trail ride?"

"We do give them now and then, a couple of hours and most people have had their fill of horseback. It keeps some of the older stock exercised. Besides…it's fun. Martha assures me a day or so in her box and this girl'll be right as rain." He rubbed the mare's neck as he said it.

There was that crooked grin again, accompanied by the crinkled corners of his eyes that seemed to be teasing. She turned away from him.

"And this beautiful girl is what—" she made a cursory examination "—sixteen? Seventeen?"

"Sixteen." Brody's smile had faded slightly.

Lucy ran her hand down the gleaming neck, her gaze taking in the shape of the ears, the forehead, the wide-set eyes. There was no doubt about it. She'd know that head anywhere. A smile flirted with her lips. What a pleasant surprise.

"Which would make her…one of Pretty Colleen's," she announced triumphantly. His flirtatious grin wouldn't get far with her, and she would make sure he knew it. She knew her business, and he needed to know that. She wasn't just an emissary sent to broker a deal.

Brody's smile disappeared completely. He stared at Miss Farnsworth, trying to puzzle her out. How on earth could she tell that? He'd bought Pretty Piece from a farm in Tennessee when she was eight…one of his first purchases on his own. This little moppet with the red curls, Lucy, she would have been a child when Pretty foaled. And she was from Marazur. The Mediterranean was a long way from backroads Alberta. Yet her accent didn't bear it out. She wasn't native to Marazur. He was as certain of that as he was that Pretty Piece was indeed of Pretty Colleen. A fact she couldn't have known before today, not unless she'd had a look at his records.

Who was Lucy Farnsworth? His brows snapped together. There was more to her than first appeared. He wondered how much more.

"How did you know?"

"It's her head. Looks just like her mum."

Brody shook his head while Martha laughed. "Congratulations, Miss Farnsworth. I think you've rendered him speechless. Quite a feat, because most of the time he has *something* to say."

"Martha!" Brody frowned. Never mind that at one point, Martha had been his babysitter and had changed his diapers.

Martha reached down for her bag. "Oh, pipe down, Junior. The girl knows her stuff, that's all. I'll be back in a few days to check on the mare."

She blustered out leaving Brody and Lucy in the gap, each with a hand on Pretty.

Somewhere outside a soft whicker echoed.

"I'll admit, Miss Farnsworth, you surprised me just now." He put his hat back on his head.

"I have that effect on people."

"Maybe sometime you'd care to explain that." He let a little humor sneak into his voice; she piqued his curiosity plain and simple. She'd clearly been around the industry a long time. Despite her youth, she seemed knowledgeable. And her accent was State-side. Southeast somewhere, he gathered. "Where are you from, anyway?"

For a moment their eyes clashed and he sensed she was deciding how to answer what should have been a simple question. He tried a smile, inviting her to speak. To his surprise her eyes immediately cooled and her lips thinned.

"You must have work to do," she offered stiffly.

"There's always work, but I expect you know that." She didn't want to answer. He wondered why, but there'd be time to get that information. She was supposed to stay several days.

"I'll just—" She swallowed, let the sentence hang.

"You've had a long flight and drive. You probably want to rest. I'll take you up to the house."

"You said you had work."

He angled his head slightly. He couldn't quite figure out Lucy Farnsworth. She was younger than he'd expected, especially to be so involved with such a renowned stable. It was clear she'd been sent because she could do the job. He wasn't sure why, but he'd expected someone taller, with dark hair and a remote manner.

The only thing that bore out his expectations was the

manner. There could be no mistaking the coolness, the only warmth she'd shown was in the caresses she'd spared Pretty. But tall and elegant she was not. She was barely up to his shoulder, and her hair was a tangle of gingery ringlets that flirted with her cheekbones until she tucked them behind her ears.

"I do, but that doesn't mean I can't get you settled in the house first."

Lucy looked away from him, as if what she was going to say next was so uncomfortable she couldn't meet his eyes. She instead looked Pretty in the eyes and scratched between the mare's ears. "I assumed I'd be in a guest house."

"We don't have a guest house, but then there's no need. There's more than enough room." He had a fleeting thought of running into her in the hall at sunrise, her curls in disarray and her cheeks still pink from the warmth of her bed....

Where the hell had that come from?

"I don't mean to impose on you, Mr. Hamilton. I can stay at the hotel in the town I drove through. What was it called... Larch something or other?"

"Larch Valley, and it's a twenty-minute drive." Perhaps not a bad idea, come to think of it, but the agreement had been made that he'd provide accommodation. He didn't want it said that he didn't provide proper hospitality. This was an important deal. And part of that was providing all that the ranch had to offer.

"That's a short commute in most places." Her voice interrupted him again.

Brody walked to a nearby hook and grabbed a lead, snapping it on to the mare's halter. "If you're more comfortable there, I understand. I'm sorry the arrangements weren't made clear. But why drive it if you don't have to?"

"I don't know..."

He sensed her hesitation and pressed on. "At least stay

for dinner. If Mrs. Polcyk can't convince you with her roast chicken…"

He let the thought trail off. Why was he insisting, anyway? The hotel back in town wasn't *that* bad. It had its good points—it was clean.

But he'd given his word to King Alexander. That his representative would be shown every hospitality. That whoever was sent would be received as an honored guest. He just hadn't expected it to be a sharp-tongued slip of a girl.

Brody didn't do well with girls. At least not beyond sharing a dance on a Saturday night. Especially one he tried to charm with a smile and who saw clear through it.

"I don't want to be in your way."

"The day starts early here, and sometimes finishes late. It's much more convenient, but of course, it's whatever makes you most comfortable. You are our guest, Miss Farnsworth. I'll leave it up to you."

Brody tried very hard not to wrinkle his brow. He'd seen her eyes when she'd first stepped into the corridor. He and Martha had taken her by surprise, and for a tiny moment Miss Farnsworth had looked small and vulnerable. Her eyes had gone a little wide and then darkened with a whole lot of assessment. She probably didn't even realize it but she'd bitten down on her lip and he'd been tempted to laugh. A cute little thing, he'd thought. A little out of her element, pretty and fresh, and he'd wanted to make her blush.

But then he'd realized who she was. A representative sent to assess his stock. A woman who knew horses, supposedly better than most men he knew. His Highness had said so when he called. Brody couldn't dispute that fact…it took a keen eye to identify an offspring by its parent, and the way she touched Pretty was confident and kind. For some reason Lucy Farnsworth was willing to sacrifice comfort for isolation. Why?

Lucy stepped away from the horse and backed up a few steps. Hamilton was right. She'd known the agreement included accommodation, and to drive to and from town when she didn't have to didn't make sense. The only reason not to stay here—the only one—was that she already felt awkward around Brody. Which was foolish.

Here she was representing the royal family of Marazur and she was astute enough to know that staying in town would be a deliberate snub against her host. And in the days ahead she might want Brody in good humor during negotiations.

"Of course the house will be lovely. I just don't want to be an inconvenience to you."

"You won't be, I assure you. The house was built for a large family and is a little lonely with only two in it.

"Two?" She had a fleeting thought of a wife and, for one ridiculous moment, felt more awkward than ever.

"Me, and Mrs. Polcyk. She's the housekeeper and cook. She's been looking forward to having someone else to do for, other than grumpy old me."

She looked up into his eyes—dark like the warm molasses her mother used to put on her bread. Right now he didn't look grumpy *or* old. The tummy-turning deliciousness was back, helped along by a breathlessness so foreign to her she didn't recognize it at first.

Brody Hamilton was sex on a stick, from his delicious eyes to his long legs to his manner that somehow managed to convey energy *and* a lazy ease. There was no escaping the facts; the only thing she could control was her reaction.

She took a deep breath and pasted on her polite-yet-distant royal smile…the one and only aspect of her new life she'd mastered. She remembered how big the house was and nodded. She probably wouldn't even run into Brody most of the time. "I appreciate it."

"Let me finish up with Pretty and I'll take you up. You can have a look around if you want."

"I'll do that."

He led the horse away, and Lucy watched them depart down the corridor, boots and hooves echoing through the quiet space. His faded jeans fit him as if they were made for him, the dark T-shirt emphasizing his broad shoulders. The black brim of his cowboy hat shaded his neck.

She squared her shoulders and set her jaw. Life had been full of enough complications lately. And she'd be damned if she'd let Brody Hamilton be another one.

# CHAPTER TWO

Lucy perched on a wooden stool, sipped on a cup of strong, rich coffee and came to two important conclusions.

Number one, Brody Hamilton ran a good ship. Everything was kept in tip-top shape, and from what she'd seen, that extended to his horses. This was a good thing. You could tell a lot about a man's stock by the state of the rest of the farm. Prairie Rose was neat, tidy and organized. Brody Hamilton paid attention.

And number two, Mrs. Polcyk ran the house. Full stop.

Lucy smiled into her mug, remembering how the housekeeper had put Brody firmly into his place. Brody had introduced her to the round, apple-cheeked woman who had instantly bustled her inside. Mrs. Polcyk had then ordered Brody to bring up Lucy's things, and he'd obeyed without batting a single one of his obscenely long eyelashes. He'd done it without a grimace or an eye roll but with an innate respect and acceptance of her, and Lucy liked that about him as well.

Lucy, on the other hand, was ushered through to the kitchen where she was now watching Mrs. Polcyk take some sort of pastry out of the oven. The room smelled of coffee grounds and cinnamon and fruit.

All of it filled her with such a sense of homesickness she thought she might cry. She missed afternoons like this. Tea in the drawing room was not quite the same as hot coffee and cookies in the kitchen.

"Your bags are in your room."

Brody's rich voice came from behind her, and she swallowed coffee and the tears that had gathered in her throat. She hadn't realized that coming here would hurt her so much. Hadn't realized that it would remind her of a place where she no longer belonged. And it was clear Brody took all that for granted. She wondered if he realized how lucky he was.

But she couldn't say any of that, of course. She put the smile back in its place and spun on the stool to face him. "Thank you."

"My pleasure."

He took a few long steps until he was at the stool next to her. He hardly had to move at all to perch on its seat and Lucy was reminded again how very tall he was. His voice was deep and full of teasing as he leaned forward, egging on Mrs. Polcyk. "If you tell me that's cherry strudel, I'm yours forever, Mrs. P."

She flapped a hand in his direction, but pulled a thick white mug out of a cupboard and poured him a cup of coffee.

Lucy felt his eyes on her and she refused to meet them again. If she did he'd see the tears that still glimmered there, and the last thing she needed was for him to see her vulnerable. And with him watching her so intently, there wasn't an opportunity for her to wipe them away. She opened her eyes as wide as she could, willing the moisture to evaporate. She'd thought of this trip as a chance to escape. Instead, the grief she'd tamped down for the last months rose up, leaving her raw and breathless.

For a few minutes they sipped in silence. He seemed to be waiting for her to speak, and she couldn't come up with anything to talk about. Her personal life was strictly off-limits. For one, she would fall apart, and for another, he would treat her differently, and that was the last thing she wanted. Maybe it was jet lag, because she knew she should ask him about Prairie Rose and his breeding program and hundreds of other relevant questions. Instead her brain was riddled with personal questions. Why was he the only one here? Did he run this place completely on his own? How was Mrs. Polcyk related to him? But for her to ask him those questions would be opening herself up to ones of a similar nature, and she couldn't have that.

Instead she stared into her coffee cup, fighting off memories and twisting her lips. It had to be fatigue, nothing else made sense. Certainly the feeling of resentment that was bubbling underneath all the other emotions didn't add up. He was teasing and comfortable. And she knew he had no idea how he was taking his situation for granted. No one ever did until they'd lost and then they were left with regrets. She'd bet any money that Brody didn't have regrets.

At least that made it easier for her to dislike him. Disliking him was vastly easier than liking. If she didn't like him, she wouldn't be tempted to reveal more than she should.

"Miss Farnsworth?"

She chanced a look up. He was looking at her over the rim of his cup, his eyes serious. "We've got plenty of time to talk business. If you're tired, you don't need to put up a good front. The jet lag alone has got to be killing you."

He was giving her an excuse; being kind to a guest. And it would be a good opportunity for her to create more distance between them. She should take it. Yet the thought of facing an empty, unfamiliar room wasn't that attractive. She'd spent enough time alone lately.

"You can start by calling me Lucy." The staff in Marazur reluctantly called her Miss Farnsworth after she'd dressed them down for using her official title. She couldn't abide the "ma'am" they'd come out with on her first day, either. Even

"Miss Farnsworth" made her feel like a stranger; she was used to her stable mates calling, "Hey, Luce" down the corridor. But she hadn't been able to convince the staff to call her Lucy. She didn't want to be Miss anything or Princess anyone. She wanted to be Lucy. Maybe if Brody would call her by her name she wouldn't feel like such a fraud.

"I like your house," she offered, an attempt at civility. "It's very…homey."

Something dark flitted through his eyes even though his tone was teasing as he responded, "As the head of King Alexander's stables, I expect you're used to finer accommodations."

"Not at all. It's not like I grew up in the palace." That much was true. She hadn't laid eyes on Marazur until a few short months ago. And arriving at the palace had been a shock. She'd grown up in a very modest middle-class neighborhood. She was used to worn furniture and chipped dishes, not antique settees and fine china. She was torn jeans and T-shirts; Marazur was linen and lace. "I had a typical middle-class upbringing, you might say. I'm just…ordinary," she conceded.

"How *did* you get the job, anyway? You're awfully young."

"Too young?" She bristled, familiar with the refrain. It was easier to do battle on the age front than admit she was there because of Daddy.

"Obviously not. I get the feeling you know exactly what you're doing."

He didn't make it sound like a compliment, but it was wrapped in politeness so it was hard to tell.

"I grew up around quarter horses, and I…" She paused, considered. She didn't want him to know. He couldn't know. There would be no more coffee breaks in the kitchen, and she'd missed them desperately. Even if southern Alberta was vastly different from Virginia, this kitchen held the same feel as the one she remembered, and she was hungry for those

feelings again, no matter how bittersweet. Mrs. Polcyk refilled her cup, and the scent of the brew drew her back to the
smell of strong coffee in the office at Trembling Oak; to the
tin of cookies that had always seemed to make its way to the
scarred wooden table. These were the feelings of home.

She didn't want to be treated any differently. As long as
he thought of her as Lucy, she could pretend she'd escaped,
even for a little while. If he knew who she was, he wouldn't
take her seriously. And the truth was she needed him to believe in her competence. Needed him to know she was fully
capable of doing this job.

"It was a case of knowing someone who knew someone,
that was all."

Brody's jaw tightened. First she'd called his house "homey"
as if she couldn't come up with a better word. Then she'd
all but admitted she'd got her job by knowing someone.
*Nepotism.* He despised the word. It reminded him of someone else. Someone who'd once considered Prairie Rose Ranch
a little too rustic for her taste. His fingers tightened around
the handle of his cup.

Mrs. Polcyk put plates of warm strudel in front of them
and bustled away to the refrigerator. Brody examined the
square and told himself to forget it. It didn't matter who or
what Lucy Farnsworth was. She was not Lisa, and all that
mattered was concluding their business. Being allied to the
House of Navarro and King Alexander was what was important. It would mean great things for the ranch and the breeding
program he'd worked so hard to improve since taking over.

Brody cut a corner off with his fork and popped the buttery pastry into his mouth. "Cherry. God bless her." He sighed
with appreciation.

Lucy smiled thinly, almost as if she were unaccustomed
to it. What he really wanted to know was more about King
Alexander and his plans. Allying himself to one of the great-

est stables in Europe would be a huge coup. He'd be able to grow his breeding program the way he wanted, really put Prairie Rose on the map. He owed that to his father. He owed it to himself, and to Mrs. Polcyk.

"What's it like? Working for someone so high profile?"

Lucy picked up her own fork to hide her surprise. Briefly she'd sensed Hamilton's withdrawal and got the uneasy feeling he was somehow mad at her. Now he was asking questions. Prying veiled in small talk. If he really wanted to know about her, all he'd have to do was a bit of navigating online and he'd get the whole story. She would have to give him enough to keep him from doing that, and not enough to let the cat out of the bag.

She was in such a quandary that she took a second bite of strudel before answering, pressing the buttery layers with her tongue, letting them melt. She'd been around a lot of livestock men in her life, and conversation was usually not one of their finer points. She had to acknowledge that he was making an effort, and for the sake of amicability, she considered how to answer.

Working for King Alexander was stifling at times, knowing why she was there in the first place. Being told she belonged there, when she knew she didn't. Yet it was glorious at others, like when she got to go riding through the fields without asking permission. Being able to hand pick her own mount, with no restrictions. That little slice of freedom was all that had kept her sane.

She couldn't reveal any of that to Hamilton, not if she wanted him to respect her capabilities. Not if she wanted him to see her as more than Daddy's girl flirting around with the horsies. She knew ranchers. Knew that was exactly what he'd think.

She squared her shoulders and forced a smile.

"His Highness has fine stables and the best in facilities

and equipment. His tack room alone is half the size of your barn, all of it gleaming and smelling of rich leather. Navarro horses are in demand all over Europe, from riding horses for the privileged to show jumpers to racing stock. His staff is dedicated and knowledgeable. It's a manager's dream come true."

"But?"

She put down her fork slowly, met his eyes while pursing her lips in puzzlement. "What do you mean, 'but'?"

"But what are you leaving out?"

"Nothing. It's a great operation."

"Then why aren't you meeting my eyes when you tell me about it?"

"I beg your pardon?" She felt color rise in her cheeks and took a deliberate sip of her cooling coffee. She'd been deliberately vague, and now he was calling her on it. She never had been good at hiding her feelings. Her mother always said Lucy had no face for poker and that Lucy had come by it honestly, as she hadn't had one, either. It had been years before Lucy understood what she'd really meant.

"You're avoiding looking at me. My mother always said that was a sign of a liar."

She bristled. An hour. She'd known him barely an hour and he was calling her a liar! The mug came down smartly on the countertop. He couldn't know who she really was. And if he did, pretending he didn't was downright rude. Mrs. Polcyk looked over, then calmly went back to cutting vegetables.

"Are you accusing me of something?"

"Of course not. I'm just wondering what you're not saying. This is my operation and my stock you're looking at. I don't get to travel to Marazur to check things out first. And when I get a sense that there's more to a story, I want to know before I sign anything on a dotted line."

She stood up from her stool. Dammit, even sitting he was

slightly taller than she was. "You're insinuating that I'm with-holding something about the Navarro stables. I don't appreciate that. The hotel is looking better and better. Navarro stables doesn't need Prairie Rose Ranch, not as much as..." She looked around her and then back into his face, lifting her chin. "Not as much as you need Navarro. You aren't the only stud operation in the world."

The anger felt good, releasing. Even if she knew provoking him would be a tactical mistake.

His eyes glinted like dark shards. "Perhaps not. But I was under the impression King Alexander wanted the best."

She met his gaze, admiring his confidence despite how annoying it was.

"And you're the best, I suppose."

"You wouldn't have come all this way if I weren't."

Her lips thinned. He had her to rights there. She *had* come a long way, and it was all to do with Hamilton's Ahab. That horse was the main reason she was here, as well as having the discretion to negotiate further stud fees and even add to Navarro with Prairie Rose stock.

"You're very sure of yourself."

"Don't get all in a dander over it. You described the stables like a brochure would, that's all. I'm just curious to know more. I like to know who I'm dealing with."

His implacable calm fueled her temper. Who was he to question the integrity of Navarro? She shoved her hands in her pockets to keep them from fidgeting. She knew she shouldn't rise to the bait but with the exhaustion and surprising emotionalism, she seemed incapable of ignoring it. "All you need to know is that I'm here to do a job. A job I'm more than qualified to do. Nothing else is up for discussion."

She spun to walk away, but his voice stopped her.

"Run away, then."

Everything inside her froze.

Run away? Her breath caught at his casual tone. If only she could. If only she could run away from what her life had become. She was so sick of everyone telling her how wonderfully things had turned out in the end. It didn't feel that way *at all*. Everything, *everything* she thought she'd known had been taken away with one conversation. Life had changed irrevocably, and right now all she could see was what she'd lost along the way.

Her job. Her home. Her mother.

Yes, she wished she could run away. But instead she was back to trying to prove herself and find *something* to anchor her again so she wouldn't feel as if she were drifting in this endless sea of loss and grief. And that something was her job at the stables, and her task was clear: the breeding program here at Prairie Rose.

And that meant that in the present she had to somehow deal with Brody Hamilton.

She turned and looked at him, sitting there, his black eyes watching her keenly, waiting for a response. Waiting as if he could see through every wall she'd built around herself and knew what she was hiding on the inside.

And for one brief, irrational moment she did want to run. Not away, but into the circle of his arms. They looked like strong arms, arms a woman could get lost in and forget the rest of the world existed. For months now she'd been standing on her own and she was tired. Tired of feeling she had to apologize for not being happy. Tired of pretending, when all she wanted was life back the way she'd had it. Tired of knowing even the past she'd thought secure had been based on a lie. For a few moments she wondered what it would be like to rest her head on his strong shoulder and just *be*. To let someone carry the weight for a while.

She swallowed. This was ridiculous. She hardly knew him and what she did know she resented. It had to be exhaustion, it was the only reason that made sense to her. There was no other reason for her to feel drawn to Brody Hamilton. None at all.

Looking at him…he just knew where he belonged. He was solid and steady, and he *fit* in a way she never had.

That was reason enough to resist the urge to step into his arms. Reason enough to resent him for all he had and the fact that he probably didn't even know it. The thought of stepping into his embrace was laughable.

This was a man who'd just questioned her integrity. She should be taking him down a peg. Instead she was bone tired of all of it. Her gaze dropped to his lips, and something intimate curled through her core. She mentally took a step backward.

"It's hardly productive for us to argue," she said, as icily as she could muster. "I believe you were right about the jet lag. I'm not myself. If you'll excuse me…I'm sure by tomorrow I'll be squared away and ready to get to work."

His eyes revealed nothing.

"Of course." The words were cold with empty manners.

"I'll take you up, dear." Mrs. Polcyk came around the corner with a gentle smile. Lucy turned her back on Brody again, forcing yet another smile for the kindly housekeeper. She could still sense his dark eyes on her, and they made her feel naked.

"You'll be wanting a nice hot bath, and a good meal—dinner's not far off."

What Lucy wanted was to disappear for the rest of the night, but she couldn't help but be comforted by the motherly insistence that somehow food would make everything right.

"That sounds wonderful."

She followed Mrs. Polcyk to the stairs but turned back at the last moment, displaying some sense of good manners her mum had instilled in her.

"I'll see you at dinner, Mr. Hamilton."

"Yes'm."

The housekeeper led her to the last room along the hall; a large bedroom with a window facing due west. "The bathroom is next door," Lucy heard, though her gaze was caught by the view of the mountains hovering in the distance. She'd seen them on the highway coming south from Calgary, but since turning east at Larch Valley, they'd slid from view. Now from the second floor window they jutted, gray, dark teeth, up to the hazy blue sky.

"Can you always see the mountains from here?" Lucy spun toward Mrs. Polcyk, who was standing with her hand on the doorknob.

"Most clear days. Wait'll you see the view from Wade's Butte."

"Wade's Butte?" Lucy couldn't recall seeing that on her map.

"Get Brody to take you out. It's probably a couple of hours ride, just on the edge of the ranch land."

"The name's not familiar."

"'Course not. You won't find it on any map, though most from around here know it right enough. It just sort of got named that, after Brody's granddad."

Mrs. Polcyk aimed a bright smile. "You just go relax now, and put on your eatin' legs. I made roast chicken tonight and there's peach cobbler for dessert. Cally brought back two cases from BC last week."

Lucy had no idea who Cally was and wasn't quite sure what "BC" was, but peach cobbler sounded heavenly. "I'm looking forward to it," she replied, with as much warmth as she could muster.

Mrs. Polcyk shut the door and left Lucy alone.

She looked around the room. It was different from any place she'd ever stayed. The floor looked like original hardwood, polished within an inch of its life, and the furniture gleamed from a fresh cleaning. The spread on the bed was homemade, a brilliant cacophony of bright colors and fabrics that made a patchwork pattern of flowers. Fresh flowers sat in a vase on the side table. Lucy went over and dipped her nose to sniff at a nasturtium. These weren't purchased at any store. These had been cut from a garden, today. For her.

The deliberate welcome touched her, despite Brody's gruff manner. He'd all but accused her of lying, but he'd been right. Perhaps that was what had annoyed her so much. It would be a cold day in hell before she would admit it.

She took out fresh clothing and wandered next door to the bathroom, delighted to find a small basket of little toiletries on the vanity next to a pile of fluffy towels. She put the plug in the tub and added some salts, breathing in the fragrant steam. Summertime or not, after a full day's travel added in with the time difference, a hot bath sounded like luxury itself.

An hour later, refreshed and dressed with her damp curls framing her face, she made her way back downstairs to dinner.

Brody was in the kitchen. And he was mashing potatoes.

Lucy stopped at the bottom of the stairs, watching the scene without being noticed. His hat was off, his dark hair lying in fine whorls around his skull, his dark T-shirt clinging to his wide shoulders with each push of the masher. Behind him Mrs. Polcyk wielded a set of electric beaters, whipping cream in a clear, cold bowl. Lucy's mouth went dry at the sight of his muscles flexing as he lifted the huge jug of milk and dumped some into the pot, scooped up some butter on a spoon and stirred it all together with a sure hand.

She really had been without a date too long. Because the sight of big Brody Hamilton whipping potatoes was doing things to her insides that she hadn't felt in a very long time. He was *tempting.* So physically powerful that her body betrayed her, and when he smiled at Mrs. Polcyk, a dimple popped in his left cheek.

Oh, my.

He reached over Mrs. Polcyk's head for a serving bowl and muttered something; Lucy nearly laughed out loud as he then skillfully dodged an errant female elbow that came flying his way.

She'd had time to think while in the bath and she knew that Brody had been right. She had been deliberately hiding something and it was natural he'd be suspicious. There was no way for him to know that she'd rather have her old life back than be ensconced at some cold stone palace in Europe. She'd also realized she needed to volunteer information about the stables and not herself. It was all a matter of slanting the focus to put him at ease.

She'd made a promise, and she wouldn't go back on it. Even if it was the last thing she'd wanted.

Brody put the bowl on the table and turned, spying her standing by the stairway. His happy, unguarded look faded as he saw her, and she wondered why it was he disliked her so much already. "Dinner's on," he said blandly.

Mrs. Polcyk took a platter of chicken to the table, followed by vegetables and a boat of golden gravy. "Please sit down, Lucy," she invited.

Lucy took the chair at the end; for some reason it seemed like the vacant spot. Brody took the other end while the housekeeper perched herself in the middle.

Mrs. Polcyk dipped her grayed head and to Lucy's surprise began a prayer in a language she didn't understand.

When it was over Lucy lifted her head and met Brody's eyes. Something warm passed between them, something that spoke of a unity and recognition even though they were strangers from different lives.

And Lucy knew she had to back away from it as fast as she could. Nothing good could come of it. She couldn't get close to Brody Hamilton.

She couldn't allow herself to get close to anyone.

# CHAPTER THREE

BRODY woke to moonlight tracing a pale line along his bedroom wall. He rolled to his back, rubbing a hand over the stubble on his face.

He'd been dreaming of her. Dreaming of her corkscrew hair falling over his hands the moment before he pressed his mouth to her defiant lips.

He raised up on to his elbows, shaking his head a bit in the dark. He wasn't a man prone to dreams, especially about women he'd just met. But something about Lucy pushed his buttons. She was stubborn and abrasive, and damned smart if he were any judge at all. Carrying a chip on her shoulder the size of Marazur.

Yet there was something behind it. Something he couldn't quite put his finger on. It was in the way she'd looked at him just before dinner tonight; the way their eyes had met after Mrs. P.'s saying of grace. She could be as icy as she pleased, but there was *something* about her that called to him.

And he would ignore that call. Her life was vastly different from his, and there was no way he'd forget it. Once burned… Well, that had been enough for him.

It was crazy, thinking about her this way. It was ridiculous to even admit to himself that he felt a physical attraction to her. It'd come plain out of nowhere and had hit him square in the gut. He'd disputed it to himself earlier but there was no arguing with the dream.

He rose from the bed and moved to the open window. Cool, crisp air fluttered over his skin. The hot, dry breezes of July nights were gone; in their place were the cold, clear nights of August, chill and full of stars. The air rushed in through the screen and he let it clear his head.

Then he saw the light.

The windows at the front end of the barn gleamed in the inky blackness. And he was positive he'd turned everything out before going to bed.

He pulled on his jeans in brisk, quiet movements. He carried his boots in his hands and crept down the stairs, checking his watch as he went. The luminescent hands gleamed at the two and the four—two-twenty. When he got to the door he saw Mrs. P.'s jacket hung precisely beside his denim one. He snagged the latter, shoved his arms in the sleeves and slid out the door into the brisk night air.

He crept toward the barn door, which was opened a few feet, letting out a rhombus-shaped slice of yellow light. A quiet shuffle sounded; someone was definitely inside. He turned back toward the house for a moment, suspicion forming in his mind. Lucy's room was dark, no light from the bedroom windows at the west end of the house. As another shuffle sounded, he turned again to the barn.

She'd arrived today and now someone was in his barns in the middle of the night. Coincidence? He didn't think so.

What was she up to? What could she possibly be looking for? Brody exhaled slowly. All important records were locked in the office up at the house. And she likely knew that. Which meant…

Which meant she was sneaking around his horses. Tampering, sabotage—whatever she was doing he was going to put a stop to it right now.

He squeezed through the opening between door and wall and slowly made his way through the shadows, toward the office. A light was on inside, but another shuffle told him that whoever had turned it on was no longer inside. Instead the sound came from a stall on the right. He held his breath… there was the sound again, followed by the hollow echo of shifting hooves. Pretty's box. The horse she'd met earlier. His heart gave a heavy thump.

Brody squared his shoulders, took four silent, long strides that took him to the stall door.

It, too, was open.

He slid it open wider, bracing himself for who or what he'd find, inhaling and filling the doorway so whoever was inside would have to go through him first.

A woman's voice stopped him. "It's not fair" he heard over the sound of shaky breaths. "You're the princess, Pretty. Not me."

*Not fair.* The words seemed to bounce around in his head as his heart clubbed. If she was in there to hurt Pretty…

He leaped into the stall. And stopped at the sight of wide brown eyes staring up at him in shock and fear, still clinging to Pretty's mane and standing close to her withers.

Brody's mouth opened but he had nothing to say for the first few seconds. The lashes above her eyes were wet with tears, and as he watched in fascinated horror, one slid down over her pale cheek and dropped off her jaw into the straw by her feet. Her lips were puffy, the way he'd imagined them being after he'd kissed them in his dream, soft and fragile. And her fingers were twined in Pretty's mane as the chestnut stood quietly at her side.

"What in the world are you doing?"

"I…I, uh, it was…" Lucy stammered, a guilty flush adding to her already red and chapped cheeks.

"Eloquent." He blocked the doorway, determined to get

answers and equally determined not to let her tears influence the conversation. Pretty was a valuable mare and more than that, she was his. Nope, Miss Farnsworth had some explaining to do. And fast.

"I came to be alone." She shot the words out all in one go, attempting a defiance that fell completely flat.

"So you're sneaking around in the middle of the night? What are you really after? If you're here to harm my horses…" He took a menacing step. "No king will protect you here, Miss Farnsworth."

She gawped at him with what looked like disbelief. Good, he thought. Calling her out might just get him some answers. She blinked back the remaining tears, and his shoulders relaxed a little. Relief. He didn't deal well with tears and histrionics.

"After? You think I'm after something?"

"Are you kidding? You arrive today and your first night here I find you snooping around my stock while you're supposed to be asleep? What would you think?"

He watched, utterly entranced as she swallowed, casting her eyes on her feet. She was caught. Guilt was written all over her pink cheeks.

"I'm sorry. Of course you would think that. I…please believe me, Mr. Hamilton. I had no…untoward intentions by coming here tonight."

"Then, why are you here?"

Stoically she looked away, focused on Pretty's neck, smoothing her hand over the gleaming hide.

"Isn't it obvious?"

"Not exactly. Beyond that you're upset." He stepped another foot forward, shortening the distance between them. He would look in her eyes. Then he'd know for sure if she was telling the truth. "That's a given."

Her lower lip trembled until she bit it, worrying it with her teeth. Brody stopped, shoved his hands in his pockets.

"I came here to be alone. To…to have a cry out, okay? I never meant to disturb you."

A stranger was in his barn in the middle of the night bawling all over one of his horses. This was a first. His brows knit together. Granted, he'd been short with her a few times today. But she'd gone toe-to-toe with him and he'd respected that. He hadn't gotten the impression she was the weepy sort.

But she was definitely weepy now, and he had to admit her story rang true. Those tears hadn't been manufactured when he'd burst through the stall door. And he remembered doing handkerchief duty for Lisa and stepped backward. He'd done his time with crying females and didn't care to again.

"Mornin' comes early. Why don't we go back up to the house now."

Her eyes slid to his, and he felt the impact straight through his gut to his spine. A few strands from her curls stuck to the dampness of her cheek.

"I'll be up in a bit."

Brody stared at her. She obviously didn't get the hint that he didn't want to leave her in the barn. Granted, he'd told her to make herself at home earlier, but this was stretching it just a little. More than a little. He didn't like her snooping about, no matter who her boss was. His first care was for his horses. He'd learned that a long time ago. And it had cost him.

"I insist. I insist you leave with me now. There will be time for you to look around tomorrow. With me."

He had nothing to hide, but he did have Prairie Rose to protect.

"Please…I just want some time to pull myself together."

"I'll just keep you company, then." He folded his arms.

She looked past his shoulder, out the door of the stall as if trying to figure out how to get away. Annoyed that she'd stopped giving her attention, Pretty dipped her head and nudged Lucy's hand.

"She likes you."

"I like her." Lucy pressed her face into the mane again. It was obvious she wasn't ready to leave yet, and he'd be damned if he'd leave her down here alone. Brody stepped a little to the side, leaning back against the fragrant wood of the box.

"Why?"

Lucy looked up. "Why what?"

"Why are you so interested in Pretty Piece? She's got years left, granted, but she's not what you came for."

Lucy rubbed her hand down the velvety nose. "No, she's not. She's a delightful surprise. I knew…I knew her mother."

To his chagrin her voice broke on the last word. Lord, not more tears.

"Let's get out of here," he demanded, stepping forward and gripping her arm. It was warm through the fleece she was wearing. "Before you upset the horses as well as yourself."

He led her out of the stall, and when she paused he tugged on her elbow.

"Stop." Her voice was sharp as she pulled out of his grasp.

"You want to talk about why you're crying, then? Because I want answers. Satisfying ones."

"I'm not crying for any specific reason." Her chin jutted out. "I just couldn't sleep."

He snorted something unintelligible.

She looked up at him then. "I *did* travel halfway across the world, you know."

Brody watched her keenly. This had nothing to do with jet lag, he knew it. And even though they'd argued earlier, he knew it wasn't about that, either. There was something else at the heart of it. What had she meant earlier when she'd muttered it wasn't fair?

He'd never been able to watch a woman cry, and he'd done

his share in years past. That had been one of his biggest mistakes, and even knowing it he couldn't help the need to help that rose up in him. He wanted to believe her. To believe her motives were true even though her actions were suspect.

He took another step closer, close enough that if he extended his arm he'd be able to touch the tender skin of her bruised eyelids. Only inches away.

"What is it, Lucy? What is it about being here that upsets you so much?"

Lucy's fingers tightened, wrapping around each other in the absence of Pretty's coarse mane. She had to keep it together, because if she let go she'd realize exactly how close Brody was right now. The barn was so quiet she could hear the hum of the lights overhead. And still he watched her, waiting. Waiting for a reasonable explanation.

Brody was a deliberate man. She could tell that earlier. He did things a certain way and had definite opinions, and his initial one of her hadn't been favorable. And yet…he was waiting patiently for her. And she had no idea what to tell him. The truth was out of the question.

The sting of it was, when he looked at her this way, she wanted to tell him all manner of things, and she was sure he wouldn't understand.

No one understood.

Once again the feeling of total isolation. There was nothing familiar anymore, and the closest she'd gotten to it lately was here, tonight, surrounded by the scent of hay and horse and leather.

"Lucy?"

She couldn't help it. At the quiet verbalization of her name, the tears started afresh. Lucy. Who was that now? No one she knew.

"I hardly know you." It sounded pitiful to her ears but needed to be said.

He didn't answer, just absorbed everything through those black, damnably keen eyes of his. She was losing control and there was nothing she could do about it. But she would die rather than have him witness it.

"Please let me go," she tried, willing the words to come out strong and failing utterly. "I've embarrassed myself enough already. I shouldn't have come."

He stepped to one side.

She straightened her back, trying valiantly to gather what little bit of dignity she had left. Lucy blinked, sending teardrops over her lashes and down her cheeks as the homesickness overwhelmed her. She looked at the door. If she moved quickly she could get out and away from him. She'd been foolish to think she could belong here. She took one step, then another, her eyes blurring with tears.

And stumbled on a crack.

His arm was there to steady her in half a second, but her breath hitched in her chest and she sniffed. Brody turned her gently and pulled her into his arms.

The shock only lasted a millisecond. All the surprise of finding herself being held against him was swept away in the warm shelter of his arms, the rough feeling of his jean jacket against her cheek. She inhaled; the scent was somehow familiar. He was strong and steady and as his hand cradled her head, stroking her hair, she let go of all her grief in one sweeping wave.

He was a stranger. She was there on business. He'd questioned her and her integrity all in less than twenty-four hours. None of it mattered. He was a good man. He was *there*. That was what was important right now.

"Shhh." The sound rippled the hair above her ear, warming it with his breath. "It's okay."

Not in three long months had someone put their arms

around her. No one had held her. No one had told her it would be okay.

Grief hit her, jolting the breath from her abdomen. She felt for a moment like she had the first time she'd been thrown and had hit the loam of the paddock. It had been a harder landing than she'd expected, and it had been difficult to get up.

Her arms slid around his waist, her fingers reaching up and biting into the denim covering his shoulder blades.

He tightened his grip around her, and one large hand massaged the back of her neck.

And all of the desolation Lucy had been holding inside came out in a grand rush of weeping, one that crashed on to the shore like a huge breaker and ebbed away on the tide, leaving her fragile, but feeling as though a burden had been taken from her shoulders.

She sniffed, sighed. And heard Brody's voice, rough and quiet.

"Lucy."

Her heart skipped around crazily. Not Miss Farnsworth, but Lucy. Tonight, in the intimacy of the barn, she'd become Lucy.

She stepped out of his arms. This was madness. She was tired and this was the middle of the night. He was a stranger. A very handsome one. It all jumbled together.

"I'm so sorry," she breathed, horrified at the splotches of moisture on his jean jacket. She couldn't meet his eyes. He already saw far too much. She didn't want him to see any more. She didn't want to see parts of him, either. There was a danger that she just might, and she took a step backward.

"Don't be."

"Forget this ever happened."

"Why don't you tell me what caused you to cry first?"

Oh, where would she begin?

Pretty stamped behind them. Their presence there was disturbing the horses.

"There are actual chairs in the office," he said gently. "A kettle and a can of cookies. We can get to the bottom of this."

Lucy shook her head. "I've already made things uncomfortable. This won't happen again." She was pleased that her voice was coming out stronger with each word. She almost sounded convincing! "I'll just go back to the house."

But Brody persisted. "You're going to be staying here a while. You might as well tell me, because if you don't I'm going to wonder and you're going to hold it inside and it's just going to create friction. Hardly conducive to a profitable business trip."

He held out a hand. "Let me buy you an instant decaf."

She straightened her pullover. "Mr. Hamilton, I…"

But he interrupted. "You've just cried in my arms for a good ten minutes. You might as well put away the Mr. Hamilton. And if we go to the house now, Mrs. Polcyk will undoubtedly hear and you'll have to explain your puffy eyes to her."

He held out his hand. She refused to take it, instead feeling her cheeks burn with humiliation that she'd allowed herself to get caught up in what it was like to be held. She swept past him as best she could and heard him follow, ensuring the stall door was latched behind him. He passed her and led the way down the corridor, his boots echoing dully in the quiet of the night.

Once inside she took a quick inventory. There was a battered old sofa, a chair that looked as if its springs had given out a long time ago and a wooden contraption on casters behind a scarred desk. She took her chances on the springs; the sofa meant he'd sit beside her and she couldn't take that.

He filled the kettle at the tap outside and came back, plugged it in and pulled two mugs off a shelf. When the water boiled, he stirred each cup and handed her one before perching against the front edge of the desk.

She sipped; the brew was hot, strong and with the cardboardy bitter taste of instant crystals.

"So," Brody began, sounding very conversational indeed. "Quite a day. First your arrival, and now, not even a day later, here we are."

"I *am* sorry. I don't usually fall apart like that."

"I didn't peg you as the type to crumble, either. So imagine my surprise to find you lurking around my barn in the middle of the night."

"You don't trust me."

"Would you, in my position?"

"No, I wouldn't," she agreed quietly. "I'd be suspicious of anyone who felt the need to be around my livestock while she's supposed to be sleeping. I can only say that my actions were completely innocent, and hope you believe me."

"Is there a reason I shouldn't?"

Her gaze met his. She thought briefly of the secrets she was keeping.

"No, there isn't."

Brody considered for a moment, took a sip of his coffee. "Out here, everyone pretty much knows everyone else. There are people I let in and people I don't. And I haven't known you that long. I haven't decided if I'm letting you in yet or not. A little bit of truth would go a long way."

Letting her in? That was the last thing she wanted.

"I'm here to do a job."

He crossed an ankle over his knee. "Yes, you are. And now I have more questions about you than answers, and that doesn't do much to inspire my trust."

"You, trust me? My fa— King Alexander's name should be enough." She tried to hide the near slip.

"Like I said earlier, I know enough about Navarro to know that His Highness only wants the best."

"Why do you need this alliance, anyway?" She jutted out her chin. What had seemed like a simple enough assignment on paper was rapidly getting complicated. She hadn't counted on a stubborn rancher who didn't know how to mind his own business!

"Are you kidding? Everyone knows about Navarro stables. An alliance with the royal family of Marazur could change everything."

She pursed her lips, putting her cup down on the desk and folding her arms. "You clearly will gain more than we will, then. It's not in your best interest to question."

Brody raised an eyebrow. "And if you went back empty-handed?"

Her scowl faded. That was out of the question. This was all she had left. She had to prove herself to her father. And that meant proving herself to Brody now.

Brody persisted. "He's sent you to me. Face it. We need each other."

"What do you want from me?" She hid her face behind the rim of her mug. She was still feeling too raw, and their verbal sparring had only been a placebo against the pain; the reason why she'd sneaked down here in the middle of the night in the first place. She'd wanted to be away from prying eyes. To be somewhere that she felt even a little bit at home. She had wanted to have her cry—the one that had been building all day—in private. Get it over with, with no one the wiser. Now she was having to deal with that *and* an angry Brody.

"I want to know why you were in my barn in the middle of the night, crying."

"It's private."

With an impatient huff, Brody stood and put his cup down

on the desk. "Have it your way," he said shortly, turning to the door.

Had she honestly thought he'd accept that answer? She supposed it would have been too much to ask for some understanding. Maybe he'd used up his quota holding her outside Pretty's stall. But she could tell by the set of his jaw that the next days were going to be very difficult if they were working from different sides.

Her mouth opened and closed several times but no words would come out. Instead the only sound was Brody's boots on the cement floor.

She couldn't let him leave. If he refused to negotiate, she'd go back to Marazur a failure and that was the one thing she *couldn't* do.

"Brody, wait!"

She ran to the door and braced her hands on the frame. "Wait."

He stopped. Turned back around.

And her heart did that skip thing again.

It was supposed to be easy. An escape. Not a sexy cowboy who felt a need to pry into her personal business and was using her professional needs as blackmail.

"If you must know, I grew up in Virginia. Around horses. My mum…she was a bookkeeper for a farm there. That's how I knew Pretty's dam, Pretty Colleen. She was at Trembling Oak when I was a child, before she was sold. This place…it reminds me of there."

"You're homesick?" He didn't sound as if he quite believed her. His voice echoed hollowly through the barn.

"Yes…but there's more. My mum…" She paused, swallowing against the sudden lump that lodged in her throat. "My mum died a few months ago. There've been so many changes…" Her words drifted into ether. She blinked once, twice. Inhaled, gathering strength. "So many changes lately that I haven't had time to grieve. Being here today seemed to set me off, that's all. And I needed to be with…with someone who understood."

"Pretty," he replied, an indulgent smile in his voice.

"Don't make fun of me." Her eyes flashed at him. Was it so hard to understand that she'd found a link to her home in the horse, in Prairie Rose? Surely he wasn't that blind.

He came closer. "I'm not making fun." He stopped, the toes of his boots mere inches from her sneakers. "It's the first thing you've said that made perfect sense."

She lifted her gaze and met his. With the animosity and grief suddenly drained away, there was nothing standing between them, and Lucy felt the unadulterated pull of attraction.

"Was that so hard?" His question was a soft murmur.

"Yes," she whispered back.

"I know," he replied, those two words evoking so many questions she now wanted to ask.

He cupped her jaw, ran a rough thumb over her cheekbone. "Thank you for telling me. It explains a lot."

She swallowed, tried to inhale, but the air seemed thin. Another inch and he would be in kissing distance. She shouldn't be thinking about kissing him….

"Let's go back up now. Tomorrow's a long day."

Lucy stepped back, offered what she hoped passed for a smile and followed him out of the barn.

She'd said more than she'd planned…how could she have mentioned Trembling Oak? And she'd been talking to the horse when he'd burst into the box. Had he overheard any of what she'd said?

He already knew too much. She'd have to be much more careful. No more midnight revelations. From now on it had to be strictly business!

# CHAPTER FOUR

Brody looked up from his breakfast when he heard her steps on the stairs.

And then looked down again, spearing another chunk of scrambled egg on his fork and ignoring the queer lifting in his chest. He wasn't looking forward to seeing her. He couldn't be. That was just plain ridiculous.

He'd been crazy last night. Finding her in Pretty's stall had raised all sorts of alarm bells, but by the end of it...

He scowled. He'd been a fool. A soft touch. He should know better by now. Instead he'd listened to her story and he'd...hell, he'd even *touched* her at the end. His fork dropped to his plate. Touched her soft, white skin with its faint smattering of freckles.

And he'd thought about kissing her.

Yup. A fool. A fool to forget who she was, where she was from. A fool to be distracted by the sight of tears on her lashes, and a fool for wanting somehow to make it better. He picked up his fork again and defiantly shoved another piece of egg into his mouth. Oh, no. He'd fallen into that trap before.

"Good morning."

He looked up, schooling his features into what he hoped was a general expression of disinterest. "Good morning."

Her cheeks were pink and her lips were slightly puffy, as

though she'd been chewing on them. "Breakfast was fifteen minutes ago." He couldn't resist adding the shot.

He was gratified to see her blush a little before he looked back down at his plate.

"I'm sorry. I...I overslept."

Yeah. As if he didn't know why. He stretched out his legs, glad that he wasn't the only one who was running on short sleep. He raised an eyebrow in her direction.

"I didn't sleep that well."

"I'm sorry to hear that." And then felt about two inches tall as he saw the confused, wounded look on her face. He was being a jerk and he knew it.

"It doesn't matter, Lucy." Mrs. Polcyk came from the kitchen with a plate in her hands and a smile on her face. "You just sit right up now. Brody's out of sorts this morning."

He scowled. There were disadvantages to having a housekeeper that had known him since he'd been a boy in boots too big for his feet. First Martha yesterday and now Mrs. P. Yet he knew the women around here well enough to know they always considered the men their "boys," thinking that living with them excused lots of things. He looked up at Mrs. P. who merely angled an eyebrow at him. They'd been through hell together, and he had to admit it did excuse a lot. He wouldn't dress her down for the world. He gritted his teeth but said nothing. He knew he was reacting unreasonably. But he'd be damned if he'd give an apology. It was probably better to keep Lucy at arm's length anyway. He looked away and grabbed the carafe of coffee from the table, refilling his cup.

Lucy spread jam on her toast and looked up at him. "I thought this morning maybe I could have a look at your files."

She was speaking directly to him and he was obligated to look at her. He did, noticing how her tongue ran out over her lip even though she tried to make her eyes look brave. So she was nervous. Good. She'd taken enough liberties last night. He folded his hands in front of him and faced her squarely.

"I've got things to do."

"If you'll just point the way…"

Brody's eyebrows snapped together. "Point the way? And leave you alone?"

"What do you think I'm going to do, Brody?" Her toast dropped back to her plate and she stopped worrying her lips. They were plump and prettily pink. Like they'd been last night in the barn.

What did he think? He ignored his fascination with her lips and leaned back in his chair. What he thought was that those who trusted too easily got burned, and that his trust had to be earned, not expected. He'd spent enough time doing damage control because someone got a little bit nosy with the particulars of Prairie Rose Ranch. He wouldn't let that happen again.

"Who knows? After last night…"

Mrs. P. banged a pan in the pantry, and both Brody and Lucy fell momentarily silent. He looked at her across the table. The truth was he'd been able to understand her actions last night more than she knew. How many times had he taken solace in the barns when things got to be too much? He understood the need for connection. The need to grieve and not feeling able to.

But this was a new day. It was not shadows in a quiet barn, instant coffee and confessions. There could not be anything personal between them. The last thing he wanted was for her to delve too deeply, and the thought of her riffling through his records and files made him set his jaw. He'd hoped she wasn't one of those people who put more stock in paper trails than in horseflesh. He didn't put much credence in that, and he was a long way from trusting her.

He looked away from her steady eyes and instead added

pepper to his already sufficiently peppered eggs. The truth was, he didn't know exactly what she planned to do with whatever information she found. There was more to Lucy than a simple emissary. He just didn't know *what*. That was the problem. He doubted it was just about breeding records. Yet what more could she want?

"I thought you might like to go for a ride this morning. See more of the ranch."

Lucy forced herself not to sigh. She'd thought she'd made some headway last night in getting Brody to trust her, but he was clearly putting her off this morning. The halfhearted invitation to go for a ride was simply to offer a diversion. She knew he didn't want to be near her any more than she really wanted to be near him. He just didn't want her snooping around. What was he hiding?

She wanted to ask him, but she knew he wouldn't answer. And right now she had to bite her tongue and try to keep things civil.

It was completely reasonable for her to want to look at his breeding history. She had to make the right decisions for Navarro if she was going to prove herself. She wanted to see bloodlines, combinations, strengths and weaknesses before she signed on the dotted line. He should know this. He should trust her to do her job.

Which meant he had another reason for putting her off. She didn't like the thought of that very much.

She sliced through a piece of fried ham. "And I'd like to do that, but another time. I'd like to get an overall picture of your program here first." She wanted dates, names, records. To see his strengths and weaknesses and think about how they could benefit Navarro. And even…how Navarro could benefit him.

"And if I refuse?" He raised an eyebrow.

"Then I'm wasting my time." Heart in her throat, she

pushed back her chair and started to put her napkin beside her plate.

"Fine."

She stopped, half up and half down. Relief rushed through her; he wasn't calling her bluff.

"Finish your breakfast, princess. When you're done I'll dig out the files you need."

For the tiniest second she froze, immobilized by the idea that he'd somehow clued in to who she was. Struggling to compose herself, she sat back in her chair and silently steamed. Nothing she had said could have revealed her true identity to him. Which meant…which meant he was using it as a nickname. And she didn't like the snarky twist he added to it, either. It certainly wasn't meant as a compliment.

She met his gaze coldly. "Thank you."

Wordlessly Brody got up, gathered his plate and coffee cup and took them to the kitchen before stalking out.

Lucy sat for a moment, thinking she should feel as if she'd won a victory, but somehow didn't. Brody wouldn't know why she felt she had to succeed here, or why she needed to prove herself.

He was making it difficult right from the get-go. He intimidated her and she hated that. It made every rebellious fiber in her rise up and want to be counted, a trait that had got her into trouble too many times as a child. Which didn't necessarily help in the "get what you want" scheme of things. She drained her coffee cup and put it down. Yet…it wasn't in her to simper and play at pretending. She wasn't good at it.

Which is what made this whole farce even more difficult.

She turned the cup over in her hands, running her thumb over the Prairie Rose insignia on its side. She'd come downstairs wondering if they were going to be awkward with each other and had been met with annoying belligerence.

Perhaps that was good, because he wouldn't ask personal

questions. But this trip was rapidly feeling as if she was beating her head against a wall and making little progress. She put the mug down.

Why had he been so angry this morning? Last night he'd ended up being kind...even gentle. For a moment she'd thought he was going to kiss her.

Mrs. Polcyk stopped by her shoulder and refilled her coffee cup.

"Mrs. Polcyk, did I do something wrong this morning?" The housekeeper reminded her of Mrs. Pendleton, the wife of the owner of Trembling Oak. Mrs. Pendleton had never given herself airs; she'd baked pecan pie and cooked grits and had always made time for talks with Lucy in her kitchen. It was easier for Lucy to ask it of the motherly housekeeper than Brody. Mrs. Polcyk patted her shoulder, and Lucy almost thought she heard a sigh.

"Brody's a private man, Lucy. That's all."

"But...but I'm here to *help* his business. I don't understand why he made such a point of not wanting me to have a look at the breeding records. I need to see where Ahab's progeny have gone and how they've performed." She stopped short of mentioning the previous night in the barn.

Mrs. Polcyk went to the cupboard and took out another mug, poured herself a cup of coffee and took the seat Brody had vacated.

"I think you're a good girl, Lucy, and I'm not the suspicious type like Brody is. But he's got good reason to be careful."

She took a drink of her coffee and looked down the hall toward the study.

"You're not going to explain that further, are you."

The housekeeper smiled thinly. Lucy thought she saw a hint of sadness in the grayish blue eyes. "In this case I don't think it's my story to tell. What I *can* tell you is that Brody has put his heart and soul into making Prairie Rose what it is today. It's everything to him."

"I can understand that."

"I know you can." She reached over and patted Lucy's hand. "For what it's worth, he wants this deal to work. He needs to up our profile, and an alliance with you will do that."

"Then why does he keep fighting me? I've been here less than twenty-four hours and I already know if I say black, he'll say white."

Mrs. Polcyk got up from the table, taking both their cups. "Because the only thing more important than an alliance with King Alexander is protecting what he loves. If he thinks that in some way you'll threaten Prairie Rose, the choice will be easy for him. He's put his heart and soul into this place." Mrs. Polcyk paused and gazed out the window for a moment, and Lucy could have sworn she saw the older woman's lips tremble a little as she murmured, "Perhaps too much."

She cleared her throat and nodded at Lucy. "You go on to the office now, just down the hall at the end. Brody'll have everything set out for you, despite his earlier attitude."

Lucy smoothed her hair and ran her hands over her T-shirt, down the thighs of her jeans.

Mrs. Polcyk meant well, but now Lucy had more questions than answers. What had Brody sacrificed for the ranch? What had been threatened before? What was it that made him build a wall around himself whenever she was around?

She looked down the hall at the closed door. Perhaps a morning spent with breeding records would tell her more than she could get out of either the housekeeper *or* Brody.

Lucy rubbed her eyes; they were drying out in the hot prairie air. She'd been most of the day going over Brody's files, and the only thing she felt was impressed.

Over the past several years, he'd taken Prairie Rose Ranch

and moved it from strength to strength as far as she could tell. His decisions made sense, for the most part. She liked how he kept his own quarter horse stock fairly undiluted and with solid bloodlines. It was a grassroots approach that clearly worked for him and he knew it. She could see it in his decisions right here on paper.

And she could see it in what she'd seen of his horses. She'd caught a glimpse of a stallion last night that had been breathtaking. She could already envision the offspring from him and their newly acquired Thoroughbred mare. Her father—King Alexander—had emphasized his desire to breed quarter horses with his Thoroughbreds, and she agreed with him completely. Each had qualities that, when combined, would make wonderful polo ponies. King Alexander was looking for those traits of speed and agility.

She closed the last file folder and checked her watch. Nearly six. Where had the time gone? She noted the mess of notes she'd taken on the desk and knew she should tidy it up, leave the office as neatly as she'd found it. She tamped the papers together and lined everything up on the blotter. If she just had a paperclip to keep her notes straight.

She slid open the first drawer, but it had nothing in it but a brick of pristine paper, presumably for the printer. She slid it closed and opened the next one. Bingo. Pens, a stapler, a pair of scissors.

She was putting everything back in order when she realized she'd missed a file. It was inside one of the others, and she tapped her bottom lip as she opened it and scanned the records within. Everything Brody had given her this morning had gone back about six years, maybe a little more. But this file was older...closer to eight years. She saw the signature on page after page—not Brody's but John Hamilton's. Then there were a few pages with Brody's scrawl across the bottom. Her brow wrinkled as she rechecked the date. There was a gap of nearly a year—nearly a year of records missing. She knew it was impossible that he hadn't bought or sold any horses in that time, or hadn't participated in any breeding whatsoever. It was almost as if…

Lucy chewed her bottom lip. Almost as if the ranch had ceased to exist for a solid year. She wondered what story the bank records would tell, but she had no access to them, nor did she imagine Brody would give them to her.

A door slammed, and Lucy quickly shut the file, putting it back at the bottom of the pile. She was just putting the clip over her sheaf of papers when Brody stepped into the office.

He spared her a look, raised his eyebrows slightly and asked, "Did you find what you were looking for?"

She wondered, not for the first time, what had happened to put that distrustful chip on his shoulder. Did it have something to do with the lapse she'd found in his filing system? She itched to ask him, but looking at his scowling face, she knew this wasn't the time. "I did. And then some," she couldn't help adding.

His eyes narrowed a little, and she couldn't help but laugh. The imp in her—the part she'd been hiding for so long—wanted out to play. The best thing would be for him to offer the information voluntarily, and there was no way that would happen if they kept snapping at each other. "The only thing I didn't find in your files is evidence of your shoe size."

She'd wanted him to laugh, to lighten up. But at his continued quizzical glare, her own smile faded.

"I'm not going to win with you, am I." It was a statement rather than a question. She gathered up her sheets and came around to the front of the desk. He stepped aside but not far enough. When she went to go through the door, his body was too close to hers and she quivered with sudden awareness. It was as if she was back to the night before, in the dark intimacy of the barn. His size didn't intimidate her; perhaps it would be easier if it did. But in the moment that she paused at the door, she felt the strength in him and wondered what kind of woman could possibly resist his sort of sexy stability.

"Problem, princess?"

She swallowed, feeling the blush flood her cheeks at his dark, knowing words. They were meant as a taunt, but he couldn't know how they added fuel to the fire already flickering within her. "Uh, no," she murmured, and headed out the door and away.

"Dinner's on in five minutes," he called after her as she fled to the stairs. She took them two at a time and hurried to her room, closing the door and leaning against it.

First last night, and now in the study. This was not in the plan at all.

Because she was curious about Brody Hamilton. And not all of it had to do with Prairie Rose or Navarro. A good healthy portion of it was a woman responding to a man. Desire. And she had no idea how to deal with it and still do her job.

When she went downstairs, she could smell dinner rather than see it. She followed the delectable scent to the deck and found Brody flipping steaks with a set of metal tongs. She moved past him to lean against the railing of the small deck. It faced south; she looked slightly to the right and could just pick out the hazy ridge of the mountains. It was so flat here. A person could see for miles and miles.

And feel very small and insignificant. She should be used to that feeling by now. Lord knew she felt that way most of the time in Marazur.

"Is there anything I can do to help?" She pasted on a polite smile and hoped she didn't blush again. Brody'd put his hat back on out in the afternoon sun and it shaded his face too much. She couldn't see his expression.

Mrs. Polcyk bustled through the door, carrying a tray of dishes and cutlery. "Let me take that," Lucy insisted, jumping to help, and hiding from Brody's gaze behind the weight of the tray. "I feel silly doing nothing."

"How do you like your steak?"

She paused from putting out cutlery and looked up. Lord, he was ornery, and his reticence was driving her insane, but she couldn't deny his good looks or his physical presence, or her reaction to them. Even scowling, he was impressive. "Medium," she answered.

He nodded beneath his black hat, and she wished he'd take it off again so she could see his eyes. And she wished they would stop arguing all the time. Her pride dictated she go toe-to-toe with him. But the lonely girl in her wanted to see him as an ally, a friend. She'd been going it alone for some time now. She wasn't sure she could keep it up much longer without turning bitter. She finished laying out the plates and went to him.

"Brody." She laid her hand on his arm, surprised to feel the muscle tense beneath her fingers. She stared at the spot where their skin met for a fleeting second, the warmth shooting through her veins. She swallowed. Forced herself to look him in the eye beneath the brim of his hat. She'd been seeing this all from her point of view. What if she were in Brody's shoes? She'd never considered herself selfish before, but her thoughts over the past few months changed her mind. She'd spent so much time resenting what her life had become that she'd forgotten to put herself in other people's shoes. She had so many questions she wished she could ask him: about the family he didn't seem to have, about the ranch. But she got the feeling he was hiding hurts, and she needed to remember she wasn't the only one who'd been dealt a cruel hand. She needed to apologize to him and perhaps start them over on a new footing.

"I didn't mean to make things tense this morning. I...I only wanted to see your records so that when I see the rest of your operation I can put it in context. I want to make the best decision for Navarro and that means learning as much as possible. I hope you understand that's where I was coming from. It wasn't meant to be...oh, I don't know what I'm trying to say. I just want you to know I'm not out to hurt Prairie Rose." *Or you,* she thought, but held the words inside.

Once the words were out, her breath caught for a second before she inhaled again. His eyes, those lovely dark onyx eyes, slid over her face. The meat sizzled on the grill beside them and a kingbird called from a nearby shrub, but for a few suspended seconds their gazes caught, held, while her hand remained on his arm. During those seconds Lucy had the same crazy sensation she'd had last night when she'd thought about kissing him.

Her tongue ran over her lip. Kissing big Brody Hamilton.

Now that would be a learning experience.

Her breath shuddered inward, and Brody took a step back and away from her touch.

"Yes, well, in my opinion you don't learn about an operation by trusting what you see on paper. You've got a long way to go to inspire my trust, Miss Farnsworth."

Last night she'd been Lucy. Now it was back to Miss Farnsworth, just as in the study.

It was probably for the best.

"Do you trust my...King Alexander?"

"I don't know."

She stepped back, unsure of how to proceed. Mrs. Polcyk returned and put a couple of salad bowls on the table, seemingly oblivious to the tension shimmering around them.

"Those steaks about ready, Brody?"

He spared Mrs. P. a glance, then looked back down at the grill. "Not quite."

Lucy turned toward the housekeeper. "Is there anything I can do, Mrs. P.?"

Brody's head snapped around so quickly she wondered that he didn't give himself whiplash.

"Not a thing, dear. Once the steaks are done, we'll have a nice dinner." She looked at Brody who was scowling darkly. "Though Brody's beer's almost gone. You could get him another, and one for me, too, if you don't mind. This heat…"

Lucy escaped to the coolness of the kitchen. She could hear Brody's voice and Mrs. P.'s sharp reply through the window, but not what they were saying. When she returned to the deck with three bottles, Mrs. P. was settled in a chair with a satisfied air, and Brody smiled stiffly as she twisted off the cap and handed him the beer.

"Thanks."

It was polite, but she could tell he didn't really mean it.

Lucy sat at the table across from Mrs. Polcyk, wondering how this could possibly be any more awkward. She'd apologized and he'd basically handed it back to her. Politely, but handed it back just the same. The only thing that would make it worse would be if he knew who she really was, she thought with a grimace. At least now she could kick back with a beer and enjoy a steak.

"One medium." Brody placed the steak on her plate and moved on to Mrs. P. The smell was tantalizing. At Mrs. P.'s urging, she added potato salad and tossed salad to her plate.

For a few moments no one said anything. Lucy wondered if the sounds of chewing were going to take the place of polite mealtime conversation. She wished it had when Mrs. Polcyk decided that the time should be spent finding out more about *her.*

"How do you know King Alexander, Lucy?"

The potato salad got thick in her mouth, and she chewed, tried to swallow. Suddenly her earlier explanation to Brody wasn't enough. And briefly she considered telling him exactly what her relationship was to His Highness. But he already didn't trust her, and he would trust her even less if he knew she was on a daughter's errand. He didn't believe she knew what she was doing. And telling him she was the king's daughter would wipe away any hope of credibility.

She paused so long that Brody put down his fork and knife. He'd removed his hat before sitting down to eat, and there was no evading his piercing eyes this time.

"Yes, Lucy, exactly how *do* you know the king?"

Mrs. P. angled him a sharp look at his caustic tone, but Lucy knew she was well and truly caught. Her mind worked feverishly, trying to find a way to tell the truth without *really* telling the truth.

"He knew my mother," she managed, trying to make her voice casual and demonstrating her outward relaxation by spearing a piece of cucumber and popping it in her mouth. If only they knew how uncomfortable she was on the inside, perhaps they'd stop asking questions!

Then she looked at Brody and realized her discomfort was probably a fringe benefit to him. She chewed with gusto and pasted on a smile. If ever she needed acting ability, now was the time.

"King Alexander has always dabbled in the horse business," she explained as breezily as she could muster. "I mentioned that I grew up in Virginia—" she looked at Brody for confirmation "—and my mum ran the office for Trembling Oak. She'd met Alexander—still a crown prince at the time—when he was on one of his extended trips.

"I spent years working in the stables. When the time came that my mum was ill, she thought perhaps I'd like to travel, see the world. Thought perhaps King Alexander would hire me in Marazur. I could travel and work at what I loved at the same time."

"Which he obviously did. But why would he do it? He didn't really know you, did he?"

"No, I'd never met him before."

Suddenly she couldn't push down the lump that formed in her throat. Both Brody's and Mrs. P.'s eyes were on her, and she forced a bright smile. "Why does anyone do anything? The main thing is he *did* decide to hire me and so far he hasn't regretted it. I'm good at what I do. I have a good eye."

There, she'd done it. She'd laid out the history without Brody being the wiser. Anyone who saw her would never put two and two together. She looked nothing like her father. He had the Navarro dark, Mediterranean looks, and she had her mother's curly burnished hair and pale skin.

Brody pushed back his plate. "Great salad, Mrs. P. But then, it always is."

"Aren't you staying for dessert?"

He shook his head, pushing back his chair and standing. He grabbed his hat from the knob on the end of the deck post. "No, thanks. I have some things to do. I'll grab some later when I come in."

"Do you want some help?" Lucy looked up. She'd really hoped that her partial story would be taken as an olive branch. After all, she knew next to nothing about Brody, and already he knew more about her than she'd wanted to tell. But he shook his head.

"No, you enjoy your evening." He paused. "You've got free rein in the office tomorrow. I have some business to take care of away from the ranch."

He spun on his heel without a further goodbye and hopped off the deck, leaving Lucy gaping at his snappish exit while Mrs. Polcyk calmly ate her potato salad.

# CHAPTER FIVE

SHE'D had enough of looking at paperwork.

Lucy closed the cabinet and pushed back in the rolling chair, the casters settling in comfortable grooves in the plastic mat beneath the desk. There was only so much to learn from paper, and even after searching today, she still didn't have any answers as to what happened to the missing year. And she'd been inside long enough. She knew Brody didn't want her snooping around—not after the other night in the barn. He seemed quite territorial that way. But it was a gorgeous day, and she had a need to be outside in the fresh air with the birds and the scent of grass and the horses.

She pulled on her boots at the door. Maybe she'd pay a visit to Pretty and take her an apple. The poor girl had been cooped up just as she had—inside on a beautiful summer's day.

The sky was a heartbreaking blue and the air hot and dry as Lucy wended her way through the yard to the barn. She filled her lungs, absorbing the smell of sweetgrass from the surrounding fields. She didn't mind the isolation here. It was welcoming. She thought briefly about her new home in Marazur. More people around, more activity. Servants and business, parties and meetings. All things so foreign to her that it was no wonder she hid in the stables most of the time. She definitely felt more lonely there than here. Even with Brody's surliness, Prairie Rose was far more familiar to her than the high-class Navarro stables. Loneliness wasn't about people, she realized. It was about being comfortable with your place in the world. Now she lived in a palace where the occupants were distant strangers. Trembling Oak had been her place. Prairie Rose was the closest she'd been to that in a long time.

Pretty's box was empty when she arrived, and she wondered if the farrier had come back to check on the hoof. The barn was quiet; in the middle of summer most of the stock was outside. She smiled, trailing her hand along a smooth railing. Why wouldn't they be? That would have been her choice, too.

As she got close to the middle of the barn she heard voices coming from the riding ring.

She left the railing behind and made her way to the double doors leading to the enclosed ring. It was cool inside, and her feet sunk a bit in the soft loam. For a moment she paused and smiled. It reminded her so much of her childhood days, training for her pleasure classes. Putting her horse through the paces after school, then heading back to the kitchen for a snack on the sly.

A couple of hands were standing in the center of the ring, with Pretty attached to a long lead. And that's when Lucy's smile faded.

"She looks good, Bill. Might as well call Martha and save her a trip. No harm in lettin' her out for a bit now."

Lucy approached, her eyes on Pretty even as the words registered. Martha was the farrier. It had only been a few days since Pretty had picked up the bruise. Did Brody know what these men were about to do?

The mare should definitely be seen before being set loose. At the very least, Brody should be the one to pronounce her fit. It was what she'd do if it were her operation.

She set her lips. Something wasn't quite right.

"Lengthen your lead and take her up and back," she commanded from across the ring.

The two men turned to her, eyebrows raised as she strode forward.

"Beg your pardon?"

"You heard me. Give her more lead, take her up and bring her back."

The one she assumed was Bill touched his cap but his eyes were cold. "And you are?"

She paused only feet away. "Lucy Farnsworth."

He smiled politely but she knew she wasn't getting far. Her name meant nothing to them.

"Well, Miss Farnsworth, unless we hear from Mr. Hamilton…"

"You'll what? Forgo a visit from the farrier and then be responsible for a lame horse? A prize-winning mare? Be my guest. But I wouldn't want to be on the receiving end of Mr. Hamilton's anger when he realizes you've crippled her because you were lazy and taking shortcuts."

She stopped and shoved her hands in her pockets.

The man met her eyes steadily. She knew she was right and she could see the mention of Brody had him doubting his wisdom.

"I guess I can humor you. Though you'll just see she's doing fine." He looked over his shoulder at his companion. "Give her more lead and trot her out."

Lucy stepped forward, watching closely as Pretty moved away from her. When she came back she noticed it, but she had to be sure.

"A couple of turns, please."

Wordlessly they took Pretty in a half circle, turned and came the other direction. Yes, there it was. She had no doubt now.

"That mare is still lame."

"I didn't see nothin'."

"Then you're blind. Look how she lifts her head. It's not big, but it's there."

She strode over to Pretty, gave her a pat and rubbed her nose. "Hey, girl. What's up?"

She looked over at the men. "One of you going to help me or what?"

The man named Bill came over, scowling. "Mr. Hamilton doesn't like outsiders messing with his stock," he growled.

"And how does he feel about incompetence?" she asked coolly. "Here, hold her a moment."

With Bill's hand on the mare's halter, Lucy bent and ran her hands down the foreleg. No tenderness here, but...she paused. There was heat, on the hoof. She nudged and Pretty obliged by lifting her foot, and Lucy did a brief inspection. There didn't seem to be any cuts, but that didn't mean she couldn't have been pricked and it had been missed. Infection? Hard to know. She stood, moved over to the other side and went through the same procedure.

"What's going on here?"

Brody's voice rang through the ring and Lucy jumped, went back and started over. She could hear his boots approaching but focused on her job at the moment. No, she'd been right. There was definitely heat on the other hoof wall and slight swelling on one side only. This side was cooler.

"Bill. What's going on?"

His voice was hard and Lucy shored her shoulders for the blast she knew was coming and for the courage she'd need to face it.

"She came in and started giving orders. I told her you wouldn't like it."

Lucy stood, wiping her hands on her jeans. "Hey, Brody." She made her voice deliberately casual but it failed miserably. His scowl was more pronounced than ever.

"I thought you were in with the paperwork."

"I was. I finished. I went for a walk and ended up here. Good thing, too."

"Is that right."

He was outright scornful and her temper flared. "That's right. Your men were going to give Pretty Piece here a clean bill of health. And that would have been a huge mistake."

"Says you." He snorted, starting to turn away.

"Says you, if you listen for two minutes!" she shouted.

Bill and his companion backed away slowly.

Brody turned back and treated her to a look of pure bored indulgence. "Look, Bill and Arnie have been with Prairie Rose for years. I trust their judgment."

"So you won't even listen to what I have to say? You arrogant jerk! You'll risk a lame mare because you're too proud to what? Take advice from a whippersnapper like me?"

His lips quivered. "Whippersnapper?"

"Shut up." The words she was thinking of were much more pithy but she didn't utter them.

The men's mouths had dropped open at the word *jerk* and had yet to close, but she ignored them and the heat that flushed her cheeks at knowing she'd lost her cool. His obvious humor at her choice of words bugged her, too, but she pushed it aside, trying to make her point.

"You think that I don't know what I'm doing because why? Because I'm young? Because I'm a woman? You decided the moment I got here who I was and you put me in a convenient little box."

For the moment he looked so nonplussed he didn't speak. Well bully for him.

"You judged me and decided I didn't have anything valuable to add. You would have sent me on my merry way if King Alexander hadn't been involved. And you know what that makes you?" Her eyes flashed as his darkened and a muscle

ticked in his jaw. "One of the good old boys. A chauvinist.
I've seen lots of them in this business. It didn't stop me then
and it won't stop me now. I'm good at what I do. I'm really
good! I've earned my place and I know it even if no one else
does!"

She broke off abruptly, her heart pounding and the backs
of her eyes pricking painfully. That felt good. For months
it had been about being Mary Ellen's daughter, or Princess
Luciana. As if who she was inside didn't really matter. As if
all the work she'd put in over the years meant nothing compared to a promise.

"Are you done?"

She nodded. "For the moment."

He stepped forward. Bill and Arnie were long gone; once
she'd started her diatribe they'd fled. Her heart fluttered as he
stepped through the soft loam of the ring until he was close
enough she had to look up to see his face.

"My trust needs to be earned. And I don't trust easily and
certainly not with my livelihood. Your affiliation with the
king is all that's kept you here, you do realize that."

She swallowed. She'd been right on that score, then. It in-
furiated her. She hadn't even met King Alexander until a few
months ago!

"You weren't what I expected, that's true. I *was* surprised
that Navarro had sent a very young, very pretty girl to negotiate an important deal. That was flag number one. Then
you came and I caught you snooping the first night. That was
flag number two. And then you were determined to spend
time with my files. I've seen people like you. Ones who are
more concerned with bottom lines and what things look like
on paper rather than reality." His arm swept wide. "*This* is
reality. And it's the *last* place you've come, rather than the
first."

She took a breath and exhaled slowly, knowing another

outburst wouldn't help her case and she was still reeling from the fact that he'd called her young and pretty. She pushed her female vanity aside; it was as irrelevant as her age or her gender. "Just because I took a different approach than you would doesn't make it wrong. And it doesn't mean I don't know what I'm doing. If you take the word of those men over mine, it'll make for larger problems later. You want a chance to trust me? This is it."

"All right then. What makes you think they are wrong?"

"I had them trot her out. It's not that obvious, but it's there if you look. I think she's developed an infection. The hoof wall is hot and she's showing signs."

He regarded her carefully. She still had her hand on Pretty's halter and she met his gaze fully. She could tell he was curious but not entirely convinced. This was her chance to prove to him she knew her stuff. "Don't take my word for it. Let me show you."

Lucy paced off a few steps and trotted out the mare, pointing out the tiny bob of the head each time she stepped on the affected hoof. Bringing her back, she showed Brody the hoof. "It doesn't look like anything, but the wall's warm. Warmer than the other. I used the same hand to be sure. I'm not imagining it, Brody."

Brody put the hoof down and straightened, rubbing Pretty's withers and frowning.

"No you're not. You're right."

"Thank you."

"I suppose you expect an apology now for what I said."

She smiled wryly. "You don't strike me as the apologetic type." She lifted her chin. "You meant every word you said. So did I."

His eyes warmed. "Then I won't say I'm sorry if you won't."

"That's fine, then."

"How about if I just concede that you are right about the mare and that you seem to be more knowledgeable than I originally thought."

Her lips curved slightly. "That'll do."

He took one more step. Her breath caught at his nearness and he lifted his hand. She wondered if he was going to touch her. She wanted him to touch her. Even after the words they'd hurled at each other, she still wanted it.

But his hand moved past her shoulder and gripped Pretty's halter. Lucy took her hand off the nylon.

"So in your opinion, what she needs is…"

He waited for her to answer. He was giving her a chance to show she could make the right call.

"Antibiotics and anti-inflammatories. Probably a five-day course of each. If that doesn't clear it up, then call the vet. But I really think that will do it."

"I agree."

She had to go now. It had been difficult to argue with him but it was more difficult to stand there and act unaffected. The trouble was, she'd meant all she'd said. And she still found herself drawn to him. To his strength and conviction. How could that be?

She nodded and started to walk away.

"Lucy."

She turned back. He had his hand on the halter but was facing her. "Thank you."

It would have to do. From Brody there wouldn't be praise and acknowledgment of her expertise. She'd been correct and he'd said thank you. It was all she'd get and she knew it. But she wanted more. She'd come here to do a job and here in the ring it had been about Pretty and about proving something to him. She'd done that. And now she found she wanted approval, not just of her skills but for herself.

Brody was starting to matter. And he couldn't, not when

she had to leave so very soon. She couldn't let his opinion of her matter. It would only hurt in the end, and life had hurt her enough lately.

"You're welcome," she replied, but spun on her heel and kept walking until she was back outside in the heat again.

"I've saddled the gelding for you."

Lucy stared down the corridor at Brody. For several days they'd crossed paths as she learned more about the ranch, and he'd been slightly warmer, with perhaps a hint of grudging respect. Last night he'd been quiet at dinner but at the end had suggested they go for a ride around Prairie Rose so she could see more of the outlying areas of the ranch. He hadn't said as much, but she had supposed it was his way of showing his approval of her. Of admitting in a roundabout way that she knew what she was doing. Only now she wasn't sure at all, because he'd picked a past-his-prime gelding for her to ride out on.

"Seriously?" She'd had her eye on the bay, the large magnificent one she'd seen the other night. Brody led the gelding out, a gray appaloosa with a blanket of gorgeous spots on his hindquarters. A beautiful boy just the same, but she could tell he was slowing down. He'd be tame. Too tame for her. She wanted to feel the wind in her hair and the power beneath her. She gritted her teeth. She thought they'd cleared the air yesterday, but his choice of mount for her was patronizing. Clearly her job wasn't done if he thought the gelding was the best she could handle.

"If you think I can't handle a more spirited mount, think again."

Brody smiled slowly. "You know, I get the feeling life is never boring with you, Lucy. You have this need to challenge *everything*."

"And you think that's funny?" She planted her hands on

her hips. His grin was a surprise, a teasing, lopsided smile that was hard to resist. He ran hot and cold, she realized, and wondered why that was. Since that day in the corral, he'd been cool and remote, almost angry at her picking up on Pretty's injury. Even at the end when he'd admitted she was right, praise had been sparse and certainly not teasing. Today he seemed to have shed all that animosity and at least seemed equitable. What had changed between last night and this morning? "You're very lucky I challenged your men."

His smile faded into seriousness. "I know that. You picked up on what they missed. I'm grateful."

"But you still don't trust me with your prized horses?" She raised her eyebrows at the gelding. "You don't think I can handle them?"

"That's not it at all!" He scowled. "Lord, you try to do a girl a favor and she can only find fault." He put his weight on one hip. "Women!"

Lucy opened her mouth to respond but shut it again. He was winding her up. The thought hit her and she was shocked. He was expecting her to react. Her eyes widened as his looked on her, expectant.

Brody Hamilton was using the age-old technique of argument to *flirt*. With her. And, oh, it was tempting to return the favor.

"I thought after the incident with Pretty you would have learned that the way to score points with me isn't to pamper me but to treat me as an equal."

His grin widened at their banter.

"Did you hear that, Bruce?" He looked at the horse and shook his head with mock seriousness. "I think she just insulted your manhood. And here my intentions were pure." He sighed, put upon, and with a chuckle, tilted his head and delivered the final riposte: "Bruce here needs some exercise. And he's pouting because I haven't given him any lately.

He thinks senior status entitles him to certain privileges. I thought today I'd make peace by offering him a pretty lady. Perhaps I was wrong."

Lucy's lips twitched. Obviously Mrs. P. had slipped something in Brody's morning coffee because he was cracking jokes and flirting as though all their animosity had never happened. She couldn't help the grin from dawning over her face. Was it so simple as that? That the horse had needed a workout, and that was Brody's only motivation in choosing him? Perhaps she'd been taking things too personally. She'd been defensive about everything for so long it was second nature. Perhaps it really was as easy as a ride on a summer's day with a cowboy she was starting to like way too much.

"Does that line work for you often?"

He leaned close to the gelding's ear and whispered something, and the horse nudged Brody's shoulder.

"Bruce says not as often as he'd like."

Lucy couldn't help it…she laughed. She wouldn't have guessed that Brody had a playful side. She strode up the corridor, carrying her cap in her hand. "So what's with the change in mood? You haven't—" she broke off as Brody's left eyebrow lifted. "You haven't seemed very happy I'm here. To put it mildly. Or that I put my oar in about Pretty's injury."

Brody came forward, Bruce clopping steadily behind him until he halted right in front of her and handed her the reins.

"I was rude. I'm sorry. I'm not usually that grumpy. Or closed minded."

He actually looked as if he meant it. The crinkles were gone from the corners of his eyes as he regarded her seriously.

"My word, did I just hear an apology?"

His eyes twinkled. "Must have been the wind."

Bruce was getting impatient and nudged Lucy's shoulder with his head, pushing her toward Brody. It put her off balance and Brody's hands came out to steady her. And stayed, just above her elbows. "Lucy I—" he cleared his throat "—I am sorry. About your mother and about being so rough on you and quick to judge. I'm usually not so hard to get along with."

Her eyes dropped to his lips. They were crisply etched, with a perfect dip in the top one. This was madness. She had to do something to get out of his arms before she did something foolish.

"You're not?"

She raised one brow just a bit in sarcasm, though there was little malice in her now. She'd said it so he'd let her go, but his grip remained firm. They weren't sniping, they were...

She bit down on her lip as she looked up in his eyes. They were *waiting*. Waiting for one of them to make a move. Lucy knew it could never be her. She relaxed her shoulders and took a small step back so he'd let her go. Of all things. Using an aged gelding to set off sparks. She wasn't entirely sure she didn't prefer the nasty Brody. It made distance a heck of a lot easier. Because this Brody—the human, caring one—was a man she'd like to know a lot better. And to do that would mean revealing things about herself she didn't want him to know.

"No, I'm not," he said huskily, his hands still in the air where moments before her arms had been. The intimate tone reached inside her and she wanted to back away. But that would mean letting him win. He would expect her to, and she needed to stand her ground.

"Why were you, then? Why did you judge me so harshly?"

He finally turned away. "Hop on. You're none too tall and your stirrups will need adjusting."

She knew pestering him wouldn't get answers, so she put the hand holding the reins on the saddle horn, her left foot in the stirrup and hopped, sliding into the saddle. Once she was seated she realized that indeed, the stirrups were a few inches too long for her feet.

Brody's hands worked the first buckle and she watched him from above, his strong, capable fingers partially hidden by the brim of his hat.

"Why were you so angry with me?" She repeated the question softly, needing to discover the real reason behind his actions. He could be kind and funny. She wanted to believe that was the real Brody and not the exception. His hands stilled on the leather strap.

"There are just a lot of pressures right now. And…because I don't like people nosing around in my life."

She thought of the discrepancy in the records and knew if she brought it up he'd consider it an invasion of his privacy. And rightly so. How would she feel if he went through her things? He finished the first stirrup and went around to adjust the other.

"Why not? I thought all cowboys were an open book. The uncomplicated type."

He didn't look up at her. She wished he would so she could see his expression. But he kept fiddling with the strap. She relaxed, leaning ahead and resting her hands on the saddle horn.

"I'm not that complicated," he explained. "Doesn't mean life hasn't thrown me complications. Ones that I don't choose to broadcast. Still have to be dealt with, though."

He finally looked up. "Don't you have any of those, Lucy?"

His hand landed on the ankle of her boot and she felt the pressure of it through the leather, connecting them in this one moment. She had so many questions she wanted to ask, and no right to ask them. He wasn't teasing anymore. He wasn't flirting. This went deeper than that. She wanted to reach out and touch his face, just once. To smooth the tiny wrinkle that formed between his eyes, telegraphing his worry.

What could he be dealing with to cause him such distress? Did it have anything to do with when he took over the ranch? Or how his father's signature had suddenly stopped appearing on the official records? But she held back. He was entitled to his secrets as much as she was entitled to hers. And getting too close to him wasn't part of the plan. No matter how good his hand felt. Maybe she needed to know, but this wasn't the way to go about it.

"Then can we agree on one thing, Brody? I'm not here to dig into *your* past. I am only here to forge an alliance, if you will. Between Prairie Rose and Navarro. Whatever deal we broker should benefit both operations, don't you agree? I was just getting up to speed with records. That's all." She paused. "I didn't go through your files with any other intention than that."

Brody moved away from her leg. "Okay."

"Brody, I…" She swallowed. "Look, I tend to judge on what I see. And, yeah, I also need to know who's running Prairie Rose. It matters. It doesn't mean I need to know every detail."

She met his gaze evenly while Bruce waited patiently for his cue to walk on. Lord, Brody was handsome. More than that, he was steady. She didn't know what he was dealing with, but she knew he'd do it standing tall or not at all. She liked that.

"I'm running Prairie Rose. Just me."

More than ever she wanted to ask about his father, but the words stuck in her mouth. What if he asked about hers?

"I think you're a good man, Brody, and one dedicated to Prairie Rose. That's all I really need to know."

She nudged Bruce and turned him, walking out of the barn into the yard. Maybe that was all she needed to know, but it wasn't all she wanted. She wanted to know about his connections, about his family. Where was his family? Mrs. Polcyk was only a part of it. But she knew that whatever she found out, it was going to have to come from Brody. She wouldn't lower herself to snooping.

# CHAPTER SIX

BRODY caught up with her a few moments later, riding the bay she'd been hoping to ride herself. It was the first time she'd seen him sit a horse, and he did it with an unmatched naturalness and ease. He was born to be in the saddle. A nearly nonexistent cue from him and the stallion broke into a trot, coming to meet her by the fence.

"Okay, so now I'm jealous."

He flashed a grin at her again, as if the tense moments in the barn hadn't happened. She was beginning to realize that the Brody she wanted to know existed when he was most in his element. He was easier, less guarded. She recognized it because she felt it herself. She got in the saddle and all her troubles seemed to melt away. She could just *be*.

"Ahab's my pride and joy."

It was easy for Lucy to see why. He was tall for a quarter horse—she'd guess at slightly over sixteen hands—with beautifully muscled hindquarters and a broad chest. She remembered the bloodline from the files yesterday—solid. A little mixing of Thoroughbred, which gave him his leaner, taller build. Ahab wasn't a stock horse. At the way his hooves danced impatiently, she knew he'd be agile and fast. Exactly what Navarro was looking for, exactly as her father had said. But at the look on Brody's face, she knew. "He's not for sale, then."

Brody patted Ahab's neck. "Nope. Not for sale." He inclined his chin at a field ahead. "You wanna head out?"

"Why not? Though I doubt Bruce and I will be able to keep up."

"Don't underestimate Bruce. He's got a competitive heart."

Brody nudged Ahab into a canter and Lucy followed, letting out all her pent-up oxygen in a rush as Brody led her out of the lane and into a meadow. She watched him from behind. Perhaps Ahab wasn't for sale, but she definitely wanted to talk to Brody about stud fees. He was far and away the finest piece of horseflesh she'd seen in months. But it wasn't just Ahab. It was Brody. Yes, he was a pain in the neck. He was also dead sexy. Definitely a complication she didn't need. She had an obligation to fulfil. She'd promised King Alexander that she'd do this job properly, and that meant going back to Marazur and...

She frowned. And what? Taking her place as princess? Is that what Alexander had planned for her? It didn't seem possible. And it was the last thing she wanted to think about on a beautiful morning like this.

She nudged Bruce along, only slightly behind Brody, and her chest expanded in the clear air. This was what she'd missed over the past week. In the few days before leaving she hadn't had any time to escape. Now, with the warm summer breeze in her face and the familiar rocking motion of Bruce beneath her, the stress she'd been holding on to dissipated into the prairie breeze. They rode for several minutes in silence, following the fence line north, up over a small knoll and toward a thin line of trees in the distance.

Brody stayed slightly ahead with Ahab, which was fine with Lucy. She was more than enjoying the freedom and wide-open space. The sky here was so huge, like a giant blue ceiling that went on far beyond the walls of her vision. There was room here, in the drying grasses and the calls of the birds and the gentle hills. There was room to simply exist. There was a wild freedom here she hadn't experienced in a long time. Like spring-cleaning day when her mother had thrown open all the doors and windows and let the sunshine and fresh air in. It almost felt like a new beginning. But that was silly. She'd had all the new beginnings she'd care to have for a long time. For a fleeting moment she almost wished she were back in Marazur, running the stable and keeping a low profile at the palace. There was only so much change a girl could take. At least there she knew what the expectations were. Here, at Prairie Rose, they constantly seemed to change with Brody's mood.

Brody turned along a fence line and she caught sight of several horses grazing below. She kept trying to puzzle him out. The very first day he'd been teasing with her, and then almost angry when he realized who she was. She wondered if it had to do with her, or if it was just because she was there and digging into his past. She didn't like the twist he put on the nickname "princess," either. She was sure he hadn't realized the truth of her identity, but that didn't stop the resentment and guilt she felt whenever he used it, even if it was in jest.

Brody slowed Ahab to a walk and halted. As she came closer, she saw him relax in the curve of the saddle, lean his head back and let the sun warm his face. With utter fascination she showed Bruce to a wall and watched as Brody took a deep breath and let it out.

This was why she cared. She understood what that breath meant. There was something about Prairie Rose, something about being here and being with the horses that she recognized and responded to. She'd tried to capture the same freedom in Marazur but had failed. Every time she tried to sneak away for a ride on the cliffs, King Alexander had security follow her. She supposed it was his idea of being an attentive father. But there was no one here now. She was *free*.

Prairie Rose Ranch was different, yet much the same as the life she remembered. She could tell Brody felt the same bone-deep appreciation for it. The gorgeousness of a summer sun soaking through a T-shirt. The pungent warmth of horse and worn leather, the wide-open space and the something that was elemental about all of it brought a catch to her chest. What would it be like to be here all the time? To be a part of a ranch like Prairie Rose? To be with Brody? She licked her lips. Perhaps it would be easier to imagine if she could figure him out.

She came up beside him and stopped, looping the reins over the horn and turning her face to the sun, as well.

"I'd had you pegged as an English girl, princess."

Eyes closed, she chuckled softly. There wasn't any derision in his use of the name this time, only teasing.

"Naw, Western. When I was eight years old my mum finally decided something had to be done with me and asked if I could take lessons at the Oak. I did a lot of western pleasure riding, right up to my teens. Once I started working, though…"

"You?" he prompted. He turned in the saddle to look at her, eyes curious. She opened her eyes and caught him staring.

"I'd been hanging around the stables for years, first riding, then helping the grooms. I started working part-time in high school and then got more involved. The owner was dabbling in racing a bit and I wanted more action. I changed my manners and discipline for speed."

"You surprise me."

She looked over at him as a crow cawed in the trees ahead. "By the time Mum got sick, I was assistant manager."

"Then why did you leave?" Brody shifted in the saddle, the leather squeaking softly.

Lucy couldn't meet his eyes. So many choices to make about what truths to tell and yet…talking with Brody today and in the barn the other night helped her feel more connected to herself than she had in a long, long time. "I made a promise to my mother. She wanted me to explore other areas of my life. I promised her I would. I can't go back on that promise. It…"

But she broke off, suddenly grieving again. She hadn't realized what a grounding force her mum had been when she'd been alive. And now she was gone and had taken Lucy's touchstone with her. How Lucy wished her mum could be there to talk to now. Lucy could have apologized for the things she'd said at the end. Things she would always regret.

But if her mother had still been alive, Lucy wouldn't have gone to Marazur. She wouldn't even be at Prairie Rose. Funny how things worked out. She wasn't even sure if it was a good or a bad thing. And she still felt guilty for going to Marazur in the first place. To get away from her mother and from the lies. She'd been so angry. At her mother for lying. At her mother for getting sick. And even at Alexander for making no demands on her at all. It was almost as if he didn't quite care what she did. He was so perfectly agreeable she felt completely useless. Redundant.

"I know about making promises. Even when they're tough ones. She'd be happy you are following through with it, Lucy."

Lucy turned tear-filled eyes to him. She remembered her mother telling her about Alexander and then revealing that she'd invited him to come to the States to see her. The words Lucy had said…she couldn't take them back. And when she'd told them—together—that she was dying, all Lucy had been able to feel was anger and helplessness and she'd lashed out about being manipulated. She'd apologized, but the words could never be taken back. When her mother had made her promise to go to Marazur, she couldn't refuse. The day after the funeral she'd actually been glad to get away.

"It was all she ever asked of me. I couldn't very well refuse her."

Brody saw the tears and wanted to reach out and hold her, like he had in the barn. It wasn't her fault he was angry. He'd been angry for so long, he almost forgot what it was like to be anything else. And yet…there were times when he caught himself teasing her and wondered how she'd snuck past his guard. He didn't want to care. It would only complicate things.

"I'm sorry about your mother, Lucy."

She brushed away her tears with the back of her free hand. "I didn't mean to get weepy. You brought me out here for a ride and here I am getting all girly on you."

Girly, indeed. Because he couldn't help but notice the dusting of freckles over her nose or the way her firm breasts looked in a plain T-shirt. There was something more natural about Lucy today. A princess? Hardly, but no less alluring. Her unruly red curls were pulled back and tucked through the hole at the back of her cap. Her jeans were faded, as though she'd worn them often, and her T-shirt was tan-colored, making her pale skin look even paler. Delicate.

Damn.

That line of thinking would only get him in trouble. She was here to do a job. And today he felt better about her— at least in a professional capacity. She'd been honest with him about her purpose, and then she'd demonstrated that she wasn't just another flunkie sent to analyze charts and records. She *was* a horsewoman. Only someone who knew what they were about could have picked up on Pretty's injury. He'd like to think he would have noticed right off but wasn't sure.

He looked at her long fingers, the leather reins threaded through them and longed to touch them, to reassure her it would be okay. Feeling drawn to her wasn't right, but he'd wanted her with him today anyway. She'd earned the right to see the rest of the ranch, and he'd needed the break himself. Going into town yesterday hadn't been fun, and he was glad she hadn't pressed him about where he was going. Details. Details that needed attention and that reminded him of how much responsibility he had. And Lucy somehow reminded him that there was more to life than endless responsibility. He could say that it was part of the job, showing her around. But the truth of the matter was, he'd needed to escape for a while and he'd wanted to do it with her.

He'd wondered if the rolling prairie would bore her, but she looked free and happy. He recognized that look. It wasn't one he wore very often, but today, playing hooky and going for a joy ride reminded him of why Prairie Rose was a labor of love rather than obligation.

He had enough obligation to worry about, anyway. And right now that didn't include making eyes at Lucy Farnsworth. It certainly didn't include the crazy thought that she looked *right* sitting there astride Bruce. Like she belonged. Again he was reminded of how he'd thought that once before, only to be proved completely wrong. Things weren't always as they seemed. Lisa had taught him that.

He swallowed the bitter taste in his mouth and nodded toward the trees. "You want to see the old homestead?"

She nodded, but he heard the telltale sniff that she tried to hide. Her feelings were still raw. Her mother hadn't been gone that long. He remembered how that felt, how the moments snuck up on you when you realized everything had changed forever.

He tried a teasing smile, hoping to cajole her out of her doldrums. "I'll race you."

Before he could blink, she'd dug her heels into Bruce and set off down the hill, her head low over his neck. At his signal, Ahab leaped forward, his long stride stretching over the tall grass. She shoved her hat further over her eyes and bent low, urging him on, her knees tight against the saddle as her laughter danced back to him on the wind. With a whoop, he gave Ahab free rein. They caught Bruce and Lucy halfway and galloped side by side the rest of the distance, the bright sound of their laughter chasing them.

They pulled up in a pouf of dust at the border of trees around a small dilapidated building. Lucy walked Bruce forward, turned him by a poplar tree and brought him back, both of them winded. Her grin was wide and free, and Brody let the answering laughter come, let it feel good after months of it being a stranger. "I guess you were right. Bruce didn't stand a chance."

Lucy's breath came in bursts of exertion. "Yes, but Bruce has got a valiant heart, don't you, sweetheart." She leaned forward and pressed a kiss to his gray, damp hide. Bruce halted beside Ahab, so that she was face-to-face with Brody.

She sat up and lifted the brim of her ball cap a bit. "What is this place?"

Brody smiled again, more at ease than he'd expected to be. Lord, she was beautiful. And not in any flashy, extravagant way. There was something so natural about her. She reminded him of the flower that was the ranch's namesake. A wild rose. Beautiful, but in a take-me-as-I-am, unostentatious way. Her hair set off the creaminess of her skin. He touched the tip of his finger to her nose. "The sun is making you freckle."

He had touched her without thinking, and shifted in the saddle as her lips dropped open with surprise.

"Sorry," he muttered, and slid out of the saddle, putting his back to her. Stupid, stupid. Noticing her *skin,* of all things!

Her laugh floated on the breeze behind him. "I'm embarrassingly pasty for someone who lives in the Mediterranean.

Blame it on my Irish roots—red hair and pale skin. But I burn easily, so the secret is SPF a zillion. Apparently today I missed my nose."

He imagined her smoothing the lotion over her arms and swallowed thickly.

He narrowed his eyes. Her reference to her home reminded him that she was only here to do a job and she'd be leaving in a matter of days. He'd do better to remember that she was here at the request of the king of Marazur and stop weaving fancies that didn't exist. She didn't belong here. She had no idea what Prairie Rose was really about. She certainly wouldn't have found it in the files from yesterday. Or even with Bill and Arnie and Pretty.

"This is a sod house, isn't it!" Curious, Lucy made her way through the weeds to the small structure. She turned her head briefly to look at him, and his heart constricted.

Yeah, he was testing her. He'd forgotten that in the joy of racing, but her remark about Marazur reminded him. He'd figured she'd bear out his expectations and that'd be that. Lisa had taken one look at the soddy and had turned up her nose, laughing. She'd wondered why they'd kept it, a pile of dirt in the middle of the prairie. But Lucy was looking at him as if he'd given her a precious gem, when the reality was that it was just like Lisa had said. A mound of dirt in the middle of nowhere.

It would have been easier if she, too, had turned her nose up at it, rather than looking at it with such interest.

She stepped gingerly around the structure, peering in through the opening where the door once was. "Who lived here, Brody?"

He stepped forward, unable to keep from recounting the story. It was one his mother had told him often after his grandmother had passed on.

"My great-great-grandparents. They settled this land in the

late nineteenth century. And lived in a soddy as they built it up and raised beef."

"Can you imagine living here? My God, the hardship." Her voice came from around the other side, and he looked toward where the sound came from. All he could see was waving grass and scrub brush. Her voice came, hollow on the wind as she circled the structure. "We complain when the power goes out for a few hours. And they lived and loved each other right here in a home made of dirt and grass."

She reappeared on the other side, her smile wide. "Amazing, isn't it! You must be so proud."

"Proud?" Proud, of a family that was poor as church mice? Of a family who'd been foolish enough to lose so much? He looked away. There was no distaste in her eyes, just curiosity. He'd wondered, considering she now lived in such luxury. But Lucy *got* this place. He could see it in her. The way she valued roots, the way she talked about her mother and Trembling Oak. And he'd been prepared for her to turn up her nose.

"Of course, proud! Think of how strong they must have been to stick it out. Not just here, but with each other. Marriage is…"

She broke off the sentence and looked uncomfortable. He tried to meet her gaze but she averted her eyes. "Marriage is…?"

His heart pounded. She couldn't know about Lisa. He'd said absolutely nothing to make her suspect he'd been married before, and he doubted Mrs. P. would have, either. The subject of his failed marriage was a no-go zone.

"I was just going to say that marriage is difficult enough without throwing hardships into the mix."

Throw in a few hardships and marriage did get difficult. Too difficult. He knew that all too well.

"And you're basing this on…?"

Brody shoved his hands in his pockets but he didn't waste time waiting for an answer. "Have you been married, Lucy? What about your mum? You've mentioned her before, but not your dad. I take it that wasn't a happy family unit, either."

She angled her head, watching him closely. He didn't like the way she was looking at him. As if she was on the verge of asking questions he didn't want to answer.

"I didn't know my dad, growing up."

"Really. So they were divorced?"

This time Lucy looked away. "My mum and dad split up when I was a baby."

Brody ignored the little voice inside him that said he was pressing too much. "Do you even know who he is?"

Lucy's nostrils flared. He'd touched a nerve, apparently. Good. He'd heard enough about what everyone thought had caused *his* marriage to fall apart, when he knew the truth: Lisa hadn't loved him. She'd loved something she'd thought he was, and when it wasn't true she'd cut and run. Fast.

"I do know my father, yes. Though you're really being an insulting ass right now."

"And is he married?" He kept on, undeterred.

Lucy's eyes snapped and her cheeks turned red. "Why does it matter?"

Brody snorted. "All this makes you a judge of marriage, I suppose? You didn't grow up with one and you haven't experienced it yourself."

She stepped away from the soddy and came closer. "You don't need to get run over by a tractor to know it's gonna hurt," she remarked, stepping over a large stone. She stopped in front of him. "People can imagine themselves in situations, good and bad, and have something of an understanding of what it would be like."

"Really."

Lucy let out a growl of frustration. "Honestly, Brody, you

change direction more than the wind out here. You're joking and happy one moment, and an absolute bear the next. Haven't you ever imagined something wonderful and you knew exactly what it would be like without having experienced it?"

His gaze dropped to her lips and stuck there. Yeah, he had. Because right now he was imagining what it would be like to kiss her. To taste the sunlight on her lips and hear her sigh against him. To touch that silky-soft skin of her arms as he held her close.

Was she right? Was he really that miserable? It was true he'd felt the strain of running everything single-handedly more the last few years. And he didn't trust easily. But had he really become so crotchety?

"You might want to get back on that horse and head on home," he muttered, unable to tear his eyes away from her mouth.

"Why? Because you're going to snap at me again? Insult me and my family?" She puffed out a derisive breath. "By now I'm almost immune."

"Damn it, Lucy…"

She laughed at him then, and it made him so mad he could only act. He grabbed the brim of her cap, pulling it off her head and sending the gingery curls springing around her face. Her lips dropped open in shock the moment he dropped the cap on the ground and shoved his hands into the rippling mass. The surprise in her eyes was instantly replaced with something new. Passion. Desire. He let it feed him as he tilted her head back and pressed his mouth to hers.

Lucy's hands hung limply at her sides momentarily as Brody's lips hit hers, not asking but demanding a response. His mouth was firm and hot and very, very agile. She lifted her hands and pressed the fingertips into his shoulders, standing on tiptoe and finally curling her fingers around the back of his neck. He teased her mouth open wider and tilted his head, the brim of his hat shading them both from the glaring sun.

He eased off, nipping her bottom lip between his teeth, and all her nerve endings shot to her core. She put her weight back on her heels as his hands withdrew from her hair, leaving the curls in a wild mess.

"You were wrong." His voice was gravelly, and a shiver went through her despite the heat.

"Wrong about…" she squeaked, cleared her throat, and started again. "Wrong about what?"

"You can imagine things all you want, but they're rarely what you expect."

Her cheeks flushed. The insult was clear. She'd just made a complete fool of herself. Crawling all over him as if he was irresistible. A magpie cackled in a nearby poplar, taunting her.

*He* had kissed *her,* she reminded herself, not the other way around. He'd been the one to pick a fight. He was the one who kept changing his mind. She'd been the one to keep her head—for the most part. She lifted her chin.

"You, Brody Hamilton, are mean." She wasn't about to let anyone play her for a fool, not again. "You did that deliberately. Well, congratulations on proving your point. You can go on being miserable, just the way you like it."

The last word broke but she didn't care. She picked up her cap out of the dust and shook it off. "From now on let's just talk about your stock, shall we? I'll start putting together a proposal based on what I've seen and we can talk fees. That's what I came for, and that's what I'm taking back with me."

"Where are you going?"

She glared at him with one foot in the stirrup. "You'll have to find someone else to argue with, it wasn't in my job description." Tears of humiliation pricked the backs of her eyelids. She slid into the saddle and shoved her hair haphazardly through the cap once more.

Then she spun Bruce around and urged him into a gallop, flying over the prairie, heading back to the barns.

Brody Hamilton had played her for a fool. She was relieved she hadn't told him the truth after all. Right now all she wanted to do was do her job! And then catch the first flight home.

Bruce rebelled at the pace and she relaxed, letting him slow down. Home. It struck her that she'd just referred to Marazur as home. How had that happened?

## CHAPTER SEVEN

For two days Brody and Lucy maintained a cold, polite relationship that consisted of examining stock and negotiating
stud fees. No more insults, no more joking, and definitely
no more kissing.

Never would Lucy have imagined herself wishing to go
back to Marazur and the palace. She was only there because
of guilt and promises to begin with, and because she had
known in her heart it was a wonderful opportunity professionally. She certainly hadn't taken the job out of loyalty to
her father.

Her mother had waited until almost the end before telling her about Alexander, and then had used her illness to
make Lucy promise to go to Marazur. Alexander had come,
and Mary Ellen had told them both what the doctors had
told her—that she was terminal. She hadn't wanted Lucy
left alone. And at Lucy's resistance, she'd then pointed out
Navarro's reputation and that she had to think of her future.
Lucy had promised, too afraid to do anything else. But Lucy
had said things…awful things…to Alexander. And her mother
had heard every hurtful word.

Lucy sighed and sipped her coffee. The dew still lay thick
on the grass and a cluster of ducks flapped overhead, flying
toward the pond beyond the barns. Despite all she'd said,
Alexander had still asked her to come. He'd still entrusted

her with his prized stables. And he'd trusted her to do this job. She couldn't imagine why. She'd heard him all but admit to her half brother, Raoul, that he was at a loss as to what to do with her. But then he'd sent her here, and he would never have done that if he didn't think she was capable of it. He took his stables too seriously.

It was Saturday, and back in Virginia she'd be putting in a half day with the horses and then likely going out with friends for the evening.

Not today. Today she was stuck at Prairie Rose wondering about Brody. Not very productive.

"Lucy?"

Brody's voice stirred her and she took her feet off the empty chair and put them back on the deck floor.

"Yes?"

"I'm going into town later this morning. Thought maybe you'd like to come. See civilization, such as it is."

It was a polite invitation. He probably didn't even mean it; Mrs. Polcyk had probably put him up to it. But it might be a chance for her to do something nice for the housekeeper who had brokered a peace between them for the past few days. They'd have hardly spoken at all if Mrs. P. hadn't been there urging things along.

"Is Mrs. P. coming?"

"No, she's got a bit of a summer cold and she's taking it easy."

Lucy turned around in her chair. Brody was standing by the sliding door, neither smiling nor frowning. Waiting for her answer.

Brody was holding secrets. And it wasn't like he was going to sit down and have a big heart-to-heart with her, now, was it? Curiosity bubbled inside her. Since he'd lived here all his life, maybe she'd be able to put some pieces together by going to Larch Valley with him. Get some answers. If there was news about Prairie Rose, a community this small would surely know about it.

"I might like that. If Mrs. P. puts together a list, I can pick things up for her."

"That's generous of you."

Silence fell, uncomfortable.

"Lucy, I…"

"Brody…"

He stepped out on the deck, his hat in his hands. "I was way out of line the other day. I was deliberately insulting and hurtful. I'm not usually. My mama would kick my behind to know I'd spoken to a woman that way."

Her lips curved the faintest bit. Ah, mothers. Did they have any idea how much power they exerted even after they were gone? She thought of her own mother. Where was Brody's? But the peace between them was too tentative for her to ask. She looked into his eyes. He seemed earnest.

And she realized he was apologizing for what he'd said, not about what he'd done. Her heart fluttered. She was finding it difficult to regret the kiss, too, even if she had failed his test. It had been a long time since she'd been kissed like that.

"We seem to goad each other without even trying."

"We've both had a lot on our minds, I think."

Lucy thought for a moment. She knew what her problem was. She was angry. She wanted something she didn't have and she was downright mad about it. Maybe he was angry, too. Maybe he'd never planned his life to be this way. The paperwork showed he'd taken control of the ranch several years ago, but no inkling why. She couldn't presume to be the only one with hurts and regrets. What regret did he hold inside?

"You want to talk about it, Brody? About why you're so angry?"

She tilted her head back so she could see him properly, raising her eyebrows.

"Not really. You?"

She thought about just saying, *Hey Brody, my dad's really King Alexander of Marazur but I didn't know that until three months ago.* And she nearly laughed at what she imagined his expression would be, especially given the nickname he'd dubbed her with. She had to give her father credit. He'd seen her unhappiness and had sent her here. She'd gotten the impression it was to placate her, but she was determined to go back and show her worth, to exceed his expectations. She didn't want to be simply Princess Luciana. She wanted a place she'd earned.

And to do that, she had to earn Brody's approval first.

"Nope. I'm not really a sharing type of girl, if you haven't noticed."

He chuckled. "So let's take a day off from being mad and from working. I have some errands to run, and I'm going in, anyway. You might as well come with me. There's a farmer's market and some shops for you to visit if you like."

"That sounds nice."

"I'd like to leave in an hour."

"I'll be ready."

He slid the door shut behind him and she went back to her coffee.


Larch Valley was exactly what Lucy expected from a small western town. A little like stepping back in time, with the stores still sporting false fronts, and antique-style streetlamps along Main Avenue. She looked out the window of Brody's half-ton truck and smiled. Here was a place where children played in the park before being called home to supper and you'd get your week's worth of gossip at the local hairdressers on a morning such as this.

"I can drop you off here, if you like. Follow the avenue down to the end for the market. There are shops all along here, though. If that's okay."

She looked over at him as he pulled up to the curb. His lips were thinned and tense and she wondered why. What was he doing in town today that caused him to be so uptight? Was it personal or business? He'd already been to town once this week. Her mind raced back to the file she'd mulled over, sensing something wasn't right but not able to put her finger on it.

"I could come with you. I don't mind waiting."

He turned his head away from her and stared out the windshield. "You'd be bored to death."

She didn't want to pick another fight, not when they had such a tenuous truce going. She'd have to find her answers elsewhere. "Okay. I'll meet you at the market then?"

"In about an hour."

She opened the truck door and hopped out. He gave a wave of his hand, but still wasn't smiling as he drove off. It definitely wasn't an errand he was looking forward to.

She glanced around her. The avenue *was* quaint. Across the street was a small gazebo, bordered with some sort of weeping tree…one she'd never seen before. The bark reminded her of birch, but the leaves were tiny and hung toward the ground like silvery green curtains. A group of children played soccer in a small area, their shoes trampling the grass. It was lush and green—obviously watered, because on the drive in, most of the fields had been dry and brown in the late-August climate.

She turned her attention to the sidewalk before her and smiled. In Virginia they'd always been close to Norfolk and now in Marazur…she was used to urban centers.

She'd never been one for small towns really. But Larch Valley was pretty in its quiet, take-me-as-I-am way. All along

Main Avenue, iron and wood benches waited to be occupied in the summer sun. Baskets of gaily painted petunias and lobelia hung from the streetlamps, and urns of geraniums sat near doorsteps or beamed from window boxes.

Brody had been in this town his whole life. He'd probably gone to school here. She thought about it for a moment. He'd probably had girlfriends from here. Girls he'd known his whole life.

She frowned, surprised at her own line of thinking. She began to wander down the concrete walk. It shouldn't matter to her about Brody's love life. There was nothing between them. There couldn't be.

She sat heavily on a bench. This was silly. She had a fantastic job, money in her pocket. Lived in a palace. So why was she unhappy? And why did suddenly walking down a street in Larch Valley make her feel as though she was coming home? She'd never been here before. She didn't belong. Brody had made that clear the other day at the soddy.

No, in a few short days she'd be going back to Marazur. And if Alexander was happy with her performance, she'd be in charge of one of the most successful Thoroughbred racing stables in Europe. It was what she wanted. It was her way of subtly thumbing her nose at her father, to show him she'd done just fine without him. She'd go back and show him she was worthy of the job. This sort of position had been her goal as long as she could remember.

Except, back in Marazur there wouldn't be any Brody.

She covered her eyes with a hand. She shouldn't be thinking about Brody. Not after one disastrous kiss. It couldn't be Brody's fault. It was this place. It did funny things to her, that was all.

She got up and continued down the street, fighting the weird sense of familiarity, stopping before a white door. It was opened partway, and delicious smells wafted out: cinnamon and fruit and bread all mingled together. She knew what was on her shopping list, but she couldn't resist the urge to buy a treat.

The bell above the door tinkled as she pushed it the rest of the way open. "Be right with you!" came a shout from somewhere in the back of the building. Within seconds, a red-faced woman bearing a tray of buns bustled in.

"Morning! Sorry about that." Her hands flew as she arranged the buns behind the glass counter. "What can I get you?" she asked, straightening and dusting off her hands.

Lucy smiled. "Something that tastes as good as it smells in here."

The woman flashed a grin. "I'm afraid you'll have to be more specific."

Lucy laughed. "I was afraid you'd say that."

The woman couldn't have been more than thirty, Lucy realized, and she wondered how on earth she'd managed to stay so slim surrounded by sweet treats and breads all day. "Chocolate. I'd like something chocolate."

"Brownies. Made them first thing this morning and iced 'em hot." The woman pulled a pan out from a steel rack behind her. "I haven't even put them out yet."

Lucy could smell them—moist, rich chocolate. Her stomach turned over. Today had been coffee and a slice of toast for breakfast. She was already imagining a slab of brownie with a glass of cold milk.

She wondered if Brody liked brownies.

"I'll take them...and..." She paused. Maybe it would be silly to ask.

"And?"

"Do you know Brody Hamilton?" she blurted out.

The woman laughed. "'Course I do. Everyone knows Brody."

And Lucy felt that damnable blush heat her cheeks again.

"Oh," the woman said. Her smile grew.

"Oh, no," replied Lucy quickly. "It's not…no. I mean, I just should've known you knew him. It being a small town and all."

The woman handed over the brownies and raised an eyebrow.

"I mean…" Lord, she sounded like an idiot. She supposed that asking about Brody like a besotted fool would look less like she was prying. Yet she was at a loss as to what questions to ask. "I'm staying at Prairie Rose on business, and Brody brought me into town. I told Mrs. Polcyk I'd pick up a few things, seeing as she's not feeling well…"

"Betty's under the weather?"

The interruption didn't surprise her nearly as much as the use of Mrs. P.'s first name. "Uh, yes. She's got a bit of a cold."

The young woman's brow creased. "That woman, working too hard again." Her hands flew once more as she put a selection of items in a paper bag. "I'm sending you some herb bread and a bag of buns. You stop at the market and pick up some sausage, even if it's not on the list. It's Betty's favorite."

Lucy wasn't put off by the order; it amused her. This was a place where everyone looked after each other, it seemed. She blinked. Why was it, then, that Brody seemed to feel responsible for everyone else and so bent on doing things himself? He'd mentioned obligation. It made her wonder. What sort of obligation was he under?

"One last thing," she said lightly, her heart pounding like a schoolgirl's. "Do you know if Brody has any favorites? Mrs. Polcyk always seems to be baking, and it would be nice if she didn't have to, for once."

A pie box was added to the bag with the brownies. "How well do you know Brody again?"

She would not blush. She would not.

"I'm just visiting from another stable. That's all."

"I see." She rang up the total, and Lucy paid the bill. "Well, you tell Brody that Jen says hi, and that he'd better save me a dance at his barn dance next Saturday."

Jen? A dance?

She swallowed, smiled as her mind raced. "I'll do that. Thanks."

Outside she breathed the morning air and wondered who Jen was to Brody and what dance she was talking about. It didn't matter. Lucy would likely be gone by then, anyway. She adjusted the bags in her arms and lifted her head. She'd just make her way to the market and wait to meet Brody. She'd done enough of being silly this morning. If she had questions she should just come out and ask him herself. She didn't have much time, she might as well wander and explore. She wouldn't have time for it again before she left.

On the way to the market she couldn't help but be charmed. People on the street nodded hello; a couple of old men sat outside a diner and drank coffee, gesturing with their hands as they debated. Children sat on benches outside the ice cream parlour, licking cones that were melting in the warm morning sun. She was almost to the market when a sign caught her attention—Agnes's Antiques.

She went inside.

It was a treasure trove of items, from the flea-market quality to true finds. Old cola paraphernalia next to gorgeous willowware dishes. Sepia pictures and handmade dolls in nearly new condition.

"Hello, dear."

The woman was Agnes. There was no possibility of her being anyone else, Lucy concluded. Her gray hair was pulled precisely to the back of her head in a tight bun, and little glasses sat on her nose. Her eyes were sharp as tacks and Lucy, short, petite Lucy, felt somehow large and ungainly.

"Anything I can help you find?"

"I'm just looking, thank you."

Agnes came forward. "Why don't you let me take those bags for you. Wouldn't want you bumping into things."

She reminded Lucy of an old schoolteacher she'd once had. Kind, but oh, so particular. She put the bags on the counter and smiled. "I'm new to the area and was passing by."

"Of course. You're the young lady staying out at Prairie Rose."

Lucy's lips dropped open. "How did you know that?"

Agnes's eyes twinkled. "Small town, dear. News travels."

Lucy found she didn't mind the intrusion. In some small way it made her feel as though she belonged.

"Prairie Rose is lovely. I haven't had time to get much into its history though." She ignored the guilt sneaking through her at the obvious prodding. "I did gather from Brody that it's been in the family a long time."

Agnes smiled. "Oh, yes. Not always quarter horses, mind you. That was John's idea—Brody's dad. He was a real horseman through and through. I taught him in elementary school, you know."

Lucy smiled widely. So she had been right—a schoolteacher. She had that look and way about her.

Agnes beckoned with a finger. "Come and see this. You might find it interesting, seeing as how you're out at the ranch."

Lucy followed her through the dim store to the back, where Agnes took a picture down from a hook. "This isn't really an antique, but it sure is about history." She smiled. "That's Brody." She pointed to a small dark-haired boy in a miniature cowboy hat. It seemed he always wore one, even then. Lucy smiled at the image of him. He couldn't have been more than four years old. "And this here's his mum, Irene, and dad, John, and Hal and Betty Polcyk. Of course this was way before…"

Her face dimmed as she sighed.

"Before?" Lucy tore her eyes away from the picture and looked at Agnes.

Agnes peered over her glasses. "Woulda thought Brody had mentioned it. His mum, dad and the Polcyks were in an accident several years ago. Irene and Hal were killed."

"And his dad?"

Agnes took the picture from her hands and hung it on the hook again. "Oh, he's still at the nursing home. But it took Brody a long time to get things right at Prairie Rose after everything that had gone wrong. Boy darn near worked himself to the bone. But then," she peered over her glasses at Lucy, "men have been doing that in this part of the country for years. Ranching's hard work. Brody knew that and he's done a fine job putting things right."

An accident and the nursing home? Lucy had so many questions she wanted to ask, but not of Agnes. She wanted to ask Brody what the woman meant when she said putting things right. She wanted to know why he never mentioned the accident, or that he had any family at all. She'd shared bits and pieces with him, perhaps not a whole truth but parts of herself, yet he'd backed away when she'd asked a simple question about his parents. She wanted to know why he'd neglected to mention a father that apparently lived...

It clicked into place. Here. His father lived here. Brody had taken over Prairie Rose. And there was the gap.

At her silence Agnes peered at her with hawklike eyes. "You just go ahead and browse around, dear, and if you have any questions, ask."

Lucy had plenty of questions, and still another twenty minutes before she would meet Brody at the market. Mrs. P.'s husband, Brody's father, Brody's mother. Where had Brody been? And was Mrs. P. the only one who'd gotten out in one piece? Was she the only family Brody had left? Her heart ached for what he must have gone through.

She wandered through the store, thinking back to the two days she'd spent going over files. Brody had mentioned he'd bought Pretty seven years ago—his first solo purchase. She'd just taken it as a sign that Brody had assumed control as sons were wont to do. But now she got the feeling there was something more. Something had gone wrong, and she wanted to know what. And this time it had nothing to do with protecting the Navarros's interests. She wanted to know about Brody. Perhaps if she stayed on a few more days...

She stopped before a clothing rack, a motley selection of vintage blouses and dresses and skirts. Her eyes fell on a long skirt in navy. She reached out and touched it, realizing the stitching was done by hand. The tiny stitches were fine, intricate and exact. Every seam lay flat in the fitted waist, then flowed out toward the hem. Agnes had paired it with a blue flowered blouse...complete with fine white satin fringe along the breast and mother-of-pearl buttons.

"Gorgeous, isn't it." The older woman's voice came from behind her. "Been here for ages. Used to belong to Mathilda Brown. She did lots of rodeoin' in her day. And, land, could that girl dance. She was the belle of the Stampede during the war."

Lucy reluctantly let go of the fringe and turned. Even coming from Virginia, she knew all about the Calgary Stampede. "The Greatest Outdoor Show on Earth," she quoted, gratified when Agnes smiled.

"That'd just about fit you, you know."

Lucy looked at it longingly. For years there'd been little money for extravagance, and buying a vintage outfit certainly qualified. But now she didn't need to be concerned about money. She smiled. She could afford to do this now. And perhaps someday when she was back in Marazur she could put it on and remember her time here. Could pretend to be Mathilda Brown and feel the skirt flirt with her calves as she danced…

Danced. What would it be like to dance with Brody? She remembered the feel of his hard chest against hers as he'd pulled her close to kiss her. So hard, yet so very gentle, too. What if what Jen said was correct? Was there a dance? If she stayed on a few days, she would be able to go.

She wanted to be with him again. To see his eyes fall on her the way they had in the barn that first night, to feel his lips on hers as they had at the soddy. It wasn't rational and it wasn't smart, but it was what she wanted. She wanted to be able to take that bit of him with her.

"I'll take it."

Agnes beamed. "Oh, you'll look lovely in it." Her keen eyes peered over the frames of her glasses. "And I hear the annual dance out at Prairie Rose is next weekend. Perfect time to try it out."

Lucy smiled at the older woman warmly. "That's the general idea."

Agnes took the outfit from Lucy's hands and bustled behind the cash register to wrap it. "Of course, the former Mrs. Hamilton would never have worn such a thing, but I think it's just right."

"Mrs. Hamilton?" Lucy puckered her brow. "Why not?" Lucy looked at the navy skirt again. It was very traditional, very western. Not that she knew much about Brody's mother, but somehow it just seemed to *fit* with Prairie Rose.

"Oh, she was too fine for this sort of thing. Always felt sorry for Brody, though. Lots of head shaking happened when that wife of his left him for greener pastures when things got sticky."

Lucy's hand froze on her purse. Not his mother, as she'd thought.

Wife. He had been married.

Suddenly his hot-and-cold moods made perfect sense. The way he looked at her as if she'd made some grievous mistake, and then at other times as though there was something more. Clearly he wasn't over his ex-wife. All these days... and it hadn't been about her at all. It had been about his wife.

Knowing it cut into her far more deeply than it should have.

After all she'd learned today, she knew that Brody had to be hurt by his past. And if he knew the truth about her it would only pain him further. And yet...she still wanted that dance. One chance to be held in his arms, in Mathilda Brown's skirt and fringe.

Staying at Prairie Rose permanently wasn't an option; there was no reason for her to. Brody didn't need a stable manager and he certainly wasn't in love with her, nor would he ever be. A weight settled in her stomach. If he wasn't over his wife, he certainly wouldn't acknowledge any feelings for Lucy. And she did want to prove her mettle to her father, which meant resuming her position at Navarro. But a dance with him...would be a lovely memory to take back to Marazur. Something to hold on to.

She checked her watch. In only a few moments, Brody would be expecting her, and she would pick up what Mrs. Polcyk had requested. She thanked Agnes and put the bag with her other purchases, hurrying out the door.

And saw Brody's truck turning out of a parking lot on to Third Street and coming in her direction.

She hurried to the entrance of the market just as he was finding a parking spot. When he came around the hood of the truck, she noticed the lines in his face had deepened. It made her want to reach out and smooth them, to ask him what put them there and try to make it better. To tell him that whoever she was had been a fool to walk away and leave him to deal with everything all alone.

She couldn't fathom why she cared so deeply. The last few days he had been merely polite. He'd all but come out and said that her kiss hadn't been up to scratch.

The problem was, his had been. And she wanted the chance to try again. In the skirt and blouse she'd just bought.

"I'm sorry I'm late. I haven't even been inside."

He eyed her packages. "But you have been shopping."

"Well, yes." She lifted one arm slightly, putting a paper bag into relief. "I couldn't resist the bakery and then the antique shop."

His lips barely moved, though she got a glimpse of what might have been a smile. "Jen there this morning?"

She ignored the spurt of jealousy. For one, she had no claim on him and for another, he had probably known "Jen" since they'd been in diapers. "Yes, and she sent along some things for Mrs. P. With instructions to get sausage."

Brody did smile then. "Mrs. P.'s favorite. I should have thought of it."

*But you have enough on your mind, don't you.* The thought rushed to the surface of her mind but she kept it there. She'd save it for another time. When they were alone at the ranch and could talk without half the town sending curious glances their way as they were doing now.

"She also mentioned a dance. You know anything about that?"

The lines dissipated slightly, replaced by a warmth she suddenly realized she'd missed over the past few tense days. "Yeah. Annual barbecue out at Prairie Rose. Steak and pie and the Christensen brothers come out and play for a barn dance." He eyed her curiously. "You should stay. Unless you need to get back to Marazur. It's always a good time, and..."

"And what, Brody?" Her heart leaped at what he might say next.

"And if Mrs. P. is still under the weather, she could probably use a second set of hands."

Of course. Her excitement deflated, taking any shred of hope she might have had with it. Of course it was about Mrs. Polcyk and not about dancing with her at all. It all made perfect, depressing sense.

She forced a bright smile. "Speaking of Mrs. P., she did send a list." Lucy tried to adjust the bags to get out the sheet of paper.

"Here," Brody said, taking them from her hands. "Let's put these in the truck first."

He carried her bags to the truck and returned, gesturing to the entrance. "Let's go pick up what we need and head back."

Lucy had never been to anything like it, and she shook off her doldrums. There were stalls of home-grown vegetables, a fruit vendor from British Columbia with glorious peaches and apples, cherries and apricots. Another of baked goods and a huge tent filled with herbs and vegetables from a Hutterite colony. She picked up a bunch of dill and remembered her mother's cucumber salad. There were crafts and the sausage maker and a flower stall.

At the end of it their arms were full. Wordlessly they went back to the truck and headed out of town, back toward Prairie Rose.

Lucy looked over at Brody, unable to forget what she'd learned—and what she hadn't—this morning. Maybe talking to him would help.

"How was your morning?"

"It was fine." He stared straight ahead. The radio played in the background, and she wanted to reach over and turn it down, but figured it would only make him more wary.

"Where did you go?" she tried again, even though she had a suspicion about where he'd been anyway.

"Just around."

"Brody, why don't we try something new. Why don't you just come out with the truth and we'll take it from there."

She was aware how much of a hypocrite she was being. If he'd asked her the same probing questions, she would have evaded them, too. But she *had* told him some of her past. Certainly more than he'd shared with her, and it was clearly wearing on him. What Agnes had revealed this morning only made her more curious. More concerned. If it was causing him this much stress, maybe she could help. He'd gone through most of it alone. And if she were any judge, he'd have refused any sympathy or coddling.

"Right. Like what?"

She smiled faintly. The wife they'd save for another time. "We could start by you admitting you were visiting your father today."

She hadn't known his face could be so hard.

"Who told you that?"

"No one. I mean, I did hear that your dad was in a nursing home, and I put two and two…"

"Well you can stop it."

"Why?" She pressed on, wondering why after all this time it should bother him so much.

"Lucy…"

"Are you still angry with him?"

Brody braked and pulled the truck over along the shoulder of the road. He shoved it in Park and half turned to face her.

"Angry? Why the hell would I be angry?"

The words slashed through the cab of the truck. "You tell me," she bit back. They both knew he *was* angry, whether he should be or not.

After a few interminable seconds, Lucy said more quietly, "It's okay, you know. I understand being angry. I'm really angry with my mum right now. And angry at myself for being angry. Pretty screwed up, huh."

Brody stared at her.

"Yes," he said finally, and the word sounded exhausted. "Yes, I'm angry. I'm angry that he left Prairie Rose vulnerable, and I'm angry he took matters into his own hands, and I'm angry how much it cost me to have to clean up the mess myself."

Without another word, he put the truck back in gear and they drove to the ranch in utter silence.

# CHAPTER EIGHT

Brody shut the door to the truck and exhaled for the few seconds it took for Lucy to get out. He should have known taking her to town would be a mistake. He should have foreseen that anyone she met would wag their tongue. But he'd been deliberately insulting the other day and he didn't like the cool way she'd treated him since, so he'd thought getting away might thaw the ice a little. Might make up for the way he'd treated her and make it easier for them to work together. The polite silence that marked their relationship lately felt awkward.

He realized Lucy wasn't like Lisa, and the longer he spent time with her the more sure of it he became. He'd taken her to the soddy to test her, to confirm his suspicions that she considered herself above a hovel of dirt. Instead she'd felt the same way about it that he used to feel. She was continually surprising him, and it threw him off.

"I'll just take these things in," he heard her say, and turned his head. She was standing at the back of the truck with the bags in her hands. A tiny puff of wind ruffled her curls and sent one fluttering against her cheek. But there were no more questions. For once what he'd said had shut her up completely. If he didn't know better, he'd think he'd hurt her feelings. But that was silly, wasn't it?

"You got your ears filled in town, I expect."

She shifted her weight. "Maybe a little."

"And you're curious now. I should have known better than to take you with me."

She put the bags on the ground and stepped forward. "And you don't want me asking any more questions, do you, Brody."

"No."

He looked past her shoulder, not wanting to look into her knowing eyes and see pity there. Someone had told her about his father but she didn't know the half of it. He couldn't stand the thought of how she'd look at him if she knew all the details.

The morning had been hard enough. His dad had been having one of his bad days. Brody's fingers clenched. Seven years. Seven years and the weight of it still lay heavily upon him.

He remembered Lucy's dancing eyes as she'd looked over her shoulder at the soddy. Would she think less of him, of Prairie Rose, if she knew what had happened all those years ago?

His eyes dropped to her lips. Kissing her at the soddy had been a mistake. He'd known it from the moment he'd put his mouth on hers. And what was worse, he wanted to do it again. Badly.

Maybe it *would* be good to trust someone, to have her understand. "But maybe I should answer them, anyway," he said softly. "When you're done unpacking, come out for a ride with me," he suggested. His fingers itched to touch her hair. The fresh floral scent of it reached him on the breeze. Maybe being with her was what he needed; to take his mind off everything his father had said…and hadn't said…this morning.

Something flickered in the depths of her eyes. A little bit of fear, and maybe a little bit of resentment. He couldn't really blame her after the way he'd treated her. He smiled then, knowing exactly how to bribe her. "I'll let you ride Ahab."

Her nose crinkled a little, scrunching up her freckles as the smile dawned on her face. He didn't know how he'd missed that before. It made him want to kiss that particular spot.

But she stepped back, walking backward along the side of the truck until she reached the tailgate, the impish grin still lighting her face.

"You'll let me ride your prized stallion," she asked, tilting her head to one side. "You'll *trust* me."

"If you don't want to…" He nearly laughed at the look on her face. He needed to get away, just for a little while. And he wanted to do it with her.

"That's an offer I can't refuse," she replied, picking up her bags. "Give me ten minutes."

Lucy put the groceries away and dashed upstairs for a hat. She dug into her bag, pulling out a straw cowboy hat and punching it back into its proper shape. She wore ball caps most days to keep her hair tamed and the sun from her eyes. In Marazur she'd gotten a few wry smiles when she'd gone to the barns in her cowboy hat. But it was a part of who she was. And today it would keep the sun off the back of her neck.

She quickly changed into proper boots at the door. She couldn't deny that she was excited about riding Ahab. It meant Brody was beginning to trust her. After his outburst in the truck, she'd nearly despaired of getting answers, and had known she couldn't pry them out of him. But something had changed. Something between them, and as she strode to the stables in the blinding sun, she made herself forget about going to Marazur or brokering deals.

It was Brody she wanted.

He was waiting, standing at the gap of the sliding doors, a set of reins in each hand while the horses stood quietly behind him. Waiting for her, and she wondered briefly what it would be like to have it this way all the time.

"You were fast."

His deep voice echoed and her pulse fluttered. "Oppor-

tunity knocked," she replied, a little breathlessly. She pulled
a pair of gloves out of her back pocket and slid them on.
When he handed her the reins, their fingers touched, burning through the leather.

They mounted up. Brody adjusted his hat and dashed her
a wicked grin. "You won't have trouble keeping up today,"
he grinned. And he set off at a trot, this time heading dead
west.

They rode that way for a long time, not speaking, yet somehow connected. When he'd snapped at her in the truck, she
had figured she would never know what had happened at
Prairie Rose, or about his wife. But Brody verbalizing his
anger had somehow opened a door, one where he was offering to let her in. She'd meant what she said about helping
him. Understanding him.

They reached a promontory and Brody stopped. There was
a large boulder to one side, but nothing else besides waving
prairie grass. Straight ahead lay the jagged line of the Rockies.
They were devoid of snow now in August, but somehow their
sharp peaks were softened by a hazy summer glow. She slid
out of the saddle and merely dropped the reins…it would be
enough for Ahab to stay where he was.

"Wade's Butte," she murmured, turning in a circle.

"You knew."

He'd dismounted and come to stand beside her.

"Mrs. P. mentioned it when I first arrived. Said something
about getting you to bring me here before I left. I thought
maybe we were going there the other day, but you showed
me the soddy instead."

She turned a quarter turn and looked at him. It was hard to
believe anything could get to him. There wasn't a weak spot
to be seen. His dark T-shirt showed where muscles dipped
and curved through his arms, back and chest, his trim hips

and long legs were steady and sure. His jaw was strong, un-relenting. He was, in a word, splendid.

"What?"

His lips formed the single word as he stared out toward the mountains.

"I was just thinking how appearances can be deceiving."

"Oh?"

She nodded. "Looking at you, Brody Hamilton, no one would guess you were hiding a broken heart." His head snapped sharply, his gaze clashing suddenly with hers as he opened his mouth to deny it. "Unless," she continued quickly, "they had also had their heart broken."

"I don't do broken hearts," he insisted, looking away again.

"Oh, I think you do," she said softly. "And I think your father is the least of it."

Brody sighed heavily. "Let me turn the boys out, and we'll sit down."

He slid the bridles off the horses, letting them graze on the fresh grass free of the bits in their mouths. Lucy perched on the boulder, the surface cool through her jeans even through the glare from the sun. "Wade's Butte was named after my grandfather," he said, coming to sit beside her. "He used to come here a lot. He used to take a few days every fall, come out, pitch a tent and go hunting."

Lucy craned her neck around, searching the grass for evidence that didn't exist. "He did?"

"He was a real man of the land, Granddad. My grandma…" He paused and swallowed. "My grandma used to come along sometimes. They'd build a fire and…"

Again he broke off. Lucy lifted her knees and folded her arms around them.

Brody leaned forward, the gleam in his eyes intense. Lucy's hands came away from her knees. Her voice was a husky whisper. "They'd build a fire and…"

"You can guess," he answered, his voice a sexy rumble that came from the center of his chest. His fingers plucked her hat from her head, dropping it to the dry grass. As his hands sank into her hair, her heart trembled. She could well imagine what his grandparents had done around a blazing campfire with the wide-open prairie spread out beneath them. Had he brought his wife here, too? The thought slid away into oblivion as his dark gaze centered on her lips, clung there.

She took off his hat, too, dropping it beside hers and running her fingers through the short black strands of his hair. His eyes closed briefly, and when they opened they stared right into her core. There was no point in denying the attraction now or making excuses. It was all too clear to both of them; it was bigger than any of the secrets they'd been hiding.

They both leaned forward, meeting in the middle. His mouth met hers hungrily, his hands moved to link his fingers with hers, and she felt the connection to her toes. She heard a moan and realized it was her own as he released one of her hands to reach around her back, cradling her ribs.

The shift in weight pushed her back until she was lying on the flat surface of the boulder. "Luce," he whispered, looking down at her as his weight pressed her into a natural cradle in the stone.

"This is why you brought me here," she said, looking up at him, wishing he didn't thrill her so, but unable to deny it. His using the shortened version of her name drew them even closer together. She knew that any time someone called her that ever again, she'd think of him. And remember. Remember this moment, of feeling strong and protected and *wanted*.

"Yes," he replied, the word a dark confirmation as he lowered his head again and her lashes fluttered shut.

For long minutes they kissed, hands exploring over cotton clothing, taking their time.

Her fingers grabbed on to his T-shirt, crumpling the jersey as his tongue swept down the curve of her neck. Images of making love to him here under the sun surged through her brain, making her blood race hot. His hand slipped beneath her shirt and pushed it up, revealing the hollow of her belly, and he slid down, his mouth leaving a hot trail from the neck of her T-shirt down her cotton-covered breasts to the skin along the ribs, making her shudder with want. He kissed the soft skin there, then dipped his tongue in her navel and she gasped, arching her back as desire made her limbs heavy.

And she knew what it was to lose all sense. The sun seeped through her eyelids and she lifted her hands to cradle his head. Somewhere in the back of her mind she knew she should stop this and get him to talk, as she'd intended. But being in his arms felt too good; too right.

He had to stop, before they couldn't. Sex would be a mistake, one she couldn't take back.

She froze, and thankfully Brody seemed to understand. He paused, braced up on his hands above her. Letting out a breath, he pressed his forehead to hers. "I'm sorry," he murmured.

Her pulse leaped again. "You don't have anything to be sorry for." If anyone did, it was her. His conscience was clean. He wasn't the one lying about who he was.

He pushed up and away and she felt momentarily naked, which was silly since she was still fully clothed. There was something seductive about being sprawled on a rock in the middle of nowhere. She found she couldn't be sorry they'd done it. But neither would she make the mistake of letting it go further.

She brushed her hair out of her eyes and sent him a flirty smile. "Thank god for glacial deposits, huh."

The corners of his eyes crinkled.

She smiled up at him, but felt it waver. She was starting

to care for him, too much. "You brought me here, knowing this was going to happen, didn't you."

He didn't answer. Perhaps a fling wasn't that big a deal for him. She didn't know him well enough to know for sure. But she wouldn't have guessed it. And she didn't do flings. Under any circumstances.

"Brody? Did you bring me here to have sex with me? Did you think I would?"

He hopped off the rock and grabbed his hat. Had he thought that? It shamed him to think perhaps he had. He'd needed her. Needed to feel close to someone again.

He hadn't really considered making love to her, and when she'd frozen in his arms, he'd backed away. It wasn't fair what he was doing and he knew it. And yet…he'd wanted to be with her.

She straightened her clothing and he couldn't help but feel a bit sorry.

"Maybe we should stick to nice, safe topics," she suggested dryly. "Like your family."

He snorted. "I'm not sure I'd call that a safe topic."

"How did your dad end up in a nursing home?" She asked it quietly, as if she would respect whatever his answer was.

Something about her made him want to just say it and get it over with. She knew less about him than anyone he knew, but somehow she *got* him. He wanted to trust her.

He plucked a blossom from a bush creeping up against the rock, twirling it in his fingers. He'd rather she hear it from him than someone else, and the longer she stayed, the more likely it was that someone would say something. Perhaps it was time.

He cleared his throat, wondering how to begin. "There was a car accident. My mum and Hal—Mrs. P.'s husband— were killed. My dad wasn't. Sometimes—" he lifted his chin, stretching out his neck "—I wish he had. It would have been easier than seeing him this way."

"I'm very sorry." He sat back on the rock, and she reached over, putting a hand on his thigh. The denim was firm and warm. "That must have been very hard on you."

He didn't move, didn't put a hand over hers or turn his head to look at her. "You're here from Navarro stables, and you want—or rather King Alexander wants—to establish some sort of relationship between our two operations. I don't think you understand exactly what that means for Prairie Rose, Lucy. It's not a deal I wanted to jeopardize. But I've done that already. I kissed you when I shouldn't have. I brought you here…" He looked away. Never had he used seduction to get his own way. "This isn't how I normally do things."

"That has nothing to do with the relationship between Navarro and Prairie Rose."

"Thank you for that."

Her dark eyes met his once more. "Please, don't ask me to regret it."

His body surged at her words. He'd expected her to be offended, angry. And instead…his gaze dropped to her full lips. With very little persuasion he'd have her flattened on the rock again. He swallowed. And it still wouldn't be any more right.

She breathed in the sweet air. "I think I understand exactly why this particular place could be special to someone. The prairie's spread out like a giant floor, isn't it. You can see for miles in all directions." She tucked a curl behind her ear. "It's a beautiful paradox…how something so vastly empty can fill a soul so fully."

"I've never heard someone explain it in quite that way before." Indeed, it was as if she'd read his mind. Yet another thing that tethered them together. Lisa had never understood it, not like this.

"You came here a lot, didn't you. After it happened."

"Yeah. Yeah, I did. To clear my mind. Decide what to do next."

Lucy sighed and leaned over, resting her head against Brody's shoulder. He tried to ignore how natural the gesture felt. "It's terrible," she continued, "like living without the compass you've used your entire life. Everything you knew— suddenly it's all gone, and you don't know which direction to turn, and there's no one to tell you what to do or to look to for guidance."

"Like when you lost your mother."

"Yes, like that."

She understood. And knowing it, feeling that connection, made him feel for the first time like talking about it.

"Do you have a Wade's Butte, Lucy?" He turned his head and tilted it down, so that his lips were nearly against her hair.

For the first time in months, Lucy didn't feel alone. She closed her eyes, soaking in the feeling of his hard, solid body up next to hers.

"Sometimes I go for a ride in the mornings. If I manage to wake up early, I take out my favorite mare and watch the sunrise from the cliffs. It comes up over the ocean, everything pink and purple and blue and green. Somehow it keeps me from feeling completely disconnected."

For several minutes they simply sat, shoulder to shoulder.

"How bad *is* your father, Brody? What happened?"

Brody shifted, sliding back on the rock and making space for her in the lee of his legs. She leaned back, every bit of stress that had been lurking in her body shimmering away on the wind as his arm came around her, holding her in place. He held out the pink blossom and she took it in her fingers, admiring the fragile petals. They'd gone to the two extremes, on one side arguing bitterly and at the other, kissing. Now it was as though everything was in balance.

"He's paralyzed from the waist down," Brody murmured in her ear. "But he had head injuries, too. Some days are better than others. And my mother and Hal—" he shook his head slightly "—they were just gone. It didn't make any sense. After it happened, it was Mrs. P. who kept things together. She'd just lost her husband, and yet she stepped in until I could take over. I owed her. Prairie Rose owed her. And the first thing I did was tell her that as long as she wanted it, there was a place for her here. She's stayed ever since."

"Why did Prairie Rose owe her?"

He paused. "You might as well know all of it, I guess. Dad owned Prairie Rose, but Hal had a stake in a new venture… Dad wanted to expand. They'd also taken on a third investor…only it became clear that he wasn't as trustworthy as they thought." Brody's muscles stiffened as he remembered. "He'd been a little too generous with himself. Once the paperwork had been signed, he'd been able to play with the books. Dad found out and he and Hal were determined to look after it themselves. They were all going up to Calgary for the weekend. Mum and Mrs. P. to do some holiday shopping. Dad and Hal to set things straight with the partner. Only, they never made it. They were broadsided, and Mrs. P. was the only one to come out of it with minor injuries. Mum and Hal were on the passenger side where they got hit."

The ramifications hit her squarely. This then, explained not only when Brody had taken over, and his signature on all the paperwork, but also the gap in the files. He'd lost his mother and essentially his father, he'd inherited a ranch, a widow and a set of legal problems she could only imagine were a complete nightmare.

She twisted out of his arms and turned, staring up at him with her mouth open in shock. "How much? How much did he take? That's what happened, isn't it. He embezzled."

"Too much," Brody admitted.

"Tell me you got him."

Brody smiled thinly. "Eventually. I hadn't known anything about it. But I didn't try to do like Dad. I didn't go after him myself. I let the RCMP do that. We didn't get any money back, though."

Lucy lifted her hand and touched her fingers to his cheek. There was a rough layer of stubble along his jaw. She imagined what it must have been like to be as young as he was and to lose everything. And to have that much responsibility placed squarely on his shoulders. Her mother had asked that she go to Marazur with Alexander. To give him a chance. That was nothing, nothing compared to what Brody had faced.

He pulled away from her touch, and a muscle ticked in his jaw. "And this is why I didn't want to tell you. Because of the way you're looking at me right now. I never wanted you to feel sorry for me."

But Lucy didn't back away. "Of course not. You're too busy being responsible for everyone. You don't have time for pity."

His black eyes bored into her for long seconds. He hadn't expected her to understand, she could tell. But she did. She understood more about Brody than he realized.

"I *am* responsible. I had a responsibility to Mrs. P. To Hal and Dad. To my mum. To Prairie Rose."

"No one can possibly expect themselves to carry all that alone." No mention of the nameless wife. Where had she been through all of this? When had she abandoned him? And why?

"There was no one else. My father—" For the first time his voice broke and Lucy knew just how much strain he'd been under. "My father wanted Prairie Rose to be the best. He'd wanted to move forward with a new breeding program and build a reputation for us. He did, but not in the way he wanted. It was up to me to do that for him."

"And so an arrangement with Navarro accomplishes that."

"Yes, it does. And it's why I didn't tell you this before. I didn't want to ruin it."

The noon sun deepened, losing its sharp glare and mellowing over them. A hawk circled overhead, soaring higher and higher. Lucy followed it with her eyes for a few moments.

He needed Navarro. And she needed Prairie Rose.

"It occurs to me, Brody, that we've been fighting each other when it would have been better to work together. Only…"

"I didn't trust you."

She realized she was still partially within the circle of his arms. A few inches forward and she could be in his embrace again if she wished. This explained so much. And it only served to make her want him more.

"But you trust me now."

"For some reason that escapes me." For the first time he pressed his lips together in a small smile. She answered with a smile of her own, which grew and widened until they were both grinning at each other.

"Well I'll be damned," he muttered, and she thrilled to see his eyes twinkle at her.

"What?"

"I didn't want to tell you. I thought you'd see it as a reflection on the ranch. But you don't, do you."

"Of course not. It was hardly your fault. I told you before. I judge by what I see."

"Thank you." The words were simple, but Lucy heard the heartfelt meaning behind them. It was like one of the barriers between them had crumbled away.

"Let's work together, then. You need me to establish a relationship with His Highness. And I need you to prove that I'm capable of this job."

"Oh, I bet King Alexander already knows you're capable."

She was unable to stop the glow that spread through her at his easy praise. "I wouldn't be so sure." Only she knew the conversation she'd overheard between Alexander and her half brother the night before she'd departed. "I'm new, I'm young, I'm a woman in a male-dominated industry. And I'm also sure that we can come to an arrangement that will benefit both of us."

"I thought if you knew, you'd take your business elsewhere."

*And if you knew who I really am, all bets would be off.*

She dropped her eyes, staring at the flower in her fingers. The ranch had been aptly named. Prairie Rose. Beautiful. Strong. And resilient.

He trusted her. She pushed away the stab of guilt. She wished she could trust him, too. And she knew she could, about some things. But how could she possibly tell him now? Tell him who she was. If today had shown her anything, it was that Brody was a man of integrity. He'd definitely think twice about signing with someone who'd misrepresented themselves. What she'd told him was true, all of it. But she wasn't naive enough to believe that there weren't such things as lies of omission.

If she told him the truth they wouldn't be sitting on a boulder in the summer sun. And she wanted that desperately. Men like him didn't come along every day. And all too soon she'd be gone. Did she really want to waste what little time they had? Or could she keep quiet and work with him without the resistance that had plagued them thus far? She'd go back to Marazur with an agreement to prove her competence to her father, and Prairie Rose would have the prestige of a professional relationship with the King of Marazur.

"Lucy?"

She forced herself to look up and tried desperately to ignore the guilt of perpetuating her own deception. Maybe if she'd said something earlier…but now it was too late.

"I'm sorry," she whispered, wondering if those two words could possibly cover everything she was feeling.

"Come here," he commanded, opening his arms. She went into them willingly, the need for him overriding everything. She pulled her knees up to her chest and let him cradle her in his arms, her forehead against his neck so that his pulse beat reassuringly against her skin. The horses grazed, unconcerned at the turn of the afternoon, their hides gleaming as their tails swished the flies away.

And being held in his arms, Lucy realized the one truth she'd never expected: she'd been waiting for Brody all her life. Someone strong and secure and reliable. Someone who could face life's challenges and come out stronger and better. She'd never had that. Not in the whole time growing up. Alexander and her mother had made sure of that.

She pushed back, tilting up her head. The last time he'd kissed her. This time she wouldn't wait.

She touched her mouth to his, felt his breath mingle with hers as they hovered there. His lashes settled on his cheeks and she had the absurd urge to kiss his eyelids.

His teeth caught her lower lip before he pulled away.

"This probably shouldn't happen again. It makes things complicated."

"No, of course not. Neither one of us needs complications." She knew it was right despite the disappointment that settled heavily in her chest.

He thinned his lips and let out a whistle, calling the horses, and tucked his shirt back into his jeans. She slid off the rock and picked up her hat, jamming it on her head.

He put the bridle back on Ahab, slipping the bit into his mouth and giving him a pat before handing the reins to Lucy. But when she grabbed them, he didn't let go.

"I didn't mean for any of that to happen today," he said, and she knew the note of apology in his voice was genuine.

"I know that."

"And it shouldn't happen again. Letting this get too personal…"

"Brody." She knew what he was going to say and wanted him to stop. He couldn't be nice on top of everything. It would only make everything more difficult.

He looked her square in the eyes. "We both know this can't go anywhere. You're going back to Marazur and I'll never leave the ranch. I don't want you to get hurt."

She nodded mutely.

"It's for the best."

He turned to retrieve his mount's bridle, leaving her standing holding Ahab's reins, her eyes wide.

This wasn't in the plan at all.

She'd gone and fallen in love with Brody Hamilton.

# CHAPTER NINE

How it had happened she wasn't sure. It certainly hadn't been part of the plan and it was silly for it to have happened after only a few short weeks. But there it was.

She'd fallen for a man she could never have.

Lucy made her way back from the barns, her heart heavy. She'd thought her life in Marazur had been complicated. Not wanting to fit in but trying anyway, resenting her father yet trying to please him at the same time. Feeling shut up in the palace and yet having the freedom she'd been given at the stables. All of it was extremely uncomplicated next to her feelings for Brody.

And he'd done nothing but revert back to his cold, businesslike self since the afternoon at Wade's Butte. For days she'd wanted to ask about his ex-wife but couldn't find a way to without prying. He had a right to his own secret, even if not knowing was driving her crazy.

She shut the screen door quietly behind her. Tomorrow Prairie Rose was holding the annual barbecue and barn dance; the one Jen at the bakery had mentioned. And Lucy was seriously considering finishing up her business at Prairie Rose and leaving in the morning, before the festivities.

She entered the kitchen and found Mrs. Polcyk wrist-deep in pie crust and the unconventional sight of Brody peeling apples. She watched his strong wrist rotate the fruit as his paring knife cut thin curls of peel, the coils dropping onto a newspaper.

His smile stopped her in her tracks. It was more open than she'd ever seen it, teasing and warm. "You didn't think I knew how to peel an apple?"

Her lips quivered as Mrs. P. worked the pastry. "I didn't expect to find you here, that's all."

"Tomorrow's a big day. I've got the boys getting the loft ready for the dance and setting up the stage for the band. But before that, there's food."

"The boys? Those men are old enough to be your father."

Mrs. P. interjected dryly. "Yes, but aren't all men really boys, Lucy?"

She giggled as Brody's hip shot out and gave the housekeeper a definite nudge, making her adjust her balance.

Then Mrs. P. turned her head, her hands still in the mixing bowl, and sneezed into her own shoulder. "You're still fighting that cold," Lucy observed. "You're sure it's not hay fever or ragweed or something?"

Mrs. P. shrugged. "I've been taking over-the-counter stuff all week. It'll pass."

But Lucy saw her eyes looked red rimmed.

"I was thinking...you've been so great to me, but I don't need to contribute to the workload any more than I already have." It sounded logical to her ears. "I thought I'd leave in the morning and drive to Calgary, and take a flight out later in the day."

"Before the dance?"

She nodded. She could feel Brody's eyes on her but didn't want to look at him. Everything had changed for her since the trip to town and the afternoon at the butte. What she wanted from him and what was to be were two very different things. It would hurt less just to make a clean break. Brody didn't love her. And even if he did...the situation was impossible.

"You should stay. It's a fun day. You'd get to meet other ranchers, neighbors…"

But Mrs. P. broke off, tucking her head against her shoulder again. She slapped the ball of dough into the bowl and went to the sink to wash her hands. "I'm going to take something," she grumbled, and left the kitchen.

Brody calmly sliced apples into a bowl. "So you want to leave."

"I think that's best." When he didn't look up, she continued softly, "Don't you?"

Plop, plop. Slice after slice hit the bowl. He threw away one core and picked up another peeled apple. "You mean after the other day."

She swallowed. How could they talk about what had happened? To verbalize what they'd done…what she'd felt lying there in his arms…was impossible.

"Yes, after the other day. Nothing can happen, right? I mean I have to leave eventually. A day or two early shouldn't be a big deal."

"Mrs. P. was right about tomorrow. It's a lot of fun, and a chance for you to experience real western hospitality. Steaks on the grill and a night of dancing. Our way of celebrating the end of summer."

A night of dancing. She could imagine dancing with Brody, being held in his strong arms. It would be sweet. Bittersweet, knowing she was leaving. Why torture herself when she didn't need to? Being with Brody was a beautiful dream, not reality. And she'd learned not to indulge in dreams. It wasn't worth the thud at the end.

"You don't want me here, Brody." She paused. "You never have."

He finally looked up from his apples and their gazes caught. He looked on the verge of saying something for several seconds, then his shoulders relaxed as he changed his mind. He tossed away another core and picked up another apple. "If nothing else, think of Mrs. Polcyk. There's a lot for her to do, and she could use your help. I've never seen her under the weather for so long before."

Lucy stepped forward, concerned. "Do you think she might be ill?"

"I don't think so. But perhaps run down a bit. When she got sick I suggested postponing tomorrow but she insisted."

"Which is why you're paring apples."

He looked up again, his smile small and lopsided. "Exactly."

The knife grew still in his hand. "Stay," he said softly, and her heart turned over. If he only knew how much she wanted to do just that. "Stay and go back on Monday as you planned."

When he spoke to her that way she wasn't sure she could deny him anything.

"All right, then. I'll look after what I need to and ask Mrs. P. what I can do to help."

"Thank you, Lucy," he replied.

She got the sinking feeling she was making a mistake. But she'd agreed and now she had to send all the information to her father by e-mail rather than in person. He'd been already waiting to hear what she'd negotiated and his last message had sounded a little impatient.

"Tell Mrs. P. I'll be back down later to help," she murmured. "Excuse me."

The upstairs was quiet. It was just as well, anyway.

Lucy was going to go over her notes one last time and then type an e-mail to her father to finalize arrangements. Then she'd be able to focus on helping Mrs. P. and enjoying herself at the dance. Once that was over, she'd have to pack for her departure.

For leave she must, and they both knew it.

She opened her closet to get out her laptop and spied the skirt and blouse she'd bought from Agnes.

Straightening, she ran a finger over the soft floral print and beneath the satin fringe. She knew tomorrow was just a barbecue and as suited to jeans and boots as not, but she wanted to wear it. Wanted Brody to see her in something other than faded denims and her customary T-shirts. She wanted… she smoothed a hand over her wild curls. She wanted to feel pretty. Like a woman. The way she'd felt lying beneath him at Wade's Butte.

She shut the closet door with a firm snap, closing the outfit away. Nothing was going to happen between them again. She knew it was the right thing even as her body tingled, remembering his hands on her. She closed her eyes and opened them again, for when they were closed she could only see how his face had appeared above her in the moments before they'd kissed. Dark and dangerous and oh, so alluring.

No, she had to stay focused on business. Anything else would make leaving on Monday far too difficult. She turned to find Brody standing in the doorway to her room.

She shouldn't be glad to see him, but her heart thumped out a welcome anyway.

"Busy?"

She wished he didn't look so good. Seeing him there on the heels of her thoughts doubled the effect. Somehow his tall, dark looks had become her ideal. She shouldered the laptop and tried to smile.

"About to use your Internet connection, if I may," she answered.

He leaned lazily against the door frame, his face partially shadowed by the brim of his hat. A frisson of irritation flickered through her. He always wore it, and it lent him a sense of mystery she reacted to whether she wanted to or not.

"You're a little out of sorts, princess," he commented glibly, but never moved from the door, blocking her exit. She huffed out a sigh of exasperation.

"I wanted to e-mail King Alexander the latest news quickly. Before he's gone for the day." At his continued use of her nickname her temper flared. "Because of the time difference," she snapped. "You're obviously finished with your pie making."

"Tsk, tsk," he teased, leaning back even further. "No need to bite my head off. You know you're welcome to use the office anytime. I've told Mrs. P. that you'll be along shortly to give her a hand. But perhaps you should wait until you're not so hot under the collar."

He couldn't possibly know how much his words hurt, scoring her heart. Perhaps he was teasing, but he was right, she'd been sharp with him when he hadn't really done anything to warrant it. He couldn't know how much she felt as though she could belong here. Except, to do that she'd have to belong to him, and that wouldn't happen.

To compound her humiliation, tears clogged her throat.

She coughed to clear them. She'd never been a waterworks and she'd done enough crying since arriving at Prairie Rose.

"Hey." Brody pushed away from the wall, and the teasing curve left his lips. "I didn't mean to upset you. I was only kidding. What's wrong?"

Lucy bit down on her lip. There was no way she could tell him she was upset at having to leave. They'd shared some kisses and Brody had proven himself to be strong, resourceful, responsible. But…it wasn't as if he didn't still have secrets of his own. And for him to reveal what he had and omit his ex-wife…that told her exactly how deep the hurt went. She couldn't compete with that. Staying for the weekend was just prolonging the inevitable.

"I'm just tired, and anxious to get home again. Living out of a suitcase isn't my thing."

His words came out with a sardonic twist. "I'm sure you are. And I'm sure when you get there all your needs will be attended to."

"I didn't mean it that way!" The shoulder strap to the case slipped and the laptop thumped to the floor. "There has been nothing lacking in your hospitality." She stared into his cold eyes and couldn't resist adding, "Mrs. Polcyk has seen to that."

His gaze ignited. "Yes, she has. Still, not the equivalent of the House of Navarro, is it."

Her blood fired. "You know it isn't." What was he trying to accomplish? He knew as well as she did that Prairie Rose was lovely but it was no Mediterranean palace. Nor would either one of them have wanted it to be. He was baiting her and she wasn't sure why. If he was trying to push her away he was going the right way about it.

"I bet you live like a real princess, don't you, Lucy!"

She froze. The nickname was one thing but this was a little too close for comfort. She felt the color leach from her face. Two more days. Surely he wouldn't guess the truth so close to her date of departure. Wouldn't that be a kick in the pants.

The only thing she could do was call his bluff, to see if he meant it the way it had sounded. "Naturally. His Highness treats everyone equitably and with the greatest courtesy."

She sensed, rather than saw, his eyebrows lift. She'd heard her own words, haughty and dismissive and for the first time realized she'd *sounded* like a princess. She faltered, embarrassed. But she couldn't let Brody see her weakening. She covered her mistake with an added barb. "King Alexander never resorts to pointless arguments."

"Dammit, Lucy, you go too far!" He took a step into the room and she planted her hands on her hips. The haughtiness fled only to be replaced by temper. Lord, the man knew how to push her buttons!

"What are you going to do, Brody? Kiss me? It occurs to me that you have three gears—argue, kiss or the cold shoulder!"

She paused. She wanted him to kiss her. Her eyes dropped to his lips, knowing how deceptively soft they really were. Remembering how each tiny touch had ignited her skin. She wanted it again so badly that she could already feel his mouth on hers, even though he was glaring at her from four feet away.

She didn't want to argue. She didn't want him to walk away from her. What she wanted was to forget about all the reasons they were apart and simply launch herself into his strong arms. Feel his body against hers, the heat of his mouth on the soft skin beneath her ear.

"And what if I did? What if I kissed you?" His voice became soft, silky.

What he said only fueled her further. Her tongue slipped out over her lips. She had to stop this now. She was leaving in a few days, and to have anything more between them would be a mistake they would both regret. For him it would be kissing. For her it would be putting feelings into actions, and that was a whole other issue. She couldn't bear for history to repeat itself. Alexander and her mother had set an example she didn't want to follow, and it was impossible to miss the similarities in situation.

"We both agreed that was a bad idea," she stammered, taking a retreating step. She wanted it so badly she ached, but if he kissed her, she'd be lost…and tempted to tell him how she felt.

"You're right. It is a bad idea. And I'm not in the habit of making bad choices."

Oh, that stung.

"So now I'm a bad choice," she defended tartly, lifting her chin. He was giving her what she wanted…an escape route, and all she could do was to be angry with him for it. The man was so exasperating! Just when she'd decided to keep things as calm as possible before she departed, he had to come in here and push all her buttons, good and bad.

"Absolutely."

Her nostrils flared. "Worse than *she* was?"

The words flew out before she could think, and her lips sealed shut again as Brody took another menacing step.

"Her who?" he asked, the question low with warning, but she couldn't turn back now. It might be her only chance to know.

"You know who," she whispered. It was difficult to hold his gaze but she knew she must. "Your ex-wife."

He looked away first, staring out her window even though she knew he couldn't see anything at this distance.

She hadn't meant to blurt it out. He was entitled to his own secret. Now she'd gone and revealed that she'd known about his previous marriage.

She'd felt that same panic of discovery only moments ago when he'd made the princess comment. And now she was unfairly turning it on him. The obstinate set of his jaw told her he was loath to discuss it. And the way he avoided her gaze told her how much it still hurt him.

"Damn Mrs. Polcyk." The words were quiet and bitter.

"It wasn't her. She didn't betray your confidence. I'm sorry, Brody. I shouldn't have mentioned it. It was low. You provoked me and I blurted it out."

His head turned slowly toward her. "Taking you to town was a bigger mistake than I realized."

He was making this more awkward with every word.

"I didn't go prying, I promise. There was a picture of your family at the antique shop…"

"Agnes. And you didn't say anything."

"It wasn't my place, Brody. You have a right to your own secrets." Even though it hurt her to know it.

To her surprise he sighed and went to the window. She had expected him to argue and rail, but he didn't. He just treated it with a calm acceptance. Somehow she preferred the argument. It was what she understood. Especially since her own life had been turned upside down.

She waited, biting back the burning questions bubbling within her. The fact was he'd trusted her with the truth about Prairie Rose and his father, but he hadn't trusted her with this. And the past with the ranch was very painful, so that told her very clearly how much his divorce had cost him.

And now she'd fallen for him and wanted him to trust her with everything, knowing full well she had no right. Not when she was keeping such an important secret from him. "Do you want to talk about it?"

His reply was a dry, sardonic huff. "What do you think?"

Lucy bent and picked up the fallen laptop, putting it on the bed.

"I was right," she said finally, "when I said you had a broken heart. Because if she hadn't hurt you that much you'd be able to look at me right now."

He turned, the jut of his chin angled, trying to prove a point. "Do I strike you as the kind of man who talks his feelings to death?"

Lucy went to him, laid a hand on his arm. "You look like you'd rather be doing anything else."

His eyes fell on the spot where her hand met his arm.

It was pale against his darker skin. "It doesn't matter anymore. It was over a long time ago."

"You don't trust me, and that's okay." Her fingers glided down and linked with his. She got it. She didn't trust him with the truth, either.

"We've only known each other a few weeks."

"I know." She circled her thumb over his fingers. "Crazy, isn't it." Yeah, crazy that she cared about him so much in such a short amount of time.

"And this isn't part of your job."

"As much as we try, this stopped being about the job a long time ago."

"I know."

Brody pulled her into his arms. She felt good there, tucked against his chest, the flowery scent of her hair filling his nostrils. He wanted to trust her but knew why he didn't. And each time he held her, he knew it would be that much harder watching her leave. He argued with her because it was so much easier than admitting his feelings for her were more than they should be. Or could be. Yet she had this crazy way of keeping them together and making him tell her things he normally didn't speak of to anyone. He wasn't sure how she did that.

"Lisa married me expecting one thing and getting another. The ranch was profitable. It was expanding. We were making plans to build a new house for us. Something big, that's what she wanted. To make a statement. I loved her and was too blind to see she wanted that more than she wanted me."

"When?" Lucy asked simply. The warmth of her breath seeped through his shirt, and he closed his eyes.

"A few months after the accident. I was in charge of the ranch, and the money issue had come out."

Lucy pushed away and looked up at him. "You mean the fraud."

"Yes."

"You're kidding. She left you then?"

"She hadn't signed on for that, you see."

Lucy's lips pursed as if she'd just tasted something sour. A bubble of laughter rose in his chest. "For God's sake, Lucy.

You don't need to get all indignant on my behalf. It's over and done."

"But that's cruel."

"It was at the time. But at least she was honest about what she wanted in the end. She wanted a life I couldn't give her and had the sense to leave rather than drag things out and make us both unhappy."

Lucy went strangely quiet. She walked over to the bed and sat down. After several moments she looked up again. Her dark eyes were the most serious he'd ever seen them. "Is that why you resent me so much? You think I'm like her? You think the *kind* of life I have is more important to me than the people in it?" She blinked. "Is that why you call me princess?"

Though it could well be a mistake, he went to the bed and sat down on the spread beside her.

"Yes," he admitted, "but only at first. I don't think you're like Lisa now. I realized that the day I took you to the soddy and you didn't look down your nose at it. But the fact is we *are* from different worlds. And you must go back to yours soon. You wouldn't be happy somewhere like Prairie Rose." He looked away. He couldn't meet her eyes as he delivered one last truth: "I'm not sure I even believe in love, anyway."

He felt her shift beside him but continued on. He was right about this. Prairie Rose couldn't compare with Marazur and he wouldn't have believed her if she'd said it could. She had the job of a lifetime there and all the comforts she could ever want. And he wasn't in love with her. He couldn't be; he hardly knew her.

"Look, Lisa said she loved me but she didn't, not really. I'm not sure I was really in love with her, either."

"You don't mean that."

"I do."

Lucy spun on the bed, tucking one leg beneath her. It was the damnedest thing. She had him talking about things he'd never spoken to anyone about. It wasn't exactly a comfortable feeling, this outpouring of honesty.

"But, Brody… it's not in you to be in anything halfway. You put one hundred percent of yourself into everything you do. If I know anything from my time here it's that you care too much!"

He jumped up, spinning away from her. That was preposterous. This would all be better once she was gone for good. He wouldn't have to worry about a dark set of eyes tempting him to talk about things that couldn't be changed. Momentarily he hated her for it.

"Look," he said, stopping at the door and attempting to make his face as normal as possible. "You only have a few days left and it's pointless to spend them arguing or talking about stuff that doesn't matter." He ignored the wounded look on her face. Monday she'd be gone and over whatever it was that was between them. "Tomorrow is the barbecue and dance. Let's just enjoy it, okay?" He didn't wait for her to agree, but turned away and walked back down the hall. Dammit, he'd come here with the idea of teasing her about the dance and they'd ended up arguing again. There was no *normal* with them. Anytime he attempted it he either ended up fighting with her or, like today, getting in too deep.

The sooner she was gone the better, because each day she spent here was one more where his feelings grew more complicated.

# CHAPTER TEN

LUCY stared at herself in the full-length mirror. She should just take the outfit off and put her jeans back on. Brody had said they should enjoy today, but she hardly felt as if she could. How would it look to him now, for her to get all dressed up? Like she had designs on him?

The trouble was she did. Even though she knew she shouldn't. And her feelings grew stronger each time they were together.

She spun in front of the antique mirror and frowned. The secret of who she really was weighed even heavier these days. Perhaps she should have been honest with him from the beginning. It certainly would have made things less complicated between them. But she'd needed the time to just *be*. And it was too late to go back now.

Lucy sighed, smoothing her hands over the cotton of the skirt. She looked about fifteen years old in the outfit. She'd gathered her hair back from the sides with a clip and the rest of her gingery curls rioted around her shoulders. It made her appear even younger.

It was foolish to dress up for Brody, anyway. Day after tomorrow she'd be catching a flight back to Marazur and leaving Prairie Rose behind her for good. She'd finally sent that e-mail detailing stud fees and arrangements she'd made on Navarro's behalf. All that was left was to pack her things and drive back to Calgary for her flight home.

There was no denying, though, this place got to her. It was simple and uncomplicated, with no expectations. Here she was just Lucy Farnsworth, pain in the neck. She smiled a little to herself. Perhaps that was why she'd been drawn to it from the beginning. Prairie Rose—and Brody for that matter—seemed to take things to a common denominator. Hard work, loyalty and honor. Without the mess of family drama that marked her life in Marazur.

She turned away from the mirror. The outfit had been purchased in a moment of whimsy, and she'd wear it tonight regardless. It fit her, and made her feel like she fit in here, as well. She'd be back to reality soon enough.

A knock sounded on the door frame and she looked over her shoulder, seeing Mrs. P.'s sparkling eyes watching her. "Mrs. Polcyk! I was coming down to help you. After your cold, you shouldn't be doing all this yourself."

The woman had been cooking for the better part of two days, getting ready for the barbecue. Lucy had been so focused on finishing up business with Brody she hadn't had time to help put things together beyond a half hour of wrapping potatoes in foil this morning.

Mrs. Polcyk stepped into the room, much the same as Brody had the previous day. Lucy smiled. Privacy didn't seem to count for much at the ranch, but she didn't resent the intrusion, which was a surprise in itself. It made her feel included.

"You're a dear, and I appreciate the help," Mrs. Polcyk declared, smiling fondly. She stopped and gave Lucy an appraising glance. "Oh, Lucy. You are a picture."

Lucy smiled shyly. "You think so? I bought it at Agnes's."

"It's lovely. But…" She stared at Lucy's toes, bare except for the pale-pink polish on the nails. "You seem to be missing something."

Lucy looked down at her toes. "I know. I have to polish my boots."

She looked back up to find Mrs. P's eyes twinkling at her. The housekeeper was dressed in a pair of neat jeans and a white cotton shirt with *Prairie Rose* and a matching flower emblazoned on the breast. Her graying hair was gathered in its customary bun.

"I do feel somewhat overdressed," Lucy admitted.

"Nonsense. You look dressed for a dance. Stay here. I have an idea." Mrs. P. scuttled out only to return moments later with a shoe box in her hands. She came right into the room, placed the box on the bed, and lifted the cover.

Lucy reached out and put a single finger on the tip of one lovely pump.

"Oh, they're beautiful." Indeed, the fine navy leather was soft and cut in an intricate pattern, making them appear as though they were constructed of lace. One toe had a tiny scuff mark; otherwise they were unblemished.

"They match your skirt. Try them on."

Lucy sat on the edge of the bed and slipped a shoe over her foot. A perfect fit, which was a surprise. She stuck out her toes, admiring the delicate bow adorning the shoe top.

"They fit!" Mrs. Polcyk let out a delighted laugh.

"Mrs. Hamilton would have been so pleased to see them on a girl as lovely as you."

"Mrs. Hamilton?" Lucy drew her foot back, and a crease formed between her brows. She was still surprised at being called lovely.

"Mrs. Wade Hamilton. Brody's grandmother."

Lucy slipped off the shoe. "Oh, I can't, then. These must be—"

They were vintage, same as her outfit. And so perfect. But it wasn't right. It almost felt as if she was insinuating her way into something, and she didn't want that.

"Oh, sometime around the thirties I'd guess."

She put the shoe gently back in the box. "Then I absolutely musn't. They're antiques, and an heirloom."

"Did Brody tell you the story about Wade and Delilah when you rode out to the butte the other day?"

Lucy hoped she wasn't blushing; her cheeks felt warm and she couldn't meet Mrs. P.'s eyes. They'd talked of his dad, but other conversation had ceased because they'd been busy doing *other things*. "No, but he did mention it was his grandfather's favorite spot."

"It's named after his grandfather, you know. He used to go there hunting and such, and Delilah…oh, what a pistol she was." Mrs. Polcyk smiled in fond remembrance. "And a crack shot. Wade proposed to Delilah on that very spot. And they went back there every year for their anniversary."

"There's so much history here." Lucy looked longingly at the box. Brody had taken her *there?* A place that had so much family importance? What did that mean? Her heart trembled at the knowledge that he'd taken her somewhere so obviously special. Was it possible he wanted more from her? The soddy had been a test. Had that been another one?

Had she passed?

The thought expanded her chest. What would it be like to be a part of the Hamilton history? To truly belong? But that was absurd. She made herself push the shoes away. "I can't. It would be presumptuous of me."

But Mrs. P. insisted. "Life is meant to be lived, and shoes were made to be danced in. These have sat alone too long. Brody's mum had large feet, and the younger Mrs. Hamilton…" But she didn't finish the sentence.

"Lisa, you mean."

Mrs. Polcyk nodded, taking both shoes out of the box again. "Brody told me you knew."

"What was she like?"

Mrs. P. laughed, but this time it wasn't filled with her usual mirth. She put the shoes firmly in Lucy's hands. "Not worth a single hair on that boy's head, and that's the truth." She rested her hands on her knees. "Waltzed in here with her nose turned up demanding Brody build them their own place."

"So he said."

"She was beautiful, I'll give her that," the older woman conceded. "A little *too* beautiful for here. Certainly wouldn't have worn secondhand shoes." She angled a knowing look at Lucy. "He'd do better with someone more down-to-earth."

Lucy fought back the urge to laugh. It was as plain as the nose on her face that Mrs. P. meant her, and while there was a certain attraction to thinking she and Brody might suit each other, she also knew it would never be.

She thought of her opulent suite back in Marazur. It was about as far from down-to-earth as it could get. But when she'd moved there, Alexander had insisted that she be afforded the same comforts as her two half brothers. She frowned again, blinked. Maybe her father hadn't been trying to pressure her at all. Perhaps he'd only been trying to show her she belonged as much as Raoul and Diego did.

Mrs. Polcyk patted her leg and stood, her knees creaking. "You just put on your dancing shoes and come down when you're ready. Neighbors will start showing up anytime, and another pair of hands would be right welcome."

When she was gone, Lucy slipped the shoes on and did a few steps beside the bed, stopping at the mirror. She stared at her reflection. Most girls dreamed about being a fairy-tale princess and going to the ball. Tonight she just wanted to be an ordinary girl, doing a two-step. She reached up and took the clip from her hair, shaking out the curls the way she knew Brody liked it best.

He was right. Mrs. Polcyk was right. Life was meant to be lived. She should enjoy what little time she had left here.

There would be time enough to face reality tomorrow.

The yard was already filling up with half-ton trucks and cars as people started arriving. All laughing and smiling, dressed mostly in what Lucy recognized as everyday special: neat jeans, western shirts, polished boots and, of course, hats. After one look out the kitchen window, she turned back to Mrs. Polcyk. "What can I do?"

The older woman smiled warmly and held up a white cobbler apron. "Put this on so you don't mess that pretty dress. Brody's already lit the grills. All that's left to do is the coleslaw. If you don't mind grating cabbage."

"Of course not." Lucy moved swiftly, taking the apron and slipping the loop over her neck, tying the straps behind her back. A massive cutting board sat on the counter with halved cabbage heads waiting their turn to be made into slaw. She picked up the first and started grating, stopping every few minutes to fill the huge bread bowl at her side.

"Mind your knuckles, now," Mrs. P. cautioned, as Lucy got close to the end of her cabbage head.

Lucy grinned. "You do realize you can buy this already shredded, in lovely convenient bags."

"Wouldn't be any fun in that," Mrs. P. returned, her smile automatic. "Besides, it's not fresh, that stuff."

Lucy picked up another chunk of cabbage while watching Mrs. P. whisking vinegar and mayonnaise in a bowl. "And you make your own dressing?"

"Of course I do."

She was in the middle of telling Lucy her secret recipe when Brody slammed through the door, his hat set farther back on his head than usual and his eyes sparkling.

"Well, well," he said, teasing Lucy openly. "Here's our princess in an apron."

Her smile froze in place. Now that she knew the reason behind the name, it hit the heart of her even harder. She swiped the cabbage down harder than necessary and felt the scrape of a knuckle against the metal holes.

"Ow!" Her hand flew to her mouth as she sucked on the wounded skin.

Brody stepped forward as Mrs. Polcyk said calmly, "I told you to watch your knuckles."

He took her hand in his and turned it over, examining the scratch. "It appears there's going to be a little bit of you in the salad."

"Shut up," she muttered, trying to pull her hand away. But he held firm.

"You're going to need a bandage on that."

"I can get it myself."

And darn it all if he didn't laugh at her, leaning back from the waist and letting out a full-throated hoot. When he looked back at her, his eyes were gleaming. "You, Miss Lucy, look about ten years old when you stick out your lip like that."

She looked up in his mocking face and resisted the urge to stamp her foot. "Go away and quit distracting me. I can't be much help, if all you're going to do is stand here and aggravate me."

He let go of her hand and she exhaled, relieved that he wasn't touching her anymore. Each time he did her pulse leaped.

"Thank goodness it was only your hand, and not your feet," he remarked, winking. "You're going to need them for dancing later."

"Oh, go *on* with you! Don't you have steaks to grill or something?" He'd winked at her, for Pete's sake. An incorrigible flirt.

"Sure do." He grinned at her for another moment before turning on a booted heel and slamming back out the door. When Lucy sighed, Mrs. Polcyk held out a Band-Aid.

"He's an infernal tease, that boy. I'd forgotten how much."

Her words warmed Lucy. Did she bring something out in Brody he'd kept hidden? He'd seemed to loosen up since her arrival, but she'd thought at first that maybe it was just because they'd gotten to know each other better.

And now an offhand comment about his light mood. She'd like to believe she brought out some of his positive traits; he had so much to offer.

She took the bandage and doctored her knuckle. That way of thinking was pointless. She couldn't seem to reconcile the two things she wanted. Being with Brody had opened up a new world for her, one she didn't want to leave. But it had also made her think more about her relationship—or lack of it—with her father, and something inside her also wanted to explore that further. To get to know the man who had fathered her. To give him a chance. It certainly wasn't something she'd expected.

She picked up a carrot and started grating it to add to the slaw. It was Brody and his steadfastness who had made that possible, she realized. He'd made a promise to his father to look after the ranch and Mrs. Polcyk, in the same way that she'd promised her mother she'd go to Marazur and give Alexander a chance.

Hmm.

"If you're done there, I'll put the dressing on and we can start carrying things out."

"Oh, of course!" She shook away her thoughts and passed the bowl.

For several minutes they carried roasters and bowls to a string of folding tables set up as a buffet. Roasters full of foil-wrapped baked potatoes, baskets of fresh buns and butter, bowls of coleslaw and earthenware pots with homemade baked beans all made their way outside. Brody tended steaks on three separate gas barbecues at the end of the procession of tables, his ever-present hat shading his eyes from the sun. She could still feel his gaze on her every time she passed with her hands full. Finally there was nothing left to put out but the paper plates and cutlery. For a moment she allowed herself the fantasy that this was exactly where she was meant to be. As one of the hosts. As part of Prairie Rose and the community.

Brody looked at Mrs. Polcyk and said, "The first round of steak is ready."

Lucy's smile was as wide as his when Mrs. P. pulled out a rusted triangle and rang it several times, calling everyone to eat.

Lucy stayed behind the tables, helping Mrs. Polcyk to make sure everyone had what they needed. Every few seconds Mrs. P. or Brody would introduce her—to the Bancrofts, the Scholtens, a group of teenagers of various parentage who had come separately from their parents and wore trendy jeans and T-shirts rather than their parents' more traditional western wear. The Christensen brothers filed through; they'd provide the music later.

And on it went, men and women and children laughing and filling their plates and grabbing beers and soft drinks from washtubs filled with ice at the end of the tables. When everyone had gone through, the noise was horrendous, even outside: Lucy saw with some amazement that there were probably close to a hundred people seated at picnic tables all laid out between the house and the barn. It was loud and raucous, yet with a harmony to it, and she smiled to herself. Brody came behind her and put his hand on her waist.

"Get something to eat…while there's still something left."

She grinned. "Yes, boss."

He smiled back, his hat touching her curls. His face was so close to hers that she could feel the heat of his breath on the side of her neck. "Well. It only took you a few weeks to realize that."

"You wish."

The warmth disappeared but his hand remained on her waist as he leaned back at the waist, laughing. "You're never going to give in, are you."

It was meant as a joke, but the words seemed to ricochet around, hitting each of them with the truth. As much as she might want to, she knew Brody would never love her the way she wanted, and to give in to her own weakness would only hurt her further. "No, I'm not," she answered quietly, ducking away from his hand and grabbing a plate.

Mrs. Polcyk was filling her plate, and Lucy sat with her rather than with Brody, who found a place with a young couple and their kids as well as Jen, the woman from the bakery, who looked fresh and cute in a short jean skirt and boots. Lucy's eyes narrowed. She would not be jealous. She would not. It didn't matter to her one bit who Brody sat with. Or who he dated. It was absolutely none of her business.

"You want to tear her eyes out?"

Mrs. Polcyk's bland observation hit her, and she turned away from the sight of Brody laughing at something Jen said. "What?"

"The way you're glaring. If you want to put your mark on him, do it. I don't think he'd put up much of a fight."

"That's ridiculous."

"Is it?"

"I'm leaving day after tomorrow."

"We're all aware of that." Mrs. Polcyk cut into her steak with her plastic knife, slicing easily through the tender beef. "But a blind man could see there's feelings between you."

"Mrs. Polcyk…please." Lucy lowered her voice. "It's impossible. It's just easier this way."

The woman boosted herself up from her seat and gathered up her plate. "Well, hell," she said lightly. "No one said it was going to be easy, did they?"

Lucy tried to finish her meal after that, but she wasn't very hungry anymore. After a few minutes of pushing her potato around her plate, she gave up and put it in one of the trash bins set around the eating area. She went to help slice and serve pies, and thankfully Mrs. Polcyk said nothing more about it. One by one the pie plates were emptied of apple, cherry and lemon meringue. Washtubs were replenished with cans of pop. Laughter echoed through the barnyard and Lucy stood on the outside, with an untasted piece of apple pie on her plate, wondering how on earth she'd come to love this place so much in such a short time.

While Brody hitched up a small wagon and took the children for a quick hayride, all the women pitched in cleaning up; joking and teasing Mrs. P. and making their way through the kitchen as though it was their own. Lucy smiled and answered questions politely when she was asked.

This was what she remembered about Trembling Oak, too. It was a community. Everyone relied on each other. Of course, everyone stuck their noses in everyone else's business too, but that was a price that was paid. It was knowing that when push came to shove, you weren't alone. It all became too much and Lucy fled before anyone could see the strange look on her face or how she felt the need to cry.

She escaped out the back, taking deep breaths to get her emotions under control. The sun began to set, becoming a beautiful bronze ball that painted the sky with pinks and purples as it dipped toward its bed behind the Rockies. The brash light of summer softened, setting everything with a misty haze. The golden and green fields were dotted with gorgeous, gorgeous horses and railroad tracks of fences.

Music started up, the testing strains of guitar and violin finding their pitch before somehow making their way to an agreed key and song. She listened for a few minutes, her foot tapping lightly. She could skip out on the whole thing and be completely miserable. Or she could join in and enjoy herself and hopefully take back to Marazur a beautiful memory of dancing and laughing on a summer's night.

There really was no choice.

She turned the corner of the house and headed toward the "old" barn, the one that held no livestock now but served as storage below and an abandoned loft overhead. Battered wooden stairs led up to the loft, with several people standing on the platform outside the double doors that were rolled open. She climbed the stairs and ventured a peek inside.

The band was on a raised platform, nearly laughing as they played a tune and people two-stepped in circles around the floor. Boots and jeans paired up with sneakers and shorts as young danced with old. Benches were lined up against the side of the room for those not dancing, but only a handful of people were seated. The music was lively and good; it would be hard to remain still for long.

At the end of the first song, they went immediately into another two-step. Brody appeared at her side. "Care to?"

"Don't you have host duties?"

"Absolutely. As the host it's my job to dance with the prettiest girl in the place."

"Go on."

"Why else did you dress up in that outfit, anyway? It was made for dancing. Or so Agnes has bragged enough times. It is from her shop, right?"

She lifted her chin and looked away. How could he know

that? Unless Mrs. Polcyk had loose lips. After her observations at supper, she wouldn't be surprised.

"And besides, you stared at me all through supper."

Her head snapped around. "You're impossible!"

"Maybe, but I'm a helluva good dancer, Miss Farnsworth. And if you don't want to dance, there's lots of ladies here who will."

He held out his hand and lifted an eyebrow, challenging her.

"Fine," she said with a glare. "One dance. It would look funny if I didn't, I suppose."

She took his hand, shocked when he spun her around quite efficiently and settled his hand at her waist. Instantly he guided her into the easy rocking steps of the dance, the entire swirling circle of dancers moving around the floor as if they did it every day of their lives. And damn his hide, if he wasn't right after all. He *was* a sublime dancer. She'd known how to two-step since she was ten, but he made even spinning turns simple as he guided her first one way, then the other, beneath his arm and bringing her effortlessly back in step.

"I told you."

He grinned down at her as the band thumped and twanged their way on, the rough, enthusiastic quality of the music creating an energy that vibrated from the soles of her feet up. "Hmph."

"Miss Lucy, you're adorable when you pout. It makes *all* of your freckles stand out."

That did it. She stomped down hard with her vintage pump on his toe, breaking their rhythm. She attempted to twist out of his arms but his hand gripped her wrist quite efficiently and swirled her back into the dance.

"Good thing for you I'm wearing boots," he remarked. The teasing smile was still in place but something darker glittered in his eyes.

"You've been an arrogant pain in the behind for the better part of two weeks, and tonight you turn into an incorrigible tease. Go turn your charms on someone else who will appreciate them."

"Do you really want me to?"

"Yes, I think I do."

"Okay."

The music ended and he let her go. The air seemed abruptly cool, now that there was space between them, and she tried very hard not to miss his warmth.

"Thanks for the dance, Lucy."

He walked away unconcerned, and when the band started up again, he crossed the floor and led Jen out for a waltz.

# CHAPTER ELEVEN

SHE wanted to stay mad, but it was hard when he danced and smiled so effortlessly with everyone. When the Christensen brothers fired up a polka, she couldn't stop the smile at the sight of him stomping around the floor with Mrs. Polcyk in his arms. When the first group was well winded and left the floor, the band immediately went into another polka, and Lucy was grabbed by a neighboring rancher she dimly remembered meeting at supper.

The band announced a break, and it seemed everyone made a beeline for the tubs full of pop and bottled water. Lucy grabbed a water and twisted off the top, scanning the area for Brody. But he was gone.

She saw lights in the barn and wondered if he'd gone to check on the horses that weren't out in the pasture. Suddenly the cool quiet of the barn sounded more appealing than the dance and crush of strangers. For a while she'd forgotten that she didn't truly belong, but seeing the laughing faces reminded her that she was an outsider. She looked at the long structure, suddenly needing the horses. They'd never failed her before.

She made her way across the soft grass, noting that the barn door was open. What she didn't expect was the youth that came barreling out at save-my-neck speed or the sound of sobbing from within.

She peeked around the corner, and immediately saw Brody, his arms around a girl and his face looking incredibly worn as the girl did her best to soak his shirt through with her tears.

"It'll be okay, Suze," she heard him say gently. "He's a good kid. You both are. It just didn't work out."

"But I love him," came the plaintive reply, borne on hiccupy sobs.

"I know."

That was all. No trying to persuade her it didn't matter, no telling her she was too young for such an adult emotion. The girl couldn't be more than seventeen, but Brody simply offered her a shoulder.

Lucy sighed. How she'd wished for someone like Brody when she was growing up. Someone who would simply accept her and be on her side. No matter what. If she thought he'd be this way for her, she'd explain about her father. But he wouldn't understand. And so she would keep her secret to herself.

At her audible sigh, Brody looked up. He tensed, seeing her there, and the girl straightened and turned when she sensed the change in him.

"I'm sorry," Lucy offered, seeing the girl's sudden embarrassment. "I didn't mean to intrude."

"It's okay." The girl stared at her feet, clearly embarrassed at getting caught out.

"Lucy, this is Suzanne." Brody performed the introduction quietly, his hand still secure, comforting on her shoulder. Protecting her.

"Hello, Suzanne," she offered softly. "I'm Lucy."

She was still trying to get past the gentle way he was looking after the teen. It was so much the way a father would, or a big brother. Both things that Lucy had missed out on growing up. Brody would be such a good father…the thought snuck in unbidden and she chased it away.

The music started up behind them; the band's break was over. "Did you come with Matt?" Brody asked Suzanne.

She nodded, tears threatening again at the boy's name.

"But your mum and dad are here and can drive you home," he continued.

Another nod.

Brody sent a pleading look at Lucy, that said he'd suddenly run out of ideas about what he should do. She stepped in, knowing that the only thing worse than breaking up was breaking up in public and having everyone see the evidence of crying. She stepped closer. "Well, Suzanne, you can't go back to the dance like that, can you." She smiled. "Come on up to the house and I'll help you get fixed up."

"You will?"

"Of course I will."

She ignored the gratitude she knew was in Brody's eyes, instead aiming her smile directly at the distraught teen. She couldn't look at Brody with all these feelings bubbling up inside her. His teasing was infuriating, but his caring tonight only showed her what a good man he was beneath the cocky smile or stony reticence. Seeing this side of him made it even more difficult for her to run away from her growing feelings.

"I'll bring her back," she murmured.

"Thank you, Luce."

A shudder went through her as he used the shortened version of her name. She led Suzanne away, happy to retreat into the cool air of the yard as they made their way to the dark farmhouse.

It was half an hour before they returned to the dance, Suzanne wearing a weak smile and a fortifying coat of makeup and Lucy with a sort of breathless anticipation of seeing Brody again. Of maybe dancing with him. The gaiety was in full swing. Moments after arriving in the loft she was snagged for a two-step and a waltz. Her gaze sought Brody out again and again as they both danced with other people. She sat out a line dance, choosing to watch the younger people boot-scoot. But the singer announced the "barn dance," and pairs formed up into two circles; men on the inside and women on the perimeter. Lucy was captured by an older man with a huge grin and a larger belt buckle. As one couple demonstrated the steps to any newcomers, Lucy memorized them in her mind.

The music started and she faltered only once before being passed on to her new partner. After three more she had the steps down pat and relaxed.

Until she got to Brody.

He didn't smile, and neither did she. He took her hand in his, the warmth seeping through the skin, the heat of it heavy, even though he held her fingers lightly. She followed the steps, at each beat wondering how to say what she wanted and knowing she'd sound like a complete idiot if she said exactly what she was thinking.

They were halfway through the sequence and time was growing short when he said over the fiddle and guitar, "Thanks for what you did for Suzy."

"It was nothing." Their heels touched, then their knees while Lucy struggled to say what she felt before he handed her off to a spotty-faced boy behind her. "You were very good with her, Brody."

His gaze caught hers, dark and magnetic, but the steps pulled them apart.

Another half hour passed, the music getting faster and the laughter louder. She was gasping for air and fanning her face after something frenetic called the Butterfly, when the band slowed it down and called Brody to the stage.

"He thought he could avoid us all night, but it's time for Hamilton to favor us with a tune." At Brody's wave-off, the singer leaned into the mike with a lopsided grin. "Too late now, Hamilton. Get your butt up here."

Lucy watched, amazed, as Brody stepped up onto the stage and took the guitar he was offered. He cradled it against him as he perched on a plain wooden stool, and Lucy trembled as their eyes met. His, so very dark, so knowing, slightly shadowed by the black brim of his hat, yet she knew he was looking straight at her. *Inside* her. The way only he could. Just moments ago she'd been in his arms, cheeks flushed with exertion and flirtation as he took her around the floor in the Butterfly. The memory of the heat of his body close to hers was still present.

He sat on the wooden stool, one long denim-clad leg stretched out straight, ending in his boot which braced against the floor. And looking down for a moment, he started to play.

It wasn't a song she recognized, but the quiet sound of the guitar filled the loft. Every single person there had stopped to listen, to watch, as their neighbor, their friend, picked out a melody.

He lifted his head and looked straight at her as he started to sing.

*This can't be happening,* she thought, taking a step backward. He had to be too good to be true. There had to be something about him that would send her in the other direction. A cowboy dedicated to his ranch and his livestock and his family, with a ready smile and a willing hand. One who, she understood now, gave everything for his family. One who would rather die than break his code of honor. On top of all that, he could *sing*.

They'd done such a good job of denying that there was anything more than sexual attraction growing between them; or at least pretending to deny it. Even when they'd kissed out at Wade's Butte, they'd both turned away from it in the end, knowing it would be a mistake. But today he'd seemed to shed all his worries, and it made him sexier than ever. She should look away. She shouldn't be standing like an idiot on the wood floor, gazing like some groupie at the sexy cowboy in the dark hat. She should get out of the barn right now. And get far away.

But then, she knew Brody well enough to know that if she did that, he'd come and find her. She tensed as she considered that possibility. What would happen if he found her at the barn…in the house…by the pond?

Was that what she really wanted, then? Did she want him to find her? If he did she knew what would happen. Whatever this was that had been growing between them wouldn't be denied. Not on a night like tonight. Too much had happened and they were both well aware that time was growing short. So what *did* she want from Brody? A quick roll in the hay? Because anything more from him was out of the question. And anything less would never be enough.

His eyes pinned her as his voice, deep and smooth, reached out. His fingers plucked at the strings as he ended the first chorus…each word branding itself on her heart.

She blinked. It was too much. Somehow…at some point Brody Hamilton had snuck past every single one of her defenses.

Somehow, in such a short space of time, he'd become *everything.* And she had to stop it, and stop it now. She was leaving. She had to go back. She knew it and accepted it, as deeply as she understood exactly what it was she was feeling: she was completely in love with him.

The silk of his voice slid up her spine as she stood on the dance floor alone while couples circled slowly around her. Back to Marazur. Away from Brody. Away from Prairie Rose. Away.

And when his voice faded away with the last chord of the song it was just the two of them, caught in the moment, together though apart, and she understood exactly what it was her mother had meant when she'd spoken about Alexander.

Sometimes the choice was simply taken out of your hands. The thought cloaked her in fear.

She looked down at her feet, clad in his grandmother's shoes. There was no use in denying that she was connected to Prairie Rose now. But she couldn't do this. She couldn't set herself up to get her heart broken. She had seen her mother remain single her whole life because she'd given her heart to a man who didn't value it.

There'd been enough pain already. Enough dealing with her mother's death and promises she'd made. She had to leave. Leave the dance—surely Brody wouldn't walk out since he was hosting—and pack so she could get back to the life that was waiting for her. She'd dawdled enough.

The band had started up another song, a faster one, and people were crowding the floor once more. Lucy spun on her heel and headed straight for the doors and the stairs. The fairy tale—if it could be called a fairy tale—was over.

She was on the fourth step when he called out behind her. "Lucy! Wait…"

She kept going, nearly frantic now in her need to get away. She dipped around a couple of teens who were lazily leaning against the railing. Hit the dirt at the bottom of the stairs and wished she were in boots instead of heels.

"Lucy…" His arm reached out and caught hers and her eyes slammed shut.

"Don't. Oh God, Brody, please don't."

She heard the plea in her voice and was helpless. If it took begging so be it.

"Let's get out of here," his voice rumbled close to her ear, and her eyes snapped open as quickly as they'd shut.

"Are you kidding? I can't…we can't…what will…"

"Stop stammering. People are staring. Is that what you want?"

He pulled her halfway around so that she was staring up into his dark eyes.

"So help me God, Lucy, we need to talk about this, and I don't want to do it with an audience, but I will."

She nodded dumbly. He took her hand and led her away, his long strides forcing her to nearly jog in the shoes. She shivered even in the long sleeves; once the sun went down the air seemed to turn clear and cold.

Brody stopped several feet away from the shore of the pond. A few late-night ducks bobbed on the surface. The music from the dance echoed from behind them, punctuated with shouts and laughter from the partygoers inside. Instead of brash, the sounds had a misty quality about them.

"Brody, I—"

"Be quiet."

She faced him, her expression blank at his sharp tone. She didn't know what to say. His jaw ticked once, twice in the shadows and the unholy urge to touch the strong angle ran through her. "I just—"

"Dammit, Lucy, don't you ever listen?"

She opened her mouth to respond. And instead found it covered with his.

Oh. My. God. They were the only three words that she could find space for in her brain. His body was hard and unrelenting as he pulled her up against him. One hand captured her head just behind her ear, and his lips were a torturous delight as they assaulted hers. This was more demanding than any other kisses she'd experienced. His arms cinched her tightly in place and she gave up any hope of resisting. It was pointless. She wanted this as much as he did.

He planted his feet, and one hand pressed against her bottom, pulling her flush against his hips. Once she was there his hand slid up her ribs to cup a breast, and she moaned into his mouth.

"Let's go to the house," he suggested, the words strident with desire.

Lucy slid her lips away from his, closing her eyes. "I can't." The fact that she wanted to bit into her. "Please, Brody, just kiss me again."

He obliged with no resistance whatsoever, but within moments it became clear to her he hadn't abandoned his initial objective.

She pushed him away, staggering backward. "No!" she gasped. "I can't. Oh, please, Brody, stop. I'm leaving on Monday. This would be a mistake."

"Why?" He had dropped his hold on her but was still close enough she could feel the heat from his body. It was too hard to think with him right in front of her, but this was one time she couldn't walk away.

"Because I'm leaving! Because we both know it won't go any further than this one night, and I'm not the sort of person that does that."

"And you think I am?"

She covered her lips with her hand for a moment, torn between simply wanting to give in and knowing she absolutely must not. "You're the one that suggested it, so I guess you must be."

"I haven't propositioned a woman in my life, Lucy Farnsworth. I've never asked a woman for sex."

She laughed harshly. He was making it easier after all. "You mean you don't *have* to ask, right? Well I'm not going to be some doe-eyed girl ready to fall all over herself to get in your bed!"

He stepped forward again, his lips a thin line and his jaw hard with anger. "Do you think that's what I want from you? Do you?"

She stepped up so they were toe-to-toe. "That's what you said! And seeing as my time left here can be counted in hours, what else am I supposed to think! What *do* you want from me, Brody?"

He spun away, took a few steps and stopped, his hands on his hips.

For long seconds he said nothing, while Lucy waited. She could tell he was trying to think of what to say, and for some reason she wanted to hear it. Wanted to hear him justify all the reasons. If she could only make him out to be as shallow as he sounded right now, it would be so much easier for her to leave.

The dance seemed a distant event. The cool nighttime breeze filtering through the trees was the only sound, wrapping itself around them. Lucy looked up. One by one, stars dotted the black night around them. She picked out the dipper, then the line that meant Orion and the *W* shape that meant Cassiopeia. A queen of unparalleled beauty. Lucy smiled sadly. She wasn't a queen. She wasn't even a princess, not really.

Brody turned back to her, his features softened slightly. "I'm sorry, Lucy. I got carried away. I got..."

"You got...?" She pinned him with the question.

"I got scared, all right? I find myself not wanting you to leave. There's something between us, and I'm not sure I'm ready for things to go back to normal around here after you go."

"What do you expect me to do, then?"

She waited with bated breath. Would he ask her to stay, extend her time at Prairie Rose? Would he suggest something more than one night of passion? At this point she would grasp at anything. Anything to make this feeling of emptiness at the thought of going home go away.

"It's not what I want *from* you, Lucy, don't you get that? It's what I want *for* you."

She held her breath. This was madness. Utter and complete madness. He couldn't do this to her now. Now when she had no choice. She'd given her word. And he knew it. Why couldn't he be selfish? How could she want to be in two places at once? She closed her eyes, beyond confused, and with no idea how she was supposed to feel anymore.

"I know you have to go," he said softly. "I know it because it's what I'd do. I'd make the sacrifice to keep a promise."

"You already did."

"Yeah, I did. And I don't regret it, I don't. I love this ranch and I love my father, and loving them has never been a burden. It's the decisions, the responsibility that weighs heavy. But it's mine."

"I know that, Brody. I wish I could do something to help..."

"You have, Luce," he insisted, cutting her off. "More than you know. You have no idea what you have done for me. And I want you. You know it. Is that fair? No. But it's true. I want you tonight and you should know that before you walk away. You should know that you are wanted."

Tears clogged her throat. It was even more potent when he said it in that calm, rational voice. The beauty of being wanted sliced through her like a painful knife. Everything now was a double-edged sword, healing and hurting at the same time. "Brody, don't."

"If I don't say it now I never will. Lord, woman, how you got me to talk. Now I can't seem to stop. I need to say all the things now I would want to say on Monday when you're leaving and I won't be able to."

She fought back tears. This tender side of Brody called to her heart more than any other.

He cupped her cheek in his wide, rough hand: "I want you

to be happy, and chase all your dreams, whatever they are and wherever they take you."

"I gave up on dreams a long time ago."

"I know, but you shouldn't have. And I wish I could carry your burdens for you. You've already had to carry so much, Lucy, with your mum dying. I don't want you to look back on your time here with regret but with a smile, because you changed so much for me. I want you to—"

He cleared his throat, and her heart cracked a little more.

"Life is full of choices, Lucy. The secret is picking the answer that means the most to you."

Lucy closed her eyes, unable to look in his earnest face. He couldn't possibly know how torn she was. She wanted to go home. She needed to see for herself what waited for her there. At the same time, she felt as if Prairie Rose was home.

"What if I don't know what that is?" Her voice was a whisper, carried on the westerly wind that was coming down from the mountains. "What then?"

"Then you look for the answer."

She waited. If he asked her now, she wasn't sure she could say no. If he asked her to stay with him she might just do it.

But he never asked.

And he'd never said he loved her, she realized, her heart sinking. In fact, she distinctly recalled him saying that he didn't believe in love anymore.

There really wasn't a choice to make. She couldn't stay and love a man who didn't love her back.

"Okay," she answered.

She took a step away, but his hand reached out and grabbed her wrist. "Don't go. Not now."

"I'm cold."

The chill was deepening as midnight approached. The stars hung close to the earth, and as she looked up, a satellite streaked across the sky, a perfectly curved path through the inky blackness.

"Then dance with me."

In the distance they heard the last dance start playing up in the loft. They both turned their heads toward the wistful strains of "Let Me Call You Sweetheart" swaying toward them on the wind.

"Dance with me," he whispered, "one last time."

His wide hand was warm on her waist, her fingers enclosed in his as he started to lead her in a waltz, their feet making shushing noises in the soft grass. She closed her eyes, knowing that somehow a million stars shone down on them and she would have wished on each and every one if she could have figured out exactly what it was she wanted.

Their steps grew smaller and shorter, and within a few bars of the song she was pressed against the warm breadth of his chest, listening to his heart beat against her ear and knowing that at least once in her life she had experienced a completely perfect moment.

As the fiddle faded away, they were no longer dancing but simply swaying to the one-two-three rhythm of the song. Somewhere the band said good-night. Voices became louder as the barn cleared out and people made their way to their vehicles. And still she remained in his arms, unwilling to pull away. Because she knew when she did it would be the last time he ever held her.

## CHAPTER TWELVE

WHEN Brody came downstairs, Lucy was already at the break-fast table. He took his seat opposite her, noting that she looked very prim and put together in a tidy white sweater. Her hair was up, too…not a corkscrew curl in sight. Instead it was pulled back and twisted up in something elegant. He wondered what had prompted her change from the usual jeans and T-shirts. Was it a reaction to their intimacy of last night? He smiled behind a finger.

After she'd left him at the pond he had known he'd said too much. The music and moonlight had made him all senti-mental and…and needy. She'd finally run from him and he'd let her go, knowing that if he'd followed he probably would have said something he couldn't take back. And that *would* have been foolish. It was just the dance and her leaving that had made him speak the way he had.

She put a forkful of scrambled eggs on her fork and looked up at him. "Good morning."

"Good morning. How did you sleep?"

He winced at his own inanity. Good Lord. He was reduced to inquiring after her sleep now? He really was getting stupid over her. His own fault for being able to think about nothing other than her lying between the sheets last night, wonder-ing if she was as restless as he.

"Fine."

Two spots of color erupted on her cheeks, and he knew she was lying. Good. Because he hadn't slept worth a damn, either. He'd tossed and turned, not sure if he wanted to go to her room and press his case or be completely irrational and ask her to stay on.

"Brody, I'm…I've decided to leave this morning. I'm going to drive up to Calgary and catch an earlier flight first thing tomorrow."

Leaving?

He turned his head toward the counter as the phone rang, but he let it. "Surely there's not that much of a rush." A tiny thread of panic slid through him. He wasn't ready for her to go. He'd thought he would have a whole day left. The phone stopped ringing; either whoever was on the other end had hung up or Mrs. Polcyk had answered it.

"One day sooner isn't going to make any difference. Our arrangements are all finalized. I don't need to be here any longer."

Her tone was cool. He stared at her for a long moment, but her gaze remained fixed on her plate. She'd given up eating, just pushed around a few fried potatoes for show.

"Stay, Lucy," he said suddenly. "Stay here."

Mrs. Polcyk came in from the office, her face suddenly drawn. "Lucy, phone's for you. It's *him*."

Brody watched as Lucy tore her gaze from his. He would have sworn from the way she was just looking at him that she was actually considering it. But the moment was lost as she turned to Mrs. P.

"Who, him?"

"King Alexander."

Lucy's fork hit her plate. "Tell him I'll call him back, that I'm busy for the moment."

"I already said you were at breakfast and he said…he said…" Uncharacteristically, the housekeeper faltered.

"He said?" Brody urged her, his brow furrowing. It wasn't like Mrs. P. to be flustered no matter who she was speaking to.

"He said to tell Princess Luciana he wished to speak to her right now."

Brody's gaze snapped to Lucy's. Her face had gone completely white. The words bounced around in his brain. Princess Luciana. Lucy Farnsworth. Princess Luciana.

She pushed back her chair, avoiding Brody's eyes which was just as well, because he couldn't keep the shock from his features. So many things raced through his mind he could hardly process them all; things she'd said or done over the past few weeks that suddenly made sense with a clarity so intense he couldn't believe he hadn't seen it before.

"Thank you, Mrs. P."

She extricated herself from the table gracefully and walked down the hall, with two pairs of eyes watching her every step.

"Did you know?" Brody asked Mrs. P. the moment the office door was closed.

"No."

Brody pushed his plate away, feeling sick. He'd made such a fool of himself. "Not a clue, Mrs. P?"

"None, Brody. I took her for who she was."

"Who she pretended to be, you mean."

Mrs. Polcyk didn't answer, just bustled through clearing plates. It was obvious no one was eating any more.

"What are you going to do?" she asked finally.

"What I should have done in the first place," he replied darkly. And he left the table and made the long walk down the hall to the office.

Lucy hung up the phone and rested her forehead on a hand. Her father hadn't known what he'd done, she was sure of it, and he'd wanted to talk to her now instead of two days from now because one of their mares had fallen and he wanted her input before making a decision.

Who knew her father would be so sentimental? His favorite mare had stepped in a hole and broken her leg. The vet had been called and was recommending they put her down, and Alexander had called her for her opinion. She sighed. Too bad she couldn't give him the answer he wanted. She knew the mare as a lovely, gentle soul. But the recovery for an older mare was long and difficult, and no matter what his attachment, simply not fair to the animal. She'd seconded the vet's opinion without a moment's hesitation. But it was never easy putting a horse down.

Brody strode into the room and she sighed, knowing exactly why he was there. "Can we do this later, please?" she asked, exhausted. She lifted her head from her hand and studied him with weary eyes. "I've just ordered a horse put down and I'm not up to an argument with you."

"That's too bad, because you're getting one."

Lucy inhaled deeply. "You're angry. I get that. But I'm leaving anyway."

"You can't possibly think that's enough of an explanation. Not after last night."

"Last night was a moment of whimsy."

"They why can't you look at me when you say it?"

She forced her gaze upward again. His words were soft but his eyes were deadly. And she knew they were going to have this out, here and now, anyway.

"I am Princess Luciana of Marazur," she conceded. "And that's nothing more than a technicality, because I'm also Lucy Farnsworth, daughter of Mary Ellen Farnsworth of Virginia. And that's who I was until a few months ago when my mother told me who my father was."

"I see." He bit the words out like they were distasteful, and

Lucy was torn between wanting to yell at him and wanting him to understand.

"No, Brody, you don't. And I knew you wouldn't and that's why I didn't tell you."

"So you lied to me instead. You pretended to be someone you weren't."

"No!" She stood then, bracing her hands on the desk. "Don't you get it? I know who *Lucy* is. I don't know who Luciana is, and coming here I got a chance to just be *me* again! I got to be myself."

"You let me believe you were merely an employee for Navarro stables. When I asked you how you got hired, you said a friend-of-a-friend kind of thing. You lied right to my face. And that's inexcusable, Lucy."

"Of course it is," she scoffed, feeling the stirrings of anger. "You're perfect Brody Hamilton. The king of loyalty and honor and righteousness! The man who lost everything and came back better than ever. Tell me, Brody, did you make *any* mistakes along the way? Because you lost everything eight years ago and I lost it just this year and I have some catching up to do!"

"Don't." He made a slashing motion with his hand. "Don't turn this on me. You…we…I told you things, Lucy. I told you things about myself and this place because you made me trust you. And it was all based on a lie. You should have come clean with me."

Lucy came around the corner of the desk. "Don't you think I know that? Don't you think I felt guilty about it? Let me explain, Brody. Let me explain all of it, and then you can judge me however you want.

"My father met my mother when he was in Virginia, and they fell in love. Or so the story goes. He was crown prince but still very young, and recently widowed. He had two small sons at home. And she fell for him like a rock. According to my mum, he was rebelling a bit at being left a single father at such a young age. He flew her to Las Vegas and married her. And they spent a few weeks at Trembling Oak, without having told anyone what they'd done.

"He went back to Marazur with the plan to eventually tell his family that he had a new wife. But before he sent for her, the unthinkable happened. His father had a heart attack and died, and Alexander was forced to take over the throne. Imagine the PR nightmare of coronation with a new American bride at his side, fresh from a wedding at a Vegas chapel. My mum came from pretty humble beginnings, and that's putting it generously. It would have been an embarrassment.

"Oh, Mum was very generous in her opinion of him. She said that he didn't want to put her through that. That the pressures of being thrust into the position of queen and wife and stepmother were great and he wouldn't blame her for not wanting to take them on. And she didn't. Days before the coronation, their marriage was legally ended with no one the wiser."

"He didn't know about you?"

She shook her head. "No, and I knew nothing about him until the doctors said her cancer was inoperable. Even then she maintained that it had been her choice. That she hadn't wanted to be the cause of a scandal within a family that had already dealt with enough."

"So she made you promise."

"Yes, the same way you promised your father you'd look after Prairie Rose and Mrs. Polcyk. She made me promise to give Alexander a chance and I couldn't deny her, not when she was looking up at me with eyes so tired and in pain and yet with that little bit of hope. And like you, I couldn't break my word."

She licked her lips, catching her breath. At least he was listening now, and maybe understanding a little bit. "I went. And

I've never felt more out of place in my life. My half brothers are carbon copies of Alexander—tall, dark, Mediterranean looks as opposed to my pale skin and red hair. They've grown up with titles and servants, and I'm used to a cup of tea in the kitchen. In the end Alexander didn't know what to do with me, so he sent me here. And I was determined to show him that I knew what I was doing." She gave a small sad smile. "Determined to show you, too. To show you both that Lucy Farnsworth is *somebody*. And so I kept my title a secret."

She closed her eyes for a moment, then opened them, walked across the floor past him and shut the door, enclosing them in the office.

"Let me ask you something. Would you have told me about Lisa if I hadn't let it out when we were arguing?"

At the set of his jaw, she knew the answer. "I thought so. I wasn't the only one keeping secrets."

"I never pretended to be someone I wasn't!" he said, stepping forward.

"It was still a secret. It was something close and painful to you that you didn't want to talk about. And the more you didn't talk about it, the more I knew how painful it must be to you, and I tried to respect your right to your own secrets. Because I had mine. And then once you told me about her, I knew I could never tell you who I was. You already thought I was like her. And you still do. I can see it in your eyes!"

"Well, she certainly pretended to be something she wasn't in order to get what she wanted."

That stung, especially since there was some truth in it. "Yes, but her motives were different from mine."

He turned away from her, but she could see the stubborn set of his jaw.

"Don't you think an ex-wife would have been a good thing to mention after we went to Wade's Butte? Why'd you do that, anyway? Why'd you take me to that place in particular? I know what it means to this family. It means something."

"I wanted to be with you, that's all."

Her heart surged at his words until he deflated it. "Only, I guess I didn't know who I was with after all."

His voice was so bitter it caused her physical pain. Her stomach cramped as she felt herself sinking deeper and deeper yet knowing they had to get it all out so they could leave it behind them. "And I felt horrible about that. Don't think I didn't feel guilty about not coming clean."

"Right," he said coldly.

She leaned back against the desk, needing its support. "I had to get away from Marazur. I was feeling stifled and angry, and I knew there were all these expectations of me that I hadn't asked for. And so, coming here was like a chance to just be me again. And I wanted you to deal with me as Lucy, not as the King's daughter. I wanted you to respect my knowledge and expertise and not think that I was a spoiled daughter sent on an errand.

"And I think somewhere along the way I earned that respect. I'm not sure that would have happened if you'd known who I was from the start. You would have seen the crown and not the person behind it."

She stopped. Brody said nothing, which she knew was as close to agreement as she was going to get.

"But then something else happened. We started having feelings. Or attraction. Whatever you want to call it. I felt at home here…with the ranch, and Mrs. Polcyk, and with you. And every moment, I knew I couldn't let myself get too attached because I was leaving. And that I had to cling to every single moment because it would be gone all too soon and I'd have to go back to being the princess again.

"And you kissed me. More than once, and held me like I was the most precious thing in the world. You told me about your father and the ranch and I knew more than ever that we are the same sort of people. Only, I knew if I told you the truth about who I was that would all be destroyed. So I kept quiet.

"And then it was too late. We got to a point that you wouldn't ever understand. You danced with me under the stars. Do you have any idea what you've done to me, Brody? I wanted to hang on to that moment forever, even as the guilt about it all was eating me up inside! And I told myself the best thing was to pack and leave and make sure that this all stayed a beautiful memory."

"Luce—"

"Don't call me that," she snapped. "I can't bear it. Oh, I can't bear it, Brody."

Tears spurted into her eyes. Her heart was breaking bit by bit. "You opened your heart to me last night, but only as far as you would let it. Knowing that this was ending. So let it end. Please. Just let it end now before either of us gets hurt more than we already have."

"How could I possibly hurt you?" His hands burrowed into his pockets, and the lines of his face were taut with emotion. "You get to go back to your life."

She bit down on her lip. *But this is my life,* her heart cried. And he was pushing her out of it just as surely as she'd known he would. Already he wasn't seeing the woman she'd shown him over the past weeks but the facade her title provided. She loved him; that was a foregone conclusion. He didn't love her; that was fact, as well.

"I am not a machine," she whispered brokenly. "I have feelings. I have feelings for you. And I refuse to be like my mother. I understand now how her love for Alexander made it impossible for her to find someone else. The way that you're looking at me now hurts me. Leaving you and not seeing you again will hurt me, too. At least I'm honest enough to admit it."

"What's that supposed to mean?"

She looked him straight in the eyes. "You don't believe in love, anyway. So it doesn't matter."

His lips dropped open.

"You don't deny it. Can you even say the word?" He blinked, and his face became stony, hiding any expression. "And there go the shutters. I've known all along that you couldn't love me. So why would I spoil what little bit of you I could have by telling you about some title I've acquired that I didn't even want? You're the one who gets to go back to your life, not me. Well, maybe you were right last night. Maybe it's time I started looking for my life and deciding what it is I want."

She couldn't bear it any longer. If this was to be their good-bye, she had to get it over with before she lost herself completely. She could fall apart later when she was all alone. She had twenty-four whole hours before she was due on a plane and back to a life where privacy was a valuable commodity.

She darted past him and wrenched open the door. "If you cared anything about me, let me go now."

Half of her wanted him to let her escape and get away from the pain and resentment. The other half wanted him to stop her and tell her that it was all a big mistake.

But he didn't come after her, or call her name, or hold out a hand to stop her. Choking back the sobs, she fled upstairs to her room, grabbed her packed bags and dragged them out to the SUV.

She buckled her seat belt and stared at the dashboard where Bob usually sat, giving her directions in his monotone voice. She shoved the GPS in her purse and put the truck in gear.

She didn't need directions this time. She knew the way out perfectly well.

* * *

Lucy had been back several days already, but the memory of Brody and Prairie Rose was as fresh as if it had been only moments ago. She'd arrived tired and a bit broken, only to open her suitcase in her suite and find the shoebox with the navy shoes inside. Mrs. Polcyk. There had been a note too…a simple "She would have wanted you to have them." Touching them had reminded Lucy of dancing to the scrape of the fiddle, of that moment when Brody had teased her and she'd stomped on his toes. She'd cradled the shoes next to her and finally cried, releasing all the anguish she'd held in for the better part of two days. And when she'd finally stopped, she'd sent Mrs. Polcyk a short e-mail thanking her and asking her forgiveness in not saying goodbye. Lucy knew the housekeeper understood.

The arrangements with Prairie Rose Ranch had been finalized through cool, businesslike e-mails, which Lucy had sent through the official Navarro Stables account, leaving her signature off them. If Alexander noticed, he said nothing. He'd been surprisingly undemanding since her return.

The only personal e-mail to come her way from Alberta was from Mrs. P., who'd sent her a picture from the night of the barbecue. It was a candid shot of her with a piece of pie on a spatula and Brody standing just beyond her shoulder and both of them laughing. It reminded her of all the good things, before they'd been marred with the truth, and she'd printed it out. It sat in a frame now on the rosewood table next to her bed, a dried pink rose—the one he'd given her at Wade's Butte—tucked into the bottom corner of the frame. She sighed, reached out a finger and traced the outline of Brody's hat. Lord, she missed him so. Their harsh words at the end had done nothing to diminish her feelings.

A knock at her door made her look up, surprised to see her father's face peeking in. "Do you have a moment, Luciana?"

She no longer minded his use of the long form of her name—another thing that had changed. "Not at all. Come in."

He stepped inside, this man who was suddenly her father. He saw her hand on the photo and smiled softly. "You love him, don't you."

The question was so simple and intrinsically answered that a tear slipped out before she could prevent it. "Yes," she whispered. "Yes, I do."

"Oh, my daughter," he said softly, seeing her distress and taking quick steps to cross the room to take her in his arms. He was tall and strong and she let her head rest against his shoulder as she cried.

After a few minutes she pulled away, embarrassed that she'd acted in such a fashion. But he'd seemed to understand in a way she hadn't expected. He looked down into her eyes and she received another shock: they were very much like her own.

"I've been wondering if you'd ever see the resemblance," he said, squeezing her hand. "Come, let's sit. And you can tell me about this man who's broken your heart."

They sat on the edge of her bed. Lucy folded her hands and was unsure of how to begin. This was all so new.

"Do you know, the night before I left I saw Brody do this very thing. He held a girl in his arms because she'd had her heart broken by a boy, and I thought to myself how I'd never had someone like that in my life before."

"You do now," Alexander replied staunchly. "If you let me. Oh, Lucy, I want to be your father so much. I know it's been difficult. I thought perhaps Marazur was getting to be too hard for you so I sent you to Canada, thinking it would be good for you to get away. But I'm sorry. It seems all it's done is hurt you."

"No, it was something I needed to do," she said. She turned

on the bed, sitting cross-legged before him, she in her everyday jeans and he in his customary tailored dark suit. His
tie was slightly crooked, and she reached out to straighten it
with a shy smile. "I blamed Mum and I said horrible things
before she died, things I can never take back. After she was
gone I put so much energy into resenting you for abandoning
her that I never gave you a chance like she asked me to."

"You only reacted as anyone would, Lucy, you can't blame
yourself for being human. You must know we thought we
were doing the right thing," Alexander said, looking at his
hands. "I loved your mother. It was a lot to ask of her, to take
on a country and a husband and children who were still raw
from losing a parent. If I'd known about you, though, I would
have found a way. I swear to you, I would have. But then...
I never wanted her to resent the choice she'd made. I never
wanted our love to be a burden."

Lucy remembered something Brody had said their last
night together, in the moonlight by the pond. She said, "Love
isn't a burden. Perhaps a responsibility, but never a burden."

"How did you get so wise?" Her father smiled and laid a
hand along her curls.

"Someone told me that once," she whispered.

"And?"

"And then he found out that I wasn't Lucy Farnsworth but
Luciana, Princess of Marazur."

Understanding flickered in his eyes. "That's my fault, isn't
it."

"No, it's not. It's just the way it is." She sighed. "I should
have been honest in the beginning and told him who I was.
Or at least told him, once it was clear there was something
between us. I was so bent on pretending the princess side of
me didn't exist that I didn't trust him." She looked up at him,
into the eyes so like her own. "Oh, Papa, I was so wrong."

Alexander stood up abruptly and walked to the window.

Lucy's eyes followed him and saw him raise a hand to his face, swiping it over his mouth and chin. "I beg your pardon," he said, trying for control but failing as the emotion crept into his voice. "I wasn't expecting that."

He turned back to her. "We...that means Raoul and Diego and I...we want you to be a part of this family. Please believe that, Lucy."

"I do. I only needed to realize it, and my time away helped me to see that what I believed to be expectations were really just you trying to make me feel like I belonged." She went to him and took his hands in hers. "I would very much like to be your daughter. In any capacity you wish."

The acceptance was bittersweet. But she had the choice now, and if she couldn't have Brody she could at least choose to have a family.

"Of course I wish it. I only kept it quiet because I didn't think you wanted it to be made public."

"I thought maybe you didn't want the details of your marriage to my mother to come out."

"Why, when the result is so beautiful?" he asked, and she smiled.

"What do I have to do?"

His eyes lit. "My darling, you just need to be yourself. And what about Mr. Hamilton?"

Lucy turned around and looked at the picture. "It doesn't matter. He doesn't love me." She turned back and smiled up at her father. "I need to move forward. Let's do it."

Alexander pressed a kiss to her forehead. "I think it's time the world met Luciana Navarro, Princess of Marazur. What do you think?"

# CHAPTER THIRTEEN

Lucy looked at her reflection in the cheval mirror. The last time she'd done so she'd been wearing a vintage skirt and western blouse getting ready for a barn dance. Now she was wearing a gown and getting ready for a ball. Her ball.

She plucked at the filmy overskirt with her fingers, feeling the fine stitching of blue flowers and green leaves against the white background. It was a fairy dress, strapless and white and flowing to the floor in dreamy folds. Alexander's idea of combining her introduction with her birthday was lovely... lending a personal touch to a formal occasion.

And she wasn't nervous. But she wasn't completely happy, either.

There was another knock on the door; maids had been coming and going most of the day. "Come in," she called, but it was her half brother, Raoul, who came in, the crown prince himself, looking very dashing in tuxedo and sash.

"May I?"

"Of course."

She liked Raoul, even if sometimes they were still reserved with each other. She was okay with that. At least she knew when he said something, he genuinely meant it. He held out a velvet box. "Happy birthday."

She took the box from his hands. "Should I open it now?"

"Please."

She put it down on the table and with satin gloved hands, flipped the lid open with a stiff creak. Inside was nestled a perfect diamond-studded tiara.

"It was Mother's," he said gently. "She wore it at their wedding ball."

She understood what the gesture meant. "Oh, Raoul, it's lovely, but I shouldn't."

"We want you to, Lucy. You're a part of this family now." His voice was thick, and he cleared his throat. "Besides," he added dryly, "this means Diego will have to stop pestering Papa for a baby sister to aggravate."

She laughed. Diego was twenty-six and incorrigible, far more easygoing than the serious Raoul.

"Will you help me put it on?"

He took the slender tiara from her fingers and settled it atop her fiery ringlets. "I'm not sure which is brighter, little sister. The diamonds or your hair."

She hugged him impetuously. "Thank you, Raoul."

He set her back and bowed. "I know Papa has the first dance, but I'd be honored if you'd dance with me tonight, Lucy."

"Of course."

When he was gone, she sat on the bed, her hand pressed against the nerves in her stomach. There was only one thing missing now, and that was Brody and Prairie Rose. But she couldn't have both. Or could she?

She stared at the satin slippers waiting on her spread, a smile creeping up her lips. She went to her closet and instead took out the navy shoes, slipping them on her feet. "Well, Grandma Hamilton, you're going to the ball tonight," she murmured, suddenly feeling completely put together.

Alexander met her at her door and escorted her down the long curving stairs to the foyer and then to the doors of the ballroom. "Happy birthday, Luciana," he murmured, and then nodded at the footmen. The doors swung open and she entered on his arm, everything in a haze, including being announced as Luciana Navarro, Princess of Marazur.

Never had she been in such a place. Liveried servants circulated among the guests, and Lucy, her father and brothers formed an official receiving line where she could be properly—and personally—introduced. It was very surreal, being addressed as Princess Luciana or Your Highness. She smiled, thinking she should really just be called "Lucy of the Stables." But then her father squeezed her elbow and smiled at her and she was suddenly glad she had him there at her side. If her thoughts drifted to Brody now and then, that was okay. One didn't get over a broken heart in a few weeks.

There was cake, a frothy concoction of vanilla fluff and real flowers, and enough champagne to float the entire island of Marazur. Lucy was holding a glass when Alexander touched her elbow and said, "We are ready to start the dancing."

He cued the orchestra and held out his hand. She took it in her gloved one and bit down on her lip at the look in his eyes. And when he pulled her into his arms and guided her steps, she leaned ahead and whispered, "Thank you, Papa," in his ear.

At the end of that dance she was paired off with Raoul, who complimented her on her dancing, and then Diego, who made a joke about her wild hair and the tiara, which caused her to snort in a most unladylike way. Grandma's shoes made several more turns with the heads of influential families in Europe before she was passed back to Alexander once more.

"Are you tired?" he asked, as their waltz was nearly over.

"A little."

"And your feet?"

She smiled. "I've been on them all night."

His smile broadened suddenly. "Do you think they can manage one more dance?"

"I suppose, but why…"

"Your birthday present has just arrived."

He turned her a half turn toward the doors.

Brody.

Everything in her slammed to her chest. He was here. In Marazur. Standing twenty feet away from her in a tuxedo, his hat nowhere to be found, his dark eyes glittering at her dangerously. Instead of a bowtie, he wore a bolo.

To her, he was perfect.

Alexander still held one shaking, gloved hand. "When there is a choice to be made, my darling, one should always choose love." And he let her go, stepped back.

Everything in her wanted to race across the floor and fling herself into his arms. Yet she held herself back and waited, heart pounding, as he took step after torturous step until he was before her, in the middle of the ballroom, with three hundred pairs of eyes on them.

And when the orchestra started playing "Let Me Call You Sweetheart," he took her in his arms without a word and turned her around the floor.

Oh glorious, glorious day. Her heart swelled to bursting, she reveled in the feeling of his hand at her waist, the way his fingers curled around hers and the heat of his body as he led her across the floor in an effortless waltz. She looked into his eyes, unable to look away from what she saw there. "This was what was missing," she whispered, as he executed a sweeping turn.

"What?"

"You. Just you."

His eyes dropped to her lips for the tiniest of seconds before moving back up again.

She smiled, suddenly so happy she thought she might explode. "I'm wearing your grandmother's shoes," she confided.

"I wondered why you danced so well."

"Mrs. P. gave them to me."

"She told me."

"Do you two have any secrets?"

He finally smiled, a devilish curve that delighted her. "A few. Now be quiet and dance."

By the time the final bars were played, they were both grinning like fools. He stepped back and executed a perfect bow. And with one raised eyebrow, she dropped into a deep, delectable curtsy, her skirts billowing out like a white and blue cloud around her.

He held out his hand and she took it, and he led her to the balcony.

They walked to the balustrade, shrouded in darkness. Brody lifted his nose to the breeze. "It smells different here. Feels different."

"It's the ocean. And...well, it's Europe." She laughed. It faded away into the perfumed evening. "I had no idea you were coming."

"His Highness invited me."

"So I gather."

She could almost hear Brody's smile in the dark. "That man's got a tone that's as effective as any shotgun."

She couldn't help it, she burst out laughing. The picture of Alexander in his designer suit and a twelve-gauge in his hand tickled her funny bone. "He couldn't have been that bad."

"Pardon me, but it was like a long-distance Spanish inquisition."

She covered her mouth with a hand. "What did he say?"

His response echoed in the darkness. "Nothing I didn't already know."

"Like?"

He came to her, took her hand in his and tilted her chin up with a finger. "Like I was a damned fool."

"Well, shoot," she whispered. "I could have told him that."

"And to be honest, when he called I was already making arrangements. I had to come." The pad of his thumb touched the crest of her cheekbone. "I had to make things right. All I could think of on the plane was what if I had blown it?"

He smiled at her, touched the tip of her nose with his finger. "Do you know how beautiful you look tonight?"

"It took several people all day to accomplish this."

"Don't do that," he ordered. "Don't. You are beautiful. Almost as beautiful as you were when you turned the corner at the soddy that afternoon."

She was stunned. Way back then? She'd been dirty and grubby from riding. "I had on old jeans and a T-shirt and was getting a sunburn."

"And you were the prettiest thing I'd ever seen."

"Oh, Brody..."

"Gorgeous," he continued. "My prairie rose. And not like the roses from the shop. Simpler. Beautiful, strong and resilient."

She pressed a gloved hand to her lips, overwhelmed. "You really mean that."

"Of course I do. I'm sorry," he said firmly. "I'm sorry for laying all the blame on you. I was so angry that morning, and felt so foolish, and everything you said was completely right and I was too proud to see it. Too proud and too afraid."

"I don't know what to say."

The sea breeze ruffled his hair, carrying the perfume of the gardens up to them from below. "You had your say," he replied. "And now I want to have mine. And what I have to say is this. It was a mistake for me to let you walk away, Lucy Farnsworth. Or Princess Luciana or whatever you want me to call you."

Her smile was tremulous as she cupped his jaw with her satin-clad hand. "Sweetheart would do nicely."

"Sweetheart."

"I'm sorry, Brody, for everything that happened at the ranch. I never wanted to hurt you."

"I know that now."

The sounds of the orchestra wafted out on the breeze and Lucy laughed lightly. "I don't know what it is about us and dances, but we always seem to be 'out here' when everyone else is 'in there.'"

"If we were in there I couldn't do this." He traced her lips with a finger, and then replaced it with his mouth.

Nothing in the world had ever felt so right as the feel of his mouth against hers. It made every cell in her want to weep with welcoming. For a few blissful moments Marazur didn't matter. Prairie Rose didn't matter. Home was being held in Brody Hamilton's arms and being kissed as if she was the most cherished woman in the world.

When their lips parted, he rested his forehead on hers for a moment, the warmth of his breath fluttering over her skin and raising the fine hairs everywhere on her body.

He stepped back and looked at her in the moonlight. "Look at you," he murmured, his eyes dark and wide. "Like an angel. Or a princess." He smiled then, that lopsided one that made him half rogue, half prince charming. "You even have the tiara."

Her fingers flew to it out of instinct. "Raoul gave it to me today. My half brother," she explained. "It was his mother's."

"You've found a family here after all."

"Yes, I have. Things have changed…Papa has turned out to be so kind, and even the boys…" She chuckled. "They hate being called boys. They've accepted me as their sister. You helped me to see that it was me who stood in the way of having a family. I had so much resentment. And now…now I have a family who loves me. Who supports me. It's all quite overwhelming."

"You're happy."

There was an edge to the words, and she thought she understood why. "I'm contented, and that's more than I ever expected."

To her surprise, Brody walked away, moving to stand next to a potted tree, resting his elbows on the stone railing and looking out over the courtyard.

"I'm at a royal palace in Europe."

She smiled, though she knew something was off. "It's kind of surreal, isn't it."

"I told myself it was better to let you go, to let you find your own way…so things could return to the way they had been. Now when I look at you, I can't help but think that might have been right then. You're not the Lucy I knew—not tonight—and yet you are. I don't quite know what to make of it all."

"How about if you just tell me what you want?"

He tucked his hands into his pockets. She realized he did that when he was particularly nervous, and she couldn't help the tiny smile that touched her lips.

"I look at you, Lucy, and I still see that girl standing up to me about Pretty's hoof. I see the girl I kissed out at Wade's Butte and the one I wanted to make love to the night of the dance. And I don't know how that's possible, because I'm still not sure she exists. And yet…everything you said about Lisa that morning was true. And I realized that deep down I think we *are* the same sort of people. We want the same thing… someone to love us even though we're determined not to let them.…

"And I love you, Lucy. Whether or not anything comes of it, I have to tell you. I love you. And I'm not afraid of it anymore. I'm only afraid you don't love me back."

Finally Lucy did what she'd been wanting to do since she'd

seen him standing, waiting for her. She launched herself into his arms and wrapped her arms around his neck.

"Of course I love you! Why else do you think I've been tied up in knots for the last month and a half!"

Tears sparkled in her eyes as she slid down his chest, her wrists still anchored firmly around his neck. "I thought you didn't believe in love."

"I didn't. But you know what? Something funny happened. I believed in you."

"You didn't."

He gripped her waist tighter. "Yes, I did. Which is why when I found out the truth, I felt like the rug had been pulled out from beneath me."

"I've loved you since that afternoon at Wade's Butte when you told me about your family."

He pushed her back a little, his hands on her hips. "Way back then?"

She nodded. "Way back then. And I knew if I confessed you'd hate me, and I couldn't bear the thought of it. And that look in your eyes the morning I left…I knew you despised me and it broke my heart."

"I never want to hurt you like that again."

For long moments he held her in his arms. But as the evening chilled, reality crept in. "There are still logistics to consider."

Lucy heard the tone in his voice, and something heavy settled in the pit of her stomach. He couldn't have come all this way just to leave again, could he? But then she thought of her parents. They had loved each other, too, but their lives were so different that they hadn't found a way to reconcile them.

"What do we do now?" she whispered. If he were leaving again, she wanted to have this conversation and get it over with. "I know you would never leave the ranch. And I couldn't ask you to."

"You're still a princess and I'm still a rancher. Worlds apart."

Lucy angled her head and looked up at him. "Not really. If we were, I wouldn't have been at Prairie Rose in the first place."

His black eyes were piercing as he looked down at her. "True."

Another few moments, and Lucy dipped her chin.

"And you've found a family who loves you and wants you, right here. It wouldn't be fair to ask you to leave them."

Again silence.

"And there's the matter of the promises we made."

"Yes," she whispered.

Laughter and voices came from inside, and silence reigned on the terrace.

Then Lucy's voice broke the silence, and she surprised herself at the strength in it. "I also have a father whose last piece of advice was that when faced with a choice, I should follow my heart."

"Good advice," Brody replied, his voice deeply intimate in the darkness.

"Brody, I…"

"No, Lucy, it's my turn."

He stood back, and her heart turned over as he knelt on one knee. Torturously, one by one, he pulled at the fingers of her left glove until they were all loosened, and then pulled the long satin cuff off her arm. He held it in one hand while the other took a ring from his jacket pocket, slipping it over her fourth finger. "Marry me, Lucy. I think you're going to *have* to marry me because I'm pretty sure I can't do without you."

She tugged on his hand and he rose, and she cupped his

face in her hands. "What *took* you so long!" Her laugh danced off the stone walls of the palace. "Yes, I'll marry you! Didn't I already tell you Prairie Rose felt like home to me? And home is where *you* are, Brody. Nowhere else. I was just waiting for you to ask!"

"But your family here…"

"Will be my family here. Think of the marvelous vacations we'll have. Not to mention being allied with one of the premier stables in Europe."

"There is that."

She leaned up and kissed him hard on the mouth. "We should tell Papa. He'll be so pleased." She tugged on his hand, pulling him toward the French doors that led to the ballroom.

He planted his feet and stopped her progress. "Lucy, you know that's not why I asked, right?"

"Of course I know." She tugged off her other glove and laid them both on the edge of a planter filled with flowers. "I said I didn't want to be like my mother, and that's true. She gave up on the man she loved. And that's one thing I promise I'll never, ever do."

He swung her up in his arms and spun her around, and her tiara tumbled off and danced across the stone floor as he kissed her. She thought there was a very good chance she would never, ever get tired of kissing him back.

Finally he put her down and bent to retrieve her tiara. "Let's put this back on, Princess Luciana." He tucked it gently into the strands of hair that still remained pulled back in tiny diamond clips. Then he stood back and looked at her.

"For now," she whispered, unable to tear her gaze away from the admiration she saw in his eyes. "Where I'm headed I won't have need of it." She reached up and cupped his jaw, her ring sparkling in the moonlight. "I'll only need you."

He turned his head and kissed her palm, the heat of his breath warming her all over. "We should go in," he murmured, and she thought she heard a trace of reluctance in his voice. But there would be time to be alone later. Forever.

"I think this is one of the best demonstrations of multi-tasking I've ever seen," Lucy said, squeezing his hand as they reached the doors, preparing to enter together. "Just think… tonight will always be known as my coming out, my birthday and my engagement ball!"

\* \* \* \* \*

# HEART & HOME

**Harlequin®**
*Super Romance*

## COMING NEXT MONTH
### AVAILABLE JUNE 12, 2012

**#1782 UNRAVELING THE PAST**
*The Truth about the Sullivans*
**Beth Andrews**

**#1783 UNEXPECTED FAMILY**
**Molly O'Keefe**

**#1784 BRING HIM HOME**
**Karina Bliss**

**#1785 THE ONLY MAN FOR HER**
*Delta Secrets*
**Kristi Gold**

**#1786 NAVY RULES**
*Whidbey Island*
**Geri Krotow**

**#1787 A LIFE REBUILT**
*The MacAllisters*
**Jean Brashear**

# REQUEST YOUR FREE BOOKS!
## 2 FREE NOVELS PLUS 2 FREE GIFTS!

### ◆ Harlequin®

*Romance*

### From the Heart, For the Heart

**Harlequin** *Romance*

*A touching new duet from fan-favorite author*

# SUSAN MEIER

*First Time* **DADS!**

When millionaire CEO Max Montgomery spots
Kate Hunter-Montgomery—the wife he's never forgotten—
back in town with a daughter who looks just like him, he's
determined to win her back. But can this savvy business tycoon
convince Kate to trust him a second time with her heart?

**Find out this June in**

## THE TYCOON'S SECRET DAUGHTER

*And look for book 2 coming this August!*

## NANNY FOR THE
## MILLIONAIRE'S TWINS

Saddle up with Harlequin® series books this summer
and find a cowboy for every mood!

HRI7811

*The legacy of the powerful
Sicilian Ferrara dynasty continues in
THE FORBIDDEN FERRARA
by* USA TODAY *bestselling author Sarah Morgan.*

*Enjoy this sneak peek!*

**A Ferrara would never sit down at a Baracchi table for fear of being poisoned.**

Fia had no idea why Santo was here. He didn't know.

He *couldn't* know.

"*Buona sera,* Fia."

A deep male voice came from the doorway, and she turned. The crazy thing was, she didn't know his voice. But she knew his eyes and they were looking at her now—two dark pools of dangerous black. They gleamed bright with intelligence and hard with ruthless purpose. They were the eyes of a man who thrived in a cutthroat business environment. A man who knew what he wanted and wasn't afraid to go after it. They were the same eyes that had glittered into hers in the darkness three years before as they'd ripped each other's clothes and slaked a fierce hunger.

He was exactly the same. Still the same "born to rule" Ferrara self-confidence; the same innate sophistication, polished until it shone bright as the paintwork of his Lamborghini.

She wanted him to go to hell and stay there.

He was her biggest mistake.

And judging from the cold, cynical glint in his eye, he considered her to be his.

"Well, this is a surprise. The Ferrara brothers don't usually step down from their ivory tower to mingle with us mortals. Checking out the competition?" She adopted her most businesslike tone, while all the time her anxiety was rising and the questions were pounding through her head.

Did he know?

Had he found out?

A faint smile touched his mouth and the movement distracted her. There was an almost deadly beauty in the sensual curve of those lips. Everything about the man was dark and sexual, as if he'd been designed for the express purpose of drawing women to their doom. If rumor were correct, he did that with appalling frequency.

Fia wasn't fooled by his apparently relaxed pose or his deceptively mild tone.

Santo Ferrara was the most dangerous man she'd ever met.

*Will Santo discover Fia's secret?*

*Find out in THE FORBIDDEN FERRARA*
*by USA TODAY bestselling author Sarah Morgan,*
*available this June from Harlequin Presents®!*

EXP0612

# Harlequin Presents®

## Live like royalty…if only for a day.

Discover a passionate duet from

# Jane Porter

### *When blue blood runs hot…*

When Hannah Smith agrees to switch places for a day with
Princess Emmeline, a woman who looks exactly like her, she
soon ends up in some royal hot water. Especially when Emmeline
disappears and Hannah finds herself with a country to run and
a gorgeous, off-limits king she's quickly falling for—Emmeline's
fiancé! What's a fake princess to do?

## NOT FIT FOR A KING?
Available June 2012

And coming soon in July
## HIS MAJESTY'S MISTAKE

Available wherever books are sold.